Part II of the American Kitsune Series

Written by Brandon Varnell

Illustrations by Kirsten Moody

ISBN: 978-1507762073
ISBN-10: 1507762070

Content

ACKNOWLEDGMENTS

There are a lot of people who made writing and publishing this book possible, people who have helped me so much that I would have never gotten this far without them: my parents who have supported me through all my endeavors, my illustrator who's always making the most awesome cover art, and the people who have taken the time to read my stories. It is only thanks to them that this series has even gotten off the ground, and I will always be forever grateful. Thank you.

Chapter 1

The Girl in the Lolita Dress

It was the weekend after Kevin's and Lilian's close encounter of the big, ugly and hairy kind; not much had happened in that time, comparatively at least. Very few things could top nearly getting killed by an inu yōkai, except for maybe finding out that the fox you saved was also a yōkai and wanted to jump your bones. Odd how both had already happened within a two week period.

Aside from a week passing since the fox-girl and the human she had chosen as her mate were almost killed, it was also the first weekend off from school that Lilian had ever had. Having been home-schooled all her life she was, naturally, quite excited about the concept of weekends off—excited being a mild euphemism that did no justice to truly describe how ecstatic she was. The redhead had been practically bouncing off the walls for almost two days straight at the thought of having a weekend off like a regular high school student.

Kevin felt the term *regular* could hardly be applied to someone like Lilian.

Kevin's wounds had healed entirely; not just the physical damage that had been wreaked upon him when Chris cut him open via several claws to the chest—which had not even scarred thanks to Lilian's Deus Ex Machina healing technique—but also the mental scarring caused by the realization that someone from his school had been a yōkai. Given his association with Lilian, it shouldn't have come as a shock that there were other yōkai out there, or that one might have hidden amongst the students of Desert Cactus High School; yet it had, and the event had psychologically damaged him, for a time.

The entire debacle and near -death experience at the hands of Chris had really made the young man rethink everything he thought he knew about the people around him. Several times he caught himself looking at people he associated with suspiciously, wondering if perhaps they were also yōkai in disguise. Even his best friend, Eric, and not-so-secret crush, Lindsay, were subject to this scrutiny. Lilian had assured him that both were human, but that did very little to placate him. Chris had been an inu, a species that was an enemy to kitsune everywhere, and she had not even realized what he was until the boy nearly killed them.

Kevin knew it wasn't fair to blame Lilian. She wasn't omniscient. Still, for a time, a part of him did blame her for not realizing that Chris was a big, ugly dog that wanted to cause them grievous bodily harm. He felt ashamed about how he'd blamed her for what happened, even though there was no way she could have known about Chris beforehand.

He blamed it on existential trauma.

In either event, he had eventually gotten over his paranoia—at least to the point where he wasn't doing his best impersonation of a groundhog on Groundhog's Day.

Surprisingly, Lilian's reassurances *had* helped him move past the traumatic experience of last week.

According to her, most yōkai just wanted to live in peace with humans. That was the whole point of disguising themselves and living amongst humans in the first place.

Lilian's village was the perfect example of this peaceful coexistence. While her village was an all-kitsune village, meaning only kitsune lived there, they allowed humans to visit—or at least visit the resort situated several miles away. Most of the kitsune living in the village also worked at the resort, so it amounted to the same thing.

According to her, the village she lived in was a very popular tourist attraction for the elite of human society. Nearly fifty percent of her village's income came from the stupidly rich humans who spent exorbitant amounts of cash for the extravagant services the kitsune resort offered.

Those few yōkai who did not want to live with humanity for whatever reason tended to live so far away from civilization that they simply weren't a threat. After nearly a week of jumping at his own shadow, Kevin had come to accept the information she'd given him as fact, and life had returned to the status quo—sort of. With someone like Lilian taking up residence with him, the status quo had been all but obliterated from his life.

Saturday morning found Kevin waking up to a big surprise: no Lilian. This shocked him because Lilian always slept with him. *Always.* These days she didn't even wait for him to fall asleep before sneaking into his bed. She would just straight up crawl into his bed at the same time he did and cuddle up to him, which she had done again last night.

After the incident with Chris, Kevin had decided to stop sleeping on the couch, instead choosing to once again use his *actual* bed. Since Lilian was so adamant about sleeping with him regardless of where he was, Kevin felt he should at least be as comfortable as possible, especially since dealing with a fox-girl who wanted to sex him up was decidedly uncomfortable.

For a time he had tried convincing her that they could not share a bed, but he gave up after two nights of arguing. No matter how logical his words were (sleeping together is for married couples, we're not dating, or the ever-infamous "get out of my bed!"), all Lilian had to do was give him that adorable pout no female with the kind of supermodel body she possessed should be capable of producing, and he caved faster than a badass male protagonist from a popular manga that's been derailed by wimpification in a fan fiction. He just couldn't win against her.

He wondered where she had gone off to. It wasn't like he missed her warmth, or the feel of her incredible body pressing into his side. Of course not. He was simply curious. This was the first time since they'd started living together that she'd woken up before him.

Shaking his head, Kevin decided not to worry about the red-haired vixen's whereabouts. Lilian was probably just making breakfast or something. That's what she usually did when she woke up. He would always find her in the kitchen cooking breakfast after he finished taking a shower.

At least when she wasn't trying to take a shower *with* him.

Since he was awake, at least partially so, Kevin decided that he might as well get a start on his day. It was still kind of early, like, six a.m. early. Most people would have just gone back to bed, but Kevin actually had a few chores that he needed to get done. The sooner he got started, the more time he would have later that day to do what he wanted.

His chores for the day involved cleaning the apartment. It

wasn't really something he wanted to do, but he didn't really have a choice in the matter. It was an unfortunate side effect of having a parent who was almost never home and not having a maid.

Maybe he should think about getting a maid?

Somewhere in the United States, a kitsune clad in a kimono and carrying a katana and a wakizashi sneezed.

After getting out of bed, Kevin stumbled to the bathroom, his feet dragging along the floor as he tried to wake himself up. A wide yawn escaped his lips and he ran a hand through his messy blond hair, pushing several bangs out of his eyes. He absently took note that his hair had gotten a little longer. He needed a hair cut, and soon.

Kevin had only just closed the bathroom door when he realized that something was wrong. Several somethings. One: the air was very warm. Hot even. Two: there was a lot of steam wafting around, clinging to his skin, fogging up the mirrors, and coalescing along the walls and ceiling. Three: someone was humming. Four: they had a beautiful voice. And five: someone was already in the shower and she was very familiar to him.

"L-Lilian?!" Kevin squeaked. Why was she in here? Wasn't she making breakfast? That's what she usually did in the morning.

The curtain was pulled back for reasons beyond Kevin's ability to comprehend (it was almost as if Lilian had known that he would come in here, thinking that she was making breakfast), so he could see far more of the girl than was appropriate.

Far, *far* more than was appropriate.

Her long red hair lay flat against her head and traveled down her body, sticking erotically to her fair skin and stopping at her magnificently shaped rear. She wasn't facing him, but rather, her body was turned slightly to the side, so that she presented him with a three-quarter profile of herself. With her arms raised above her head to massage shampoo into her hair, Kevin was given a perfect view of her generously sized and well-formed sideboob.

"Oh, Beloved," Lilian chirped when she finally noticed him standing in front of the door, gaping at her with wide eyes and a face so red that lobsters everywhere were probably crying out in jealousy. She turned around to present him with a full-frontal view of her nude, wet body, giving him a dazzling smile full of perfect ivory teeth to let him know how pleased she was to see him.

Not that he really saw it—her smile, that is—because the moment she turned around his eyes found themselves gazing upon the two large, round *things* on her chest, which bounced and swayed every time she moved. Her breasts were very perky despite their size, and Kevin found himself mesmerized.

Such is the power of a woman with large tits. There is a general consensus among men, not all, but most, that women with big boobies were more beautiful than women with itty bitty titties. Buxom is Better, as it were. Or, big breasts equals hot chick. Eric Corrompere put it best when he said, *"Boobs weigh heavier than a man's life."*

And was it just Kevin, or did Lilian's boobs actually make a *boing* sound when they bounced? How weird was that?

"I'm glad you're awake. I was going to wake you up myself after I finished taking a shower, but I think this works out better."

No, it doesn't, Kevin wanted to shout, but found himself incapable of even opening his mouth.

"Since you're up now, would you like to help me wash my back?" After saying this, she presented her back to him, moving her long hair out of the way. With a strangely innocent grin that looked completely out of place given the context of the situation, she wiggled her marvelously-crafted derrière at him to emphasize exactly where she wanted him to wash.

Unprepared for such a lethal move, Kevin was nearly felled right then and there. His head began to swim as all the blood rushed to his face. This was far too much sexy for his teenage mind to handle.

Kevin didn't pass out, but he had to lean back against the door frame to keep upright. His legs buckled and shook erratically, showing clearly that if he didn't do something soon, he may very well have fallen into that blissful state otherwise known as unconsciousness.

"Ugh… uuuuu… ha…?" Kevin said, having been reduced to random monosyllables.

"What are you doing just standing there, Beloved? Come on. The water's perfect."

Lilian stepped out of the shower, her body dripping wet. Kevin's eyes practically bulged out of their sockets as he watched several droplets of water travel down her awe-inspiring curves. It was an arousing sight; hundreds of tiny liquid pebbles that glittered like jewels in the light as they blazed an adventurous path across her glorious body, leaving a wet trail along her skin. Her long, luxurious red hair flung water into the air as she swished it over her shoulder, creating a sparkle effect that made her look like some kind of otherworldly creature; like an angel who'd descended from heaven to grant a mortal like him a taste of what awaited in the afterlife.

Or it could just be due to how *Everything is Better with Sparkles*. No, seriously, if you want to show that something is valuable, magical or just plain special, shove an inordinate amount of sparkles on or around it and *voila!* Instant specialness.

On a side note, when a bishounen sparkles, it’s known as the *Bishie Sparkle.*

On another side note, *Mahou Shoujo* also tend to sparkle a lot, but that has more to do with censorship than magical girl-ness.

Moon Prism Power.

Right.

***

“H-hey! Wh-what are you—!? Q-quit dragging me!”

“Muu,” Lilian made an oddly pouty sound, “Stop struggling and get in the shower with me, Beloved. The water's perfect.”

“I don't want to take a shower! I'm still dressed!”

“If you don't want to take a shower, then why did you come in here?”

“…”

“I thought so. Now come on, let's get those clothes off, ufufufu…”

“Okay, that laugh is really beginning to freak me out—Eep! What are you—s-stop!”

“Ufufufu, and now to get rid of those pants!”

Cue the sound of clothing being ripped.

“You could have at least let me take those off! Those were my favorite pajamas! And stop staring at me like that!”

“Ufufufu, why? You have nothing to be ashamed of. You're quite… well endowed, ufufufu… and you still have room to grow. Oh, we are going to have so much fun together!”

“We're not going to be having any fun you—wait! No! Stop it! I don't—! Oh god! What are you—!? Iyahn!”

***

Not even fifteen minutes later, Kevin sat at the kitchen table, his head laying on the hard wooden surface. His face felt like someone had stuck it in an Easy-Bake-Oven for six hours. He could probably boil eggs on his face.

He could no longer even look at Lilian, who was currently humming a beautiful tune as she made some kind of homemade yogurt parfait with something she called Greek yogurt. He didn't know what the difference was between normal yogurt and Greek yogurt, but apparently there was one. Something about the pasteurization making the yogurt thicker… or something… he hadn't caught the explanation because he'd been too busy trying *not* to pay attention to the girl doing the explaining.

On a side note, he wondered where she got the Greek yogurt from. He knew for a fact that there was no Greek anything in his fridge.

In either event, Kevin really didn't care to know the difference between Greek yogurt and regular yogurt. He was still too busy trying to keep his heart rate under control and the blood from rushing to his face… along with another part of his body that he had adequately dubbed "Kevin Junior."

"Here you go," Lilian's happy voice reached his ears. Kevin looked up, instinctively reacting to someone addressing him. Yet, the moment he found himself gazing upon the girl most teenage boys would gladly have wet dreams about, his face flushed an even deeper shade of atomic red.

Lilian had leaned over to present his food to him. This might not have been a problem in most cases, but she was currently wearing a white, low cut sleeveless tank that showed off a good portion of her creamy, unblemished cleavage—of which the young kitsune had a plentiful amount of, which explained why his vision was practically filled with her bountiful bosom.

"T-t-thanks," he stuttered before quickly shoving his face into his food. So long as he was eating, he wouldn't have to look at her.

"You're welcome." Lilian couldn't quite contain her sigh of disappointment. Kotohime had always said that men were simple creatures; flash a little skin and they were yours for the taking. But that didn't seem to be working with Kevin—he hardly even looked at her cleavage, and she had presented the perfect opportunity for him.

It seemed Lilian would still need to work hard before Kevin was willing to bend her over this table and claim her as she wanted to be claimed.

That was okay, though. She was a kitsune. All kitsune knew that if you wanted to capture your prey—um, mate—you had to be patient. Rome wasn't built in a day and going from *"we just met"* to *"let's make babies"* took time as well.

So while she was plotting more ways to break Kevin of his resolve and get him to ravish her, Kevin was trying to deal with his mind sending him constant visions of Lilian's breasts.

Kevin didn't know why he still wasn't used to moments like this. He had seen Lilian nude plenty of times. Their very first meeting she had been completely exposed to him, for God's sake! The incident in the shower really shouldn't have affected him so much—especially because it had already happened before, several times! He'd faced much worse since the vixen entered his life.

I'm really beginning to think I shouldn't have rescued Lilian back then, he thought sullenly. *It would have certainly made my life a whole lot less complicated. But, she had been so cute! I couldn't not rescue her, right? Right?!*

He thought about how he'd rescued Lilian all of two weeks ago, back when he thought she was just a fox. His sullen mood worsened.

Even if I had known what sort of trouble this would cause in advance, I don't know if I would have done anything different. How could I not save someone when they're hurt? What kind of person would I be if I just left her to die?

Sometimes, Kevin really hated being of the Hapless Hero variety. Why couldn't he have been born with a cooler personality?

It must be genetics, he grumbled to himself, M*y dad's probably some wimp who lets women walk roughshod over him. That's why I act like this.*

"Beloved?" Lilian's voice shook Kevin from his increasingly depressing thoughts. By now, he had managed to get his blush under control, and raised his head to look at her. "Since it's Saturday and we don't have school, are we going to do something fun?"

"Something fun?" Kevin blinked once, twice, then adopted a

thoughtful expression as he rubbed his chin. "Well, sometimes my friends and I will go to the arcade on the weekend…" he trailed off when he saw the look in his housemate/pseudo-girlfriend/kitsune mate's eyes. The expression her face possessed could only be described as unadulterated hope.

And was it just him, or were those stars in her eyes?

After taking another glance, Kevin realized that, indeed, they were stars. Spanning the entire iris of her eyes were two bright, yellow, five-pointed stars that had somehow replaced her normal pupils.

What. The. Heck?

"I've never been to a real arcade before," Lilian's voice snapped him out of his incredulity. He looked up…

… And then leaned back as Lilian's stare seemed to intensify. He nearly fell off his chair when she leaned over and got nose to nose with him.

"Do you think we can go there? Please?"

"I… I don't see why not," Kevin hedged. The look in her eyes was almost as creepy as that laugh of hers. "But the arcade doesn't open until ten, so we'll have to wait for a while before leaving. There's no point in going to the arcade if it's not even open."

"Oh," Lilian's shoulders slumped. "I was hoping we could go now. What are we going to do for—" she glanced up at the clock, "—three more hours?"

"I have to clean the apartment, anyways. That's going to take a good hour and a half at the very least."

"Oh! I'll help clean!" Lilian smiled at him while Kevin just arched an eyebrow. "Then we can get it done in half the time, right? Two people are better than one and all that."

When Kevin saw how enthusiastic the girl was about helping, he agreed.

It would be one of the biggest mistakes of his life… at least until he made the *next* biggest mistake of his life. Kevin could already tell there would be a lot of those. Mistakes, that is.

***

Not even ten minutes later, Kevin was cleaning the windows and dusting the windowsills as he lip-synced to a song playing on his MP3 player. Lilian was washing their clothes.

Kevin had been cleaning this apartment for so long that he

actually picked up the habit of zoning out while he tidied the place up. Everything was pretty routine anyway: clean the windows, clean the windowsills, vacuum the floor—the usual stuff. It was boring, mundane work in every way possible and required very little thought.

When all the windows in the living room and kitchen were clean, Kevin walked into the hallway, which led to the washing room, laundry room and his bedroom. He stepped foot into the hall… and promptly stopped dead in his tracks, the cleaning supplies falling from his nerveless fingers.

His eyes widened in horror.

"What the heck is going on here?!"

"Wah! Beloved!" Lilian ran over to him, tears in her eyes and a pitiful look on her face. Her clothes and body were soaking wet and covered in white, foamy suds that looked nothing like soap. They caked to her clothes and skin, including her face. She almost looked like a snowman—erm, woman. "I don't know what happened! The washing machine just started shaking, and soap and water kept shooting out of it and I don't know what's going on!"

Kevin tried to keep calm while observing the situation as unbiasedly as possible. He looked down the hall to the washing room, which had foamy water running out of it, soaking the tile and carpet. A little further in the washing machine was going berserk, shaking and jumping like someone had decided to crank it into overdrive.

He rubbed a hand over his face. For some reason, he felt ridiculously exhausted right now—it probably had something to do with the girl in front of him.

"I'll handle this." He didn't look at Lilian as he walked past her. "You just… dry yourself off with a towel and get changed into a dry set of clothes."

"Okay," she sniffled, "I'm sorry."

Kevin just grunted as he stepped onto the ever expanding area of the now soaking-wet floor. His feet made wet, squelching noises each time he took a foot off the carpet. By the time he made it to the utility room, his socks were soaked all the way through and covered in the same foam-like substance that made Lilian resemble a snow-woman.

He entered the washing room, determined to put a stop to this insanity... only to end up getting far more than he bargained for.

"What the heck?! Woah! That was too—holy crap!"

The machine bucked and rumbled like a bull seeing red. Kevin's toes were nearly squished.

"Oh, dear sweet god! It's going crazy!"

"B-Beloved, do you want me to help? I could—"

"What the—! You're still here?! Go and get—Jesus Christ!"

The washing machine almost ran right over him, forcing him to dodge and causing his head to hit the wall when he slipped on the wet surface.

"B-but I—"

"Dang it, Lilian! I need to concentrate! Go and get—EEK!" Kevin screamed like a little girl.

"Beloved!"

Despite the difficulties he faced, he managed to shut the machine off. The intense reverberating stopped, the machine ceased jumping like a speed addict on a pogo stick, and Kevin could not keep the sigh of relief from escaping his mouth when his toes were no longer in danger of becoming pancakes. There had been several calls that were far too close for comfort. Had he been a hair slower, his poor phalanges may have actually been crushed.

Now he just had to find out why the machine had turned into some kind of raging berserker. It was a fairly new, state-of-the-art piece of equipment. It was so easy to use that even people completely lacking in intelligence and common sense should have been able to figure out how to make it work properly.

That begged the question of how Lilian managed to make the washing machine act like that. She wasn't stupid; a bit of an airhead maybe, but certainly not dumb. She should know how to use a washing machine, right?

Lilian was sitting on his bed when he entered his room. She was now dry and free of foam, and her outfit had been changed as well. While before she was wearing a pair of tight jean shorts that showed off more leg than Kevin thought was appropriate, now she had donned a red skirt that looked like it would expose her panties if she bent over. Her white, low-cut shirt had been replaced with a black tube top that left the top of her cleavage exposed and showed her wonderfully flat stomach. Settled on her feet were a pair of simple red flip flops. Her crimson-colored hair was worn in its usual style, falling freely about her face and body like a curtain of shimmering silk.

Kevin noticed right away that she was nervous as he approached; the way her fists tightly clenched the skirt and her eyes refused to meet his told him as much. Even her stiff posture and body language seemed to convey a sense of anxiety, as if she was waiting for the hammer to fall.

"Are you mad at me?" Lilian asked in a small voice.

Kevin ran a hand through his hair, inhaled deeply, then released it all in one breath.

"No, I'm not mad." Lilian looked up, her glance hopeful. "But I would like to know what happened."

Lilian's shoulders slumped as she recalled the event of a few minutes ago. It was not one of her best moments.

"I don't know. I did everything just like I was supposed to. I put the clothes in, then I put the laundry detergent in, and then I turned it on and started it."

"Um, we don't have any laundry detergent," Kevin told her. "We use those detergent pods now."

"Pods?"

"Yeah. In the left cabinet of the washing room, in a big orange bag. You can't miss them."

"I didn't see those," Lilian admitted, "But I didn't really look. When I didn't see any detergent, I just thought you might have run out and decided to use my own."

Kevin had a bad feeling, trepidation settling in the pit of his stomach. He didn't want to, but he asked anyway. "And what detergent was this?"

As Lilian reached in between her breasts, Kevin looked away. Even then, he still ended up peeking at her out peripheral. When he turned back, the fox-girl had pulled a box out of her Extra Dimensional Storage Space and showed it to Kevin who, upon reading the label on the box, gained several veins that visibly throbbed on his forehead.

"Lilian, that's not laundry detergent."

"It isn't?"

"No." Another throb. "It isn't."

Lilian blinked. She looked honestly confused. "Then what is it?"

"I'm not sure." Kevin pointed at the symbol on the box. "But I don't think laundry detergent would have a biohazard symbol on it. Just saying."

"Biohazard?" Lilian looked at the symbol on the box, noting that, yes, there really was a biohazard symbol on it. "Oh, um, whoops?" She looked at Kevin with a sheepish smile. "I guess I pulled out the wrong box, tee-hee."

As Lilian knocked the knuckles of her right hand against her noggin, one eye winking closed and her tongue poking out in an expression that he knew she picked up from the anime they'd been watching, Kevin felt like bashing his face against a wall.

"And what exactly is in this box?" He probably shouldn't have asked, but he did anyway.

"Nothing."

"Nothing?"

"Yep. Nothing."

Kevin stared at the girl for several more seconds, then sighed.

"Right. Nothing."

He decided right then and there that he was better off not knowing. He looked out of the door and into the hallway.

"This is just great. How am I going to clean all that up?"

It would take a high powered steam cleaner to get all that foam out of the carpet. Which he didn't have. Plus, the cost of renting one was expensive. Not to mention, he had no idea how he would get one home when he didn't have a car.

"I can help!"

Kevin was very reluctant to let this girl help him again after what had just happened. However, upon seeing the pleading look on her face, he gave in. Hopefully, it wouldn't come back to bite him in the ass.

***

Not very long after their conversation, the two of them stood in the hallway once again. Kevin stood off to the side, watching as Lilian dried the floor in a way he would not have thought up in a million years. Then again, he also didn't possess any Deus Ex Machina kitsune Powers, so he felt his lack of imagination could be excused, just this once.

"So what's this technique called?"

"It's a basic kitsune technique called *kitsune-bi*, or Fox Fire,"

Lilian told him as she continued drying the floor. She had made this mess and she was determined to make amends to the best of her abilities.

"Huh." Kevin scratched the back of his head. "Isn't *kitsune-bi* Japanese? I'm kind of surprised you use Japanese names for your techniques. You've been pretty adamant on saying you're from England. And you don't live in Japan either, you live in Greece. Is your dad Japanese or something?" Lilian didn't look like she had any Japanese blood in her, but maybe she just took more after her mom than her dad.

"I doubt it," she shrugged daintily. "But then, I couldn't really say, since I don't know all that much about my father. Remember what I told you at the mall?"

Kevin winced. He did, indeed, remember their conversation now that she'd brought it up. A part of him had forgotten because, well, seeing a sexy girl in equally sexy lingerie for the first time will do that to a guy.

"That's right. I'm sorry. I shouldn't have brought it up."

"No, no, don't worry about it." Lilian smiled. "It's just as I told you before, I never really knew him, so I don't have any great attachment to him or anything."

At her words and smile, Kevin gave a tentative one of his own. He still wasn't too keen on this mating business, but he appreciated her honesty and how open she was with him.

Had he been paying more attention, he may have noticed the way her eyes darkened at the mention of her father.

"Anyway, the reason the names of our techniques are all Japanese is because The Author is an Otaku."

"The what? Otaku?"

"Nothing. Don't worry about it, Beloved."

"Whenever you say that, I can't help but think you're hiding something from me."

"Ufufufu, don't think that way. I'm not really hiding anything. There are just some things that you aren't ready to know, but give it time and I'm sure you'll discover what I'm talking about eventually."

"I'm not sure whether I should be excited or terrified," Kevin replied dryly. He shook his head and changed the subject. "So, is this kitsune-bi something all kitsune can do?"

"Yes, it's the most basic of all kitsune techniques that we learn sometime after gaining our second tail. kitsune-bi is made from compressing our youki through our tails and using them to generate heat. It isn't actual fire," she added upon seeing his expression, "But it acts like fire. It can be used to warm things up, boil water, and even hurt others." She paused. "We can't use it to cook for some reason, though. No one knows why that is, but it's an accepted fact. I remember the first time I tried to cook using it—" she grimaced, "—it wasn't pretty."

"I see," Kevin mused, "So it requires two tails?" He eyed the tails sticking out of Lilian's tailbone. He was sure he should be blushing by now, but most of his attention was focused on the two bright yellow flames hovering over the tips of her tails instead of the deliciously tight derriere just below them.

"It only requires two tails because a kitsune doesn't become a supernatural creature until they gain their second tail," Lilian explained. "Before that, we're just ordinary foxes."

"Oh," Kevin blinked. "I didn't know that."

"Well of course not. It's not like you could have known that unless you met another kitsune before me and they told you." Lilian smiled as the flames hovering above the tips of her tails were extinguished. "There! All done."

"Now we just need to clean up and dry the washing room."

Lilian's shoulders slumped. "Don't remind me."

"Don't worry too much." Kevin knelt down and ran a hand through the carpet. Whatever that biohazard stuff Lilian used was, it had caked to the floor, and it was going to take a lot more than a day's effort to get the strange substance out. Forget renting out a high-powered steam cleaner; he might just have to get it professionally cleaned. "It shouldn't take as long to dry the washing room, and I can clean it just fine since we're dealing with tile. After that, you can help me clean the rest of the house." There was no way he was ever going to let her wash clothes again, and he wanted to keep a close eye on her to avoid her creating another mess. "Then we can go to the arcade."

"Really?!"

Kevin chuckled. Her enthusiasm was actually kind of infectious. "Really. So the faster we work the sooner we can leave."

"All right!" Lilian held a fist up to her face, which had gained an expression of determination. Kevin thought he could actually see flames igniting behind her irises. "Just you wait, Beloved! I'll have this room dry in no time!"

Kevin felt a lead weight drop into the pit of his stomach as he stared at the gorgeous, emerald-eyed girl with a look of mild trepidation. Despite the sudden misgivings he felt at seeing her expression, the young man decided not to let it get to him.

"I'm sure you will."

***

After cleaning the majority of the apartment, Kevin and Lilian left for the arcade. They rode on Kevin's bike, speeding down the bike lane. Trees, light posts and shrubbery passed by in a blur as they rocketed down Dunlap Road.

Being a major roadway and a Saturday, there were a lot of cars on the road that day. At every stoplight they passed, cars were packed bumper to bumper, jostling and honking and revving their engines impatiently.

It was definitely a good thing they were riding Kevin's bike and not driving. Not that they could drive anyway. He didn't have a license. Neither did Lilian, but she was a kitsune, which explained her lack of a permit. She'd probably never even seen an automated vehicle until she ended up living amongst humans.

While Kevin peddled the bike, Lilian sat behind him, arms wrapped around his torso and her right cheek resting against his back. It was a very distracting position for Kevin, who could feel her—well, *her*, pressing into him. It didn't help that her hands were shamelessly groping him as they wound around his body.

"See? I told you I would finish drying that room in no time," Lilian said, shouting to be heard over the sounds of traffic, before rubbing her cheek against the muscles in his back. He really wished she would stop. "Isn't the kitsune-bi an amazing technique?"

"It is pretty convenient," Kevin admitted with a shout of his own, glad for the conversation. It took his mind off those two large, round mountains pressing into him. "I mean really convenient. Even more so than those Power Ups that manga characters get during training arcs. It's almost Hyperbolic Time Chamber convenient."

The Hyperbolic Time Chamber: a room where someone can get a year's worth of training done in a single day.

"It is, isn't it?" A pause. "Say, how long does it take to get to the arcade?"

Kevin actually had to think about that for a second. "It's not that far. I'd say about… fifteen minutes, twenty tops. Something like that. We'll be there pretty soon."

"I can't wait to finally see a real arcade. Are the games anything like the ones we've played at home?"

"Some of them are, but they're also different than console games. For one thing, they don't use standard controllers. There are a few shooter games there, too—zombie shooters like *Dead Rising* and *House of Haunted Horrors*. But there are other games as well: dancing games and racing games and games where you have to shoot basketballs into hoops. The arcade has a lot more variety than what I have at home."

"I want to play the shooting ones."

"You know, most girls don't like those kinds of games," Kevin said, though he didn't about the accuracy of his words, since he had very little experience when it came to women. For all he knew, every female loved blowing the heads off of zombies and popping a cap in some jabroni's ass.

"Then I guess I'm not like most girls." Lilian sounded very proud of this fact. "Besides, aren't those your favorite kinds of games? It's only right that they would be my favorite as well."

"I hope you're not saying those are your favorite for my sake."

"It's not just that," Lilian said in a voice so soft that Kevin almost missed it, especially over the wind and thrum of traffic. "They weren't just the first video games I've played." Her arms tightened around his waist. She also stopped groping him, which he was thankful for. "They were the first games I played with you. That makes them special to me."

Kevin's cheeks reddened as blood rushed to his face, and not because of Lilian's twins. That had to be one of the most heartfelt statements anyone had ever said to him. His heart, which had been beating steadily against his chest, was now hammering away like a war drum. For just a second, he thought that maybe being Lilian's mate wasn't so bad.

"Plus, seeing how cute you look when you're concentrating on something difficult makes me so hot and bothered that I just want you to ravish me, ufufufu!"

And just like that, all the feelings of warmth disappeared as Lilian butchered the moment with a rusty spork.

"Ugh, there you go with that laugh again." Kevin wondered if she knew how her words had affected him. Given her last comment, probably not. "Anyway, we're here."

A large two-story square building loomed before them. Above a set of sliding doors hung a sign with the words, *Gamer's Paradise,* in giant, neon-orange lettering. In the center was the image of a small island with a claymore embedded into the ground. If that didn't say video games, nothing did.

"Wow!" Lilian looked at the building in awe as she hopped off the back of the bike. "This place is amazing! It's so much bigger than the other buildings around here!"

Kevin dismounted as well and wheeled the bike over to the bike stand, where several others were already locked up.

"Wait until you see the inside." Kevin grinned. Seeing Lilian acting so enthusiastic about something he enjoyed doing felt nice. He didn't know of any other girl who would be so excited to play arcade games.

With the efficiency of someone who had done this a million times, he wrapped the cable around the bike and bike stand, then closed the combination padlock with a deft click. Standing up, he looked over to where Lilian was standing.

"Let's go in… side… eh?" Kevin trailed off when he noticed that the redhead was no longer there. The high school sophomore blinked, then scratched the back of his head, a perplexed expression overtaking his features. "Where did she go now?"

"Beloved!" He turned his head to see Lilian standing just outside the entrance to the arcade, a dazzling smile on her face as she waved him over. "Come on! Let's go!"

Kevin sighed as he walked over to the fox-girl. "Coming!" Couldn't she show at least a modicum of patience? It wasn't like rushing around with the feverish eagerness of a child on a sugar high would allow her to play arcade games any faster.

Once he caught up to her they walked inside. Lilian's entranced eyes went wide as she found herself in what could only be described as a veritable gamer's paradise. Everywhere she looked there were large machines featuring a variety of different arcade-style games—everything from games where people shot things with large plastic guns, to games with stages that people danced on, to basketball games and casino-type games where people earned tickets that could be exchanged for prizes. Every type of game she could think of—and then some—was there, just waiting for her to play them.

In the center of the room, a set of stairs led up to a second floor. Kevin told her there was a bowling alley up there. In the back of the arcade, she could see a small bar-style restaurant that served strange foods that she had never seen before.

"Come on, Beloved!" An excited Lilian grabbed Kevin's hand, eager to go out and explore this world of arcadium that her mate was so fond of. "Let's go!"

"Hold up, Laura Croft." Kevin dug his figurative heels in, stopping the girl before she could begin dragging him off. "I need to put some credits on my card before we can begin playing any games."

"Oh," Lilian pressed a finger to her lips, her delicate eyebrows furrowing cutely in an expression of inquisitiveness. "How do we do that?"

In response to her question, Kevin pointed over to the wall near the entrance. "With that machine over there."

"That machine," as Kevin so eloquently called it, was a large, boxy contraption with a touch screen. It allowed people to select the amount of credits they wanted to put on their cards. Since they were in an age where everything was paid for with plastic, the arcade games were no longer coin-operated, but ran based on the same principle as a gift card.

Kevin put twenty dollars' worth of credits on his card. It would be enough for him and Lilian to play for at least two or three hours. At least it should be, provided Lilian didn't go crazy trying to play every game there.

They were supposed to eventually meet up with Eric, who he had sent a text message to, and received an emoticon smiley face back. However, since his pervy friend enjoyed sleeping until noon, Kevin allowed Lilian to pull him into the arcade and play some games. They of them played several different games, the first being *House of Haunted Horrors.*

"Ha! Take that evil mutant zombies!"

"I don't really think they're mutants," Kevin mumbled as he shot at the zombies on the screen in a far more conservative manner than Lilian, who blew them away like some kind of machine-gun wielding psychopath.

"Hmm? Did you say something, Beloved?"

"I said you're really getting into this."

"You think so? I guess it's because I've never done this before. I heard that my clan's resort has arcade games and tons of other cool stuff, but the matriarch never let me go there before. And our village doesn't have any of the new inventions that you humans have come up with, except for washing machines and ovens. Things like arcades and movie theaters are non-existent."

"That must really suck," was the only thing he could think to say.

"Yeah, it's pretty boring over there. Even when we went on vacation to the other villas my clan owns, they never let me leave them. That's why I'm so grateful to you for taking me to places like this."

When Kevin looked over at the redhead, he caught a glimpse of her honest smile. It was beautiful.

"Ah…" His throat constricted. He opened his mouth, but no words came out. All he could do was croak. "Ah…"

"Are you okay, Beloved?" Lilian asked, concerned when she saw his weird behavior. "Your face is all red."

She leaned over and pressed her forehead against his, which really just made his face turn an even deeper shade of red, making it take on the general coloration of a billboard in Las Vegas.

"You don't seem to have a fever." She looked confused. Kevin wondered how a girl so set on jumping his bones could be so oblivious.

"I-I'm fine." Kevin shook his head, trying to rid himself of the strange feelings that being so close to Lilian generated within him. Having had two weeks' worth of practice doing just that, he was marginally successful. "And you're welcome. Now why don't we continue playing?" He looked back at the screen, only to blink when he realized that they had both died sometime in the past few seconds when neither of them was looking.

"Eh?!" Lilian glared at the screen as the words, G*ame Over,* appeared in dark crimson, leaving trails down the screen like blood. "I can't believe we lost!"

"We did get distracted talking."

"But I was sure I paused it!"

"… Lilian, arcade games don't have a pause button."

"They don't?"

"No, they don't."

"Oh… my bad."

They then played the arcade basketball game.

"Yay! I scored 40 baskets! How many did you score, Beloved?"

"…"

"Beloved?"

"… five."

"Oh, wow. You really suck at basketball, Beloved."

It should be noted that this guy, Kevin, sucked at basketball.

"Shut up."

They played many other games as well, including *Dance Dance Revolution* and *Crazy Taxi.* Lilian enjoyed herself immensely, and though Kevin wouldn't admit it out loud, he had a good time as well.

"This place is so much fun," Lilian squealed as they finished a racing game. She had lost because she kept crashing into various walls and objects—not to mention people, but she didn't seem to care. It wasn't about winning or losing with her. It was about having a good time with her mate.

"I'm glad you're enjoying yourself," Kevin said, his voice earnest and matching the grin on his face. "Are there any other games you'd like to try out?"

"I want to try all of them!"

Kevin chuckled and blushed at Lilian's declaration. He would never tell her this, but she looked *really* cute standing there, her fists planted on her hips, eyes alight with excitement and determination. She looked ready to embark on some kind of epic quest or something.

It was the ultimate Dungeons and Dragons pose.

He wondered if she got that pose from the *Dungeon Master's Guide* or the *Player's Handbook.*

"Ah, but first, I really need to use the restroom." Lilian

suddenly looked sheepish, and it took Kevin a second to realize why—she didn't know where the restrooms were.

"I'll show you where they are." Kevin grabbed Lilian's and led her through the various arcade games and groups of people that had shown up in the past hour. He really hated how crowded it became once lunch time rolled around.

Lilian stared at their conjoined hands with a large, nearly luminescent blush and an even larger smile. It wasn't much, but the fact that Kevin had been the one to initiate contact between them brought a sense of gratification and pleasure to the kitsune. It swept through her like a storm. Her body literally shivered at the rush of emotions flowing through her.

They eventually stopped in front of two doors with signs hanging over them, labeling them as the restrooms. Turning to his companion, Kevin was about to speak up when he noticed the redness on Lilian's cheeks. "Hey, Lilian, are you okay? You look a little flushed."

"I-I'm fine," Lilian stuttered in a totally Out of Character way.

Kevin stared at her for a little longer, making Lilian squirm under his gaze, but he eventually shrugged off her strange behavior. "Alright, I'll wait here for you."

"Okay. Be right back."

Lilian was quick to make her exit after that. Kevin watched her go with a curious expression. He wondered if something was wrong. Lilian wasn't the blushing type—unless she was trying to rip his pants off or something, but that was a completely different kind of blush. In the end, he decided that this was one of those things that was just not worth knowing.

As he waited for Lilian's return, Kevin leaned against the wall and scanned the room, taking in all the people bustling around the arcade. It was almost noon, so the place was jam-packed with teenagers looking to kill time. Eric was probably in there somewhere by now.

As his gaze roamed across the many arcade games and people using them, he eventually singled out a girl with long black hair and snow white-skin. She was pressing her hands and face against the glass case to one of the claw-grabber games, admiring the many prizes inside.

The girl in question was pretty cute, but what really got

Kevin's attention wasn't her looks, but her clothes. She wore an all black, gothic lolita dress complete with frills, ruffles, v-shaped piping on the bodice, a puffy skirt, elbow-length gloves, black stockings and slipper-like shoes.

Just what a girl was doing wearing something like that in this heat was beyond Kevin. She must have been sweating up a storm in that thing, air-conditioned building or not.

The girl frowned as she pressed her face further against the glass. Kevin's curiosity finally got the better of him and he walked up to her. He stopped directly behind her, waiting for the girl to notice him. When it became clear that she wasn't going to notice his presence anytime soon, he cleared his throat and asked, "Do you want one of those prizes?"

"Kya!"

Kevin took a step back at the loud, keening wail of surprise. The girl spun around, her hair almost smacking him in the face. Her eyes widened when she saw him standing there, her right hand going to her chest, grabbing the fabric of her bodice. Her shoulders heaved as she took in deep breaths of air.

A second after she caught sight of him, her eyes widened. Then she blushed. Before Kevin could ask if something was wrong, the blush darkened and she started scowling. "You shouldn't sneak up on people like that, you jerk!"

"Sorry." Kevin had the decency to look abashed. "I didn't mean to sneak up on you or anything. I just saw you standing there, and wondered if you wanted to get something from that machine."

The girl's cheeks darkened in hue. "O-of course not! Don't be stupid!" She turned away. "Why would I want one of those stupid felines?"

"Felines?"

Kevin looked into the glass. There were several different stuffed toys that could be classified as feline, but the one that stood out to him was a creature reminiscent of a black cat with red sclera, black irises and off-white accents around the ears and tail.

"Do you mean the Umbreon?"

Umbreon was one of several hundred types of animals from an anime he used to watch back when he was a brat. Seeing that thing brought back some nostalgic memories.

The girl's face flushed as she looked at the game again, her eyes straying to the stuffed Umbreon before looking away just as quickly.

"N-no! Don't be stupid! W-w-w-what could I possibly want with such a cute—I mean, dumb stuffed animal!"

"I can get it for you." Kevin was positive the girl did, in fact, want the Umbreon, but was too embarrassed about liking something so childish to admit it. Deciding that he would get the girl her stuffed toy regardless, the young man walked straight past her and stood in front of the game.

After swiping his card through the slot, Kevin grabbed onto the joy stick and started moving it around. In response, the crane inside of the machine also began to move.

"I used to play these games a lot when I was younger," he told the girl, almost all of his concentration focused on the claw he was now controlling. "Back then I was so good at this game that I always managed to get something. Let's see if I still—ah-ha! Got it!"

Indeed, the crane managed to grab the stuffed Umbreon by the torso—a perfect catch—and pull it out of the pool of toys. As the item dropped into the small chute, Kevin reached in, pulled it out, and presented it to the girl.

"Here you go."

The girl, who Kevin noticed had the most stunning ice blue eyes, grabbed the stuffed toy with shaky hands. She held it at arm's-length, regarding the prize like it was some kind of alien entity. It was only was only after giving the girl her prize that he noticed her face was... blue? Yes, her entire face had turned an icy shade of blue.

At that moment, Kevin shivered. Maybe it was just him, but it felt like the temperature had suddenly plummeted several dozen degrees. He could feel goosebumps breaking out on his skin!

"Hey, are you okay?" he ignored the chill in favor of worrying over the girl. "Your face is, well, um, kind of, ah, blue."

"I-I-I'm f-f-f-fine! Idiot!" The girl snapped, making Kevin almost stumble back. "I didn't ask you to get this for me! I could have gotten it myself! Hmph!" With one last huff, the girl whirled around and stalked off, the Umbreon clutched tightly to her chest.

Kevin ran a hand through his hair. "What was that all about?"

"I think I should be the one asking that." A voice said from behind.

Kevin spun around to see Lilian standing before him, hands on her hips. She looked displeased. Kevin didn't know why, but he felt extraordinarily uneasy at seeing such an unpleasant expression on a face that normally appeared so cheerful.

"Who was that?" Lilian asked in a, *"you'd better have a good explanation for why you were talking to another girl while I was otherwise preoccupied"* kind of voice.

"Huh? You mean that girl?" Kevin shook off his uneasiness and shrugged. There wasn't any reason for him to feel so uneasy, right? "I dunno."

"You don't know?" Lilian's frown deepened as she stared at her mate. "Then why were you talking to her?"

"I just saw her staring at one of those stuffed toys in the prize machine." Kevin gestured to the arcade game next to him. "I thought I'd be nice and get it for her, since she seemed to be having some kind of trouble."

Though he didn't know what kind of trouble she'd been having. Not enough credits to play? Already played several times and couldn't get her prize? He didn't know; he hadn't thought to ask her.

"And that's it?" Lilian leaned forward, forcing Kevin to lean back as she invaded his personal space, her green eyes narrowing as they pierced his own blue orbs. "There was nothing else going on?"

"Going on?" Kevin scratched his left cheek with his index finger. "What do you mean? What would be going on?"

"Never mind," Lilian sighed. Her mate was clueless. Though at least she now knew this was just a simple act of kindness, and not because he knew that girl in the weird getup. "Since it looks like you were just being nice, I'll let it go… this time."

For some reason, Kevin felt a strange sense of relief wash over him, like he had just avoided some kind of disaster that would have ended in a horrifyingly erotic, yet strangely funny way. How odd.

"But I want you to get me something from that grabby game, too."

"Alright." Kevin shrugged. He could do that easily enough. "What do you want?"

"I want that!"

"The fox plushie?" It was kind of clichè'd to get a kitsune a fox plushie, wasn't it? But if that's what she wanted. "Sure."

Kevin grabbed ahold of the joystick, and a new game began.

***

Eric sat on the ground in the middle of the arcade, crying manly, waterfall-like tears as he waited for Kevin and Lilian to show up.

"Where are they?!" He wailed like a child having a tantrum. "Where are they, where are they, where are they?!"

Everyone in the general vicinity gave the perverted boy a wide berth, staying at least several meters away as they watched him warily. They didn't want to get wet from his tears, *or* the raincloud that had randomly appeared over his head and seemed to have a tumultuous storm brewing within.

"Where is my Tit Maiden?! I want my Tit Maiden!"

Many of the girls present were so disgusted that even if they *had* been inclined to go near him—which they weren't—those words would have sent them running away screaming. Some of them actually *did* run away screaming.

"Waaah!"

Chapter 2

Chris Fleischer's Big Sister

"Lilian?"

"Yes, Beloved?"

"I probably shouldn't be asking this, but why are you holding onto me so tightly?"

"You're right. You shouldn't be asking that."

"I hope that's not your way of avoiding my question."

Kevin wanted to frown. He didn't know why, but ever since they'd left the arcade—and in fact, even before vacating the arcade, Lilian had been clinging to him like some kind of limpet.

A hot, super sexy limpet, but a limpet nonetheless.

Kevin's friends seemed to be taking in a good deal of pleasure from his discomfort. Or at least Lindsay—who they'd conveniently run into after leaving the arcade to get Lilian some Greek cuisine ("I'm craving food from the country I grew up in," she'd said)—was taking a lot of enjoyment from his predicament. The expression on her face was that of someone who had prime seats to her favorite form of entertainment.

The others just gave him angry and jealous glares.

Except for Justin, who was staring at… something off in the distance. Kevin didn't know what, and he wasn't sure he wanted to.

"I can't believe this!" Eric appeared to be the most upset amongst their little group. While Alex and Andrew—who they'd also met at the arcade—were giving Kevin somewhat dirty looks, their stares were nothing compared to Eric's. His was a look of apoplectic rage that, in all honesty, looked far too funny for anyone to take seriously. He reminded Kevin of this baboon he'd once seen at the zoo when he was a kid; pinched face, puffed up cheeks and all.

"How dare that prick parade his relationship with my Tit Maiden in front of me!" Eric continued. However, because he was currently gnawing on his shirt, his words sounded more like a garbled, "Hn mm mmhm mm! Noh har hah hir mm hm!"

The group of seven were sitting at the small Greek restaurant that Lilian had chosen to eat at. Their table was round, possessed seven chairs, and was located in a gated section outside of the restaurant. An umbrella sat in the center to shield them from the sun. The table was so small that they were all forced to crowd around it, leaving little space for them to move.

Lilian had used this as an excuse to get closer to Kevin. She was practically sitting in his lap.

"I can't understand a word you just said," Alex declared.

"Neither could I," Andrew echoed.

"… Can…" That one came from Justin.

"Of course you can." Alex rolled his eyes. "With all that screamo stuff you listen to, I'm not surprised. You're probably used to translating words that make no sense."

"… Whatever…"

"So, you two look like you're having fun." Lindsay ignored the byplay between the four clowns, because that's really all they were. Lindsay often thought of them as a comedy troupe.

"We had a lot of fun," Lilian declared, giving Lindsay a frosty glare. She still didn't like the tomboyish girl. Not one bit. "My Beloved took me to the arcade and we had a blast. We shot zombies and played basketball *and* he got me this fox plushie."

Lilian used her head to gesture toward the fox plushie in question, which sat on the table next to her. She would have used her arms, but they were currently wrapped around Kevin.

"Damn that bastard!" Eric growled through his tears, not of pride—this time, of anger. Comedy Anger, to be exact. "First he steals away my Tit Maiden, then he spends all day at the arcade with her *and* he gets her a fox plushie! This is a betrayal of the worst kind! Damn you, Kevin Swift!"

"Oh, be quiet," Kevin grumbled. "Don't blame me for your own deficiencies. Maybe this is karma coming back to bite you for being such a lech. Perhaps this will teach you treat women with respect." A pause. "And stop mentioning Tit Maidens!"

While the boys held their own conversation, Lindsay eyed her fellow female cautiously. That glare really was something else. Maybe it was just her, but it looked almost like those eyes hid a strange fire behind them, one that wanted to burn her alive. It might've just have been a reflection of the light, but it still made the tomboyish blond feel distinctly uncomfortable.

"Oh… i-is that so? Well, I'm glad you two had fun." When all Lilian did was continue glaring at her, Lindsay asked, "Have I done something to offend you?"

"Not at all," Lilian assured her, though the way her eyes penetrated Lindsay like sharp swords made everyone doubt the sincerity of her words. "You haven't done anything to offend me… yet." Her lips quirked upwards into a smile. It was quite possibly the most artificial smile any of them had ever seen. "If you ever do upset me, though, don't worry; you'll be the first to know."

If the tomboyish soccer player ever offended her in any way, she would be getting punished kitsune-style. Nothing said "all my hate" like a string of the most humiliating pranks ever known to man. And yes, Lilian *was* that vindictive.

***

The loud clicking of heels on pavement resounded through the complex as a young woman walked up to an apartment. Her dark gray business suit ruffled as she moved with a confidence that could not be copied by just anyone. She had abstained from wearing a skirt—namely because she hated skirts—instead opting to wear a pair of pants with her white shirt, dark gray suit and pants combination.

As her heeled shoes ascended the stairs, her eyes surveyed the complex in utter dismay. The walls had several large cracks running along them, there was vulgar graffiti drawn on the walls, the roof needed to be re-tiled, and the doors were chipped and had paint peeling off them. The entire place had the appearance of a derelict, run-down trash heap not even worthy of being called "home" to a hobo, much less a normal person. No sane person would choose to live in a place like this.

It really made her wonder about the sanity of the person she had come to visit; just why her little brother had picked this place to live was beyond her understanding.

She stopped in front of her destination, a door labeled 2090. Like all the other entrances, the door's red paint was chipped, peeled, and had long since faded from its original color to a much lighter shade.

She was actually kind of surprised by how old, worn and damaged the door—nay, the entire complex looked. While this certainly wasn't the ritziest part of Phoenix, it wasn't the ghetto either. She hadn't realized places like this existed outside of the slummiest parts of the city. Hell, this place looked like it might've been transported directly from a third world country in the middle of a violent secession war.

She knocked on the door several times, then stepped back and waited for someone to receive her.

And she waited.

And waited.

And waited.

Eventually, the young woman got tired of waiting. With a large vein pulsing on her forehead, throbbing in a way that was reminiscent of *She-Hulk*, the woman in the business suit took a single step forward, twisted her body until she stood perpendicular to the door, lifted up her leg, cocked it back and let it fly.

There was a loud *bang!* like that of a high-grade explosive going off. The door swung inward, smacking against the wall with concussive force.

The woman stepped into the open entrance, her eyes sweeping across the living room with distaste. Stains covered the floor, several different kinds of sauce coated the walls in large splatters, making her think of a mad painter tossing buckets of paint, and the ceiling had so many cracks in it that the owner of the apartment probably had to worry about flooding whenever it rained.

Speaking of the owner…

"Did you really have to break down my door, sis? Shit, don't you know how fucking long it's going to take for me to fix that?"

Smirking, she turned her head to see her younger brother leaning against the wall. Her smirk widened when she saw the pitiful state he was in. His body was covered in ugly purple bruises that resembled polka dots, his face looked like someone had taken a branding iron to it, and he was missing several chunks of hair, leaving him partially bald. The bald spots also had major burns on them.

He had definitely seen better days.

"Hello, little brother. You look like shit. Did that temper of yours finally get the best of you? It looks like you got into a fight and bit off a little more than you could chew."

"As if!"

Her little brother scowled at her, then winced as jolts of agony went up his side. Rubbing the spot that was still lanced with pain, he glared at his older sibling for even suggesting that the person who did this was stronger than him.

"She just caught me off guard! That's all!"

"Oh ho, so it's a she, is it? You mean to tell me you got your ass kicked by a woman?"

It was only after hearing the series of rhetorical questions that the younger of the two realized his mistake.

"Chris, Chris, Chris," she repeated his name condescendingly, walking further into the room, and sitting down on his ratty old couch. She stretched out languidly, ignoring how disgusting the furniture was in favor of appearing nonchalant. Arms resting along the headrest, one leg crossed over the other, she leaned back and gave her younger brother a look of mixed disappointment and amusement. "I've told you before not to mess with a woman. Don't you know that 'hell hath no fury like a woman scorned?' We're devils in disguise when we want to be; even human girls."

"Whatever." Chris Fleischer scowled. "I don't want to hear that from you, Kiara."

Chris took several tiny, shuffling steps forward, using the wall for support as he made his way toward his sister. His face was etched in an expression of mild torment as he walked; his teeth were grit so hard that his gums began to bleed, the crimson liquid dribbling down his mouth and onto his chin.

"Whoa, this girl really did do a number on you," Kiara observed as her little brother walked into the room with all the grace of a drunken k*appa* (a type of turtle yōkai), which was to say that he had no grace at all.

"Shut up!" Chris growled as he let go of the wall and took a step forward. "I don't want to hear—ack!" His words were cut off by a loud grunt when his body flared up in pain. Without a wall to support him, he began falling to the ground.

A soft breeze rushed past him and Chris suddenly found his momentum halted. He looked down to see an arm across his chest, followed the length of the arm up to the shoulder, neck, and finally, the face of his older sister.

"Easy there, little brother. It's clear that you're nowhere near close to being healed."

"I don't need your help!" Chris growled, then yelped as the skin between his second and third lumbar vertebrae was pinched. He whimpered as the pinched skin was twisted painfully.

"Now, don't be an idiot, little brother," Kiara chided the vulgar-mouthed boy as she took her finger off the nerves in his back. "It's perfectly all right to ask for help—and you really do look like you need it. Don't let your pride get in the way of asking for help."

The foolish young man was clearly incapable of walking on his own. Just why her idiot of a brother tried to act all macho and tough was beyond her. She still remembered when he was just a brat who cried like a baby at even the slightest injury. The whole macho man act that he put on display wouldn't work on her.

"Whatever," Chris mumbled as Kiara helped him over to the couch, rolling her eyes as she did so, "Bitch."

He yelped again when Kiara pinched the nerves in his neck this time.

"And don't be rude, either. I didn't raise you to be an ungrateful little brat." Kiara set Chris up on the couch and then placed her hands on her hips as she eyed the room once more. "And speaking of raising, I didn't raise you to be a slob either. Seriously, Chris, this place is disgusting. I would say it's a pigsty, but then I'd be insulting the pigs."

"I don't see how that matters!" Kiara didn't like the look on Chris' face. "This isn't home. It's just a place for me to rest and regain my strength, nothing more. A real warrior doesn't need a place to call home."

"Don't you start that again!" Kiara barked as anger overtook her. "I don't want to hear you paraphrasing our idiot father like that, lest you become just as bad as he is!"

"Don't call our old man an idiot!" Chris bared his teeth at the older, much more powerful inu. "Our father is a great man! The most powerful warrior of our kind!"

"Our father is a selfish old prick who abandoned our mother when he found out she was pregnant with us, and only came back once he heard we were still alive!" Kiara shot back, her narrowed eyes glaring into Chris's own angry irises. "And even then, he ended up leaving after he decided we were too weak to be related to him! Our mother *died* because of him! Or did you forget that?!"

"Our mother was a weak little bitch!" Chris tried to justify their father's actions by insulting their mother. It was a big mistake, quite possibly the dumbest thing he could have said. But then, Kiara knew that he'd never been the most intelligent pup in the litter. "She was just a whore who would spread her legs for any two-bit—"

SLAP!

Chris' vitriolic tirade was forced back into his mouth as Kiara slapped him, hard. It was so hard, in fact, that not only did the powerful smack force his head to nearly spin, but he also bit down on his tongue. He whimpered as blood began gushing from the two puncture marks his canines made.

"If you ever insult our mother again, mark my words Chris, I will disown you." Kiara's voice was surprisingly calm as she spoke. "Don't forget who it is that's paying for everything you own. This apartment, disgusting as it is, is only yours because *I* pay for it. Those clothes on your back—I bought them for you. Even your food is paid for with the monthly stipend that I send you. Without me, you'd be out on the street, homeless, starving and with no way to make a living. That is what will happen if I disown you, and mark my words, I will if I ever hear you insult our mother again."

"Whatever," Chris mumbled.

"What was that?!"

"I said I'm sorry."

Kiara glared at her younger brother, a glare that looked like it could melt through solid steel, and was easily the most frightening expression Chris had ever been on the receiving end of. If it wouldn't have caused undue stress to his still-healing wounds, he would have shivered under that glare.

"Apology accepted." Kiara's voice was still only lukewarm. A moment passed and, with a sigh, she sat down next to Chris on the couch.

She wished she could stay mad at Chris, but the truth was, even if she didn't necessarily *like* Chris, he was still her brother, and he was the only real family she had left—their good for nothing father certainly didn't count. As far as she was concerned that dog was just a sperm donor unworthy of the title. They had lost their mother at a young age. She doubted Chris even remembered much of the woman who gave birth to him.

Recalling her mother brought back memories that she wished she didn't have. Their mother had always been a sweet, kind woman, not at all like most members of their species. She didn't hold to their prejudices; didn't believe that violence could solve anything—much less everything like most inu—and was always willing to forgive others for their past transgressions. Perhaps that was why their father had left her, only showing up again when he wanted to mate.

Kiara shook herself free of these unpleasant memories. They wouldn't help her. She loved her mother dearly, but that woman was long dead, and nothing she did could change that.

"So why don't you tell me who did this to you?" Kiara finally decided to get down to business. She could already guess that this was the reason Chris had called her up; he never called for social reasons, and had never asked her to personally come down before. That he had called now meant only one thing, and regardless of whether she disliked him as a person or not, Chris was still her younger brother. She wouldn't let whoever injured him get away with it unpunished.

***

It was a fairly late hour when Kevin and Lilian arrived back home. While the sun hadn't begun to set, it had certainly moved across the sky. Pretty soon it would dip behind the rocky peaks and sheer cliffs in the distance, painting the sky in brilliant hues of pinks, purples, reds and oranges.

They must have spent a good five or six hours at the arcade and strip mall, an amount of time that Kevin found surprising. He'd never spent more than a few hours at the arcade before, usually leaving around one or two in the afternoon. It was after four.

However, there were more important things on his mind than the time.

"Why were you so insulting to Lindsay today?" Kevin felt like his voice should have sounded much angrier than it did, and it probably would have, if he wasn't so distracted by the girl in front of him.

Lilian's short skirt and the fact that she was elevated above and in front of him, meant that Kevin was on the receiving end of a picture-perfect view of her panties; black lace with floral embroidery. And because her sexy underwear was partially see-through, he was seeing a lot more than he bargained for.

His eyes stared at the way her panties folded as she walked. While there was a black strip hiding her treasure, he could still see the outline, and it was causing him a number of serious problems.

The largest part of Kevin, that of the shy boy who still couldn't speak to girls very well, was embarrassed and uncomfortable by the sight. However, another part of him which seemed to be making a bit more headway these days, that of the young man undergoing puberty, was all for the view.

Both sides of him presented a huge problem. On the one hand, he felt ready to pass out. On the other, he felt hard enough to cut diamonds. Neither sensation was very pleasant. Kevin had never suffered from a case of blue balls before, but imagined that he would be getting first-hand experience tonight.

That old saying about how there was a first time for everything never seemed more true than that moment.

It doesn't have to be that way, a seductive voice whispered in his ear. He banished the thought immediately. He wasn't going to use Lilian like that, and he wasn't going to betray his feelings for Lindsay either.

"I wasn't insulting her," Lilian defended, snapping Kevin out of his discomforting thoughts.

"You were glaring at her the entire time she was with us," Kevin informed the redhead succinctly, his voice growing just a touch irritated. "And several times you made poorly-veiled insults about her choice of clothing."

"I was trying to be helpful."

"You said that her clothing made her look like a dyke."

"And now that she knows this, she can seek to correct it by buying more fashionable outfits."

Kevin's lips thinned as they finally made it to the top of the stairwell. Now that the sight of Lilian's panties was gone, he could think much more analytically.

Those panties were a serious distraction; danger in every sense of the word. Or maybe it was what they hid that presented the true danger? Something to think about for later. What was more distracting? The panties? Or the treasure hiding within them?

A question that all men have asked at some point, he was sure.

“I would prefer it if you didn't say things like that. Lindsay's been my friend for a long time,” Kevin said, “And she's a very kind-hearted and sweet girl. You won't find many people nicer or more accepting than her. She's never rude and she doesn't gossip. She was even being nice to you, even though you kept insulting her.”

Lilian paused at the door as her mate scolded her. With each point he made, her shoulders flinched. By the time Kevin had finished locking up the bike, she still hadn't moved, forcing him to stand behind her, waiting.

“Lilian?”

“Does it really mean that much to you?” she asked, her voice incredibly soft. It held a tremor that he'd never heard before. “Does *she* mean that much to you?”

“Lindsay is my friend,” Kevin told her. Sure, he wanted them to be more, but that wasn't in the cards at the moment—he was still just getting used to talking to her like a regular person. She also thought he and Lilian were an item, so it made confessing his feelings very difficult, not to mention awkward. “I dislike it when people are rude to my friends.”

Lilian remained silent.

“It's the same with Eric,” Kevin continued, since the redhead still wasn't speaking. “I know you don't like him. To be honest, I don't know any girls who *do* like him. Even Lindsay dislikes him, but she doesn't say anything because he's my best friend, regardless of how lecherous and perverted he is.”

“I see,” Lilian sniffled a bit.

“Lilian?”

“I suppose… if it really means that much to you, I can try not to be so mean to that girl; since she's your *friend*.”

“Thank you.” Kevin said, smiling at Lilian's back.

“However, don't think that just because I've decided to be nice doesn't mean I'm not going to keep my eyes on her!”

“Eh?”

Lilian spun around, her eyes narrowed in determination and possessing a fire within them.

"Just because she's your friend doesn't mean I'm going to trust her not to butt in on my territory. If anything, I need to keep an even closer eye on her now!"

"And you totally lost me."

"I won't lose to her!"

Kevin didn't know why, but seeing Lilian standing there, one fist planted on her hip, and the other near her face as she glared at something beyond his sight, gave him an inexplicable feeling of unease. A powerful knot formed in his stomach, one that he didn't think had anything to do with lunch. He could only hope that this wasn't some kind of premonition.

***

"Hahaha!"

"It's not funny!"

"Kekeke!"

"Would you stop fucking laughing!? It's not funny!"

Chris glared down at his sister, who had fallen off the couch and was now lying on her back, her arms around her middle, laughing at him. Her feet were kicking up in the air and tears of mirth streamed down her face. If she laughed any harder, she might bust a gut, as the old phrase went. That, or she might lose control of her bladder, which would be embarrassing but so worth it right then, as far as she was concerned.

"It is too funny!" Kiara gasped out in between bouts of uproarious laughter. "You… you… I can't believe you got beaten by a *two-tails*! Two-tailed kitsune are some of the weakest yōkai around, and you handed your ass to you on a silver platter by one—it's absolutely hilarious!"

Gritting his teeth in anger, Chris glared down at his older sibling, his face burning with the humiliation and shame of defeat. Bad enough that he had lost to a two-tails, but to have that fact rubbed in by Kiara? That was just not cool.

"This is why I didn't want to tell you! Fuck! Dammit!" Chris growled. As he let his anger get the best of him, his transformation began to slip. His canines sharpened to look like fangs, and fur started sprouting from his pores. He flinched, however, when an intense, burning pain shot through his body like liquid nitrogen, forcing the transformation to reverse. "I knew you would laugh if I told you. Calling you for help was a mistake!"

"No," Kiara chortled a bit more before finally managing to calm herself down. "No, it wasn't." She climbed back onto the couch. "I'm sorry." She didn't sound very sorry. "I just never expected you to lose to a two-tails. Everyone knows that among yōkai, two-tailed kitsune are some of the weakest of us. They lack the power, skill and control necessary to use their higher-tiered abilities, which is what makes older kitsune such formidable foes."

"Yeah, well, this kitsune had no trouble using those specialized powers of hers." Chris scowled. Kiara perked up at this new piece of knowledge.

"Really?"

"Yes, really." The scowl deepened. "She was throwing these strange balls of light at me… and after I hurt that boy toy of hers, she went fucking ballistic and shot some kind of weird, white beam out of her tails."

"Oh, I see," Kiara sighed.

"See? What do you see?"

"Why you lost."

"What do you mean?"

"Chris, you don't mess with a woman's man, regardless of whether they're kitsune, human or whatever. It just isn't done. Especially if that human just happens to be mated to a kitsune."

Chris frowned at his sister.

"I don't get it."

"Of course you don't," Kiara sighed again. Her brother was such an idiot.

Chris scowled, but before he could ask his elder sibling what she was talking about, the woman in question stood up. She stretched her arms above her head and grinned down at her brother.

"Don't worry, little brother." She brought her hands back down and looked at him. "As your older sister, it's my duty to help you out. I'll be sure to get even for you."

"I don't want to get even!" The scowl was back. "I want revenge!"

"Same difference." Kiara waved a hand dismissively in the air. "You just leave that little kitsune to me." She turned around and crossed her arms as she looked down at the younger inu. "Now then, I think it's time you went to bed. You're still injured, after all."

"I'm fine! It's not that late! And I'm not that hurt!"

"Oh really?" Kiara leaned down until she was almost invading Chris' personal space. She reached out with a hand, extended one finger… and then poked him in the torso.

"Ouch! Goddammit! That hurt!"

"Oh?" Poke. "I thought you weren't injured." Poke. "Come on." Poke. "Why are you shouting like that?" Poke. "What's the matter tough guy?"

"Ack! Oh for fuck's sake! Stop poking me, dammit!"

Chapter 3

Grocery Store Stress

Steam rose up within the room. It fogged the mirrors, creating swirling eddies of white streamers that drifted lazily about the enclosed space. It caused precipitation to coalesce on the walls and ceiling, forming large droplets of clear liquid that periodically fell to the floor, splashing against the tile.

Kevin Swift stood in the shower, his shoulders hunched and his hands pressed flat against the wall, fingers splayed. The hot spray from the shower hit his back, plastering his messy blond hair to his head and face. The muscles in his back relaxed, the tension slowly easing as the hot water massaged the aches and pains out of his body, dissolving them with calm efficiency. The young man let out a quiet groan as he allowed himself this tiny reprieve before life caught up to him. The likelihood that this shower would be all the peace and quiet he had today was very strong.

He eventually turned off the water, his brief period of rest finished. Not long after that he made his way into the kitchen, dressed in a pair of form-fitting black jeans and a dark red t-shirt. As his bare feet padded along the hallway, he noticed something unusual—or to be more precise, the lack of something he'd grown to expect.

There was no scent wafting on the air. Ever since Lilian had taken up residence with him, he would notice the scent of her cooking long before he actually reached the kitchen. That was missing this morning. How strange.

The carpeted floor changed to tile as he entered the kitchen, and he hissed as the coldness of the floor jolted him awake. He adapted quickly, and began searching for the fox-girl. It didn't take long. She wasn't that hard to spot.

That day Lilith was dressed in blue jean shorts that were, as always, cut immodestly, riding so high up her legs that they just barely covered her perfect, heart-shaped butt. On her feet were the gladiator sandals that he had bought for her during their first shopping excursion. She must have loved those sandals, as she wore them more than any of her other footwear.

He couldn't see her shirt, or at least not fully. The only thing he noticed was that it possessed a lot of color, but he was unable to make out the rest.

Lilian was bent over to the point where, aside from her derrière, the only thing he could really see was the crown of her head, and the long tresses of hair that trailed down to the floor. Which would also explain why he was so focused on the lower half of her attire. It had absolutely nothing to do with her marvelously crafted buttocks, or her impossibly long and sexy legs. Really.

What was she doing bent over? Kevin didn't really know, but she appeared to be looking through the fridge. The refrigerator door was open and her head was poking inside of it.

After several seconds of standing there, Kevin realized with startling clarity that he was ogling Lilian's backside.

In order to hide the growing feeling of someone taking a blowtorch to his face, he coughed into his hand.

"What are you doing, Lilian?"

"Eep!"

Kevin blinked as Lilian squeaked in surprise. He blinked again when she tried to raise her head, only to end up smacking it on a shelf in the fridge. Lilian rubbed the back of her cranium, which was now sporting an obscenely large bump.

"Ow."

"Lilian?"

"Oh, Beloved!" Lilian seemed to forget about her injury and looked at him with a fixed smile on her face, like she was only smiling for his sake and not because she was actually happy. He wondered if something was wrong. "How was your shower?"

"Uh, fine." Kevin looked at the normally peppy redhead oddly before shrugging. This girl always acted strangely, so why should now be any different? "What exactly are you doing?"

"What am I doing?" Lilian parroted the question—was she stalling? "I was, uh, that is to say I…" Lilian scratched the back of her head. "… I was trying to make breakfast."

"Trying?" Kevin raised an eyebrow. "I'm not sure I follow. Don't you usually have breakfast done by now? Is something wrong? Do you need help?"

It had been a while since Kevin had cooked breakfast. Lilian hadn't allowed him to, something about it being her duty as his mate or some weird excuse like that. He didn't get it, but hadn't felt like arguing the point and just let the girl have her kitchen time.

"All of the ingredients I had in my Extra Dimensional Storage Space have been used up," she admitted, then gestured toward the fridge. "I was trying to find what I needed to make a Greek frittata, but you don't have any of the ingredients necessary." Her face took on a thoughtful expression. "Actually, you don't have much of anything in your fridge. I'm kinda surprised."

"Well, I haven't had time to do much shopping since you came along," Kevin told her, feeling a little sheepish. After saying this, his mind registered the rest of what she'd said, and he looked at her in surprise. "Wait, so you're saying that all the food you made was from your storage space thingy?"

"Extra Dimensional Storage Space," Lilian corrected him. "And of course that's where everything came from. You didn't have a lot of the ingredients that I needed to make our meals."

That actually made a lot of sense. Kevin had often wondered where she got all the ingredients to make the many different dishes in her repertoire. He knew for a fact that he didn't have foods like lamb, feta or anything of the sort in his fridge. All he had was basic food stuff; chicken, salmon and vegetables.

"But wait." Kevin furrowed his brow as another thought occurred to him. "Are you telling me that you have all this food in your storage space, but you don't have a single article of clothing in there?"

"I do have a few clothes in there." Upon Lilian's admittance, Kevin's right eye twitched. If she had clothes, then why did he have to buy all of those outfits for her? And why hadn't she worn them when she had first revealed herself as a kitsune? That would have made things so much easier for him. "But it's all lingerie."

The eye twitching increased in intensity, and it brought friends.

His left eye began twitching as well.

"You mean to tell me that the only kind of clothing in your storage space thingy is lingerie, and yet you have what amounted to nearly two weeks worth of food in there?"

"Extra Dimensional Storage Space."

"Whatever. Just answer the question."

"Why answer a question that you already know the answer to?"

Kevin's hands clenched into fists, his knuckles turning white. His arms began shaking, and a rather large vein pulsed prominently on his forehead. He felt like he was going to explode.

Easy does it, Kevin. You need to keep calm. Yes, just remain calm...

"Can you at least tell me why the only thing you seem to be carrying around is food and lingerie?" he asked calmly.

"Don't forget my *Dungeon Master's Guide* and the *Player's Handbook."*

"Right, and those. Why are those the only items you're carrying?"

"That's easy. It's because…"

"I swear to God that if you mention The Author one more time, I'll… I'll…" Kevin scrunched up his face in thought for several seconds, before scratching his head as he realized something. "Well, I honestly don't know what I'll do, but it won't be nice," he quickly added.

Lilian looked at him with a blank expression for a full second before it turned sly and mischievous. It was enough to remind him that this girl was a kitsune; a creature that had pranking in her blood. Kevin suddenly felt dread rise up in the pit of his stomach.

"Are you saying you'll punish me if I mention The Author?"

"Uh, well, I…"

"Would you pull down my shorts, bend me over this table and smack my bum until I scream out your name in delirious ecstasy?"

Kevin, rather than getting embarrassed and turning into a blushing, stuttering mess, deadpanned. "For some reason, I don't think you would consider that a punishment."

"Oh poo." Lilian pouted. She perked up a second later. "How about you…"

"I won't be tying you to the bed, shoving a ball gag in your mouth, and having my wicked way with you until you scream yourself hoarse either."

"You're such a spoilsport, Beloved."

"Yeah, I'm a spoilsport." Kevin rolled his eyes. For some reason, he felt very out of character in that moment. He wondered if he was getting desensitized to the things this girl said. "And now that we've apparently finished this pointless conversation, let's get going."

Lilian stopped pouting, his words causing her to look at him with adorable inquisitiveness. "Where are we going?"

"To the grocery store, where else?"

***

Kiara growled as she looked in the small, dingy fridge. Not only was the exterior covered in grime and rust and stains, but it looked like someone had taken raw meat, stuck some C4 on it, and let it blow up all over the interior, too. Blood stains covered the walls and racks. Fungus grew on what little food could be found inside. Kiara swore she actually saw a piece of fungus-covered bread squirming around as if it were a living, breathing entity.

I feel like I'm at the portal to Yog-Sothoth's domain.

Standing up with a scowl, she smoothed down her business suit and marched through the living room. Her feet thudded loudly as she stomped across the grease-stained carpet, stormed down the torn up hallway, then ground to a halt in front of the door to her brother's room.

Kiara glared at the typical male door complete with male paraphernalia on it: traffic signs and a large, horrible drawing of a dog chewing off a man's leg with the words "Beware of inu" written below in sloppy hand writing. The door was also disgusting; covered in dusts, stains, dents and cracks. Seeing this really pissed her off. Chris clearly didn't realize how much money she spent on him. Ungrateful brat.

Not wanting to touch the door any longer than necessary for fear of what she might contract, Kiara latched onto the door, twisted and yanked, letting go of the handle as quickly as she could. The door swung wide open, crashing into the wall to generate a loud *bang!* With the obstruction out of her way, Kiara stomped into the room.

Much like the rest of the apartment, her little brother’s room was, in a word, abominable. Everything inside of the bedroom looked sickeningly filthy, from floor to ceiling. It looked like the room had gone fifteen years since its last cleaning, and considering Chris had only lived there for a little over a year, that was saying something.

Kiara stomped up to the bed, and cast a withering glare at the large lump underneath the sheets.

“What the fuck is up with your fridge?” She didn't swear very often, not nearly as much as her foul-mouthed brother at least, but this situation definitely warranted a bit more vitriol than normal. “The only food in your fridge is several months old and covered in mold, and it looks like someone detonated raw steak inside of it! Are you really so irresponsible that you would even let your fridge get as fucked up as the rest of your apartment?!”

The apartment being a complete and utter wreck she could understand; Chris had never been one for cleaning up his disaster-zone styled messes. She wasn’t at all surprised that his bachelor pad—if such a sty could be called that—looked like a level-five biohazard. But even then, she had expected that he would be able to, at the very least, take care of his own food.

And now she’d discovered that he had not only wrecked his apartment, but that all of the food in his fridge dated back to when he had first moved in, which was food that she had gone shopping for.

By all eight-million gods this pissed her off! He was so lucky that he was injured. If the wounds he had suffered from during his fight with the kitsune weren't so grievous, she would have kicked his ass so hard that he wouldn't be able to shit for weeks!

“Well?!” Her voice came out as an angry growl. “Answer me, dammit!”

“Shut the fuck up, sis!” Chris shouted as he slammed a pillow over his head. “Can't you see I'm trying to fucking sleep?”

Kiara's teeth bared themselves in a fierce snarl that would have had the younger inu crapping his pants had he seen it. Her eyes narrowed, and her sharp canines glinted in the low lighting.

So the brat wanted to sleep, did he? Well that was just too bad, because she had no intention of letting him sleep—not after what she had seen.

Leaning over, Kiara shifted her hands underneath the mattress and, without ceremony, yanked on it. Chris unleashed a terrified scream as he tumbled out of bed and onto the floor in a tangled heap of limbs and bed sheets.

For several seconds, Chris struggled to release himself from the tangled heap of linen, yelping and whimpering as his struggles lit all of his nerve endings on fire.

Kiara stood over him, arms folded under her chest, watching her little brother squirm and wriggle about. It was almost painful to watch. Painful, and pathetic.

Finally, the younger inu managed to free himself.

"Gods dammit, what the hell was that for?!" Chris shouted, panting for breath.

"That was for being an ass," Kiara responded in a cool voice. Now that she had gotten most of the anger out of her system, she had finally calmed down. "Now get up. I want you to clean out that fridge."

"What? Why?!"

"Because someone has to buy groceries, and you're clearly too incompetent to do the shopping yourself," Kiara informed him. Chris growled at the insult and she smirked. Hopefully, this would give the boy incentive to actually get off his lazy bum and start doing some work around the house, though she wasn't holding her breath. "When I get back that fridge better be spotless, got it?"

"Yeah, yeah," Chris grumbled under his breath, "Stupid bitch."

"What was that?"

"Nothing."

***

After stepping into the cool morning air, Kevin took in a deep breath, exhaling it all in one large gust. It was the first day of September, and the air had become a bit cooler. While still not as cold as he'd like, he wasn't going to complain.

While Lilian came behind him, Kevin strode over to his bike and proceeded to unlock it. At the same time, the two-tailed kitsune locked the front door using the spare key that he kept under the welcome mat.

"Where are we going for breakfast?" she asked as they walked down the stairs and onto the street. Kevin paused after mounting the bike, and looked back at Lilian with a frown.

"That's a good question."

Faced with the realization that they needed to go grocery shopping, Kevin had completely forgotten about how they hadn't had breakfast yet. After giving this conundrum some consideration, his face relaxed.

"I know a place we can go to," he informed the fox-girl as she got on his bike and leaned into him, her arms wrapping around his torso. "It's close to the grocery store, too, so we won't need to do any extra traveling—and stop groping me, dang it!"

Lilian pouted and, even though Kevin couldn't see it, he could imagine it well enough.

"But I can't help it, Beloved."

Kevin's right eye twitched.

"Yes, you can."

"Not when you give me such a perfect opportunity to feel your muscular chest."

Kevin felt heat rise to his cheeks at the unexpected compliment. It wasn't just the words, but the tone in her voice that made him really embarrassed. He could tell that she wasn't saying that just to be nice; she really meant it.

Talk about an ego boost. Nothing made a young man preen more than being told that he had nice pecs by a sexy girl like Lilian. Even he wasn't immune to such compliments.

Since he didn't know how to respond, Kevin didn't say anything, and instead began pedaling down the road.

The Le Monte apartment complex grew smaller as they took off down Dunlap Road. Kevin put more power into his pedaling as they rode down the bike lane; trees and buildings passed them by in a blur, the muscles in his legs working overtime to keep up the pace.

It was difficult to constantly pedal that hard with Lilian sitting behind him, but he actually enjoyed the challenge. If there was a silver lining to having Lilian go practically everywhere with him, it was that she forced the muscles in his legs to work more. He had noticed a couple of days ago that his legs, particularly his thighs, were a good deal stronger than they used to be. He could push himself much harder during track practice. While it wasn't a very noticeable difference yet, he was slowly pushing ahead of Chase in the speed department. Kevin felt positive that pretty soon his speed would completely surpass that of his rival's.

Not long after they left, the pair arrived at a small café that Kevin decided to have breakfast at. Known as *Pineapple Paradise*, the tiny café sat between a yoga gym and a pet shop. Due to the early hour, there were only a handful of people present. Kevin was grateful for that small blessing, as he didn't feel like dealing with a crowd.

He parked his bike next to the entrance, leaning it against the wall before he and Lilian entered. The door chimed as they walked in, and a young man dressed in gray slacks, a white shirt and a black apron with a pineapple on the front, greeted them from behind the bar-style register.

"Good morning. How can I help you two?"

Kevin's right hand clenched into a fist when he saw how the man leered at Lilian, who seemed completely oblivious to the attention. While she might not have noticed, he did. Like an active volcano, anger surged within him at the sight of this idiotic man, who looked well over twenty, stripping his companion with wanton eyes akin to a lecherous old fart. Didn't this jerk know the meaning of the word self-restraint?

A moment later, Kevin shook his head. What the heck had that been about? Why should he care if this man wanted to ogle Lilian? He didn't like the girl or anything, and he certainly had no romantic intentions toward her. She was just a friend.

Getting over his strange moment of irrational anger, Kevin looked at the large menu hanging above and behind the register. Considering his options, he placed his order. "I'll have your breakfast burrito, please."

The man typed up his order on the register.

"And would you like that with eggs or tofu?"

"Eggs."

"And what would the beautiful young lady like?"

Kevin wondered why he felt the sudden urge to deck the man in the face.

Lilian, still oblivious to the server's ogling, wore one of the cutest expressions of thoughtful contemplation that Kevin had ever seen. The cashier must have thought so, too, because his cheeks went pink and he lewdly licked his lips.

Another surge of anger. Kevin felt his desire to cave the man's face in grown stronger. He closed his eyes and took a deep breath.

What is wrong with me?

"I want the berries and cream parfait."

"And would you two like anything to drink?"

"Lilian?" Kevin looked at his companion, who shook her head. He then turned back to the young man and said, "We'll just have water."

"Okay. Just find a seat and we'll have your meal out in a few minutes."

"Right."

Kevin grabbed Lilian's hand and led her away before the lecherous fool could leer at her any more. He also decided that they would sit outside.

They found themselves sitting at one of the small round tables near the entrance. Without really thinking about it, Kevin pulled Lilian's chair out for her, which she thanked him for with a smile. He then seated himself at the opposite end and stared at the parking lot.

It was only a few seconds after sitting down that he became aware of the eyes on him. He turned his head to see Lilian gazing at him, her elbows on the table, and her chin resting in the palms of her hands. She wore a knowing smile, as if she'd just realized something amazing. It made him very uncomfortable, this smile, even more so than the times he caught her staring at him when he took off his shirt.

"What?" he asked, trying hard not to squirm.

"You were jealous," Lilian sang out, her smile growing wider.

"Jealous?" It took Kevin a second to realize what she was talking about, but when he did figure it out, his face took on a shade that had previously only been thought achievable by anime females. "I was not jealous! I was… I was…"

"Jealous."

"No, I wasn't!"

"You so were."

Wishing that he could do what all politicians did when faced with a situation they didn't know how to deal with—namely, bury his head in the sand and pretend the problem didn't exist—Kevin sank into his chair and tried to hide his face within the confines of his shirt.

"… Shut up…"

***

Now that she was no longer standing in her brother's dump of an apartment, Kiara's mood improved considerably. Oh sure, she was still upset—who wouldn't be after what she had to deal with? —but getting away from that garbage heap made her feel a lot better.

Still, she really wished her reason for leaving wasn't because she had to buy groceries for her brother. She clicked her tongue, feeling a mild surge of irritation. If only that idiot could take care of himself, then she wouldn't be in this position.

Kiara made a mental note to beat the crap out of Chris when he finished healing. It might not solve her problems, but damn if it wouldn't make her feel better. Kicking her brother's ass was always very therapeutic.

Walking down the aisles of a grocery store, a small basket in her left hand, she looked at the selection of food available. She didn't really know what to buy. Her brother had proven inept when it came to using fresh foods, or anything that spoiled if not eaten quickly. That meant she would be better off buying the brat canned foods.

She hated canned foods. They always tasted like tin. Still, it took a long time for them to spoil, and it wasn't like she would be the one eating them. Kiara had her own place and her own stock of food, all of which was picked fresh every week when she went shopping for herself.

She paused halfway down the canned food aisle. Blinking several times, Kiara sniffed the air, taking in a strangely familiar scent that she couldn't quite place.

"That smell…"

***

Secure Shopping had the appearance of your stereotypical grocery store; there were aisles upon aisles of shelves lined with various foodstuffs and home supplies. The tiled floor looked like a giant checkerboard, except for the bakery, deli and produce departments, which consisted of faux wooden floorboards. It was, in all regards, a very plain-looking grocery store.

Kevin and Lilian wandered down the aisles, him pushing the cart, and her walking by his side. Despite the mundane activity, Lilian's eyes shone with an enthusiastic glimmer, as her eyes surveyed the store with a child's enthusiasm.

This was the first grocery store that she had ever been in, which explained her enthusiasm. Her clan's village relied solely on their open market for foodstuffs; especially produce and meat, and there was only one bakery in the entire village for bread. They were an old-fashioned place reminiscent of a time since past. Buying products that relied on technology like a fridge to keep everything fresh was a novel concept for them.

“Do you have the list?” Kevin asked.

“Of course, just let me get it out.” Lilian reached in between her bosom and pulled out a small slip of paper.

Kevin scowled as two tiny dots of red, like nightlights in a dark room, stained his cheeks. “Do you always keep everything between your, well, you know… like that?”

“You mean between my boobs?” Lilian asked, not seeming to care one iota if anyone else heard her. Kevin was grateful that it was still early in the day, and that it was a weekend to boot. Most people didn’t get up this early on weekends. “Of course. That's where my Extra Dimensional Storage Space is.”

“Well, can't you put your Extra Dimensional whatcha mahoozit somewhere else?”

“Extra Dimensional Storage Space,” she corrected, “And of course not.” Lilian looked at her mate like he should know the reason why. He didn't, of course, so she was forced to elaborate. “It's a fanservice.”

Kevin didn't really like her explanation.

“And there you go again, talking about something that I will never understand.”

“It's okay, Beloved.” Lilian pecked her mate on the cheek before he could think of stopping her. “You just don't understand yet because you’re human, but I'm sure we can fix that. It will just take time.” A pause. “And sex. Lots and lots of sex.”

“Hearing you say that makes me not want to understand what you're talking about. Ever.” Lilian pouted at him, but Kevin ignored her in favor of changing topics. "What's our first item on the list?"

Lilian stopped trying to give him the Foxy Kit Eyes, and read from the slip of paper in her hands. "Let's see, the first items on the list are basil, cilantro and oregano."

"So seasonings first, then," Kevin determined. "Do you want it fresh or the stuff in containers?"

"I would prefer the fresh seasonings," Lilian told him. "Meals taste much better when everything is fresh."

"Though it also means we can't buy as much," Kevin informed her. "The stuff in the containers might not be fresh, but it'll last longer and it's cheaper."

"Does that mean you think we should get the container seasoning?"

"Let's get the fresh stuff," Kevin decided after a second's thought. "You're a better cook than I am, so you know better than me." Lilian was an awesome cook, so if she said that they should get fresh ingredients, then he would listen to her.

The smile that Lilian gave him thereafter had nothing to do with his decision. Really.

With their decision made, the pair walked to the produce department, where Kevin heard a voice calling out to him.

"Hey there, Kevin!"

The duo turned their heads. Standing a few feet away was a woman with short blond hair and brown eyes. She wore black pants and a khaki colored shirt, the standard uniform for Secure Shopping employees. A red apron had been thrown over her clothes, an added accessory to her outfit.

"Good morning, Dawn," Kevin greeted the friendly woman who worked in the produce department. He had known her ever since he started doing his own shopping. He still remembered how helpful she had been when he went shopping for the first time and hadn't known what to buy. "Keeping busy?"

"It's always busy here," Dawn replied with a smile. She always seemed to be smiling. Dawn was a very cheerful woman. "I haven't seen you around lately."

The smile on her face became sly when she looked at the beautiful redhead next to him. Lilian, for her part, stared at Dawn in idle curiosity, clearly wondering who this woman was.

"But I can't say I blame you for not showing up. You must have been too busy spending time with your girlfriend to go grocery shopping, huh?"

While Kevin's face became a mass of red, and he started sputtering out denials that neither female paid attention to, Lilian's cheeks took on a mild pink hue. She placed her hands against them, as if to mask her pleased response behind a demure mien.

"So you could tell that Kevin and I are a couple?"

Kevin stopped sputtering to gawk at Lilian, but recovered admirably seconds later.

"Dang it, Lilian! Don't give Dawn the wrong idea!"

The woman might look like a humble employee working in the produce department, and she might even be nice and helpful, but Kevin knew from experience that she could be also devious when she wanted to be. He clearly remembered the time he'd gotten into trouble for bringing a bird into the store; Dawn had teased him for weeks. He could only imagine how insufferable she would be if she thought he and Lilian were dating.

"I'm impressed." Dawn nodded her head up and down, surveying Lilian from head to toe with a critical eye. "You've managed to get yourself a gorgeous girlfriend. She's definitely a keeper."

Kevin buried his face in his hands as Lilian's smile widened. He was beginning to regret ever coming to this store.

The not-as-nice anymore woman thoughtfully rubbed her chin. "I don't think I've seen you around before. Are you must be new here…"

Kevin watched as the woman's eyes widened. He didn't know what thoughts were going through her head, but he had a very bad feeling. Somehow, he just knew that she would say something stupid and potentially humiliating.

"Wait! Don't tell me, you're a supermodel and this is your first time in Arizona!"

Kevin didn't know if a facepalm would be enough to express how dumb he thought Dawn's words were. He wondered if maybe smashing his face into a wall would express his opinion more clearly.

"But wait! How did Kevin get a supermodel girlfriend when he can't even talk to regular girls?" Dawn continued with a laugh.

At the insult to his masculine pride, Kevin tripped on a speck of dust, slamming face first into the floor.

"Ow..."

"No, I'm not a supermodel." Lilian smiled brightly at the woman. "Thank you for the compliment, though." Finally, she looked down at Kevin in concern, as he literally pried his face off the floor. "Are you alright, Beloved?"

"I'm fine." Kevin rubbed at his face, which now stung something fierce. At least he hadn't broken his nose. "Lilian, why don't you give me half of the list, and while Dawn helps you select the seasonings and whatever produce you need, I'll grab the other things we need."

He didn't want to be around these two as they continued talking. It would likely be far too embarrassing, and he felt humiliated enough as it was.

"I don't know," Lilian looked unsure. She didn't want to leave her mate's side for any reason.

"I'll be really quick," Kevin said, then added, "And this way we can get our shopping done faster. Then if you want we can, uh, go out for a picnic." It was only after Kevin finished speaking that he realized what he had suggested.

His eyes widened. Stupid, stupid, stupid! That was the dumbest thing he could have ever said; he might as well just ask Lilian on a date right now! What had possessed him to say that?

"A picnic with you..." Lilian's eyes had gone wide with shock, but that emotion only lasted for a second before the largest, most blindingly-bright smile that he had ever seen to date appeared on the fox-girl's face.

Kevin had to shut his eyes, lest he be blinded by the moé.

"Oh, Beloved! I love you so much!"

"Oof!"

"I can't believe my Beloved and I are finally going on a date! I'm so happy!"

It was easy to tell that Lilian was quite joyful. Kevin, on the other hand...

"Lilian... can't... breathe..."

... Not so much.

***

After just barely managing to escape with his chastity intact, Kevin found himself wandering the meat department, looking at the somewhat torn list that Lilian had given him.

"Let's see," he murmured as he studied the list, "I need to get beef loin, beef brisket, filet mignon, sirloin, porterhouse, ham, loin, Boston shoulder…" He went on to read more and more of the list, which moved on to include chicken, shrimp, crab, lamb, ground beef, mutton, venison and wild boar, of all things. The longer his irises scanned the list, the wider his eyes became.

This… this was a really long list. She didn't honestly think he could get all of this, did she? Some of the items weren't even available in America, much less a simple grocery store. Wild boar? Seriously?

As Kevin tried to decide how to tell Lilian that there was no way he could afford half of this—and that even if he could, a good deal of what she wanted wasn't available—a voice spoke from behind him.

"Excuse me, I was wondering if I could ask for your opinion on something."

Kevin turned around to see a young woman in a business suit standing before him. The woman, despite the expensive-looking suit, had the appearance of some kind of Amazon warrior princess. Her dark brown hair was short and messy, like she had been sticking her head out of a car window while driving down the highway. Two dark brown eyes were set in a face that, while nowhere near as gorgeous as Lilian's, possessed a strange sort of attractiveness to it. In a way, this woman sort of reminded him of Lindsay. The face was tomboyish and cute, but a little more… feral? Yes, it was a little more feral than Lindsay's fairer features. With a face that looked like it belonged deep within the Amazon rain forest, Kevin felt surprised by how good the suit looked on her.

"Um, are you talking to me?" Kevin pointed to himself as he stared dumbly at the woman. In response to his somewhat stupid question—because it should have been obvious that she was, in fact, talking to him—the well-dressed female gave him a feral-looking grin that, surprisingly, did make him want to run to the hills. It was odd. Her grin should have been frightening—*was* frightening. But, strangely, he didn't feel scared by it.

It must be her default look.

He wondered if she'd been taking lessons from *Zarachi Kenpoochi* from *White Out*, but then remembered that *Zarachi* scared the crap out of him and discarded that line of thought.

"Who else would I be talking to?" she asked, making a wide gesture with her hand to indicate the area around them. "Do you see anyone else here?"

Now that he was looking, Kevin didn't see anyone else around them. How strange. He could have sworn the meat clerk had been stocking the shelves just a few seconds ago.

***

Lying unconscious in the freezer was none other than the meat clerk. His hands and legs had been tied together by what appeared to be a really long hose. There was a large bump on his head, a round lump about the size of a baseball, and what looked like a pair of bandages forming an x-pattern over it. Lying on the ground by his side was a monkey wrench, the likely perpetrator for his unconscious state.

That poor, poor meat clerk.

***

"I don't mind helping you out. What did you want to ask me?" Kevin asked.

"I was wondering which type of meat you think is better?" She asked, holding up twp packages of meat. "I've got a younger brother who can't do anything for himself, so I've got to shop for him. Unfortunately, he's like a vacuum cleaner when it comes to food, and will eat just about anything, so it's hard to figure out what to buy. I want him to eat something he'll like, but I also don't want to waste money buying something expensive if he doesn't care. That's why I'd like your opinion."

Kevin scratched the back of his neck, looking at the two packages in Kiara's hands, before offering his honest opinion. "Personally speaking, I prefer the beef tenderloin. While the rib eye is much more tender, it also has a lot more fat." He shrugged. "But if your brother doesn't care about any of that, he'll probably like the rib eye more. It's also cheaper," he added, almost as an afterthought.

"Huh." Kiara looked between the two pieces of meat, her visage one of thoughtful wonder, before gazing at Kevin again.

"Thanks. It's good to see someone as young as yourself actually doing their research. It shows that you can take care of yourself, unlike some people I know." It was obvious to Kevin that she was referring to her brother.

"I live on my own…" Kevin trailed off, paused, then quickly changed his statement. "Well, I used to live on my own. Anyway, since I've lived alone for so long, I had to learn how to cook. Plus, I've got a coach who really rides us about our diet. We spent an entire track practice last year dedicated to learning things like proper dieting, and what foods we should and shouldn't eat. I swear, that man's the biggest health freak I've ever met."

"I'll bet," Kiara said sympathetically, "I used to have a trainer who was like that. She was an absolute slave driver and always went on about how 'a healthy diet is crucial for a healthy body and mind.' Trust me, I understand exactly where you're coming from."

"Thanks. I'm glad to find someone who understands what I'm going through." Kevin felt a bit of kinship with this woman. If her trainer was even half the hard-ass that Coach Deretaine was, then he felt for her.

"Beloved!"

"Looks like you're girlfriend's calling for you." Kiara gave him that feral grin of hers as Kevin began sputtering out denials. "I've got to go. Thanks again for the help, Swift."

As Kiara hurried off, Lilian came up to him, lips turned down in a mild frown.

"I can't leave you alone for a single second, can I?" She placed her hands on her hips and glared at him with one of *those* looks; the kind all men get when their significant other catches them checking out another woman—or at least *thinks* they're checking out another woman.

"What?" Kevin asked, blinking. "What do you mean? Did I do something wrong?"

"Never mind," Lilian sighed. "I see that you didn't get any of the meat we need," she observed as she put the fresh seasonings into the cart.

"Yeah." Kevin scratched the back of his neck. "That lady asked me for my opinion on something, and I guess we just got caught up talking."

"Why would she ask you and not the person working here?"

"Don't know." Kevin looked around to see that the meat clerk was *still* missing. How odd. "Maybe because the meat clerk isn't here? Or, maybe she just wanted my opinion because I'm apparently close in age to her brother? That's who she was buying groceries for." He looked at the aisle that the woman had walked down. "It's kind of weird, though…"

"What is?"

"That woman had both cuts of meat when she left, but didn't put either of them away."

Come to think of it, she also seemed to know that Lilian was talking to him, even though Lilian had been behind her when she spoke.

Lilian had also called him "Beloved," so that woman shouldn't have known who the fox-girl was talking to. There were at least five other people in their vicinity who could have been the recipient of Lilian's call.

And wait, hadn't she called him Swift? He didn't remember giving that woman his name, so how did she know who he was?

A shiver passed through him. He felt like something creepy had just happened and he missed it. Kevin didn't know if that was a good thing or not.

"Hmm," Lilian narrowed her eyes, which were now locked onto Kiara's departing figure. "That suit…"

"Lilian?"

"It's nothing."

Lilian shook her head and smiled at Kevin. They grabbed several packages of meat on the list, though she became awfully disappointed when he told her that this grocery store didn't sell wild boar. When they finished, Lilian wrapped her arms around Kevin, who pushed the cart as they exited the meat department.

"Let's finish shopping; I want to go on that picnic you promised me."

"Yeah, sure," Kevin sighed. He could already tell that this was going to be a long shopping trip, and he was not looking forward to that picnic either.

Him and his big mouth.

***

Kevin's belief that their trip to the grocery store would be a long one was proven correct when, mere seconds after leaving the meat department, they were interrupted by a loud shout of, "Woah! What is up, brother?!"

Kevin and Lilian spun around to stare at a woman dressed in black pants and a black shirt. Her dark blue eyes stared back at the pair, and her blond hair was pulled into a ponytail that went down her back.

"Hey, Cathy," Kevin greeted the woman who was pushing along a very large steel cart. Cathy worked for the online shopping program the store offered, which basically meant that she shopped for customers who were too lazy to do it themselves.

"You know, when I first saw you two, I didn't think it could possibly be you." Cathy gave Kevin a toothy grin. "Imagine my surprise when I realized that it not only *was* you, but that you were traveling with a girl, and a gorgeous one at that." She playfully punched his shoulder. "When were you going to tell me that you had a girlfriend?"

"We just started dating two weeks ago, so of course he couldn't tell you," Lilian told Cathy. "This is the first time we've visited the grocery store since we've become a couple."

"Don't go giving people the wrong impression about us!" Kevin shouted.

"I see, I see." Cathy nodded her head. "So you two are a new couple."

Several veins throbbed on Kevin's forehead. Why was everyone ignoring him? What was this, *"let's all ignore Kevin day?"*

"Whatever happened to that other girl you had your eyes on?" Cathy continued with a puzzled expression. "That one girl, the short blond with the pixie cut. What was her name again?"

"There is no other girl," Lilian declared, her eyes glowing a bright green as they narrowed almost imperceptibly at Cathy. "I am the only girl that my Beloved has ever wanted to be with."

"Lilian, what the heck are you doing?" Kevin asked, then he remembered what she had done to Ms. Vis last Monday. His eyes widened.

"Oh, I see." Cathy's eyes glazed over as the enchantment took effect. "That's right. There is no other girl. My bad."

“It's fine.” Lilian had a self-satisfied smirk on her face as she stared at the woman. “You didn't know. But now that you do, I expect that you’ll never mention this other girl again.”

“Right,” Cathy's voice reminded Kevin of a drone; dull and lifeless. “I'll never mention this other girl again.”

“Very good. You can go now.”

As Cathy began walking away, Kevin glared at the redhead.

“What. The heck. Was that?” he asked, his voice containing a hint of the annoyance he felt.

“Just correcting a misunderstanding,” Lilian tried to sooth her beloved mate. Needless to say, Kevin was not soothed in the least.

***

Kevin nearly groaned in relief as he and Lilian finally entered the checkout lane. Despite the shopping trip not taking more than half an hour, it had felt much, much longer.

What was it with everyone thinking that he and Lilian were a couple? Just because they were shopping together didn't mean they were dating or anything…

… Okay, so maybe Lilian being so close to him gave off the impression that they were a couple. And yes, the fact that Lilian kept telling everyone who would listen that they were a couple didn't help disavow that impression. Those enchantments that Lilian kept casting on people whenever *that other girl* was mentioned probably didn’t help either, but really, none of that should have mattered. They should have listened to him when he told them that he and Lilian weren’t an item. The least they could have done was give him the benefit of the doubt. He had known them longer than Lilian had—they’d only just met her today! They should have believed him over her.

As the conveyor belt began to move the woman standing behind the cash register greeted them. “Hello!” she said, her voice and manner overly cheerful.

“Hello, Susan,” Kevin sighed. This woman's bubbly nature, while normally endearing, only served to irritate him right then. He was tired and fed up and just wanted to leave.

“Oh! Kevin, how are… you…?” she trailed off when her eyes landed on Lilian, who was practically hanging off his arm. Her eyes widened. “Oh, my goodness! Kevin, you have a girlfriend!”

Kevin didn't know whether to groan or blush.

"I do not have a girlfriend!"

Susan ignored him.

"So when did you two start dating?"

"We're not dating! And don't ignore me!"

"We've been dating for about two weeks now," Lilian declared proudly, ignoring Kevin the way she usually did when he said something that she thought was silly.

"How wonderful," the woman gushed excitedly, "I'm so happy for you, Kevin and—"

"Lilian."

"Lilian. You two make such a cute couple."

Blushing demurely, Lilian gave the woman a pleased smile. "Thanks! I think so, too."

"Don't make this situation sound worse than it already is, Susan! And you!" He glared at Lilian. "Be quiet!"

"Hey, Liz! Come over here." Kevin groaned as the cashier called another employee over; a brunette with shoulder-length hair and a black apron. "Check it out. Kevin's got a girlfriend."

"I do *not* have a girlfriend!" By this point Kevin was pretty much crying tears of despair. What the heck was going on here? Why was everyone ignoring him?

"Oh, my gosh, you have a girlfriend!" Liz seemed just as excited as everyone else had been to meet his "girlfriend." Like the others, she had known Kevin since he'd begun shopping there in eighth grade. "This is so exciting! I wasn't sure if you'd ever get a girlfriend because of how shy you are."

"Why does everyone think you're shy, Beloved?" Lilian asked her on-the-verge-of-tears not-boyfriend.

"Because Kevin's always been very shy around girls," Susan answered, also looking confused, though for the inverse reason that Lilian looked confused. "Didn't you know that?"

"But he isn't," Lilian refuted, defending her mate. "He might get a little embarrassed some times, but I have yet to see him act shy around me."

If Kevin had *Spidey* senses like a certain *web-slinger*, they'd be tingling. He knew exactly what was going to happen. It had already happened at least once. Even now, a full week after it had happened, he could still remember how his secret crush, Lindsay

Diane, had face-planted into her salad after passing out from Lilian's offhand comment about how she and Kevin were engaged.

"Lilian! Don't—"

Too late.

"I mean, we've taken showers together, and whenever we go to sleep, he always clings to me. It's really quite adorable. Oh! And he sleeps without a shirt!" She frowned, then, her nose scrunching up cutely, like some kind of chipmunk, like a *Rescue Ranger*. "Though, I do wish that he would sleep naked instead just shirtless, but he insists on wearing those pajama bottoms of his. I don't know why, since they always end up getting ripped off anyway."

In response to the deathly silence that permeated the cash register, the kind of silence that made graveyards envious, Lilian smiled.

"Still, if he was as shy as everyone says, I don't think he would do all of that. Don't you agree?"

As Liz and Susan stared at Kevin and Lilian with wide, shocked eyes, the only male of the group began openly crying. He bawled his eyes as he cried out to the heavens… or at least the ceiling.

"Why me?!"

***

Kevin and Lilian left the two store employees to their shock. Even now he could still picture their eyes, wide and glazed over, showing that their minds had become overloaded from knowledge that they were just not ready to receive. They had not taken to learning about his implied sexcapades with Lilian very well, regardless of the fact that no sexcapades had actually taken place. He had tried telling them that, but after being met with only silence he'd given up. Susan somehow managed to finish ringing him up, despite being nearly catatonic.

Pushing the cart in front of him, Kevin had stopped crying and looked quite grumpy, something that his companion noticed.

"You shouldn't look so grumpy, Beloved. People will think you're in a bad mood."

"I am in a bad mood," Kevin grumbled out. "And it's all thanks to you."

"Me?" Lilian blinked several times. "Why?"

"What do you mean why?" Kevin looked at the young kitsune, who appeared to be genuinely confused. "Do you really not know?"

"No, I don't. What did I do to make you so grumpy?"

"Oh, I don't know, how about how you've been telling everyone who works here that the two of us are dating? Or, letting Liz and Susan know that we sleep in… the same… bed…" Kevin flushed bright red, his mind recalling the last time he had woken up with Lilian cuddling to him. He quickly shook the images out of his mind. "Or, how about when you told Liz and Susan that we've been taking showers together?"

"But, all that stuff is true," Lilian pointed out, still sounding and looking inexplicably confused.

"No, it's not," Kevin spat, then paused at the look Lilian gave him. "Okay, so maybe we do share a bed, but the rest of that stuff isn't true."

Lush, ruby red lips turned downwards into a frown. Lilian opened her mouth to respond, but Kevin had no intention of letting her say anything before he finished.

"And even if it was, you shouldn't go telling everyone about it! That kind of stuff is supposed to be private!"

"Oh." She paused. "I didn't know that."

"That much is obvious," Kevin sighed, running a hand through his hair. "Though you should know not to reveal private information like that. It's just common sense."

"*Human* common sense maybe," Lilian defended herself. "But not *kitsune* common sense."

Her words earned Kevin's inquiring gaze.

"What do you mean?"

"I'm not sure how to put it." Lilian pressed an index finger to her lower lip as she looked at the ceiling. "I guess the best explanation would be that kitsune don't have any of those silly taboos that you humans seem to have. Things like our sex life, gender preference and nudity aren't seen as some great sin or something to be hidden from others."

"So, basically, what you're saying is that kitsune don't really care whether others know who they're having sex with?"

"More or less." Lilian shrugged. "It's a bit more complicated than that, but that's the gist of it. To a kitsune, sex just isn't that big of a deal. My family's Matriarch, for example, is well-known for her promiscuity. She has seven daughters, and all of them were born from a different mate. And that's not even going into the number of mates she has taken that *didn't* end in pregnancy."

Kevin felt his face heat up.

"How is it that we've gone from talking about our private life to your Matriarch's sex life?"

"I was just explaining that it's not a really big deal if other people know about us," Lilian explained to him.

"It might not be a big deal to you, but it is to me." Kevin gave the girl a very pointed look. "And I would appreciate it if, from now on, you didn't tell anyone about our, um, our, uh, private life," he finished lamely, unable to think another word that described their home life. Really, how did one describe a lifestyle where some girl with fox tails and ears sleeps next to you, and tries to seduce you every chance she gets? Never mind the fact that Lilian, for all her beauty and general sexiness, didn't seem to know how to seduce anyone.

The girl couldn't seduce a flagpole.

"Now that's just mean," Lilian huffed indignantly.

That doesn't make it any less true.

"You're such a horrible person. I'll show you! One of these days, I will convince Kevin to ravish me!"

They do say that persistence leads to success. Though you should be careful. They also say that insanity is the act of repeating the same thing over and over again and expecting different results each time.

"Hmph, I'll take that into consideration."

"Lilian, who are you talking to?"

"No one."

Kevin deadpanned.

"That didn't sound like no one."

"It was no one," Lilian persisted, "Just some jerk who doesn't know how to keep his mouth shut."

"Uh huh…"

"Anyway," Lilian changed the subject, "Since you're the one asking me, I'll stop revealing our sex life to others."

"I would appreciate that." Kevin paused, the rest of her words catching up to his brain. "And would you stop calling it our sex life? We're not having sex!"

"Yet, Beloved. Yet."

"Ever!"

"Muu, Beloved, you meanie."

Kevin rolled his eyes.

As they neared the exit, Lilian's attention was drawn away from Kevin to something over his shoulder.

"Hey, Beloved, what's that?"

"What?"

"That stand over there."

Kevin followed Lilian's finger as she pointed to a large stand near a set of sliding doors. Sitting on the countertop near a register was a large glass display case full of pastries and cakes. Behind the booth were large machines used for making coffee and other drinks, their gleaming steel finish glinting under the light.

"That's Star Smucks," Kevin answered, "It's a popular coffee shop that sells drinks like cappuccinos and frappuccinos." He looked at his redheaded companion, his expression inquisitive. "Do they not have anything like this in your village?"

Lilian shook her head.

"We do have a small café that sells coffee, cappuccinos and lattes, but all the machines are really, really old there. Like, ancient."

Kevin struggled with himself for a moment, but eventually, his innate kindness won out. "Would you like me to buy you a drink?"

Lilian's gaze was hopeful. Her eyes shone like two big, bright florescent bulbs. "Can we?"

"Sure."

"You're the best, Beloved!"

Kevin wondered if perhaps he was being too nice to the girl. This was, after all, the very same female who'd barged into his life with all the subtlety of a tsunami in Arizona. But, seeing her face light up in a dazzling smile that brightened the entire store, he decided that he didn't have it in him to regret this decision.

They walked in front of the Star Smucks cash register, where a young man stood. He had olive skin, dark eyes and black hair tied into a ponytail that was hidden underneath a hat. He wore the standard Star Smucks attire; black slacks and a white shirt under a green apron.

"Hey, Kev, wassup man? You keepin' it real?" The young man, who went by Mark, greeted Kevin, before his eyes fell on Lilian. He looked her over, a long up and down glance, before staring back and forth between the two. Kevin saw Mark's eyes linger on the way Lilian clung to his arm, and felt fear mixed with resignation. "Woah, you finally found yourself a girl? And such a fine one, too." Mark gave him a congratulatory nod. "Good on you, man."

"Ugh, she's not…" Kevin sighed. Chances were even if he denied having a relationship with Lilian, Mark simply wouldn't believe him. It had been that way for everyone else, so why should he expect that to change now? "You know what, forget it. Lilian, do you know what you want?"

"Um, what size is the grande?" Lilian asked. Mark pulled out the medium sized cup and showed it to her. With a nod, the girl made her decision. "I'll have a grande Caramel Brulée latte."

"Do you want whipped cream on that?"

"Yes, please."

"What about you, Kev?"

"I'm good today." He had already spent over two-hundred dollars on groceries, which wouldn't go unnoticed by his mom—he was still waiting for the other shoe to drop regarding all the money that he spent on the clothes he had bought Lilian.

"Suit yourself." Mark shrugged. "Your drink will be up in just a few minutes."

"Let's wait over by the tables," Kevin suggested, grabbing a hold of the cart.

"Okay."

As the two made their way over to the small sitting area, Kevin looked at all of the groceries in their cart, which was practically overflowing. There were way more than he could carry on his bike, especially since Lilian would be riding with him.

"How am I going to get all this home?" he wondered out loud.

"Don't worry about that, Beloved," Lilian reassured him. "I can fit all of this into my Extra Dimensional Storage Space."

Kevin blinked several times. He had forgotten about her ability to store things in her Extra Dimensional Storage Space. And was it just him, or did that sound like a really bad sexual innuendo?

"Don't worry, Beloved, I can stick all of this into my Extra Dimensional Storage Space?"

A really, really, *really* bad sexual innuendo.

"One grande Caramel Brulée latte!"

"That's us." Kevin pushed the cart forward while Lilian went up and grabbed her drink. She removed the lid to lick the caramel drizzled whipped cream. Smiling, she took a drink as she followed her beloved mate out of the grocery store.

"This isn't bad," she commented as she took her mouth away from the cup. "It's a bit too sweet for my taste, but still good."

"I'm glad you like it." Kevin looked over at her, then just as quickly looked away. "Uh, Lilian, you have some whipped cream on your mouth."

"I do?" Lilian tried to look down, but couldn't see much more than the very tip of her cute button nose. She looked over at her mate and smiled. "Can you lick it off for me?"

Kevin nearly tripped, but caught himself before his face could smack against the cart handle. "What?!"

"I can't see it, so I need you to lick it off for me."

Kevin really hoped he wasn't developing a permanent eye twitch. "I am not going to lick anything off your face," he declared, causing Lilian's cheeks to puff up in a pout.

"Come on, Beloved." Lilian gave him a large, teary eyed pout. "I can't get it off if I can't see it. You have to get it off for me."

"Yes you can," Kevin spat, "And that's not going to work on me this time. There are some things that I just won't do. Licking something off your face is where I draw the line."

"Oh, poo."

***

While Lilian and Kevin were having their lover's quarrel, high above them, standing on the roof and looking down at the pair, was none other than Kiara. With her arms crossed under her chest, she watched them banter back and forth with an air of amusement. The two of them were definitely a riot.

"So that's the kitsune that beat my younger brother," she murmured to herself; naturally, since she was the only person on the roof.

"Gah! Do you really have to put our groceries there?!" Kevin's exasperated voice filled the air.

"But that's where my Extra Dimensional Storage Space is located."

Kiara snorted in an effort to stifle her laughter as she watched the kitsune, Lilian, proceed to stuff all of the groceries they bought between her cleavage.

Of course, the comedy of this situation was not what the girl was doing, but Kevin's overly dramatic reaction to it.

It should be physically impossible for people to turn that shade of red.

The steam rising from his ears was also a physical impossibility.

Kiara wondered if these seemingly impossible things happening to the boy had something to do with Lilian. She knew that kitsune tended to affect the world around them in strange ways. They were, after all, a very strange bunch themselves.

"But what if people see you?!"

"Don't worry, Beloved. I put up a small illusion around us. No one can see what I'm doing right now."

"Ha, whatever. Let's just go home."

"And then to our picnic, right?"

"… Right. I had almost forgotten about that."

"Then it's a good thing that I'm here to remind you."

"She doesn't look like much," Kiara mused, smirking as she watched them ride away on Kevin's bike. "It's too bad you had the misfortune of running into my younger brother. Had you not fought and injured him, we wouldn't have any problems. Ah, well, such is life."

"Hey! What are you doing on the roof!?" An angry voice behind her startled Kiara out of her reverie.

"It looks like this is my cue to make my own exit."

Kiara ran to the other side of the roof, ignoring the manager shouting at her. She jumped off the roof, landing on the roof of the next building, then leaped from that building onto the ground. As she swiftly moved to where she had parked her car, her mind went back to the two-tailed kitsune.

“I wonder why that girl looked kind of familiar?”

Kiara thought for a moment, and then shrugged. If she couldn't remember where she had seen that girl, then it obviously wasn't important.

“Whatever, either way, she and her little boy toy are doomed.”

Chapter 4

The Hapless Stalker

Kevin sighed, barely masking his relief as the shrill, piercing sound of a whistle resounded across the track field, signifying an end to practice. He loved track as much as the next runner, but Coach Deretaine had been running them ragged these past few sessions. It had gotten so bad that he and Chase had stopped staying after practice to trying and beat each other's times, such was their exhaustion.

Another reason he had stopped staying late might have been due to Lilian, who had taken to watching him from the bleachers while he practiced. She wouldn't leave if he didn't leave, and the last time he and Chase had one of their showdowns, she'd sat there cheering him on and demeaning Chase.

Kevin had been quite surprised by the width and breadth of Lilian's vocabulary.

And while he was all for people verbally demeaning his rival, he didn't want Lilian acting as the peanut gallery.

With track practice called to an end, he and his archrival joined up with the others, including Eric, Justin and the twins, Alex and Andrew. They formed a large group in front of Coach Deretaine, who was only now taking the whistle out of his mouth.

"All right, everyone." The track coach made eye contact with each of them, a serious expression etched onto his face—which really wasn't saying much, since his face *always* looked like that. "Our first track meet is next Wednesday. All the schools in our district will be coming here, so we've got the home field advantage, but I don't want any of you growing complacent!" He added the bit at the end as if he expected some of them to slack off, even though they knew what would happen if they did.

Laps around the track. Lots and lots of laps.

"I don't want any of you getting lazy! From now on we'll be working twice as hard during practice until the track meet!"

His words were almost met with a chorus of groans. Almost. No one wanted to run laps, so they all kept their mouths shut, though a few looked ready to protest. "Now get outta here and do your homework! Academics are important, too!"

The track members soon broke up. A few eyes trailed up to Lilian as she walked toward Kevin, causing him to roll his eyes at the number of males he caught staring at her. He got that she was pretty, even agreed with them, but people really should learn some self-restraint.

Kevin refused to admit that he might be feeling a little protective of the girl. What did he care if these dirty, disgusting, filthy jerks wanted to strip the redhead with their eyes? It wasn't like he felt anything for her. Lilian was just a friend.

"My Tit Maiden!" Eric beamed at the girl as she walked up to their group. "My love! My dear! My sexy friend whose bazookas I want to suck! How are you doing this fine day?" Lilian continued approaching them. Eric, thinking she was coming his way, carried on. "Would you like me to walk you home? Or about how I take you out for dinner? Perhaps a moonlit walk through the park? I'm particularly fond of that last one. It will be dark outside and we could… hehehe… then we'll… kukuku…"

"Beloved!"

Lilian walked right past the lanky sophomore, who was giggling his lecherous old man giggle, completely ignoring the boy.

While the redhead didn't notice, the moment she passed Eric his body turned a deep shade of gray. It wasn't quite fifty shades, but it came close. He also went very still, his now stone-colored body reminiscent of a statue. To further give the impression of having turned to stone, several cracks appeared all over him. Kevin almost expected him to crumble into dust any moment now.

Lilian stopped directly in front of her mate and handed him a water bottle. "Here you go." Her face broke into the loveliest of smiles as Kevin's hand touched hers when he took the water bottle from her.

"Thanks." Kevin took a long swig of water, before pulling it back in surprise. "It's still cold."

"Of course," Lilian said in a tone that suggested the reason should be obvious. "All items that go into the Extra Dimensional

Storage Space are placed in a form of stasis, meaning that when you take them out, they are in the same state as when you first put them in."

"Huh." Kevin took another swig of the chilled, refreshing water. "That's pretty interesting. Makes me almost wish I had my own storage space."

"But then you'd be a girl," Lilian told him, as if that was enough explanation as to why he shouldn't want his own storage space. "Only women have storage spaces and, well, I wouldn't be able to fall in love with a female."

Kevin gave her an odd look.

"Weren't you the one who told me that your first kiss was with a girl?"

Lilian's cheeks took on the barest hint of pink. "I had hoped you'd forgotten about that," she mumbled lowly.

"Right…"

Kevin and Lilian began walking back towards the locker rooms. Alex, Andrew, Justin and Kasey followed them. Only after they'd gone several feet did Kevin realize their little group was missing someone.

Turning around to look at his best friend, Kevin wasn't really sure what to think when he saw Eric crouched down, rocking back and forth on his heels, one arm wrapped around his leg while he drew circles in the grass. The boy seemed awfully dejected, like he might break out in tears any second.

If that wasn't enough, there was also what Kevin had dubbed *Eric's Personal Raincloud* hovering over the lecherous boy's head. The tumultuous, stormy looking cumulonimbus was unleashing a downpour upon the sophomore, soaking his hair and clothes. Several of their peers did their best to avoid the boy, lest they also become sopping wet.

"Are you coming, Eric?" Kevin called back to his friend. The tall teen lifted his head and looked up at him with haunted, bloodshot eyes that had bags under them. They were hollow eyes; the eyes of someone who had lost their will to live.

Eric could be such a drama queen when the mood struck him.

"Yeah," Eric hiccupped and sniffled as he wiped away a few stray tears from his eyes. "You go on ahead." Sniffle. "I'll be along in just a minute." Sniffle. Hiccup. "I just need to cry about the unfairness of my life." Sob. "Don't worry about me."

"We'll do that then. Have fun." Kevin turned and began walking again, Lilian still attached to his arm.

His words caused Eric's head to snap up so quickly it was a wonder he didn't get whiplash. He stared at his departing friends in shock for several seconds before snapping out of his stupor.

"H-hey! Dammit, Kevin! You're supposed to be a pal and stay with me until I'm feeling better!"

"Yeah… not happening." Kevin said, continuing to walk away.

Lilian was much more mature about the whole thing. She stuck her tongue out at Eric, even going so far as to pull her eyelid down and blow him a raspberry. That just caused Eric to begin wailing.

She then decided that this was another perfect opportunity to use her mate's shoulder as a pillow.

"Do you always have to do this?" Kevin asked the moment Lilian placed her head on his shoulder. They ignored Eric's wail of anger and despair behind them. The group had grown pretty used to those by now. They happened fairly regularly these days.

"Do what?" Lilian asked, not bothering to lift her head as she spoke. It wasn't as comfortable because they were walking, and her head kept getting jostled, but she had never been one to sweat the small stuff.

"This," Kevin sounded frustrated as he gestured at them to showcase how close together they were. "Do you always have to be so close all the time?"

"You're my mate," she answered in a tone that suggested her reason should be obvious. Which it was, to Lilian. "I always want to be close to you."

"But aren't you bothered by how sweaty I am?"

Kevin really couldn't understand why this girl always wanted to be so close to him. The redhead was almost always stuck to him like glue. He would even go so far as to say they were attached at the hip, the number of times Lilian's hips had been pressed to Kevin's notwithstanding.

Had Lilian been dealing with any other male, they would have undoubtedly lost all self-restraint by now, and taken advantage of the beautiful and seemingly naïve kitsune's devotion to them. Not

Kevin, though. The thought didn't even cross his mind.

It had nothing to do with girl-shyness anymore, but more that he just didn't love her. And Kevin Swift wasn't the kind of guy who played with a girl's emotions. He would never take advantage of someone else's feelings for his own gratification, especially when that someone seemed to truly love him.

"Not really," Lilian answered, "I mean, you are kind of smelly, but I figured this would be a good chance for me to get used to your masculine scent." Her words were met with a blush and a groan from Kevin. "Does it bother you when I do this?"

"It is kind of uncomfortable to walk like this," Kevin informed her. "Awkward, too. I'm afraid I might trip over your feet or something." It was only half-true, but he didn't have the heart to tell her the real reason he didn't want her clinging to him. Or rather, he already *had* told her, but Lilian seemed to get a major case of selective hearing whenever that happened.

"Okay, then. How about this?" Lilian took her head off his shoulder, before lacing her fingers through his.

In spite of his lack of romantic interest for the fox-girl, Kevin could not help but marvel at how soft her hands were. He'd never felt anything so smooth before. They were like velvet, especially against his calloused palm.

Lilian looked at him with a bright smile as she squeezed his hand affectionately.

"Better?"

"Um, yes," Kevin admitted. He dutifully ignored the way his heartbeat sped up, and also the way all of the blood began rushing to his face. "Thank you." Lilian just smiled, swinging their conjoined hands between them.

"Is it just me, or are you guys also having a hard time believing that this is real?" Alex asked his brother.

"You mean do I think it's impossible for Kevin to have such a hot girlfriend when I'm still single? Of course. I'm way better than him. If any of us should have gotten a girlfriend by now, it's me."

"As if! I'm better than the both of you combined! I'm handsome and smart and—"

"An asshole."

"An asshole." Alex paused, his face scrunching when his mind registered his brother's words, and then he realized that he had just agreed with them. His eyes narrowed into an angry glare. "Wait a damn minute! I am not an asshole! You take that back!"

"No, I don't believe I will my dear, naive, stupid brother."

"That does it! You're going down!"

The two began to slap each other silly. Several people stopped to watch the duo go at it. It was sort of like watching two clowns fighting, which would have actually been pretty awesome to see.

Kevin and Lilian did their best to ignore them.

"… Fight…" Justin did not.

"Those two are complete idiots." Neither did Kasey.

"God damn you, Swift! How dare you steal my Tit Maiden!" Eric just ignored the whole "twin brothers fighting" thing in favor of glaring angrily at Kevin.

Kevin and Lilian ignored them. This was pretty much how every track practice went.

"Kevin! Lilian! Hey!" a female voice called out.

Kevin's body stiffened at the familiar voice. He turned with Lilian to face Lindsay. His not-so-secret crush looked like she had just come back from her own practice. Her skin was covered in a light sheen of sweat that gave her body a healthy glow.

To Kevin, she looked perfect. Granted, his opinion was kind of biased… and he was ignoring all of the grass stains on her skin and clothing, not to mention the twigs and leaves in her hair, which appeared reminiscent of a bird's nest. Those were small details that he didn't feel were worth mentioning.

It had nothing to do with the fact that he'd had the biggest crush on her for several years. No sir. Nothing at all.

"Lindsay!" Kevin felt a moment of panic. Not good. He hadn't expected to run into her after practice today! He hoped he didn't smell too rank. Had he put deodorant on before practice? Oh, dang it! He should have thought about wearing some cologne!

"Hey, you two." Lindsay grinned at them, her cheeks flushed from practice. Kevin thought the light dusting of pink made her look even cuter than usual. "Just got back from track practice, I see."

"I… yes." All right, Kevin, just calm down. You can do this. Lindsay's been friends with you for years. Talking to her should be easy. "What about you? You just finished soccer practice, right? How'd it go?" Good job. Talk about something that she's interested in. Girls love talking about their interests, right?

Lindsay played on the high school girls' soccer team in the center forward position. He had actually gone to a few of her games last year, and knew she was really good. Definitely the best on her team.

His opinion was only slightly biased.

“It went fine.” Lindsay tucked a strand of blond hair behind her ear. The action drew Kevin's attention to the soft curvature of her jaw, which invariably brought his attention to her lips. They were chapped, and slightly cracked from being outside and running around on the soccer field for so long, but Kevin still felt his mouth go dry at the sight of them. Or maybe his mouth was dry because of dehydration? All that running had made him rather parched. “We only had a bit of trouble with one of the newbies.”

“O-oh?”

“Yeah.” Lindsay huffed and crossed her arms. “This one girl, Cassidy Fergus, kept bragging about how she had been the center forward on her last team and would do a much better job than me.” A satisfied smile crossed her face as she thumped her chest with a fist. “Don't worry, though. I put her in her place.”

“That's good to know… I think.” A highly uncomfortable silence grew between the pair. Come on, Kevin, think! Don't let the conversation end just like that! “So… when's your next game?”

Lilian played competitively, so her soccer was year-round. Kevin had always admired her dedication toward her chosen sport.

“Not for another week. Our next game is next Wednesday.” She leaned forward, hands clasped behind her back, grinning. “Are you going to come and cheer me on?”

“Ah ha, w-well, I'll certainly try.”

Straightening, Lindsay crossed her arms under her chest and pouted. “You haven't been coming to my games lately. I'm beginning to feel like you don't care anymore.”

“I-I'm sorry about that.” Kevin scratched the back of his neck uncomfortably. “I've been… busy.” Yeah, busy dealing with a certain crazy fox-girl.

“Is that so? I guess it can't be helped, then.”

While Kevin attempted to engage Lindsay in conversation, Lilian glared daggers at the soccer playing tomboy. If looks could kill, or, you know, produce heat seeking missiles or something,

Lindsay would have been smote by now.

Kevin didn't notice this, which also explained why he hadn't said anything about it. There was no way he would have let Lilian glare at his crush.

But while Kevin did not see the look Lilian sent his crush, Lindsay sure did.

"Is something wrong, Lilian?" she asked, wondering what she'd done this time. Had she said something offensive? She didn't think so, but then, it was hard to tell with that girl sometimes. Hadn't Lilian nearly bit her head off when they first met? And then there was that time at the mall…

Lindsay still felt depressed just thinking about some of the things the other girl had said to her.

"Nope! I was just thinking about something."

Lilian smiled brightly, showing off her sharper than average canines to the soccer player, who shifted uncomfortably, no doubt feeling wary in her presence. Good. Lilian couldn't just let this girl keep talking to her mate without suffering any consequences. It was important for her to let all the competition know that her beloved was hers and no one else's.

"Ah… okay…" Lindsay looked a little unsure, not that anyone could blame her. "So…" She glanced between the two of them, her eyes flickering back and forth. "I guess I'll see you two later, okay?"

"What? You're leaving so soon?" Kevin winced at how whiny he sounded, almost like he was desperate for her to stay—which he was, but he didn't want to appear that way.

"Time waits for no one." Lindsay winked. "Or so they say. Besides, my parents are expecting me home soon. Not all of us have an apartment all to ourselves and no curfew."

"I guess," Kevin sighed, "I'll see you later then."

"Bye!"

The rest of the trip to the locker room was done in silence. During their time spent walking, Kevin couldn't help but notice that Lilian looked a bit discouraged about something. He thought about making an inquiry, but decided against it. Whatever was bothering Lilian wasn't really any of his business, and he honestly wasn't sure he wanted to know.

"We're here," Kevin announced as they stopped in front of the men's locker room. He gave Lilian a look, which she managed to interpret correctly, for once.

"I'll wait for you here." Lilian smiled. Again, something seemed slightly off about it, but if she wasn't going to say anything, then he wouldn't address it either.

"Alright. I should be out in a few minutes."

Kevin walked into the men's locker room to wash off the daily accumulation of grime and get changed.

***

Lilian watched Kevin enter the men's locker room with a disheartened frown. While she had been doing everything possible to keep her spirits up, she was beginning to feel discouraged by her lack of progress in regards to her beloved.

They had been living together for a while now, but so far nothing had happened. Lilian had tried every trick Kotohime taught her to make him lose all sense of self-restraint and mate with her. And yet, he still refused to take advantage of any of the opportunities she'd presented him with.

Not even prancing around his apartment in skimpy lingerie worked. Not even posing in that lingerie worked! Posing! Sexy poses that should have had him eating out of the palm of her hands! Or between her legs. Whichever came first.

For a while, she thought something was wrong with him. Maybe he was gay? Or perhaps he had performance issues? Insecurity maybe? She didn't know, though she had hoped it wasn't that first one. There were a lot of ways to help him with performance issues—she was a kitsune. Enough said. And if he was insecure, well, she knew the best way to deal with that as well. There wasn't much she could do if he was gay, however. The Matriarch had lesbian twin daughters, and none of the men that old hag threw their way made either twin desire hotdogs over tacos.

That's why she had decided to go to his school as a student—to observe Kevin and find out what made him tick. Perhaps then she could find the best way to make him respond to her affections. Because what she was currently doing obviously wasn't working.

Some good had come of going to his school; she'd found out that he wasn't gay, for one. Nor did he seem to have any insecurity issues. He was definitely shy, but she'd discovered that fact when introducing herself to him in human form.

It was all that passing out he did. It was such an obvious sign that even someone like Lilian, who knew almost nothing about humans as a whole, could recognize the signs of a boy suffering from a bad case of *Cannot Talk to Women.*

Learning that her mate wasn't gay or experiencing insecurity should have been cause for celebration, but it wasn't. She'd run into another problem in her quest to gain her mate's love, and it was even worse than something simple like insecurity. Much worse.

A breathy sigh escaped her lips. Thinking about her current love life, or lack thereof, was depressing. She had already chosen her mate—she even lived with him—but he wasn't responding to her seduction attempts the way she had been told a normal man would.

Lilian was sure that if he were anyone else, she would have already made him fall in love with her. *"Men are easy,"* Kotohime had told her. *"They are creatures of lust and sex; just show them a little skin and they are yours for the taking."*

She had shown Kevin a lot of skin, *a lot*, but he still wasn't hers. It appeared her beloved mate was different from other men in that simply showing off some skin (or appearing before him completely naked) didn't work the way it normally would. He wasn't like other members of his gender.

It was frustrating. But it was also the reason she had chosen him—well, one of the reasons. If he were like any other man, Lilian wouldn't have fallen in love with him in the first place. She loved him for who he was. His kindness and compassion and shyness were all endearing and cute in their own way. Yet even so, Lilian sometimes wished he would just respond like a regular guy, throw her on the bed, rip her clothes off and ravish her.

It was a confusing conundrum, one that she did not know how to solve. And she'd been so excited when she found out it was him, too. Talk about depressing.

"Such a heavy sigh," a deep, articulate voice with a heavy faux-Spanish accent said from somewhere behind her. "*La bella mujer*, perhaps I could be of assistance and alleviate whatever ails you?"

Lilian turned and promptly found herself wondering if the person standing before her had been transported from Spain—or if maybe she had just fallen asleep and was experiencing a really bad dream. Those were the only two reasons she could think of to explain what this person was doing at a high school in America.

The boy in front of her was a very eccentric-looking young man, with bright blond hair and olive colored skin. That wasn't so odd. The odd part—emphasis on the odd—was his very large pompadour style haircut. It was quite possibly the largest head of hair she had ever seen. It had to be at least a foot tall! And it was all shiny! Shiny hair! Like he had dunked his head in a bucket of hair gel for several hours and then let it dry.

And don't even get her started on his clothes; skin-tight red pants that stopped halfway down his calves to reveal ugly pink socks. He wore a white, long-sleeved shirt with a high collar, ruffles at the end of the sleeves, along with four straps across his chest and shoulder pads. On his feet were a pair of brown boots and finally, white gloves covering his hands. He looked like a Spanish bullfighter gone wrong.

"What is it that ails you, *señorita*?" The boy asked while Lilian gawked at his attire. He seemed rather oblivious to the "wtf?" look on her face.

"Wha…?"

"Ah, forgive me. I have not even introduced myself."

The strange pompadour boy bowed formally from the waist, like one might expect from a prince asking a princess to dance with him.

With this guy, it just looked dumb. As he bent forward, that ridiculously large hair bounced and flopped as he moved, wiggling like jello on his head. It even made a sound that, if it were put into words, would read something like *boiyoiyoiyoing.*

It was one of the creepiest things Lilian had ever seen, easily reaching the top ten most disturbing things she'd laid eyes on. Even *Nue* would be afraid of that hair.

"My name is Juan Martinez Villanueva Cortes."

Wow, that was a really long name. And did he have two last names or was she just hearing things?

"And what is your name, my beautiful *señorita*?"

"Um…" Lilian found herself hesitating under this boy's intense stare. It was kind of unnerving. "… Lilian?"

"Lilian," Juan breathed in the name deeply, his nostrils flaring. Lilian tried taking a step back, horrified, but the creeper knelt down on one knee and grabbed her hand before she could get too far. "Such a lovely name for such a beautiful, young *flor*."

Lilian twitched. Did this guy just call her flour? As in that stuff she used to bake? How rude.

"Now." The strange boy with the weird hair began stroking the back of her hand. Lilian shivered in revulsion. "Why don't you tell me what ails you?"

Quickly jerking her hand out of Juan's, Lilian glared at the boy. "Why would I tell you anything? I don't even know you!"

"But I just introduced myself, *sí*?" Juan's expression became puzzled, like he didn't understand why Lilian was getting so upset at him.

"That's not enough to say that you know someone!"

"It is not?"

"No," Lilian's voice was clipped as she spoke. "It's not. I don't know anything about you other than your name, and that's not enough for me to say I know you." She tilted her head, then frowned as she added, "And why are you even talking to me? You don't know me."

"Ah, but that is where you are wrong my lovely *azucena*."

Lilian wrinkled her nose in disgust at this new nickname. She didn't know what *azucena* meant, but she doubted it was good. He *had* just called her flour seconds before, after all. And why wasn't her ability to understand any language spoken kicking in yet?

"I know much about you," Juan restarted his spiel, "Long have I watched you from afar, admiring your beauty." This guy had been watching her? What the hell? "However, it is only now that I have had a chance to speak with you."

"Okay. One, that's just creepy," Lilian told him bluntly. "And two, I don't want to talk to you, so you might as well stop while you're ahead."

"Come now, *la flor silvestre*."

"And there you go calling me flour again!"

"There is no need to be shy," Juan continued, completely ignoring everything she said. It was really beginning to piss her off.

Now you know how Kevin feels.

"Shut up!"

"Now, now," Juan spoke in a soothing tone. "There is no need for such harsh words. I am only here to help you."

"I wasn't talking to you!" Lilian snapped. Juan blinked, once.

"Then who were you talking to?"

"No one," Lilian replied sullenly, "None of your business."

Juan looked at her for several more seconds, then shrugged and began advancing on her again. Lilian glowered at the boy who tried closing the distance between them. She took a step back, but this did not deter him in the least. He continued stalking toward her, until soon, her back was pressed against the wall and he was right in front of her. He placed his hands against the wall on either side of her head, keeping her pinned in place.

His face, just inches away from hers, had the young two-tails wrinkling her nose in abhorrence.

"I understand that you are intimidated by my magnificence, but you need not worry. Your beauty easily stands on par with my own *masculino*."

Lilian was forced to stare into the boy's eyes, which she noted were a very dark black that clashed horribly with his bright blond hair. What was with that hair, anyway? It looked like it was alive. Sentient hair? What the hell?

In either event, she was beginning to seriously consider going kitsune on this boy, and smacking him with her youki-infused tails.

"Lilian? Who is this?"

"Beloved!" Lilian ducked under the strange boy's arm, darted around him, and hurried toward her mate. Kevin only had enough time for his eyes to widen before she collided with him. A second after that, her lips were on his, kissing him hard.

"D-dang it, Lilian! W-what are you doing?!" Kevin hissed as he pulled his mouth away from Lilian, who whined petulantly at the loss. Why must her mate be so stubborn when she was trying to show him her love? Couldn't he see that she had to let the creepy boy know she was taken?

Deciding that she had not gotten nearly enough from that short kiss—which should have lasted much longer and involved a lot more tongue, as far as she was concerned—Lilian began placing tiny, butterfly kisses along her mate's jaw, smiling when his body shivered against hers. He may be resistant to her charms, but he certainly wasn't immune.

“W-would you stop that!” Kevin grabbed her by the shoulders and pushed her away. Lilian frowned, but complied. She didn't want to make him angry. “What's gotten into you?”

“What do you mean?” Lilian asked, confused.

“I told you not to get all kissy and stuff, especially when we're in public.” Kevin tried to sound patient. Tried, because he failed and his exasperation rang clearly in his voice.

Lilian ignored the tone in his voice, naturally; she had a lot of practice doing just that.

“No, you just said not to be so open with my affection in public. Not to stop entirely,” Lilian corrected him. He’d told her that a few days after she had joined him at school. She didn't see why, especially when she needed to ensure that any hussies encroaching on her territory knew that Kevin was taken, but she listened nonetheless. Her mate had requested it, and she would do as he asked.

“Right, I did say that, didn't I?” Kevin gave a long-suffering sigh. “Yeah, well, we're in public now, so you need to tone it down.”

“Yeah, but it's after school,” Lilian pointed out. “There aren't that many people around anymore, so it shouldn’t matter if we get up to anything naughty, ufufufu…”

“Doesn't matter.” Kevin shook his head. He couldn't believe they were having this conversation. “We're on school grounds. Besides, what about him?” Lilian looked over to where Kevin was pointing, scowled, then turned back to look at him, her hair whirling like wisps of fire.

“Who cares about him?” She declared angrily. Kevin looked perplexed by her vexation. He’d never seen her this angry before. Naturally, he was a tad confused about why she was acting so choleric toward the boy in the weird outfit.

He opened his mouth, but didn’t get a chance to say anything, because another voice spoke up first.

“So you are Kevin Sweeft.”

Kevin and Lilian turned to look at Juan, who stared at the athletic young man with an expression that disconcerted the pair. It wasn't necessarily a piercing expression, but it unsettled them nonetheless.

“I have to admit, I expected someone a bit more… .” The boy with the super-sized hair sniffed derisively, “… impressive.” A vein pulsed on Kevin's forehead as Juan continued. “You are just a tweeg.”

“Yeah, well, sorry for not meeting your expectations.” Kevin rolled his eyes. Why did everyone think that just because he was thin, it meant he was some kind of eighty pound weakling? He might not be one of those star quarterbacks, but all that meat on his bones was pure muscle. Besides, this boy was even thinner than him. “And just who are you anyway?”

“I am—”

“Nobody cares who you are,” Lilian snapped in a surprisingly rude voice. Kevin stared at her in shock. There were a number of times when she had been somewhat hostile—usually when Lindsay was around—but even then she’d never been *this* rude.

Just what had this boy done to piss her off so much?

Lilian grabbed Kevin by the arm and began yanking him along behind her. “Let's go home, Beloved. I want to spend more quality time with you. Alone.”

The way she said that made shivers run down Kevin's spine. Call it a hunch, but he didn't think being alone with her right now would be very good for his health.

***

Juan Martinez Vallenueva Cortes smirked as he watched Lilian drag the young man away.

“That did not go as expected.”

Not that he had really known what to expect. Lilian was like a whirlwind. She had appeared in this school out of nowhere and took it by storm, which was actually the reason he was so interested in her. Well, one of the reasons he was interested in her. The other had to do with his job, but he figured that mixing duty and pleasure wouldn't hurt, just so long as he accomplished the tasks assigned to him.

“Then again, the chase is the most exhilarating part of catching any prey.” And he would catch her. Juan Martinez Vallenueva Cortes always caught his prey in the end!

“Dammit! Someone stole our matador outfit again!”

Juan heard shouting from a nearby door that led to the theater.

“I bet you it was that Juan Pompadour guy!”

"Let's show him what happens when you steal our costumes!"

"Hm, I suppose zees would be a good time to make my exit," Juan mumbled before bolting from the building like a bat out of hell. Good thing too, because mere seconds later, the theater doors burst open and a horde of angry thespians ran into the hallway.

Juan was still wearing the matador costume when he left the building.

***

"Are you going to tell me what that was all about?" Kevin asked. Lilian let go of his arm and allowed him to walk next to her.

"It was nothing," she said, turning her head away at the flat look Kevin gave her.

"That was most definitely not nothing."

"That guy was just creeping me out. He kept on calling me flour, and I think he was trying to ask me on a date or something, despite the fact that I'm already taken."

"Flour?" Kevin blinked. "You mean that stuff we use to bake with?"

"Yeah. Can you believe his nerve?" Lilian huffed. "I can't believe he called me that, and then to ask me on a date afterward. I swear, some people just don't seem to understand that I'm not interested in them."

"You don't say…" Kevin felt there was a certain irony to that statement, but chose to ignore it. "So, if you didn't want him hitting on you, why didn't you just, you know, use an enchantment to make him leave?"

"I did." Lilian scowled, her nose scrunching up in a rather adorable expression of frustration and bafflement. "It didn't work."

Kevin almost stumbled, but caught himself at the last second. "It… didn't work?" He looked at the young woman beside him, shocked.

"Don't you remember what I told you? If a person is stubborn enough, they can resist an enchantment," Lilian said. "I'm guessing that pompadour guy was just really determined to date me, and his desire was strong enough to override my enchantment." She shrugged. "I can't imagine why he would want to date me, though."

Kevin could.

"Besides," she hugged his arm to her chest, pushing it between her two heavenly mounds. “I'm already taken.”

“You're really not going to let this go, are you?” Kevin said, sounding resigned.

“What do you mean, Beloved? Let what go?”

As Lilian gave Kevin a genuinely confused look, the young man sighed and let his shoulders slump.

“Nothing. Let's just go home.”

“Okay.”

***

As Kevin and Lilian left the school, neither realized that they were being followed. Their pursuer had grown suspicious of the red-haired girl. She had also become very disgruntled by the sexually overcharged female's sudden appearance and disruption of her class. Worse still, that vile redhead had somehow managed to ensnare one of the students!

Ms. Vis had known there was something unusual about that red-haired female from the moment she had laid eyes on her... okay, so maybe she had only begun suspecting something after the pair had served detention with her, but that was neither here nor there.

Ms. Vis still didn't know what happened during that detention exactly one week and two days ago. The only thing she remained certain of was that they had managed somehow to skip out without her knowledge. Even worse, she knew they had come to serve detention, yet still managed to give her the slip.

She did not remember what transpired after assigning them a punishment. The last thing she recalled was a pair of bright green orbs, and then nothing. She had woken up several hours later, asleep on her desk, in the middle of the night, with no memory of what happened, and not a single clue as to why she was still in her classroom.

Something had obviously happened, and seeing as the last person she had interacted with was Lilian Pnéyma, that something had to be her. That infuriating girl with long red hair; there was something odd about that girl, and Ms. Vis was going to find out what. It was her duty as a teacher.

She had been sitting in her car ever since school let out. Ms. Vis knew that Mr. Swift and that girl would stay for an extra two hours after school. She had followed them to the track field every day since they had duped her.

Ah! B-but it wasn't like she was stalking them or anything. It was… it was… research! Yes, research. It was important to learn more about the girl—students!—the two students who had managed to evade punishment. She couldn't allow them to get away with disrupting her class like that. They needed to learn discipline.

It had absolutely nothing to do with the fact that they had somehow managed to befuddle her and escape detention. Not at all. And she *certainly* wasn't following them in the hopes of learning something that would give her leverage over them. Of course not. This was about teaching them right from wrong. It was about learning responsibility.

Nodding to herself, Ms. Vis reaffirmed her belief in the righteousness of her cause. She was doing this for their own good.

It was September, so the air was a bit chillier than it had been, as she waited in her little Toyota Corolla. Her car was parked near the school entrance, where she knew Mr. Swift and that girl arrived and left on his bike.

She had entertained the idea of waiting in the teacher's lounge, but thought better of it. What if they decided to leave early? She could miss them, which would be unacceptable.

And so, Ms. Vis had staked out the school entrance in her car for two and a half hours. She knew they usually stayed at the track field until four-thirty, but there was never any guarantee that this would always be the case. For all she knew, Mr. Swift's coach might decide to let practice off early, and then she'd miss her chance to stalk—follow them, and gather more dirt.

Mr. Swift and the girl eventually showed up. As the pair came into sight, a prominent scowl marred her face. They were walking far too close for her liking. That girl was holding Mr. Swift's arm to her chest as they walked, hugging the appendage so close that it was literally smashed between her cleavage!

H-how shameless! This girl was far too shameless!

Starting her car as Mr. Swift and that girl left on his bike, Ms. Vis followed them, maintaining a good distance from the pair so as not to arouse suspicion.

She studiously ignored the many cars honking at her as she drove twenty miles below the speed limit. Such things did not concern her. Didn't these people realize that the education of her student was on the line?!

Kevin and Lilian appeared blissfully unaware of the long line of honking cars several hundred meters back. It may have been due to their conversation.

“Ne, ne, Beloved, have you ever wondered what it would be like to have sex on a bike?”

Kevin nearly crashed his bike into a potted cactus.

“W-w-what the heck are you saying?! Of course not!”

As she watched the pair, she couldn't help but wrinkle her nose in disgust. That girl was draping herself over Ms. Swift like some kind of scarlet woman, and the way she nuzzled the back of his neck with her nose… it just wasn’t acceptable! Unacceptable! Such vile acts shouldn’t be committed in public!

What an immodest girl! There was no way Ms. Vis could allow such audacious behavior. This was a gross violation of the school's “no public displays of affection” policy, and needed to be corrected immediately. Once she found enough dirt—erm, evidence—on them, she would use it as leverage. Yes, yes, it was all coming together now. She would find out all of that girl’s shameless secrets, then force her to stop acting in such a shameless and abhorrent manner.

She continued to follow the duo as they finally made it to Mr. Swift's apartment complex, or maybe it was that girl's place? He had to drop her off before going home himself, right?

The two hopped off the bike. Ms. Vis parked her car around the corner and out of sight. Exiting, she crept along the wall until she reached the corner, peeking her head out as the young man and that girl walked up the stairs.

When they reached the top, he locked the bike against the rail, while the girl unlocked the door. Ms. Vis furrowed her eyebrows. Confusion set in. What were they doing? Why were they entering the same apartment? Wasn’t Mr. Swift just dropping the girl off? That had to be it, unless…

Her eyes widened as one possibility entered her mind, but that couldn't be it… could it? Surely not even they would… but no, she shook her head. Of course they wouldn’t. Not even that girl would be so shameless as to commit carnal acts with another at such a tender age. They were only teenagers.

Maybe they were studying together? Yes, that sounded plausible. She had heard that young people sometimes got together after school in order to do their homework and, what was that term teenagers used these days? Hang out? Perhaps they were hanging out.

Regardless, she now had a new dilemma. They were in that apartment and she could no longer see them. She needed to find some way to continue watching them without their knowledge.

Fortunately, she had the means doing just that.

She still wasn't stalking them, though.

Going back to her car, Ms. Vis opened the back door and pulled out a very large, very impractical-looking telescope. It was two feet long, conical in shape, and widened until it was nearly four times as thick as her wrist at the end. It looked like a giant's version of a pirate telescope, only without all the grime and rum stains.

Now she just needed to find an appropriate place to set up shop, where she could further observe the duo.

Taking a quick look around, she found exactly what she needed: a ladder that she could use to climb onto the roof of the adjacent complex. Once on the roof of the building, she set up her ridiculously-sized telescope with her just as ridiculously-sized tripod, and aimed it at the window to the apartment.

Ms. Vis frowned when she peeked through the telescope and noticed something bothersome. The blinds to the window were shut. She couldn't see in.

Okay. That was fine. They had to open the blinds sometime. It was a beautiful evening. The sun was painting dark reds, oranges and pinks across the sky, setting the desert landscape ablaze. Surely they would open them to properly appreciate the sight? She had read in her romance novels that couples found that kind of thing, well, romantic.

Not that she cared for romance. She didn't. The only reason she had not had a date in over ten years was because of her, uh, her, um… passion! Yes, she was simply too passionate about teaching children math to be concerned with romance. It had nothing to do with the fact that every man she had dated was turned off by her obsession for numbers, her love for long, hard equations, and her desire to talk about those equations for hours on end. Nothing at all.

Reaffirming her belief that they would eventually open those blinds sometime soon, Ms. Vis settled into position and began the waiting game that all people who've ever played as a sniper in any first-person shooter game are familiar with.

It was going to be a long wait.

***

"Would you like me to start dinner before we do our homework?" Lilian asked as they entered the apartment.

"Yeah, sure. Just make something simple though," Kevin told her as they took off their shoes and set them by the doorway. "You don't need to make something extravagant like that rack of lamb with rosemary you made the other day." He shook his head. "I still don't know how you made that so quickly. Isn't that supposed to take around half an hour just to set up?"

"I can't say." Lilian winked at him. "A girl's got to keep some secrets."

"Right…"

"So what should I make?"

Kevin paused for a moment. "I bought some pasta the other day. It's in the pantry. Why don't we just have that?"

"Okay." Lilian nodded in agreement. "And in the meantime, you can dump those dirty clothes in the hamper."

"Yes, Mom."

Lilian swatted his arm playfully, and Kevin gave her a small grin. He took his dirty clothes, which smelled like twenty-year old socks that had been left out in the sun—at least to him—along with their book bags, to his room. Meanwhile, Lilian went into the kitchen to start dinner.

This had become their usual routine these days. Kevin didn't know when he and Lilian had picked up a routine, but he wasn't complaining. It made living with her much easier.

And, even though he would never admit it, he kind of liked having her around. Kevin had been living on his own for so long. He had forgotten just how nice it felt to have someone helping out around the house.

He still wouldn't let her clean without his supervision, though. That was just asking for trouble.

After he put his clothes in the dirty hamper (his hamper; there were two now), and grabbed the books and supplies they'd need for their homework, he adjourned to the small table in the kitchen, where Lilian had already set out the food—two steaming plates of pasta with marinara sauce—with a flourish.

He still didn't know how the girl managed to cook everything so fast. That pasta should've taken at least ten to fifteen minutes to prepare—just boiling the water took at least three—but she had somehow finished cooking it in less than three minutes.

It must be some kind of strange kitsune power.

Dinner was always an interesting affair at the Swift apartment. It was mostly done in silence, though Lilian did enjoy talking quite a bit. However, because they both had the same classes, and spent over ninety percent of their day together, there wasn't a whole lot to talk about.

Conversation wasn't what made dinner interesting anyway.

"Gah! Lilian, would you stop that!"

"Stop what?"

"That! Stop rubbing your foot against my leg!"

Dinner was made interesting because of Lilian's constant attempts at playing footsie with him.

"Do you not like it when I do this?" Lilian caressed his leg with her toes. Kevin shivered as all kinds of wonderfully strange sensations bombarded him. There must be something seriously wrong with him if he thought this was pleasant. "I was told that men like this."

"I do—I mean don't! I don't!" Kevin jerked his leg back when Lilian suddenly caught some of his skin between her toes. He glared at her, but she just smiled innocently. "Who told you that anyways?"

"Kotohime," Lilian answered. Kevin twitched at the reminder that her family was apparently rich enough to have a maid. If she was so rich, just what was she doing here? And where *was* her family anyway? "She told me all kinds of stories about how she and her mate used to play footsie a lot."

"Okay, first of all," Kevin began, pinching the bridge of his nose to stave off his coming headache. This girl could be such a handful. "Those two were married, or mated or whatever, and we're not. Second, not all guys like that kind of stuff. And third, I think you need to be one of those feet people to like something like that." And he was most definitely not one of those feet people. At least, he didn't think so. He hoped to God he wasn't a foot person. That would just be weird.

"That's silly, Beloved," Lilian chided her mate. "Neither Kotohime nor I are feet people, but I still enjoy doing this." She gave him a smile that, even after having seen it for a little over two weeks, never failed to make his mouth go dry, and his heart try to beat its way out of his chest. "I enjoy it because it's with you. If anyone else did this with me, I wouldn't like it, but because it's you, I do."

Was it messed up that Kevin felt both pleased and guilty at the same time? Probably. This girl's words were undoubtedly touching, but he felt guilty because he wished they were coming from Lindsay instead of her.

His love life was so screwed up. He felt like one of those Harem Protagonists in some kind of twisted Shōnen love comedy—only without the bevy of beautiful women chasing after him for reasons that only they could possibly understand.

On a side note, he really, *really* hoped that didn't happen. He didn't think he could handle more than one girl—heck, he had trouble handling just Lilian! God knows how much trouble he'd have dealing with several women; just thinking about it made a shiver run down his spine.

"Well, could you stop, please?"

"Ha," Lilian sighed. "Fine, but only because you asked me to."

"Thank you."

"Spoilsport."

"You say something?"

"I asked if you liked the food."

"It's good." As if to emphasis his words, Kevin twirled more pasta onto his fork and took a bite. As he stuck the food in his mouth and began to chew, some of the sauce dripped onto his chin.

"You're making a mess, Beloved." When Kevin just blinked at her, Lilian smiled sweetly and grabbed the napkin. "Let me get that for you."

And thus, Kevin's face took on enough color that it looked like a miniature red sun, as Lilian leaned over the table and dabbed his mouth with a napkin. It was such an intimate gesture—and so different from the way she usually tried getting close to him—that his entire body felt like it was being cooked in a furnace.

"There," she whispered, her tone sensual enough to cause temporary paralysis. He wondered if she knew what she was doing, but a glance at her face revealed nothing more than innocent intentions. She honestly had no idea what her actions were doing to him. "All clean."

She smiled at him, and Kevin's breath became hitched. She was so close; close enough that her warm breath washed over his face. Truth be told it wasn't all that pleasant. Her breath was normally reminiscent of a winter's breeze, crisp and refreshing, but right then, it smelled like pasta sauce. Regardless, Kevin still felt himself becoming hot under the collar, which was strange because his shirt didn't have a collar.

For a second, Kevin actually thought Lilian was going to kiss him. It certainly wouldn't be the first time. Likely wouldn't be the last, either.

He knew that he shouldn't want this, knew that it was wrong. He liked Lindsay, of that he was sure. And yet, as he stared at the girl's face, at those big green eyes, at those lush pink lips, all thoughts of Lindsay fled. His body, his mind and his heart, it seemed, were eager for whatever this girl had to offer.

Fortunately (*or was it?* The voice that he ignored whispered), Lilian did not kiss him. Sitting back down in her chair, the two-tailed kitsune went back to eating, seemingly satisfied that she'd wiped the sauce off his face.

Kevin felt a strange sense of disappointment, but quickly shook it off. He should be happy that she hadn't kissed him… shouldn't he?

After dinner they took their dishes into the kitchen and cleaned them in tandem; one washing while the other dried. It was very efficient—if the Olympics had a competition like dish washing in them, they would have won hands down.

When they finished washing the dishes, Kevin turned the TV on for some ambient background noise. As *Kaidoku Funo*—one of several opening theme songs to one of his favorite anime—began playing, he and Lilian sat down and worked on their homework.

Kevin had discovered early on that Lilian was very good at English and anything involving literature. She was incredibly well-read, which surprised him, since he'd never seen her read anything, aside from his manga collection. He guessed that meant she used to read a lot at home.

"Lilian?"

"Hmm?"

"I was wondering something."

Lilian looked up from their homework; they had to write a five-page report on the original Magna Carta. Large green eyes blinked several times. Were her eyelashes always so long?

"Wondering what, Beloved?"

"How come you're so good at English literature? Is it like that kitsune ability that you have to speak any language without an accent? Can your eyes translate any language you see or something?"

"Good guess, but no." Lilian smiled. "I just worked really hard to learn how to read and write in English. I actually had a lot of help with that. I've been staying at our manor in Tampa Bay for the past five years. I was never allowed to leave, but when I expressed an interest in learning how to read and write in English, Kotohime hired an independent kitsune to teach me."

Kevin stored the term "independent kitsune" for future inquiry. He also took note of her comment about staying at a manor in Tampa Bay. However, it was her other comment that really caught his attention.

"So wait, your mom or matriarch or whatever never allowed you to go into the city? Ever? Why?"

"Ah. Well... my mom is... she's..."

Kevin became worried when he saw Lilian hesitating. Had he just stepped on some kind of land mine?

"Lilian?"

"Kotohime said it's because I didn't have enough training to interact with humans properly," Lilian huffed, crossing her arms under her chest. "I don't know how she expects us to learn how to interact with humans when she won't even let us go into the bigger cities. The only place I've ever been allowed to visit was the beach right outside of the villa, and that's only because it's privately owned by our family, so humans never go there."

So her maid told her that? What about her mom? Where did the woman who gave birth to her figure into all this? Either way, he felt pretty bad for Lilian. It must have been chafing to have such an overly protective family—uh, maid.

"What about when you lived in Greece? You mentioned that humans would occasionally visit your village."

"Humans aren't allowed into the village proper, just the resort off the coast, and I never got to see them," Lilian grumbled. "Even when I was walking through the village, I always had Kotohime with me, and she would never let me past the village border."

"So you never saw a human back then? Not even once?"

Lilian smiled, and Kevin wondered if the bitterness he saw in it was his imagination.

"I do remember one time when I met a human—a little boy who somehow managed to wander away from the resort. To this day, I don't know how he did it, but he managed to break through the barrier that kept both humans and other yōkai out. I ran into him when I was, well, when I was going through a rough period in my life."

She shook her head.

"But that's all in the past. Aside from that boy, the only other humans I've met were the ones that I enchanted to get me all the way to Arizona." She frowned. "And a lot of those people were jerks. The only reason I even enchanted them was because they kept acting like that Juan idiot."

"Hm," Kevin hummed, "You know, I remember going to Greece once."

Lilian looked at him, her eyes more attentive than usual. "Really?"

"Um." Kevin nodded. "It was a really long time ago, so I don't remember much. I think I was five? Maybe six. Anyway, Mom was doing an article on a fashion show that was being held there." He gave her a look, half-amused, half-disturbed. "I remember, the people watching over me were always getting run ragged. I kept leaving the resort we were staying at. I think I just wanted to find my mom, since she was always gone. I didn't learn until later that she was traveling to the mainland in order to conduct interviews."

"Hmm."

A pensive silence descended upon them. Lilian's brow furrowed, and her artistically crafted ruby lips turned downwards into a frown. She seemed disappointed by something.

"Are you all right, Lilian?"

Lilian blinked, her eyes sharpening as her mind snapped back to reality.

"Yes, I'm fine." She gave him an unconvincing smile. "I was just thinking about something."

Kevin was tempted to ask what she was thinking about when another thought occurred to him.

"Is something wrong, Beloved?" Lilian asked when Kevin began looking around, his eyes blinking in confusion and his brow furrowed.

"No." Kevin shook his head. "Just had a strange thought, that's all."

Lilian looked at him for a second longer, worried. Her mate was acting a little weird. Still, if he didn't want to talk about it…

"All right. Why don't I finish helping you with those notes, then you can help me with my math."

Lilian Pnevma was excellent at English. However, she absolutely sucked at math. She was so horrible at it that every time she tried solving an equation, thousands of math teachers felt a disturbance in the *Equation* and cried out in agony.

"That's not a very nice thing to say."

Sorry.

"Whatever, you're not sorry at all."

"Lilian, who are you talking to?"

"No one! Come on, let's get back to work!"

The duo of human and kitsune focused on their work after that. By the time they finished, it was nine pm.

"Time for bed!" Lilian cheered. She even gave a little fist-pump to show her excitement. Even her two tails, which she had brought out the moment they entered their apartment, were wagging around like hyperactive children on a sugar high.

Kevin looked askance at the girl, then shook his head. "Why are you so excited? We're just going to sleep."

"Yeah, I know." Lilian pouted, her lips pursing. Kevin gulped and looked away. "But that's just because you refuse to do anything else to me. I would be more than willing to explore our relationship if you weren't such a prude."

"W-whatever. You didn't answer my question."

"Isn't it obvious? Even if we don't do anything, I still get to sleep with you."

"Auu," Kevin moaned pathetically. "Can you please not say it like that? You make it sound so dirty."

"Ufufufu, you're so cute when you're embarrassed."

"And would you please, please, *please* stop laughing like that?"

"Ufufufu, laughing like what?"

"Like that!"

"I don't know what you're talking about."

"Of course you don't," Kevin sighed.

He and Lilian entered the bathroom to brush and floss their teeth. There were now two automatic toothbrushes sitting on the marble counter top.

After ensuring their breath was minty fresh, Kevin went into the small walk-in closet in his room, and changed into a pair of boxers and his fifth pair of pajama bottoms. He prayed to God, Allah and Kami that this pair wouldn't get ripped. He really didn't want to buy any more.

When he came out, Lilian was already dressed.

"Gah!" His face burned as if it had suddenly caught on fire. "What the heck are you wearing?!"

Even though he had seen her sleepwear dozens of times over, he didn't think he would ever get used to it. She wore some kind of spaghetti strap shirt that stretched taught against her bust. It had a floral-patterned lace silhouette, and a pink bow at the bust line. The fabric flowed out the lower it went, stopping at her midriff, exposing an expansive amount of her flat tummy. On her hips, composed almost entirely of lace, partially translucent and scarcely covering the parts of her that should've been covered, were the laciest panties he had ever seen.

Lilian's coquettish smile looked surprisingly innocent. Kevin knew this because, despite hiding his face behind his hands, he still peeked at her from between his fingers.

A prude he may have been, but Kevin was still a guy.

"Do you like it?"

Lilian's vibrant red hair flew around her body as she spun, causing Kevin to rear back as if struck. The flowing cloth of the baby-doll split at her back, allowing an extensive view of her fair complexion and her small, shapely buttocks.

Kevin stared, his mind almost freezing in place as it tried to memorize every aspect of Lilian's gloriously tight rear end. Located at the small of her back was another pink bow, which had six small strips of lacy cloth flowing out from and connecting it to the rest of the undergarment. This left a large diamond shaped cut-out in the center of her rear, showing off a good deal of her interglutial cleft.

That... was just a really scientific way of saying her butt crack.

Her tail stuck out of the diamond-shaped cutout. Kevin, as an animal enthusiast, had a hard time resisting a girl with such a mighty fine tail. It didn't help that he was a teenage boy with slightly Otaku tendencies.

Kevin could have sworn his life flashed before his eyes as he gawked at this unfettered glimpse of Lilian's perfectly shaped twin cheeks.

It was only after his brain managed to reboot that he realized something.

"Where did you even get that?"

She had never worn this piece of lingerie before. Then again, she seemed to have something new to wear each night they went to bed. Was this another special female ability? Generating random lingerie whenever they wanted? What a Dangerous ability. Capitol on the D.

"Wait. Is this one of the outfits that you have in your storage space?"

"No, I got this one when we were shopping." Lilian smiled and walked over to him. No. Not walked. Walking was far too simple a term for what she was doing. Stalking would be more accurate. She slinked over to him like some kind of jungle cat that had just found their prey, and Kevin was the one she wanted to pounce on.

"W-what are you doing?"

Kevin took a step back. Lilian took a step forward.

"I feel like this relationship has been moving far too slowly," Lilian told him, taking another step forward, her voice low. Kevin moved back again.

"What relationship?!"

Kevin took another step back. Unfortunately, in his desire to keep away from the twin-tailed vixen, he never bothered looking behind him.

His legs knocking against the bed, Kevin tumbled backwards with a startled yelp, landing on the mattress with a bounce.

Lilian did not stop her forward advance, much to Kevin's horror. The gorgeous girl in sexy lingerie continued closing in on him, her hips swaying enticingly with each step she took.

"For a while now, I have been waiting patiently for you to make the first move and properly ravish me."

Kevin's face couldn't possibly get any redder than it was now.

"What do you mean ravish you?! I'm not ravishing anyone!"

"But, since it seems you are far too shy to initiate our first sexual experience together, I'm beginning to see that I need to make the first move."

Lilian had realized that if she ever wanted this relationship to advance, she would have to step up and take charge. This was the answer she had come up with for her earlier quandary, the one she'd had before her close encounter with the pompadour haircut kind.

"Stop ignoring me! There will be no sexual experiences here!"

"Ufufufu, come on, Beloved. There's nothing to be afraid of."

"It's when you say things like that, that I'm the most afraid—EEP!"

***

"EEP!"

Ms. Vis' jerked her head up, startled by the sudden and loud squeal. It eerily reminded her of a mouse after it's been caught by a cat.

She looked around, frantic, her head turning this way and that. Where was she? What was going on? What was she doing here?

It was only after several seconds of staring that she remembered: she was on top of an apartment building, her trusty telescope sitting on its tripod, aimed at the window to the apartment Mr. Swift and that girl had entered. It was dark outside now. She must have fallen asleep.

"WHAT THE HECK DO YOU THINK YOU'RE DOING?!"

Ms. Vis' head jerked again at the shrill shout. It didn't take her long to realize where it was coming from. Excitedly, she looked back through her telescope, wondering if she would finally have that blackmail material she needed to coerce that redheaded she-devil with.

The excitement left and a scowl crossed her face when she saw that the curtains were *still* closed.

“Ufufufu, you're so cute when you act all shy and embarrassed!”

So that girl was still there? How atrocious! Didn't she realize it was past curfew?

“I'm not cute—EEP! GET YOUR HANDS OUT OF THERE!”

“Ufufufu, now why would I do that?”

Ms. Vis's eyes widened as she continued listening. What was going on in there? Why couldn't someone open those curtains so she could see what was happening? It sounded absolutely scandalous!

“WOULD YOU STOP TOUCHING ME THERE!”

“Ufufufu, why? It's clear you like it.”

“NO I DON'T!”

“Your mouth says one thing, but your body says something else.”

“Ugh… N-no…”

“Ufufufu…”

Ms. Vis paled as she continued listening to the conversation. It sounded like that girl was trying to take advantage of Mr. Swift! She knew that girl was bad news! Forget trying to coerce her! She was going to call the authorities and make sure that girl was gone for good!

Unfortunately, when she reached for her cellphone, it wasn't in her pocket. She searched through all of them, even going so far as to turn them inside out and still couldn't find it! Where was it?

“OH, DEAR GOD!”

Kevin's scream reminded her that she needed to be quick. Haste makes waste. Now, where did she put her cell phone… where was it, where was… ah! She must have left it in her car! Perhaps it had slipped from her pocket when she exited the vehicle?

“Ahn! L-Lilian! Stop it! No more! I can't… ha… take it—ahn! Anymore!”

Frantic, Ms. Vis shot to her feet. She had to hurry if she

wanted to catch that girl in the act!

In her haste to stand up and leave, Ms. Vis' knees slammed against her telescope, sending it clattering to the floor. She stumbled backwards, the back of her heel striking against the lip of the building.

Her arms windmilled. She released a loud, blood curdling scream of terror. Then she pitched over the side.

Within their apartment, Kevin Swift and Lilian Pnéȳma stopped what they were doing.

"Did you hear something, Beloved?"

"Um, no?"

"Good, then neither did I."

As more screams emitted from the Swift residence, a certain math teacher lay in a tangled heap of limbs, insensate to the world around her. Tomorrow morning, Ms. Vis would wake up in a hospital bed, with no recollection of how she got there or what she'd been doing the previous night.

Some people had the worst luck.

Chapter 5

(Un?)Fortunate Meetings

There had been many times in the past few days where Kevin wondered if the last month had all been a strange dream.

This was a very logical thought, one that anybody else would have had, too, if they'd gone through the zaniness that he had via one super peppy redhead. And that was just when taking Lilian into consideration. Throw in being introduced to a world where supernatural creatures lived amongst humans in secret, and you add a whole new level of insanity to the equation, one that he didn't even want to consider.

And speaking of red-haired fox-girls…

Kevin looked down to see the girl in question snuggled against him. Her red hair fanned out against his chest and the white bed sheets. The sun peeking in through the window caught each strand in its light, causing her silken tresses to gain an incandescent glow, taking on the appearance of ardent flames from a powerful wildfire. Those beautiful crimson locks created a sharp contrast with the white sheets of the bed and his lightly tanned skin.

He could actually see her face this morning. Lilian hadn't taken to lying directly on top of him last night, like she was often wont to do. Instead she was cuddled into his right side, her head using his shoulder as a pillow.

Her face was very peaceful in sleep; eyes closed and lips parted ever so slightly as she rhythmically breathed in and out, making odd but cute noises as she slept on. She looked nothing like her usual energetic, vibrant and oftentimes chaotic self. Kevin hadn't known it was possible, but she actually looked even more beautiful now than she did when she was awake.

It may have had something to do with the fact that she wasn't trying to kiss him.

Or seduce him.

Or strip him of his clothes.

Or strip off her own clothes.

There were a lot of things Lilian did that he didn't like.

The second he thought about how beautiful Lilian was, however, he regretted it. Guilt welled up inside of him. He should not be feeling this way, not about Lilian. He already liked someone else, and despite the fact that they weren't dating, thinking about Lilian this way made him feel like he was betraying Lindsay. Or at least his feelings for her.

Of course, they weren't dating, so he wasn't actually betraying anyone. He just felt like he was.

Sighing softly, Kevin shook his head and dispelled those thoughts, setting his mind straight. Regardless of his love for Lindsay, he couldn't deny that Lilian was quite possibly the most beautiful girl he had ever seen. Anyone with a set of eyes could see the girl possessed an unearthly, inhuman beauty, and he knew that many of his peers thought the same thing he did.

He was often forced to listen to them talk about her. For some reason a good deal of their comments angered him. He did not know why, though.

It was Monday morning, the start of a new school week. Nothing special there. A glance at the clock revealed the time to be five am, two hours before he and his housemate had to leave for school.

Two hours was plenty of time to get ready. He could probably afford to get a bit more sleep if he felt like being lazy. Too bad the word "lazy" didn't exist in his vocabulary. Kevin was a very hard worker. It came with the territory of having no father and a mother who was always out of the country.

Feeling that it would be better to get a head start on his day, he glanced back down at the girl sharing his bed… and promptly twitched. Like always, Lilian had wrapped herself around him like some kind of super-sexy limpet, holding him as if he were a life-sized plush toy. Her arms were woven so tightly around his torso that if she were to squeeze him any harder, Kevin feared she may emaciate him via Death Hug™, which was an even worse way to die than being killed via a notebook that automatically kills anyone whose name is written in it. Her legs also had a strong grip on his right thigh, feet locked together at the heels like a clamp.

In short, it would be impossible to break out of her hold.

Kevin wondered if Lilian was doing this on purpose to keep him from leaving the bed, or if it was a subconscious gesture of some kind. The girl was awfully clingy, after all, even when awake. *Especially* when awake.

He started shaking the girl to rouse her back into the world of conscious thought. It was harder than it looked; his arms were currently pinned under hers. Just wiggling his left arm out from the redhead's hold was a task in itself.

"Lilian. Come on, you need to wake up now."

Lilian didn't wake up. She did nuzzle her face into his shoulder, however, and Kevin squeaked when he felt warm, soft lips press against the bare skin of his shoulder in an accidental kiss. Thankfully, he had gained a lot experience with stuff like this, and so, he ignored the pleasant sensations and tried again, speaking louder this time.

"Lilian. It's time to get up. Come on, we've got to get ready for school."

The girl using him as her body pillow stirred reluctantly, shifting her body against him. This elicited another squeak from the young man as her almost-but-not-quite bare breasts rubbed against his torso. Lilian cracked a single eye open, then shut it just as quickly.

"Lilian can't wake up without receiving a kiss from her prince."

Kevin blinked. Did she just refer to herself in the third person?

He shook his head. He must be hearing things.

"That's not going to happen."

"What?" Lilian opened her eyes to look at him in consternation. "Why not?" Realizing what she had done, the fox-girl just as quickly closed her eyes and pretended to still be asleep. It was a bit late for that, but Kevin had to give the girl points for trying. "Lilian needs her kiss to wake up."

Kevin blinked again. It seemed he was not hearing things. She was definitely speaking in the third person. Was this a new verbal tick of some kind? He sure hoped not, that would be annoying. Almost as annoying as someone with a silly catch phrase.

And on that note, he really hoped Lilian never picked up a catch phrase. The last thing he needed was some naked fox-girl running around his house saying *desu* all the time.

"Yeah, well, Lilian's going to be disappointed, and you know why not. Now, come on, it's time to get ready for school."

Finally realizing that her "Beloved" wasn't going to follow along with her whims, Lilian opened her eyes and gave him her most adorable pout.

"Come on, Beloved." Despite the fact that Lilian wasn't feigning sleep anymore, it was clear that the young kitsune had no intention of letting this issue go any time soon. She wasn't letting *him* go anytime soon either. "Don't you know how these things are supposed to work? The handsome prince always kisses the princess in order to wake her up. That's how these things go."

"Oh, yeah? Then I guess it's a good thing I'm not a prince and you're not a princess."

Lilian puffed up her cheeks at the insinuation that she was not a princess. She might not have a tiara, but she belonged to a rich clan. At the very least, she was a beautiful *ojou-sama*, a girl from a rich clan with a long history, which was close enough.

Kevin, undeterred by her cuteness, continued. "You also haven't been placed under a magical spell that keeps you asleep until receiving a kiss. This isn't Disney."

"Why do I have to be in a magical sleep in order for you to kiss me?"

"Don't look at me. *You're* the one who mentioned the prince and sleeping princess scenario. The only time the prince ever kisses the princess awake is when she's locked in some kind of magical coma. That's how these things work."

"In Disney movies, maybe, but that's never the case in anime and manga," Lilian argued.

"Anime and manga?"

"Of course."

Lilian placed her hands on Kevin's chest and pushed herself into a sitting position, so that she could properly lecture her mate. Kevin squawked in indignation as she put her weight on his chest, then flushed in embarrassment as her sexy lingerie was revealed—her sheer nightgown was semi-translucent, and he could see that she wasn't wearing a bra.

"It usually starts out in the bedroom, where the main hero and heroine are. One of them, usually the heroine, will be unconscious, having been either knocked out, feverish, comatose or simply sleeping, while the other character, usually the hero, falls for their attractive sleeping face and, unable to resist, leans in to give them a kiss," Lilian lectured in a very studious voice. She almost sounded like a school teacher.

The effect was totally ruined by the mere fact that she was lecturing him while wearing skimpy lingerie and straddling his stomach.

"Uh huh."

"You know what I'm talking about, right?

Kevin did indeed know what she was talking about. He'd read and watched plenty of *shoujo* romances and *shōnen* love comedies.

"You're talking about '*Dude, She's Like, In A Coma!*' right?"

"Uh huh." Lilian nodded her head enthusiastically. "Every character in anime and manga do this." She placed her index finger on her lips and pushed. "I think Duke Devlin put it best when he said: 'Wanna know the best thing about unconscious chicks? They can't say no… What!? Like I'm the only one thinking it.'"

"Not all anime characters do that," he spat. "And Duke Devlin didn't say that!"

"He didn't?"

"No!"

"Are you sure? I could've sworn I heard him say that…"

"He didn't!"

"Gya!" Lilian jumped. Kevin's eyes practically bulged out of their sockets when her breasts bounced. "There's no need to shout, Beloved. And it does happen in romance anime. I've seen it."

"Yeah, well, this isn't an anime either." Kevin turned his head. "This is real life, and in real life, it's not happening."

"Muu," Lilian pouted at him. Even her normally upright and pointed fox ears were drooping. "You're no fun, Beloved."

Despite the sheer cuteness of the act, which had a +20 bonus effect on Kevin due to his weakness for animals and Otaku tendencies, he managed to resist the girl's natural charm. He had been getting a lot of practice lately doing just that. In fact, it seemed to be getting easier every time it happened.

“Yes, yes. I know. I'm a horrible person and a spoilsport.” Kevin rolled his eyes. “Now could you get off me so I can take a shower?” He tried to give her a stern expression, but then remembered what she was wearing, and quickly turned his head. “And for the love of god, put some regular clothes on!”

“Hmm, no.”

Kevin had just enough time to widen his eyes before he suddenly found himself pinned to the bed. Lilian straddled his hips, her hands gripping his shoulders, pushing the majority of her weight onto him, keeping him from being able to sit up. Even her tails had decided to get in on the action, and were wrapped tightly around his legs like some kind of furry bondage gear.

“W-what the heck?!” Kevin started to struggle, but it was too little, too late; he was already trapped. His body shook and writhed within the emerald-eyed beauty's grip. His hips bucked and jerked in his attempt to throw her off. None of it worked. The girl wouldn't budge. It was almost like…

Enhancement! She's using enhancement to strengthen her muscles!

“Lilian, let go of me!”

“No,” Lilian said concisely. “I'm not getting off. I want to have my fun, and since you won't ravish me, or even kiss me, ufufufu…” Her creepy laugh caused tendrils of fear to worm their way into Kevin's gut. “I'll just have to be the one who fuels our unearthly lusts and unbridled passion.”

***

“What lust?! What passion?! The only one feeling that way is—eep! What the heck do you think you're—eek?!”

“Ufufufu, did you like that?”

“No, I did not like that! Stop it right now!—eep!”

“Don't worry, Beloved, there is plenty more where that came from.”

“Dang it! I already told you I don't like that—eek!”

“Ufufufu, doesn't this make you feel good?”

“NO! I am not feeling good! I am so not feeling good right now!”

“It looks like I need to step up my game then, ufufufu.”

“Step up your—what are you—are you licking me?!”

“Do you really need me to answer that question?”

"What? I mean no! I mean stop licking me!"

"Ufufufu, don't worry, I may be inexperienced like you, but I learned from the best. Kotohime told me that all men like this."

"No they don't! We don't like this at all! AND STOP LICKING ME THERE!"

"Ho? Are you sensitive here? Ufufufu, how cute."

"OH MY GOD! YOU'RE BITING MY NIPPLE! WHY ARE YOU BITING MY NIPPLE?!"

"Ufufufu."

"AND STOP LAUGHING! THIS ISN'T A LAUGHING MATTER—EEP!"

***

In the apartment directly below the odd duo, there was a young woman.

Her name was Woman A. She was a very plain-looking gal, this Woman A, as one would expect from a background character who wouldn't even rate a proper CG if this was a video game.

Woman A had been sleeping peacefully in her bed when loud shouting from upstairs reached her apartment and woke her up with a start.

"EEK! Dang it, Lilian! Get your hand out of my pants!"

"Ufufufu, why? There's nothing wrong with a little intimacy between mates."

"We're not—oh! Ah! Un!"

Since then, Woman A had been forced to stay awake, listening with a face that looked like it might spontaneously combust at any moment, as the pair above carried on with their antics.

"Ufufufu! See? You like this."

"I do not like it! I am not liking this at all—yeek!"

"So you say, but I know you secretly love it when I do this. You're just too shy to admit it."

"No, I'm not—h-hey! L-Lilian! Don't tell me you're—no! Stop! DON'T!"

The loud sound of clothes tearing echoed around her room with ominous finality. Woman A would have wondered how such a sound could be so loud, as well as how it could echo so ominously, but she was too busy trying to keep her face from exploding to really think about it.

"MY PAJAMAS! That's the sixth set you've ruined! At this rate, I won't have any more left to wear!"

"That's fine by me. If you have nothing to wear, then you can start sleeping naked."

"Never!... Still, I suppose I should just be glad that you haven't destroyed any of my boxers..."

"Oh my, you're right... ufufufu. Maybe I should correct this oversight right now."

"You wouldn't!"

A moment of awkward silence. Several crickets chirped in a most annoying manner.

"Okay, you would. But don't! I need those boxers! I don't just wear them to bed, you know!"

"Like I said, if you don't want me to keep tearing your clothes off, then you should just sleep naked."

"Not happening—gya! Dang it, Lilian, would you stop doing that?!"

"You say that now, but I'll convince you to see things my way. Now then, let us begin this chapter by letting our unrestrained lust for each other explode! Ufufufu..."

"There will be no exploding of unrestrained lust here! And what the heck are you talking about?! Chapter five has already started!"

Another pause.

"Beloved...?" There was a tremor in the girl's voice.

"Wait, what did I just say?"

A squeal erupted from above. Woman A tried to cover her ears to lock the noise out... and then remembered that her ears already were covered and started to seriously consider slamming her head against the wall. Maybe if she were knocked unconscious, she wouldn't hear those two anymore. Then again, maybe not.

"You just broke the fourth wall!"

"I did? Wait, the fourth what now?"

"Oh, I love you so much, Beloved! I just can't stand it anymore! Take me now!"

"Wha—hold on now! Don't act so—oh! Oh no! Lilian! Don't!"

"Yes, that's it! Ufufufu! Make me your woman, Beloved!"

"I have no intentions of—Oh! OH!!"

"That's it! Yes! YES! How do you like that!? HUH?! DO YOU LIKE IT?! DO YOU LIKE THAT, BITCH?! WELL?! DO YOU?!"

A really, really, *really* awkward silence ensued after that.

"… Uh, Lilian?"

"… Too much?"

"… Just a bit, yeah."

"I'm sorry, I guess I was experiencing one of those Out of Character moments. Or maybe the time has finally come to unleash my inner dominatrix or something. Strange. I didn't even know I *had* an inner dominatrix."

"I hope to all eight-million Shinto gods that you don't have an inner dominatrix. And what the heck are you talking about?" Another moment of silence. "No, you know what? Never mind. I'm not even going to ask anymore."

"That's probably a good idea, Beloved. At least for now. You seem to be doing better though. At least you're breaking the fourth wall. I'm sure that with a little more time and a lot more sex, the fourth-wall breaking force will be so strong with you that kitsune everywhere will be green with envy."

"You know, I get really worried when you say things like that." A pause. "And there will be no sex! Stop mentioning sex, dang it!"

"Ufufuf, now why would you be worried? This is a good thing."

"It is not a good thing! And stop ignoring me when I tell you something that you don't want to hear!"

The voices from above trailed off. After several seconds of silence, Woman A dared to hope that the two had finally stopped. She wanted to get some more sleep before going to work.

"Now then, let us continue where we left off."

It was not to be.

"What? Continue where we—Wait! No! Lilian! LILIAN!"

And so Woman A sat there, her legs curled up to her chest and her face buried between her knees. Her entire body had managed to reach a shade of red that has yet to be cataloged by humans.

"HOLY SHIT! IS THAT YOUR TAIL!?"

"Did you just curse, Beloved? I don't think I've ever heard you swear before. Ah! Are you having an Out of Character moment, too?"

"NEVER MIND THAT! GET YOUR TAIL OUT OF MY BOXERS!"

Little did Woman A know that Kevin was being literal when he spoke of Lilian's tail. She thought it was just a euphemism of some kind, some sort of teenage slang to denote how talented the girl was at… whatever it was she was doing.

"Ufufufu!"

"LILIAN!"

It was going to be a long two hours.

***

Kevin had never been so glad to see the gates of Desert Cactus High School. He normally saw school as an obligatory nuisance, a necessary evil if he wanted to get into a good college and have a successful career. Now, school was very much a safe haven for him. So long as he was at school, Lilian couldn't do anything untoward to him.

No kissing. No licking. No pants-ripping.

That last one had become especially important to him. He had already lost six of his favorite pajama pants. He didn't want to lose any more.

After Lilian let go of his torso and hopped off the bike, Kevin followed suit and locked it up. The two then proceeded to class arm in arm. Actually, it was more like Lilian clutched Kevin's right arm to her chest. Of course, that was merely semantics that only Kevin believed mattered, and no one actually cared what he thought, so it didn't count.

"There it is again," Kevin muttered, stopping in the middle of the sidewalk. He and Lilian received a few curious looks from people walking by, but most seemed content to ignore them, save those few who were still enamored by Lilian's beauty.

Lilian, having heard his muttering, glanced at her beloved mate inquisitively. "There is what again?"

"This feeling," Kevin replied absentmindedly, his lips thinning in annoyance. "I have this intense urge to strangle someone, but I don't know why."

"Hmmm."

Lilian glanced at her mate in idle curiosity. She wondered what feeling he was talking about. And just who did he want to strangle? And why?

She really hoped that person was Eric. She didn't like him very much; he was just so annoying.

And speaking of people she would like to see strangled…

"Ah, there you are my *Flor Preciosa.* Long have I been waiting for the chance to see you again."

Starting from the tips of her toes and traveling all the way up to the crown of her head, Lilian's body visibly shuddered. Kevin could actually feel the tremor as it traveled through her body, and even though they were hidden, he could imagine her tails and ears quivering in the same way. It was actually kind of a cute image.

It was also enough to make Kevin nearly slap himself in the face.

Dang it, Kevin, he thought. *You need to stop thinking about Lilian like this! Sure, she's pretty and nice and—no!* He shook his head. *Don't go down this road, Kevin Swift. Don't you dare go down this road!*

He needed to think about something else. He needed to get his mind off the gorgeous redhead with her amazing body, succulent breasts, beautiful hips and shapely butt—

Kevin squeezed his eyes shut. *Think about Lindsay. Think about Lindsay. Think about Lindsay. Lindsay in a bikini.* His thoughts paused. His eyes glazed over. *Oh... oh, that's nice.*

While Kevin went to his happy place, Lilian turned toward the source of the voice with a growing sense of dread. Kevin snapped out of his happy place when he was forced to turn with her. Two sets of eyes, one of emerald and the other light blue, landed on the young man who had spoken.

"You!" Lilian shouted, glaring at the boy in the Spanish bull-fighting costume. Kevin recognized the teenager. It was the one that Lilian had been having trouble with on Monday—there's no way he could forget that hair. And why was he still wearing that matador costume?

"I am glad to see you remember me." The young man with the stupidly large pompadour haircut gave Lilian what he hoped was a suave smile, completely ignoring Kevin.

Kevin didn't know whether to feel insulted or grateful.

Lilian's glare intensified. She stared at the olive-skinned teen, attempting to burn a hole through him with her eyes. Oh, how she wished looks could kill. This boy would be so dead if they could.

Her eyes narrowed further as the boy—Juan something or other—stood there with an infuriating smile plastered on his face. Tension hung in the air, so thick that Himura Kenshin could've sliced it to pieces *Hiten Miturugi-Ryū* style. It felt like one of those old-fashioned, Samurai stand-offs. Kevin was almost expecting the two of them—or at least Lilian—to whip out a gun and start shooting.

"You!" Lilian's already narrowed eyes seemed to narrow further, the tension increasing around the trio. The air was so thick with the stuff that if anyone were watching, they'd see the bright golden aura of Lilian's clashing with the muddy green of Juan Who-has-too-many-last-names. "You..!"

A tumbleweed rolled by. It blew between the trio. Kevin tracked its progress until it disappeared around a corner.

"The heck?" he mumbled.

"You!" Lilian's glare, which had been potent enough to melt metaphorical steel… dropped. "… Who are you again?"

Had Lilian not been gripping Kevin's right arm so tightly, he would have probably fallen flat on his face from the shock. Fortunately for him, she did have a good hold on his arm, and thus he managed to stay upright.

Juan What's-his-face did not have this luxury. Too bad for him. He fell flat on his face, the pavement denting, a series of cracks like a spiders web growing from the point of impact, and his feet sticking straight up in the air, twitching erratically.

It seemed Kevin was not the only one that the face-faulting force was strong in.

Face-faulting. For when a facepalm simply wasn't enough.

Juan recovered admirably from his close encounter of the face-on-concrete kind, though Kevin did notice that his features looked kind of like a pancake. They were flat and stretched.

Juan grabbed his face and pulled, somehow making his two-dimensional features look 3D again.

"How could you not remember me, my beautiful *señorita*? Do you not remember the beautiful moment we shared together? It was the other day that you bore your heart to me and I offered you my undying love and support."

Lilian tilted her head to the side. Meanwhile, Juan looked at her hopefully.

"You remember now, si?"

"Hmm…" Lilian's nose scrunched up cutely as she tried recalling the moment this boy spoke of. Her face cleared up a second later. "Nope!" she replied cheerfully. "I don't remember that happening!"

Cue a second round of face-faulting from Juan.

"But it was just yesterday!"

"Are you sure you didn't imagine it?" Lilian asked. "Maybe you were having a strange dream."

"Of course I'm not imagining it! It was just after school; you were standing there in the hallway, looking so *triste*, and I offered you my ear."

Juan went off into his own little world, eyes glazing over in a look that sort of resembled nostalgia, only a lot more creepy. He stared off into the distance at something only he could see, hands clasped together almost like he was praying.

For some reason that was beyond Kevin and Lilian, sparkles surrounded Juan, shimmering in the air like someone had shot him with a glitter cannon. They didn't know why. He wasn't a *Bishounen*, or a *Mahou Shoujo*. At least they really hoped he wasn't a magical girl; a magical transformation of that nature would've been disturbing, even *with* the censorship.

"It happened exactly as I had foreseen; that moment when you were troubled, and I offered you my aid to help ease the pain you were feeling."

Kevin and Lilian could only watch on, a bead of sweat running down the left side of their faces. The boy ignored everything around him, including the people that were pointing at him and whispering to themselves. Or laughing at his hair, which flopped and jiggled like Davin Monstrang's six chins. Juan's body also began undulating, almost as if he were boneless, which shouldn't have been possible with an anthropomorphic body.

"You told me of your troubles and desires, and I bore witness to a side of you no one else had ever seen before."

He unclasped his hands and brought the left one to his chest, closing his eyes as a small smile appeared on his face.

Kevin stared at the boy with increasingly wide eyes. He didn't know everything that had happened between this fellow and Lilian, but he doubted the picture being painted was accurate.

This kid… just how delusional was he?

"It was a truly beautiful thing, a memory that I shall cherish until the end of time."

Lilian poked her lower lip with her index finger, tilting her head with an introspective expression.

"You remember now, don't you, *mi bella flor*?" Juan implored the girl, looking at her. His eyes were shining, literally, like two stars on a clear night sky.

It was all kinds of freaky.

A small tic mark emerged on Lilian's forehead while her right eye twitched in obvious agitation.

"You know, if you're going to give me compliments in another language, don't use Goongare Translations to get them. They're never accurate."

"Wait." Kevin interrupted before Lilian could continue. "You've never been to a mall, you've rarely gone out before coming here, and they don't have computers or any form of advanced technology beyond basic household appliances where you grew up, so how come you know what Goongare Translate is?"

"Hmm." Lilian pondered the question. "This must be one of those plot holes that people are always talking about."

"Plot holes?"

"Oh yes, there are tons of plot holes all over the place if you know where to look." Lilian pointed at Juan. "See?"

Juan twitched.

"Wait, how is he a plot hole?"

"Just look at him? How could he *not* be a plot hole?"

Kevin looked at Juan… and then slowly nodded. "I can kind of see your point. I mean, anyone with hair that looks like it belongs on a *Yakuza* must be a plot hole."

"Oi!"

"Exactly." Lilian's sage-like nod was accompanied by a smile.

"Still, I'm sure his appearance will be explained later on somehow."

"Of course." Lilian's chuckle sounded almost condescending. "Isn't that how these things always work?"

"Would you two stop ignoring me!" Juan cried out.

"Also, I still don't remember that happening," Lilian snapped, continuing her original tirade. Juan face-faulted for a third time. "The only person I would ever bare my heart to is my Beloved. Not you." She gave the boy with bright blond pompadour hair a mockingly cheerful smile as he climbed back to his feet.

While Juan stood there, gawking like some kind of idiot, Kevin closed his eyes.

"The only person I would ever bare my heart to is my Beloved."

The words bounced around in his head. He didn't understand how Lilian could sound so certain, so sure of herself. It's like she didn't even consider the possibility that he might not be her mate, that she might be mistaken. At the same time, her words were almost like a ray of sunlight piercing the clouds of his troubled mind, sweeping across the landscape of his soul and encompassing his heart in a warm glow.

He felt sick. He was leading this girl on, too cowardly to tell her no, too spineless to set her straight, and that wasn't even taking his feelings for Lindsay into account. That was a whole other can of worms that he didn't want to open right now. How could he set this whole twisted love story right?

Kevin sometimes forgot that he wasn't the one who chose to ignore the many times he told Lilian they weren't dating.

"There he is! There's the idiot who stole our costume again!"

"Let's get him!"

Juan narrowed his eyes.

"I guess that is my cue to leave, but do not think this is the last time that we will see each other." He pointed at Kevin. "I shall return, and when I do, I will steal the lovely *señorita* away from—doof!"

Something beaned the matador boy in the head; a microphone, Kevin noticed. Juan bolted, realizing that he had finally overstayed his welcome, but not before tossing one last parting comment.

"Do not think this is over! One day, I will pluck you from your vine, *mi hermosa flor*!"

"I don't even know what that means!" Lilian shouted back. "And stop calling me flour!" Unfortunately, Juan was unable to hear her over the shouts, demands and screams of anger from the pursuing theater club students.

"Get back here with our costume, Juan-Pompadour!"

"You're going to pay for stealing from us!"

"It's not Juan-Pompadour!" Juan's yell could be heard in the distance. "It's Juan Martinez Villanueva Cortes!"

"I don't care what your name is! It's going to become Juan Road Kill if you don't give us our costume back!"

"I will never let you have this back! I need it to properly show off my *encanto*; my manly charm!"

"WE DON'T CARE!"

Seconds later, the horde of enraged thespians passed by Kevin and Lilian, leaving a large trail of dust in their wake.

The two nonplussed housemates stood there, matching looks of *"what the fuck just happened?"* on their faces.

Several seconds of silence passed.

"Why don't we just pretend this never happened?" Kevin suggested. Lilian nodded her head.

"Agreed."

Putting the encounter out of their minds, the two were free to make their way to class. Fortunately, Juan had not taken up too much of their time, so they would not be late.

Not that it mattered. Lilian's Deus Ex Machina ability to manipulate a human's mind could get them out of nearly any kind of trouble. It would be especially easy since their homeroom teacher seemed unusually susceptible to kitsune powers.

"Do you really not remember meeting that Juan guy last week?" Kevin finally decided to let his curiosity get the better of him.

"Of course I do." Lilian clutched Kevin's arm tighter to her chest as she went into another full-body shudder, making Kevin think of the frenzied beating of a hummingbird's wings. "I could never forget meeting someone so creepy."

"Then why did you say you didn't remember?" Lilian gave him a sly smile, and it took Kevin a second or two to understand the meaning behind it. When he did, the young man chuckled. "You're definitely a kitsune, alright."

"Tee-hee, of course."

"Still, that was pretty mean of you."

"He deserved it," Lilian declared fervently. "He's such a jerk, thinking he can keep calling me by those ridiculous names and expecting me to go out with him."

Kevin felt a bead of sweat run down the left side of his head.

"Isn't this a case of the pot calling the kettle black?"

"What was that, Beloved?"

"Nothing." Kevin quickly looked away. "Still, I'm surprised you would pull a prank on someone. You've been so nice since you've arrived…" He trailed off for a moment as he realized what he had just said. "Well… for the most part. I haven't seen you pull a prank on anyone since we've met, at least."

"That's because I haven't really had the opportunity to pull a prank." Lilian pouted before a small, genuine smile appeared on her face. "And besides, I also wanted to make you smile. And look!" She exclaimed, freeing her left hand and gesturing to his face. "You're smiling."

"Ah," Kevin felt a familiar heat appearing on his face. "I guess I am."

As they continued walking to class, neither of them saw the figure clad in gothic lolita garb, peering at them from just around the corner.

***

Chris frowned as he stared up at the ceiling. Not like he could do much else. He'd been practically confined to this spot ever since Kiara had moved in. His body still hadn't healed for some reason, so he'd been forced to remain in bed. Even now his nerves screamed in agony anytime he overexerted himself.

It was absolutely infuriating, not being able to fight, forced to lie in this ratty little bed all day! How dare that bitch do this to him! When he got his hands on that gods-be-damned fox, he was going to—

"Hurk!"

A pained gasp escaped his mouth. His muscles twitched, sending intense jolts of pain through his body. It hurt! By the gods, it fucking hurt! It felt like every cell was being burned alive by an intense light! He could do nothing but clench his teeth and ride out the mind-shattering agony until it subsided.

Another gasp. His body, drenched in sweat, finally relaxed again.

Ever since his battle with that fox, he had been experiencing the most intense bouts of suffering imaginable. They seemed to come and go at random, but whenever his thoughts became dark, and his anger got the best of him, the pain intensified. He didn't know what that meant, but he was sure that the fox bitch was responsible.

“Kiara!” he shouted out, “make me a sandwich!” Chris was pretty hungry, and since his bitch of a sister was temporarily living with him, he might as well take advantage of it and have the woman make him some food. The kitchen was where she belonged anyway.

When his sister failed to answer he frowned.

“Kiara!” He called out, louder this time. Still without an answer, Chris swore loudly as he struggled to sit up. Even doing that much hurt. Gods dammit, he was as weak as a newborn pup!

After several minutes of struggling, he finally managed to sit himself up. He took a bit of a breather, preparing for the most difficult part: standing.

Of course, saying that standing would be more difficult than sitting was a bit of an understatement. Chris's legs didn't seem to like cooperating with him. Whenever he tried to get on his own two feet, his thigh and calf muscles would send painful jabs of muscle-tearing agony up his legs, and into his brain. It felt like someone had taken a machete still burning hot from the forge and stabbed him in the legs repeatedly. The pain forced him back onto the bed, panting and puffing as he exhausted what little energy he had recovered.

After nearly six minutes of unsuccessfully trying to stand, Chris was forced to crawl along the carpet like some kind of inch-worm, until he could get over to the wall to support himself.

It was a good thing Kiara couldn’t see him; this was humiliating enough without her.

Despite the hardships he underwent, Chris managed to climb to his feet eventually. Leaning against the wall for support, he dragged himself into the living room.

“Kiara! Stop fucking ignoring me and make me a sandwich you stupid… huh?”

Chris blinked several times as he entered an empty room that looked nothing like the living room he remembered. The once messy living room was actually clean. The stains were gone, the cracks were sealed shut, and the furniture was brand new. Was that a leather sofa?

“Kiara?” Chris' confusion turned into indignation, then anger, as he realized that not only had his sister messed with his apartment, but she wasn't even there for him to yell at. “Where the hell did that bitch go now?”

***

“I can't wait for tomorrow!” Lilian made her fervent declaration as she and Kevin walked out of the main school building. It was after school now. Track practice had ended a short while ago, and the two were on their way home.

Kevin looked down at the girl attached to his arm. Or was it the other way around? Either way, he could see Lilian's jubilant smile and sparkling, emerald eyes.

“You seem even more excited about my track meet than I am.”

“Of course I'm excited.” Lilian turned to look at her mate. “I'm finally going to get to see you in action! Your first track meet of the year! I'm sure you'll be amazing!”

“Thanks!” Kevin couldn't help but grin as well. It wasn't even that her smile was infectious—which it kind of was—but that he couldn't help but agree. “With all the training and exercise I've been getting, I'm sure I'll get first place in both of my competitions.”

“Hm hm!” Lilian nodded with exuberance. “You did really well at practice today. I saw how you beat that loser in the one-hundred and two-hundred meter dash.”

Kevin’s chuckle was like music to Lilian’s ears. “I did, didn’t I?”

That had been a moment he would cherish forever. The look on his rival’s face when Kevin beat him at both the 100- and 200-meter dashes had been priceless. And it was proof that he was getting faster.

Kevin was positive he had Lilian to thank for that; her constant presence on the back of his bike had forced his muscles to work harder than ever before. The diet he had been on thanks to Lilian's incredible cooking probably helped as well.

He would have to find some way to thank her. He didn't know how yet, because the girl only seemed to want one thing from him—and he planned on holding onto what little chastity he had left. Thank you very much. He would still think of a suitable thank you gift, though. Maybe a nice dinner or something…

His thoughts were derailed by a pair of soft, full lips pressing against his cheek.

"What was the heck that for?" he placed a hand on his cheek. It felt warm.

"For luck."

"The track meet isn't until this Wednesday. What do I need luck for?"

"Then because I wanted to."

"That does sound more like you." Kevin slowly nodded, his blush receding a bit. "Please don't do it again?"

"Eh?" Lilian whined. "Why not?"

"Because it's just…" Kevin stopped himself. Even if he told her the reason, chances were high that Lilian wouldn't listen, and unless he was willing to be a douche about it—which he wasn't—then nothing he said would work. "… Never mind."

"Okay."

A growl from behind alerted them to the fact they were not alone. They turned around to see Eric walking behind them, eyes narrowed as he stared at nothing. No, not nothing, Kevin realized as he felt the by now familiar urge to cave someone's face in overcome him.

"Eric." He held himself back, shaking his head. This was just Eric. No need to get upset. "What are you doing here?"

"I have to see my dad before I leave," Eric growled, still staring.

"You got caught peeking on the girls when they were changing again, didn't you?" Eric didn't answer, but his deepening scowl let Kevin know that he hit the nail on the head. "You do know that the principal's office is in the opposite direction, right?"

"Yes."

"Then why are you following us?"

"Because if I'm going to be forced to listen to my hypocritical old man talk about how I'm being disrespectful toward women again, then I want to have a happy memory that I can use to block him out."

"I see, I see." Kevin nodded his head calmly. "And that is the reason you're staring at Lilian's backside?"

"Yes."

The urge was stronger now. Kevin didn't appreciate how Eric saw Lilian as nothing more than an object. It bothered him, and the desire to break his fist on his friend's jaw became stronger than ever. He resisted, clenching his hands to keep from acting on his desire.

"Fancy meeting you here, kid," a familiar voice said.

Three sets of eyes turned toward the origin of the new voice. Kevin blinked when he saw the familiar woman walking up to them.

"Hey," she grinned, raising an arm in greeting.

Kevin looked at her in surprise. "You're—"

"One of the sexiest pieces of ass I've ever seen!"

Everyone blinked as Eric randomly appeared in front of Kiara, moving fast enough to shock all of them. One second he'd been standing behind Lilian, staring at her deliciously tight derriere, and the next he was invading Kiara's personal space, his face flushed red and his eyes glazed over in barely-concealed lust. His nostrils flared like a horse, and several gallons of blood seemed to shoot from his nose, splattering along the ground and the pervert's shoes and pants.

"Huh?" Lilian stared at the copious amounts of carnelian liquid pouring from the perverted boy's nostrils. "I didn't know that happened in real life."

"Me neither," Kevin admitted. He also stared at the blood spouting from Eric's nasal cavities like a geyser. "Just where is all that blood coming from?"

"I'm not sure…"

Lilian reached between her cleavage and pulled out a book, *The 100 Rules of Anime,* and began searching through it.

"Let's see… I know it's here somewhere… ah! Here it is!" Lilian coughed into her hand, and Kevin paid attention to the girl as she spoke. “Rule number eighteen, the Law of Hemoglobin Capacity: the human body contains over twelve gallons of blood, sometimes more, under high pressure.”

Kevin stared, a lot.

“That’s it?”

“Yep.” Lilian put the book back into her Extra Dimensional Storage Space.

“Well…” Kevin eyed the blood that was *still* spraying from Eric’s nose. It looked like twin jet streams shooting from a fire hydrant. “… I guess that makes sense.”

“Right.”

Kiara stared at the nosebleeding boy with a look that said, *“if you don't get out of my face right this instant, I'ma punch in your face in.”* Kevin could even imagine her speaking like some kind of Yakuza thug. How emotive.

Naturally, Eric ignored this look.

“Your tits might not be that big, but you've got an ass to die for!”

Kiara's right eye twitched.

Kevin, on the other hand, simply facepalmed. He knew where this was going.

“Those shapely legs, those buns of steel, they're absolutely amazing! Please let me rub my face in them!”

“Gotta give the perv credit,” Lilian said, “At least he asked.”

“I'll give him credit if he survives this,” Kevin retorted, “She looks pissed.”

Indeed, Kiara looked incredibly pissed. Her face was mottled with color and Righteous Feminine Fury. Her clenched hands were shaking, and blood slowly leaked out from between her fingers as her nails dug into the flesh of her palms. The woman was more furious than anybody there could possibly comprehend.

And when an inu yōkai got angry, things broke.

So did people.

Which was why, seconds later, Eric was lying face first on the ground, unconscious, his body twitching in pain. Kiara stood over him, a livid scowl marring her face as her dark, hooded eyes glared down at the boy. A very large lump had formed on his head, and two white bandages could be seen on top of it, crossing each other to form an x.

Lilian leaned into her Beloved and cupped a hand to her mouth. "I thought the lecher was a boob person," she whispered. Kevin shuddered, but did his best to ignore the hot breath hitting his ear. "So why is he after her butt?"

"Eric is the kind of person who will perv on anyone he thinks is hot," he whispered back. "He's one of those equally opportunistic pervs."

Lilian nodded in understanding. "I see, so he's *that* kind of person."

"Yep."

"Good to know."

"Secrets don't make friends, you know." No longer glaring at Eric, Kiara focused on the two before her. Walking up to the pair—and stomping harshly on Eric's back as she did so—she stopped directly in front of the two, placing her hands on her hips. "Sharing a lovers secret, are we?"

While Kevin blushed a bit, Lilian finally seemed to realize that there was an attractive female standing in front of them; one who knew her mate to boot.

"Who are you?" she asked, her eyes narrowing at the admittedly attractive woman. Sure, her breasts weren't that big—certainly nowhere near Lilian's own sizable bosom—but she still had an attractive figure, and she was athletic to boot. That business suit of hers was rather form-fitting, and anyone with a set of working eyes could see the lean, athletic body she possessed beneath.

The sight of another attractive female, and one with a body-type similar to Lindsay's, sent Lilian's possessive kitsune instincts into overdrive. She was not going to allow this other woman to try and get in good with her mate. There was enough competition for his affections already!

"I never did tell you my name, did I?" Kiara looked amused by Lilian's obvious display of jealousy. "The name's Kiara. Nice to meet ya."

"Kiara," Kevin muttered. Why did that sound so familiar?

"And how do you know my Beloved?"

"Lilian," Kevin groaned. He didn't know what was going on, but he recognized that tone. It was the same one that she used when addressing Lindsay.

"We just met at the store a while ago, and he gave me his opinion on some products I was looking to buy." Kiara smirked at the girl. "Don't worry your pretty little head. I have no intentions towards your boyfriend. I don't hit on taken men." She looked over at Kevin, who sputtered incoherently at the taken comment. "Plus, he's a bit too young for my tastes."

Lilian relaxed, but only slightly. This woman could be lying to make her drop her guard. She couldn't detect a lie, but that didn't mean much. Lilian would not allow herself to be duped. Constant vigilance and all that.

"So what are you doing here?" asked Kevin.

"I've got to pick up some things for my brother," Kiara scowled. "The idiot hurt himself playing sports, and now he's stuck at home. I'm grabbing his homework for him. Just because he's bedridden doesn't mean he can slack off."

"Ah." Kevin nodded his head and smiled. "You're a pretty nice sister to do that for him."

"Ha!" Kiara barked a laugh. "You might think that, but I doubt he will. He'll hate the fact that I'm not letting him slack off."

The femme in the business suit then turned to Lilian, who was still staring at her hard. It wasn't quite a glare, but it would certainly be disconcerting to the average human.

Good thing she wasn't average. Or human.

"Something wrong?"

"You look really familiar." Lilian's frown deepened, brows knitting in mild frustration. "Do I know you from somewhere?"

The fanged grin Kiara sent Lilian's way caused a strange shiver to run down Kevin's spine, for reasons he couldn't understand.

"Who knows," she said, dropping the grin after several seconds and giving a shrug. "We very well could have. I do so much traveling for my business that I've met a lot of people, and faces tend to blur together after a while."

"Business?" This question came from Kevin.

"Yep." Kiara nodded and puffed up her chest in pride. "I'm the owner of the largest chain of fitness centers in the United States."

"You mean Mad Dawg Fitness?" Kevin perked up. Then his eyes widened. "You're Kiara F. Kuyo!"

Lilian glanced curiously at Kevin, while Kiara gave him a fanged smirk. "The very same."

"Do you know this person, Beloved?"

"Only by name," Kevin replied, still looking at Kiara in surprise. "Kiara F. Kuyo is the owner of Mad Dawg Fitness; the largest and most popular chain fitness centers in the United States. I think they have something like twenty-thousand gyms located throughout the country. They're known for not only having top-quality equipment, but also being much more affordable than other gyms. My mom has a membership."

"We also have a lot of the amenities the more expensive gyms offer, like a spa, massage parlor, café, basketball and volleyball courts, two Olympic-sized swimming pools and an outdoor swimming pool with three water slides," Kiara added.

"You had me at massage." Lilian turned to her mate, her large eyes imploring. "Can we go there, Beloved?"

"Maybe some time this weekend," Kevin told her. He glanced back at Kiara. "I didn't know your brother went here."

"Oh, he does." Kiara smiled knowingly. "You might even know him."

"Really?"

"Well, maybe." Kiara shrugged. "It's a pretty big school, and he's a year older than you, so maybe not."

"Oh," Kevin absentmindedly wondered who among the student body could be related to Kiara. They would have to be athletic, especially with a sister like her; but he couldn't think of who that might be. There was no one at Desert Cactus High that he knew with the last name Kuyo.

"Right." Lilian smiled as she increased her grip on Kevin's arm, startling him out of his thoughts. Addressing Kiara, she said, "It was very nice meeting you, but my Beloved and I really must be going."

"That's fine." Kiara waved them off. "I have to meet with my brother's teachers anyway."

The three parted ways, Kevin and Lilian going one direction while Kiara went another.

As they were leaving, Lilian looked back to see the wild-haired woman walking toward the main school building.

"Something wrong, Lilian?" asked Kevin.

"No." Lilian shook her head. "Come on, Beloved. Let's go home."

The two began to walk again, when they were stopped by a low, pain-filled groan.

"Owwwcchhh…"

Looking down, they found the source of the agonized moaning. There, lying beneath them as they stood on his back, was Eric. He was still unconscious.

Kevin and Lilian looked back up at each other, one looking sheepish, the other wearing an amused smile.

"Um, oops," Lilian rapped her knuckles against her noggin and winked at him, "Tee-hee."

***

Almost an hour after arriving, Kiara finally finished meeting with all of Chris' teachers.

She was exhausted.

The meetings had been very trying. It was almost as bad as meetings with the board of directors for her fitness centers. She had been forced to explain why her brother wasn't attending classes, without giving away that they weren't human, or that he had gotten his ass kicked by another non-human entity. She'd used the excuse that Chris had been bullying someone smaller than him, and ran into that person's much bigger friend. Having to give the story over and over again eerily reminded her of how board meetings often went.

Her board of directors were a bunch of idiots.

Thankfully, unlike her board of directors, she hadn't been forced to repeat herself more than once per teacher. Everyone knew that Chris was the closest thing to a tyrant without actually being a ruler; they had readily believed her, swallowing her words like they were the sweetest ambrosia. She got the feeling that her brother's teachers were simply too happy knowing that he wouldn't be attending school to wonder about the how's or why's.

She didn't blame them. Her brother was one of the worst kinds of people. If they weren't related, there was no way she would have been so accommodating to the boy.

On a side note, the coach in charge of wrestling had been pretty disappointed.

As she walked back to her car, Chris's homework stacked in her hands, her mind went to the kitsune and her human mate. They were such an interesting couple, particularly Lilian. The girl was sharp; for a second, Kiara thought the redhead had actually been able to sense what she was.

She hadn't. As a two-tails, Lilian probably didn't have very good sensing abilities, and Kiara had trained herself to suppress her yōkai. A four-tails might be able to sense her, but not a two-tails.

The girl had recognized her, though, at least enough to realize they had met some time before. Kiara would have to be more careful in the future. It wouldn't do for the girl to recognize her before she was truly ready to reveal herself.

At least Kiara knew why the girl looked so familiar; they *had* met somewhere before. She still couldn't recall where yet, but figured it would come to her in time.

"I think I might actually have some fun with these two." Kiara grinned to herself as she opened the car door and sat inside. She started the car and listened as it roared to life, reveling in the sound of her vehicle's powerful engine.

Putting the car in reverse, she efficiently navigated out of the school grounds. It was time to make sure her idiot of a brother didn't lose any more of his brain cells by lazing around in bed all day.

Chapter 6

Track Meet Troubles

Wednesday heralded Kevin's first track and field event of the year. It felt a little strange to have an event so early in the year; it being only fall. Track was supposed to be a spring sport; it had been last year.

Well, whatever. Kevin didn't care about which season he ran in. This just meant that he would be dealing with slightly cooler weather, which was fine by him.

After Kevin's last class of the day, Computer Programming, he and Lilian proceeded to the locker rooms—although it would probably be more accurate to say that Kevin proceeded while Lilian just followed him around, as per the usual.

"Are you nervous, Beloved?" Lilian asked, peering at her mate as they walked through the hallway. Their feet tapped against the blue tiles of the hall, echoing in the empty corridor. The other track members were probably already getting changed.

Lilian held his hand, her delicate and feminine fingers laced through his slightly calloused ones. The fox-girl marveled at how warm his hand was. It felt nice.

"Not really." Kevin shook his head, barely even registering their conjoined appendages anymore. He'd grown so used to this happening—and finally realized the futility of trying to make her stop—that it simply no longer bothered him, even though he felt like it should. What would Lindsay think if she saw them like this?

At least she no longer clung to his side like glue; that was something to be grateful for.

You had to be thankful for the little things.

"I'm actually pretty excited. I've been doing really well during practice. Even Coach Deretaine was surprised by the times I've been getting. I'm sure I'll ace my races no problem. There's no way I'll lose to anyone this time!"

Kevin held his free hand up near his face, clenching it into a fist. His normally blue irises burst into twin balls of fire, orange and yellow flames that burned and flickered, a raging inferno being fed gasoline by several large canisters at the same time. He was emotive like that.

"Last year I got third place in the one-hundred meter dash," Kevin continued. "Chase ended up getting second, and we were both beaten by this one guy from Mountain Shadows High School."

"Mountain Shadows High School?" Lilian questioned, her head tilting slightly to the left.

"They're a school up near Peoria," Kevin told her, "Our school and Mountain Shadow have been competing against each other for years now, long before I even started going here. Our schools have always hated each other for some reason—don't really know why. I guess you could say they're like our rivals or something."

"Huh."

His school and Mountain Shadow were always trying to outdo the other in everything; from sports to academics to fine arts. There had even been rumors of a debate between the two schools' debate teams getting violent. The rivalry they had was legendary.

Not that Kevin really cared about whatever rivalry the schools had. He'd never put much stalk in school rivalries, and the only person he considered rival-worthy was Kasey Chase. It had all started before his time anyway.

"I know you'll be amazing, Beloved." Lilian smiled at her mate's obvious excitement. It was so rare to see him fired up like this. She couldn't help but become infected by his enthusiasm. "I'll be rooting for you."

Kevin grinned and swiped his thumb across his tip of his nose, appearing both mildly embarrassed and genuinely pleased. "Heh, thanks."

They soon arrived at the locker room. Kevin turned to Lilian. Overcome by excitement, body burning with anticipation, he beamed at the redhead, his smile brighter than a thousand watt bulb.

He really couldn't wait to hit the track field.

"So, wish me luck?"

That was the wrong thing to say. Or maybe it was the right thing to say. Kevin didn't know, though it would be a question he continued asking himself for some time to come.

"With pleasure."

Kevin had just enough time to spot the lustful gleam within Lilian's emerald orbs before she kissed him, hard.

As her lips hampered his own, Kevin's eyes became so wide they practically bulged out of his sockets, and his pupils shrunk into tiny dots. He opened his mouth, though whether this was to speak or scream would never be known.

If Kevin wanted her to stop kissing him, then opening his mouth was quite possibly the worst response possible. It was like a rabbit hopping up to a wolf and saying, *"please don't eat me."* He might as well have told her that it was perfectly acceptable to orally ravish him with her tongue.

Her tongue slipped into his mouth, moving between his teeth with every intention of claiming the space beyond. Kevin could do nothing more than groan as the small, pink appendage caressed and rubbed his own tongue, stirring up saliva and creating a ceaseless friction that sent his mind spiraling into a delirious state.

Everything he'd been thinking of before then vanished; the track meet, Kasey, his school's rivalry. The only thing that mattered was Lilian's soft lips on his and her tongue in his mouth.

"Hn!!"

The kiss deepened. Were Kevin in his right mind, he would have thought such a thing impossible. His back pressed against the wall, Lilian's hands placed firmly on his chest, pinning him as her lips and tongue consumed him, devouring him in ways he'd not felt since their first kiss.

Shocked at being on the receiving end of a kiss of this magnitude, especially after having gone so long without, his mind and body were unable to cope with the sensations. It didn't help that she knew what she was doing. Her lips felt incredible, and her tongue was doing some really pleasant things inside of his mouth.

She and that Iris chick must have practiced a lot.

When Lilian finally decided she'd had enough—for now—she released Kevin's mouth with a loud smacking of lips and took a step back. A small string of saliva connected them until she broke it by sensually running her tongue over her lips.

Unable to stand upright without Lilian holding him up, Kevin needed to lean against the wall for support. His face was flushed a deep scarlet, and his lungs heaved as his breath came out in ragged gasps, like a man who'd been held under water for too long and was just now breaking the surface.

While his oxygen-deprived brain attempted to reboot, his eyes stared into Lilian's, wide and round. His irises had shrunk to tiny pinpricks of bright blue, as if someone was shining a bright spotlight directly into his eyes.

It was only after a full sixty seconds of staring that Kevin finally found his voice, though it came out as nothing more than a breathy whisper.

"Lilian…"

A finger to his lips caused Kevin's response to die. The smile she gave him did not help much either. He could practically feel his heart leap into his throat at the sight of her lips curving in a manner that he could only call loving.

"That was for good luck," she told him. While most people would have already realized that—what else could a kiss like *that* be mistaken for?—it was probably a wise decision to state the obvious for Kevin's sake. His mind simply wasn't working properly at the moment, so being as blunt as possible could only be a good thing. "I'll be rooting for you in the stands."

With those parting words, Lilian walked off with an extra sway in her hips. In spite of himself, Kevin found his eyes unable to leave that small, heart-shaped butt as it swayed back and forth enticingly, until she was well out of sight.

The moment Lilian disappeared, a low groan escaped Kevin's lips. His legs wobbled, but he valiantly fought against the jelly-legs brought on by Lilian's exceedingly intense moment of passion. As he tried to keep from sinking to the floor, his mind attempted to move past what had just happened as well.

It was more difficult than it looked.

That kiss had been intense. It was like one of those kisses you see in a romance movie… or a chick flick.

Or a hentai, but Kevin didn't watch hentai.

Lilian had not been that forward with him for a long while; she had really caught him flat-footed. Perhaps that's why he'd been so unprepared for an assault of that caliber?

And was it just him, or had she gotten better at that seductress act of hers?

Maybe she'd been practicing?

"Ke-vin Swift!"

Like a live wire that had been stuck in an outlet, a jolt of something similar to electricity raced through his nervous system. It wasn't actual electricity though, just fear.

His mind screamed at him not to turn around, but his body disobeyed. Slowly, oh so slowly, as if he were about to face some kind of abhorrent abomination, an eldritch horror both ancient and unfathomable, Kevin Swift turned around.

Standing before him were five people he knew very well. All of them appeared incredibly jealous, their eyes narrowed into ferocious glares of DOOM. If looks could kill, Kevin was sure he'd be a pile of ashes by now. Even Kasey Chase looked like he wanted to strangle Kevin, and he had a girlfriend!

"Uh," Quick, Kevin! Think of something to say! "You didn't see that."

The five before him… twitched. Kevin shuddered.

"Swift…"

Standing in the center of the group was Eric, and Kevin nearly gulped when he caught sight of just how pissed the perv was. The lanky sophomore looked almost ready to start frothing at the mouth. It would have actually been kind of funny, were he not about ready to piss himself.

"Urk!" Kevin almost swallowed his tongue. Somehow, he managed to find his voice. "L-look, I know what you think you saw, but I'm going to tell you right now that it wasn't what it looked like."

"Oh?" Twitch. Shudder. "Not what it looked like, eh?" Twitch. Eric's hands made random muscle spasms. "So you're telling me that you did not just receive the hottest kiss that I have ever seen with the sexiest piece of ass I have ever met?"

"Um," Kevin would have tried backing away, but his back was pressed against the wall. "Is there anything I can say that won't end in my violent and gory death?"

Eric's gritted teeth were reminiscent of a rabid pit bull. "You are so lucky we have track right now, or I would strip you to your underwear, and stuff you in a locker filled with the wrestling team's sweaty jockstraps."

Kevin shuddered. There weren't many things in this world that he feared; his track coach when he was angry, Chris Fleischer (*especially* when he was angry), his mother, and rubber chickens (a story for another time). Kevin could now add something else to his list of fears.

Seriously, few things could be more terrifying than being stuffed into a locker filled with sweaty, smelly, disgusting jockstraps… except maybe being locked into a locker filled with *mawashi* (the loin cloth worn by Sumo wrestlers) that had not been washed for several months. It amounted to almost the same thing, except *mawashi* acted more like a thong, where jockstraps just cupped the manly bits.

Talk about gross.

"But you're not going to do that… right?" Kevin asked tentatively, doing his best to hide his trepidation. He failed.

"Not this time." Eric's glare managed to, impossibly, intensify. Kevin didn't know whether to feel relieved that he'd been saved from a most horrible fate, or worried that there might be a next time.

As the group made their way into the locker room, and Kevin continued to be subjected to his friends' angry glares, he decided to go with worried.

He really, *really* needed speak with Lilian about when it was and wasn't appropriate to kiss him, especially a kiss like *that*.

And just why was he suddenly not as bothered by the idea of her kissing him?

***

"Alright people! Listen up!"

Kevin, Alex, Andrew, Justin, Chase and a still angry Eric sat on a bench by the track field. There were roughly twenty people on the track team, so the bench was a little crowded, even though it was nearly fifteen feet long.

Kevin sat between Chase, who'd gotten over his jealousy quickly enough, and Alex, who'd thankfully decided to sit between him and Eric.

Their rival team from Mountain Shadow High sat several meters away, their dark red and black uniforms making them easy to spot. They appeared to also be getting a speech from their coach.

Coach Deretaine looked at all of them with what could only be described as a maniacal gleam in his eyes, as if he had temporarily lost his sanity and gone bat-shit crazy. And he had. For the upcoming track meet, that is.

Coaches the world over have always been temporarily overcome with madness right before their team's sporting events. It was just in their nature.

"This is our first track meet of the year," the mad coach was saying. Mad as in mad as a hatter; not actually angry. "We've been training hard for this meet."

"Doesn't he mean he's been training us hard?" Alex quipped, cupping a hand to his face so he could whisper to his friends without being overheard. "We're the ones doing all the work."

Unfortunately for him, all coaches were predisposed toward hearing any and all unwanted comments members of their team whispered, regardless of how softly they were spoken. They had ears like a fox.

Thankfully, this talent only kicked in when someone said something insulting, degrading or otherwise negative about them. Or when someone tried slipping a comment by them while they were giving some kind of pre-game spiel. Otherwise, their hearing was fairly normal.

"You got something you'd like to say, Straight?"

Alex stiffened in his seat, his back going ramrod straight. "No sir."

Coach Deretaine stared hard at the young man for several seconds, long enough to make the boy squirm.

"Hn."

He then gave a noncommittal grunt. Whatever the boy said simply wasn't worth his time. There were more important things to be thinking about—like giving his team the standard pep talk every coach spewed out right before a big competition.

"All of you have exceeded my expectations in training." As Coach Deretaine spoke, he began pacing back and forth, making a long sweep from one end of the bench to the other. He initiated eye contact with each member of the track team as he moved down the line. “And I see no reason why you should not exceed my expectations now. I expect all of you to do your best and kick ass when you get out there!”

His words were received by several shouts from the members of the track team.

“Oorah!”

All members of the track team played far too much *Halo*. They actually had bi-monthly online tournaments.

Surprisingly enough, Justin was currently tied with Kevin for first place. Who knew that a boy who seemed socially inept and slow on the uptake could be such a damn good shooter?

“Now let's get the fuck out there and show those little bastards from Mountain Shadow High who’s top dog here!”

“OORAH!”

As a great cheer went up amongst most of the track team, Kevin pinched the bridge of his nose. Whenever Coach Deretaine became… uh, impassioned? Yeah, that sounded about right, if a not little understated. Anyway, whenever their coach became impassioned about something, he would lose his composure and start swearing like a sailor who'd been grounded for several months. In other words, he swore like a very angry, irate sailor.

Those sailors had the worst potty mouths ever.

It was kind of embarrassing.

***

“All right, first up are the women's hurdles! Get out there, ladies, and show those pansies who’s in charge here!”

Kevin didn't know any of the girls on the track team (the only time he interacted with them was during the bi-annual online Halo tournament), so he didn't focus on the competition, and instead turned his attention to the stands in the hopes of spotting someone he knew.

Almost immediately a large bead of sweat trailed down his left temple when he saw Lilian up in the stands. She was holding her *“Go Beloved”* sign above her head, and her gaze was currently sweeping across the field, most likely looking for him. She was impossible to miss, what with that large and colorful sign of hers.

And he wasn't the only person staring at her. There were a large number of people sitting around the redhead doing some staring of their own, but Lilian didn't even seem to notice them. She was off in her own little world.

Must not facepalm. Must not facepalm. Must not facepalm.

"I don't want to see a bunch of bimbos jumping over hurdles! Show me my Beloved!"

Kevin facepalmed.

"Men's hurdles are up next! Get your asses out there!"

Kevin snapped his attention back to the track field; Justin was competing in the hurdles. He could see his dark-haired, pale-faced friend marching out onto the field with the others.

There were multiple differently-colored uniforms out there; their own light blue and Mountain Shadow's red, then there were dark purple, yellow and lime green. He didn't recognize some of the mascots, but they didn't have a serious rivalry with most of those schools.

Coach Deretaine had forced them to memorize the red uniforms and mascot of Mountain Shadow High, so they would know who they needed to put in their place. He was crazy like that. He also seemed to have some kind of personal grudge against Mountain Shadow. No one knew why—they were too afraid to ask.

Props had to be given to the referee; the moment everyone was on the field, he separated Justin and the other hurdler on their team from the two Mountain Shadow students, putting them on opposite sides of the track. He clearly knew of the intense hatred between the two schools, and wanted to make sure there was no foul play—in case they decided to try something, like tripping their opponents during the competition.

The gun went off and Kevin watched as his friend bolted down the field. He darted past the first hurdle, leaping over it, feet pounding on the course. Desert Mountain's first runner bypassed Justin, but the second seemed to lag behind him. Kevin thought he could see the second runner glaring daggers at his friend, but couldn't be sure because they were too far away. Justin jumped over another hurdle and picked up speed. He ran past a hurdler in yellow, then one in blue. The others were too far ahead for him to catch up. The whistle blew when the last hurdler crossed the finish line.

Mountain Shadow got third.

Justin came up to the bench, and Kevin frowned when he noticed how… not tired his friend appeared, almost as if he hadn't gone all out; he wasn't even sweating. Odd, but not unexpected. His friend rarely seemed enthusiastic about anything.

"You alright, Justin?" Kevin asked when his friend sat down. Justin gave him a blank look, eyes half-lidded, almost bored or maybe even apathetic. It was a little disconcerting.

"… Fine…"

"Girl's one-hundred meter dash is up next!"

Kevin began prepping himself, which really just consisted of him slapping his cheeks several times and taking deep, gulping breaths. His first competition was up after the women's one-hundred meter dash. He wanted to be ready—both mentally and physically—to give his all.

"Come on, ladies, get out there and make those other schools your bitch!"

At the same time, he couldn't keep the large drop of sweat from forming on the side of his head at his coach's crass words.

"Alright boys! You're up! Let me down and you'll be running laps for the rest of your high school careers!"

Kevin took a deep breath, then exhaled as he stood up. This was it. The moment he had been waiting for. Or at least one of them. He still had the two-hundred meter dash as well, but that wasn't important right now. The only thing that mattered at the moment was the current event. Now was the time for him to show his stuff! He would show everyone how fast he had gotten, and he would prove to Chase once and for all that he was the faster runner!

As if reading his mind, Chase smirked at him as they walked onto the field side by side.

"Don't go thinking that you're going to beat me just because you did well at our last practice. I'm still faster than you."

Kevin glared at his rival.

"You can tell yourself that if you want, whatever helps you sleep at night. But, we both know that I'm going to be the one leaving you in the dust this day."

Chase returned Kevin's glare with a stare to match. Sparks flew between the two, physically manifesting for all to see. Several runners gave the pair a wide berth to avoid the errant arcs of energy that struck the ground, leaving black scorch marks on the earth. One person wasn't so fortunate—an idiot who walked between the two and got zapped for his troubles.

"Oh damn! Shit just got real!"

"Was that lightning?"

"Man down! Call for a medic!"

A pair of medics rushed up and put the poor lad on a stretcher, ignoring the smell of burnt flesh, and the way the boy's muscles twitched, contracting and expanding in spasms from electrical damage.

"Damn idiot," one of the medics cursed. "He should know better than to get between two rivals like that."

The other nodded. "Un-fucking-believable."

Kevin broke his glare with Chase as they were directed toward their respective lanes. With his rival no longer near, he prepped himself for his first competition of the day. His breathing slowed as he knelt down and put his feet against the starting blocks; right knee closer to the ground, both knees bent as he stood on the balls of his feet. Kevin kept himself propped up on his fingers as opposed to his knuckles.

His head raised as he looked at his goal; the one-hundred meter mark. He tuned out almost everything around him. The noises of the crowd and other competitors died away; all of his focus, all of his attention, was on his goal and nothing else.

He was so focused that he almost missed the sound of the gun going off. Almost.

As a loud *Bang!* rent the air, signaling the start to the race. Kevin launched himself from the starting position and into a fast-paced sprint as his body reacted before his mind could realize what was happening.

He hurtled forward, opening up full-throttle, his muscles straining as he pushed them as hard as they could go. He could feel his calves and thighs and glutes burning intensely as he ran, expanding and contracting, pushing and pulling. It felt like they were being torn apart. His breathing came out in heaping, rasping pants; acid dripped into his lungs; adrenaline coursed through his body as he pushed himself to the breaking point and beyond. His eyesight blurred around the edges, creating tunnel vision, obscuring everything outside of that little circle directly in front of him in a thick haze. There was nothing on his mind except reaching the finish line as quickly as he could.

Mere seconds later, it was all over. Kevin gave one final gasp before almost collapsing. Only his desire to not look like a pansy kept him standing upright.

Ragged breaths tore from his mouth, which felt thick and dry, like he'd gone months without water and his tongue had begun to swell.

His chest burned, every breath he took felt like acid dripping through his body. Muscles ached; limbs like wet, limp noodles. He wobbled once, to the left, and then straightened back up.

He blinked when he registered the sensation of someone slapping him on the back.

Turning his head, Kevin faced the person who was doing the back slapping, Chase, who stared at him in awe, surprise and more than just a little envy.

"Holy shit, Swift! Have you been holding out on me or something?"

"Huh?" Having caught his second wind by now, Kevin looked at his rival, the dumb-looking expression on his face accurately conveying his confusion. "What do you mean?"

"Idiot." Chase rolled his eyes at the younger teenager. Kevin bristled at the insult, but didn't get a chance to retort as his rival spoke again. "Check your time."

Frowning, Kevin did just that. Looking up at the board, he found his time easily enough. It was the one on the top.

He blinked once. Then again, for good measure.

"I-is that really my time?" His voice sounded rather stunned.

"Yeah, I can't really believe it either. You've never gotten a time like that before." Chase looked up at the board again and whistled. "Ten-point-fifteen seconds, damn."

Chase had taken the words right out of Kevin's mouth. He was unable to believe his eyes. The last time he had gotten a time even close to that was last year during tryouts. Since then, he'd been unable to achieve that time again, 10.23 seconds, which he had just surpassed by a pretty good margin.

"WAY TO GO, BELOVED!"

While Chase began snickering, Kevin facepalmed.

"Your girlfriend's calling you," the older boy teased.

"Shut up."

As they walked off the track and moved towards the cheering members of their team, Chase looked at Kevin with a serious expression.

"Don't think I'm going to give up just because you beat me. The next time we race, I'll be the one leaving you in the dust."

Having gotten over his initial shock, all Kevin felt now was elation.

"You're welcome to try," he fired back, grinning at the other boy with an expression of smug satisfaction. There was no way Chase's words could get to him now. Nothing could.

"TAKE ME NOW, MY HOT BLOND STALLION!"

Cue another facepalm.

***

Lilian couldn't keep the beaming smile off her face as she watched her beloved beat everyone in his competition. If ever there was a time where she felt proud of her mate, this was it. Elation didn't begin to describe how she felt at seeing her mate do so well.

She also felt more than a little hot under the collar. Her mate had never looked more appealing than he did right now. He looked so intense, so focused on his goal; it was incredibly sexy.

By Inari, she just wanted to jump his bones!

Lilian had also been surprised by how fast her mate had gotten. She had never seen a human run that quickly before. It was surprising, to say the least.

She just hoped he wasn't that fast during other… certain… strenuous… activities…

Ufufufu…

Mind out of the gutter, Lilian.

"Right. Sorry."

S'okay. Just try to keep the inner workings of your imagination down to at least a PG-13 rating.

"Muu, I don't think that's possible," Lilian said, ignoring the people that were staring at her. "How about NC-17?"

Hm… very well, that would be acceptable.

"Alright!" Lilian grinned in victory. She would have also pumped a fist into the air, but since her hands were holding onto her sign, she just settled for the grin. "That means I can still have sexy-times with my mate!"

Everyone within Lilian's general vicinity slowly began scooting away. Not that she noticed. She was a little too busy laughing.

“Ufufufufu!”

Yes. That laughing.

Wanting to see more of Kevin, Lilian refocused her attention back onto her mate. He was being led off the field by that other boy. What was his name again? Chasey Something-or-other? Whatever. It wasn't like he mattered anyways. He was just her mate's rival. His only purpose was to make her mate look good. That's how this stuff worked.

As her beloved disappeared into the crowd of teammates who stood up to congratulate him with backslaps, headlocks and noogies, Lilian tried to find something else to keep her attention. There wasn't any point in watching the track meet when he wasn't the one competing.

Her eyes gazed out at all of the people currently in the stands. There were quite a few. While track and field wasn't as big as, say, football, it was still a pretty popular sport. The track meet had received a pretty big turn out; there was a sea of people that were standing or sitting in the stands, while a few were over at the concessions stand, buying drinks or food.

As she continued looking around, she spotted something that caused her eyes to narrow. She had only seen it once before, but there was no mistaking that outfit; a black gothic lolita dress with frills, ruffles, V-shaped piping along the bodice, puffy skirt, elbow-length gloves, black stockings and slipper-like shoes. She would recognize that clothing anywhere. It belonged to the girl that Kevin had gotten a prize for from that machine grabber-thingy when they’d gone to the arcade.

Lilian always remained wary of other women who may want to steal her beloved's affection from her.

Deciding to figure out why this girl was at *her* mate’s track meet, Lilian stood up from her seat. She then began walking down to where the raven-haired girl stood. If this hussy was here to see her mate, then she would have to make sure this loli understood that her beloved was already taken.

The girl in question was at the bottom of the bleachers, her hands holding the railing as she watched the Desert Cactus High’s track team with a look that Lilian didn't like at all. Because the goth girl was all the way at the bottom, and Lilian's seat was in the middle of the stands, she had to stride down the many stairs to reach the other girl.

"Ouch!"

"Ow!"

"Dof!"

And because she was carrying a really large and unwieldy sign, she ended up smacking several people on her way down.

"Oof! What the hell?!"

"Hey! Watch where you're swinging that thing!"

"My eye! Oh God, you poked my eye!"

"OH, THE PAIN! OH, THE HUMANITY! WHY GOD?! WHY?!"

"Shut up, idiot! You didn't get hit! I did!"

"… Oh. Right…"

Lilian ignored the cries of surprise and pain and anger directed at her. It wasn't her fault these people couldn't move out of the way in time. She had more important things to worry about than their insignificant complaints.

Yes, very important things, such as making sure that lolita-outfitted hussy knew that her mate was already taken.

"You!" That was the first word Lilian chose as approached the goth girl. It was soon followed by, "You with the lolita dress! What are you doing here? Are you here to steal my mate?"

Subtlety is a trait that all kitsune strive to embody.

Lilian has clearly never taken a lesson in Kitsune Deception 101.

The girl who suddenly found herself under Lilian's ire turned around. Ice-blue eyes blinked several times as the goth girl stared into Lilian's angry emerald irises.

"Do I know you?" The girl asked in a voice that sounded partly annoyed and partly bored, as if speaking with Lilian was beneath her.

Lilian twitched.

"No, but that hardly matters." Lilian made a dismissive gesture with her hand. She then returned her focus to the girl. "What is your relationship with my Beloved?"

"Your… Beloved…?" More blinking occurred. The girl finally expressed something other than annoyance and boredom: confusion. After a short moment, however, the emotion passed and she scowled. "I don't know who you're talking about."

"You know very well who I am talking about." Lilian pinioned the girl with a glare that could melt steel, if glares were actually capable of melting steel. "My Beloved is the one who got you that stuffed animal that you're holding. Now what is your relationship with my Beloved? How do you know him?"

If this girl had any intention of stealing her mate, then Lilian was going to get revenge on this girl kitsune-style! Oh yes, this stupid, gothic hussy, who thought she looked so cute in her lolita clothes, would be getting pranked into oblivion! Lilian was going to humiliate this girl so much, she would be forced to leave the school in shame and never come back!

Lilian could be very vindictive when it came to people trying to steal her mate, regardless of whether or not that was actually their intention. All that mattered was whether she perceived them as a threat.

On a side note, the only reason Lindsay no longer suffered this form of treatment was because her mate would be mad if she did something to the soccer playing tomboy.

This girl, however, was fair game.

The girl blinked; the time it took for her mind to comprehend Lilian's words… and then she began blushing. Unlike most people, who blushed red, this girl turned blue. The color spread across her cheeks like a bottle of spilled ink being absorbed by paper.

And was it just Lilian, or had the temperature suddenly dropped?

"W-w-wha—ah—what the h-hell are you talking about?!" The girl shrieked in mixed outrage and embarrassment. "I-I-I don't know that idiot!"

"My Beloved is not an idiot!" Lilian glared heatedly at the girl. Who did this girl think she was, insulting her mate like that? "You take that back. My Beloved is very smart, and I won't have some loli wannabe insulting him!"

"L-loli wannabe!" The girl's outraged cry was lost to the roar of the crowd. Lilian still heard her, though. "I don't want to hear something like that from someone who dresses like a slut! Especially not a fox-whore like you!"

Lilian was incensed by the insult. She was not going to let herself be insulted by this stupid little girl!

"How dare you! I'm not a whore! I'm still a virgin!"

Several men of varying age, including one really disgusting old pervert missing a number of teeth, began drooling.

A good deal of these men also ended up getting their faces bashed in by their significant others.

"Like I care about that! Ooh! I'm still a virgin! That hardly matters where *your* kind is involved!"

"What's that supposed to mean?!"

"It means that I'll call you whatever I damn well want!"

"Oh yeah? Well the same to you, little girl! I just call 'em like I see 'em!"

Lilian butted her head against the much smaller girl, who also pushed back. Sparks emitted from between their eyes. Each bared their teeth at the other, refusing to back down.

This epic stare down would continue for well over an hour, as the two argued and insulted each other for the rest of the track meet. Things became so heated that Lilian even missed her mate winning the two-hundred meter dash, which resulted in even more arguing.

Everyone in the stands did their best to avoid the duo, just in case their battle became physical.

Except for the boys, and a few older men who were not with a significant other. They were hoping for a catfight.

Those who were with their significant other tried to stick around as well, but were quickly beaten into submission by said significant other.

As several girlish screams of pain emitted from the mass of perverted men young and old, Lilian continued arguing with the girl, completely oblivious to the world around her.

***

It was much later in the afternoon. The sky had become painted with the colors of the sunset, the sun dipped below the horizon. The track meet had ended, the competition over, and Coach Deretaine had given them his "congratulatory" speech as opposed to his “you all suck” speech, which he would’ve given if they’d done poorly.

Kevin was on cloud nine as he and the rest of the team prepared to leave. Nothing could spoil this night.

“BELOVED!”

Except for, perhaps, a certain, overly-enthusiastic fox-girl.

“Lil—Oof!”

That was the sound that comes from someone who’s just had the wind knocked out of them via a red-haired missile smashing into his chest.

“Guh!”

And that was the sound someone makes when their back hits the ground because he, in his surprise, was unable to keep from being bowled over by said red-haired missile.

It didn't help that the ground was made of concrete.

And while Kevin lay on his back, gasping for breath and trying to suck in oxygen that simply would not come, Lilian sat on top of him. Her lovely thighs straddled his waist, and her hands pressed down on his chest, fingers splayed and palms open so she could better grope her mate's muscles underneath his shirt.

“You were amazing out there, Beloved!”

The smile Lilian gave him would have been enough to melt any man, maybe even Kevin. Unfortunately, he was too busy trying to catch his breath after her surprise attack to notice it.

“You looked so hot when you were racing. It was the sexiest thing I've ever seen; your hot body covered in sweat, gasping for breath as you pushed yourself to the breaking point, your clothes clinging to your skin.”

While her index fingers idly traced circles on his chest, her face was set in an expression that could only be described as smoldering. Her eyes burned with passion, half-lidded and lustful. It was easy to see what was on her mind.

“You don't know how hot and bothered I got watching you win the one-hundred meter dash. Oh, just thinking about it makes me want you to bend me over these bleachers, rip off my clothes, and forcefully take me until I'm a shivering mass of post-orgasmic bliss.”

Lilian trailed her tongue suggestively across her lips—and also used it to lick off the drool that the thought of her mate claiming her caused. Several young men walking by had to grab their nose, lest they be thrown away via the nosebleed express.

Lilian's breathing grew heavy.

“When we get home, I'm going to… show you… how proud I am of you… ufufufu…”

“Ooh! Damn that Kevin Swift! Damn him to hell! Why is it always him?!”

Eric glared at Kevin with DOOM in his eyes. His clenched fists were drawn up to his face, trembling from the force caused by his undying, if somewhat comical, rage.

He was also crying. Like, really crying. Large, waterfall-like streams of frustrated, angry tears poured out of his eyes and down his face like Niagara Falls. He also had snot dribbling out of his nose.

“I'm a good guy! I'm attractive! I should be the one getting those ginormous bazungas shoved in my face! Swift can't even properly appreciate what's happening to him right now! Damn prude!”

Eric continued to glare at Kevin, and then, as if triggering some kind of inherent defense mechanism, his mind replaced Kevin with an image of himself.

“Hee-hee-hee… now that's what I'm talking about… uhuhuhu… come to papa… heeheehee…”

Less than five seconds later Eric Corrompere was drooling like an imbecile.

He was also making really creepy squeezing motions with his hands.

And his nose was bleeding profusely.

Many of the people there, including Eric's friends, moved several feet away from the lanky teenager, as his mind went to places that none of them had any intention of ever going to.

“Idiot.”

Chase rolled his eyes at the drooling, bleeding mass of flesh that had once been known as Eric. Still, he could kind of, *sort of*, understand the pervert’s reaction. Even he could not deny that he felt somewhat jealous of Kevin; he wished his own girlfriend was that supportive and enthusiastic about the activities that he felt passionate about.

Though he could definitely do without the whole "bulldozing over onto hard concrete" thing that Lilian had going for her. That just looked painful.

"... He... idiot..."

Justin received nothing but odd looks from the people around him.

"Uhuhuhu..."

Eric continued giggling. His eyes were glazed over, and he was mumbling to himself. No one could hear what he was mumbling, mostly because it sounded like incoherent gibberish. They were all sure, however, that they didn't want to know anyway.

"What do you think, brother?"

"Hm. I feel both strangely envious and pitying at the same time. Having a girlfriend like Lilian seems nice at first, but it's actually beginning to look quite painful now. Still, the hotness factor somewhat negates her many undesirable traits."

"Agreed."

"Li..." Kevin wheezed. He still felt rather breathless. "Lilian."

"Yes, Beloved." Lilian looked at her mate with warm eyes and a soft smile.

"Can you... get off me?"

"Eh?"

Lilian almost pouted, but decided not to at the last minute in favor of giving him a coquettish, yet strangely innocent smile.

"Now why would I do that?" She leaned down until their noses were touching. "I still have to give you your reward for doing such a great job."

Already having a good deal of experience with Lilian, Kevin knew very well what she considered a reward, which, more often than not, was more rewarding for her than him—or so he kept telling himself. Either way, he knew what was coming, and knew that whatever she planned on doing wouldn't be appropriate, especially as they were still in public.

He prepared to stop her.

"Oi! What the hell do you think you're doing, you slut?! Get off him!"

Someone beat him to it.

Lilian's expression went from seductive and coy to annoyed and angry in a heartbeat. Her eyes narrowed and her brows lowered while her lips thinned into a tight line.

She turned toward the source of her ire, the girl she had been arguing with for the past hour and a half.

The pale-skinned female with blue lips and ice chips for eyes stood several feet away, hands on her hips and scowling.

"You can't tell me what to do!" Despite saying this, Lilian did get off Kevin, if only to more easily glare into the raven-haired female's eyes. "He's my mate! I can do whatever I want!"

She paused.

"And you have no right to call me that! You don't even know me!"

"I can call you whatever I want! All I need to do is look at your outfit to see that you're a complete whore!" While Lilian let loose an almost feral snarl at this, the goth girl glared back. "You can't just decide who your mate is without their consent! And it seems to me that he doesn't like what you're doing to him!"

Now that Lilian wasn't pinning him to the ground, Kevin gingerly climbed to his feet. He glanced over at the two females making a spectacle of themselves, vaguely wondering why the girl arguing with Lilian looked so familiar, but too grateful that she was distracting the redhead to really care.

"Of course my mate likes what I do to him." Lilian huffed, crossing her arms under her breasts, which did some very interesting things to them, as all of the men around could attest to. "He and I have already explored our undying passion for each other, and I've felt how much he likes what I do to him."

"W-w-w-WHAT?!" The girl gaped, her mouth and eyes both wide as she stared at the fox-girl in astonishment.

Several seconds later she was glaring again, with even more vitriol than before.

"I don't believe you! There's no way any of that can be true! And he can't be your mate!"

"Of course he can!" Lilian returned the girl's look with one of her own. "Besides, why do you care? Weren't you just telling me that you don't even know him?"

For some reason, this simple question caused the girl to become flustered.

"T-t-that's," she stuttered, "I-i-it's… i-it's none of your damn business! Whore! Slag!"

Lilian stared at the girl for several seconds, before her face became sly. She chuckled, the low tone making the other girl shiver.

"I get it," Lilian said, smiling condescendingly. "You're a tsundere."

"Tsundere?" The goth frowned. "What the hell is that supposed to mean?"

"Hmph." Lilian gave the girl a look of superiority. "If you don't know what that means, I'm certainly not going to tell you."

"Fine!" The other girl bit out. "It doesn't matter anyways. And it doesn't change the fact that you shouldn't force yourself on someone, though I suppose I shouldn't expect anything less from someone like you."

"Shows how much you know. You clearly don't understand the bond my Beloved and I share."

"What bond? I don't see any bond between you two—unless you count trying to rape him a bond."

"Hmph! That's just what I would expect from a little girl who doesn't understand matters of love." The goth girl glared. Lilian challenged her with a smirk. "Why don't you just ask my Beloved, if you don't believe me? I'm sure he would be more than happy to inform you about how madly in love we are."

"You know what? I think I will!" The pale-skinned girl turned to where Kevin was standing. "Hey, you! Are you and this fox-skank… mates… eh?" She trailed off, blinking several times in befuddlement. "Where did he go?"

As the girl began scratching her head in confusion, Lilian also turned to see that her beloved was no longer there.

Eric was still around, though. After returning from whatever licentious fantasy his mind had gone to, the teenage creature of lust and perversion had decided to stay.

"Hey you!" Lilian pointed at the boy in question. Eric blinked, then pointed to himself with a dumb look etched upon his face.

"Me?"

"Yes, you. Where is my Beloved?"

Realizing that the girl whose breasts had become his obsession was finally talking to him, Eric clenched his fists. This was his chance! He could finally convince his Tit Maiden to stop spending so much time with Kevin and spend it with him instead!

"Why don't you two forget about him?" Eric spoke in what he thought was a smooth voice. "I can show you a much better time than that idiot."

In response, Eric received two equally powerful death glares from two equally irate females. The amount of killing intent unleashed would have made even the Shinigami run away screaming like a little girl. Eric nearly wet himself.

"If you ever speak about my Beloved like that again, I will knock you out and tie you to the table of a gay bar, naked."

While getting knocked out, stripped and tied to a table by this girl definitely appealed to Eric's inner masochist, waking up in a gay bar did not.

He paled under the threat and combined weight of their glares.

"Now where is my Beloved?"

"He went that way!" Eric squeaked. The two girls didn't even spare the boy a second glance. They took off in a burst of impressive speed, heading in the direction he had pointed to.

The perverted sophomore watched the pair go—or more like he watched the large cloud of dust they left in their wake. When even the dust cloud was no longer visible, he slumped to his knees, panting as all of the adrenaline left bloodstream.

"Ha..."

Dear god that was scary. He hadn't realized that girls could be so frightening.

"Wait." Eric paused. "Did they both just ignore me in favor of Kevin?"

Upon realizing that, yes, he'd been ignored in favor of Kevin... again, Eric raised his fists to the heavens, shaking them menacingly.

"DAMN YOU, KEVIN SWIFT!"

***

"This is all your fault!"

"My fault?! How is this my fault?!"

Lilian and the goth girl raced toward the gymnasium side by side—or cheek by cheek, as their faces were smashing against each other while they ran. A cloud of dust kicked up behind them.

Several people coughed as they were engulfed when the two rushed past.

"If you hadn't interrupted us, my Beloved wouldn't have left me like that!"

"Ha! If I hadn't interrupted you, then you probably would have raped him!"

"It wouldn't be rape!"

They rushed inside of the gymnasium, a large square building consisting of more than just a gym. Consequently, this was the most likely place where they would find Kevin.

"How could it not be rape? When you have a willing and unwilling person participating in sexually explicit acts, it's considered rape!"

"My Beloved would gladly ravish me silly! And why do you care? You already said that you don't even know him!"

"T-t-that's none of your business! Wench! Skank! Whore!"

These two made for a lovely t*sukkomi.*

"How dare you insult me like that! I'm not a whore!"

"I noticed that you didn't say anything against the other things I called you!"

"They all mean the same thing!"

As they raced down one of several hallways, shaving away the distance between them and their goal, a figure stepped in front of them. This person stood in the middle of the hallway, impeding their progress, causing the two females to skid to a halt. The cloud of dust they'd kicked up did not stop, however, and kept on moving for several more feet before dissipating.

"Who the hell are you?" asked the raven-haired female.

Lilian's eyes widened. "It's you!"

***

"I can't believe you've got another one, Kevin," Alex said as they changed out of their track uniforms. "Just when were you going to tell us that you had another girlfriend hidden in the wings?"

Kevin pulled off his shirt.

"Which girl are we talking about now?"

"You know, the one arguing with Lilian."

Kevin scrunched up his face.

"Oh, right. There was a girl arguing with Lilian, wasn't there?" He threw his shirt in his duffel bag and began discarding his pants. "I wonder who that girl was."

"You mean you don't know?" Alex asked, disbelieving. "That girl was getting ready to have a throw down with your girlfriend, and you're telling that you don't know who she is?"

Kevin rolled his eyes and threw his pants in the duffel bag as well. "That's what I said. And Lilian's not my girlfriend."

"I know this is going to sound strange, but I don't believe you." These words came from Andrew.

"Wha...?" Kevin started. "Why not?"

"I don't know." Andrew shrugged. "Maybe it's because you're currently living with the sexiest girl I've ever met. Or it could have something to do with how you've been acting recently."

"... Right... living... girl... name...?"

Kevin stared at Justin like he was some kind of idiot.

The twins did as well.

"Where have you been, living under a rock? This has been common knowledge for weeks now." Kevin turned back to Andrew. "And what do you mean I've been acting differently?"

Andrew raised a single eyebrow. "You mean you haven't noticed?"

"No." Kevin twitched. "If I had noticed, I wouldn't be asking you, would I?"

Alex and Andrew shared a look. Together, they turned back to Kevin.

"Kevin," the way Alex spoke his name in such a serious tone had Kevin unconsciously straightening his back. "You have the worst case of Cannot Talk to Women that I have ever seen."

"Ugh."

"You're absolutely terrible at talking to women," Alex agreed.

"Urk."

"Couldn't talk to a woman to save his life."

"Hurk!"

Kevin almost felt the metaphorical arrows shooting into his back.

"I'm not that bad." When all he got were three deadpanned stares—even Justin deadpanned at him—Kevin blushed. "Am I really that bad?"

"Kevin, half a month ago you couldn't talk to Lindsay or any other girl without passing out. Hell, you just straight up passed out without saying a single word sometimes." Andrew's voice was half-empathetic, half-condescending. "You were so bad at talking to women that most of us had a bet going on about when you'd finally come out of the closet. Seeing you bring a sexy thing like Lilian to school was actually a relief."

"Auu," Kevin made a strange noise in the back of his throat. "It's not like I can help it. I don't know why, but I just get so nervous whenever I'm around girls."

He didn't really understand it, this strange nervousness. Having been raised by his mom, one would think he wouldn't get nervous around members of the opposite sex.

Then again, his mom wasn't exactly what he would call the most stable of parents.

"Yes, yes, we all know that," Alex said in a placating tone. "But that just proves my point. Ever since Lilian showed up, you haven't passed out once. You're even talking to Lindsay like a normal person. Well—" Alex quickly corrected himself, "—mostly normal at least."

"Have I really?" Kevin cupped his chin between his fingers, adopting a look of deep contemplation, which involved scrunching his face in ways that distorted his features.

His friends pulled out their cellphones and began snapping photos. By tomorrow morning, images of Kevin would be posted on the school's Facebook page and Twitter feed. Kevin wouldn't find out about this until several months later, much to his embarrassment.

Now that he thought about it, he hadn't felt all that nervous around any girls for a while. He hadn't even passed out during any of Lilian's most recent attempts to seduce him.

That wasn't to say he didn't still react to her; Kevin's mind went back to that moment they had shared just before the track meet. He'd definitely felt uncomfortable—and flustered—by her actions.

However, even though he had been affected by her "kitsune Seductress" act, he had not felt the light-headed oh-my-god-I'm-about-to-pass-out sensation that he would have experienced prior to meeting the two-tailed vixen.

“I guess you have a point,” Kevin sighed, then shook his head. “Whatever, I'll think about this stuff later. I'm taking a shower.”

He left his friends to finish getting changed and walked into the shower stalls, clad in just his boxers, a towel and bar of soap in hand.

The shower stalls were just that—a series of showers blocked off by large metal stalls and a curtain. Kevin liked the set up because it allowed him privacy while washing up.

Most people didn't use the showers, but he disliked the feel of sweat caked on his skin. He especially didn't like putting on a clean pair of clothes while sweating like a pig. Kevin was hygienic that way.

There were a few other people who felt the same way, and used the stalls as well, as evidenced when Kasey Chase walked out of one of the stalls, a towel wrapped around his waist.

Upon noticing that he was no longer alone, his rival stopped walking for a moment to give Kevin one last congratulations.

“You didn't do too bad today, Swift.”

Considering this was Kasey Chase, his rival in all things running, the boy might as well have told him that he was the most awesome thing since the invention of giant mecha robots.

Kevin was a big fan of mecha anime. He even had a *Gundam Wing* and *Gundam 0083* poster in his room.

Kevin walked over to the nearest stall, but stilled long enough to give the other boy a nod, acknowledging Chase's words.

“Thanks.”

“Tch. Don't get cocky now. You may have beaten me this time but, I'm not going to just let this stand,” the boy continued. Kevin hung up his towel and turned the shower on to its hottest setting. “Next track meet, I'm going to leave your ass in the dust.”

“Whatever you say, Chase.”

Steam began to rise in the small stall. Kevin heard Chase's footsteps receding as he began cleaning himself.

He stayed in there for a while, much longer than normal. He didn't feel like coming out quite yet. Kevin had a lot on his mind, and he needed some time to think, before meeting with Lilian who, in all likelihood, would be waiting for him just outside of the locker room.

He wasn't entirely sure he was looking forward to that meeting.

Most of his thoughts were actually centered around the two-tailed kitsune. Some of his thoughts were on that kiss she had given him and some were on her, um, *enthusiastic* congratulations after the track meet. But, a good deal of his wonderings were also on the girl that Lilian had been arguing with.

Just who was that girl anyway? And why had she looked so familiar? Maybe he was just imagining things, but he could've sworn he'd seen that girl before...

Shaking his head, Kevin let out a deep sigh as he finished getting clean. He would think about this later. Better yet, he would ask Lilian about it when he met up with her.

Turning off the water and grabbing his towel, he dried off as much as possible in the stall. He then wrapped the towel around his waist and walked into the changing area.

As he exited the showers and entered the changing room, his eyes blinked several times in surprise.

He stared for nearly a full minute.

There was no one else in the room. It was completely empty.

Just how long had he stayed in that shower?

Concerned by his lack of attentiveness but knowing not to dawdle any longer, he dismissed his thoughts. He walked over to his locker, opened it and got dressed in a plain white t-shirt, faded blue jeans and his black Adidas.

The sound of the door opening drew his attention and caused him to pause. The sound of three sets of footsteps drawing inexorably closer drew even more of his attention. Curious to know who else had stuck around, Kevin finished tying his shoelaces and turned to confront the newcomers.

He wasn't sure who he expected to greet him, but whoever he'd been expecting, it was certainly not the people standing before him.

Three men had entered the locker room, all of them unfamiliar, and all of them far too old to be in high school. They were muscular, with the shortest of the trio only being an inch taller than him, and the tallest towering over him by a large margin. While their muscles weren't as disgustingly hulking as

Chris Fleischer's, they all looked like they drank a pound of *Muscle Milk* every day, and spent at least two hours at the gym.

"You Kevin Swift?" asked the tallest of the trio. Kevin couldn't judge height, but guessed this man was at least seven feet. He had a deep voice, long blond hair, and a long face with lips that were disproportionately large compared to the rest of his features. They reminded Kevin of a fish's lips.

"Um, yes... i-is there something I can help you with?"

Kevin felt a distinct spike of fear rush through him, a tiny thrill that traveled along his spine, as the men on either side of the tall one cracked their knuckles threateningly.

"It's nothing personal," the tallest spoke again, also cracking his knuckles. Kevin gulped. That couldn't mean anything good. "But we've been ordered to rough you up a bit. Do forgive us."

Chapter 7

Mistaken for a Badass

"It's you!" Lilian exclaimed in shock. The raven-haired female at her side gave the kitsune a confused look, while Kiara only smirked at them.

"Yes, me."

"What are you doing here?"

"Isn't it obvious?" Kiara spread her arms, as if to encompass the entire hallway they were standing in. "I'm here for you."

"For me?" Lilian blinked several times, attempting to figure out what this woman meant. After nearly five seconds of regarding the older femme in the business suit, she scratched the back of her head nervously. "Look, I… I appreciate that you find me attractive and everything…" She looked away, uncomfortable under the woman's stare now that she knew what Kiara wanted. "… But I don't swing that way. And I have my Beloved, so…"

Now it was Kiara's turn to blink, befuddled. Fortunately, she was much quicker on the uptake than Lilian. She also came to the correct conclusion, unlike Lilian.

"That's not what I meant!" Kiara exploded, her cheeks actually turning red in mixed anger and embarrassment.

Lilian blinked.

"It's not?"

"No!"

She tilted her head to the side, confusion setting in and showing clearly on her face.

"Then why are you here for me?"

"To teach you a lesson," Kiara declared, "But before I do that." She looked at the goth girl standing beside Lilian, staring at them with increasingly obvious irritation. Kiara pointed at her. "You, because I'm a nice gal, I'm going to give you a warning; this is about to get ugly. Leave now and nothing bad will happen to you."

It took several seconds for the lolita-clad girl to respond. When she did, it was with a scowl. “Are you threatening me?”

“If that's how you want to take it,” Kiara replied calmly. “Though I like to think of it as giving you good advice. This has nothing to do with you, so there’s really no point in you sticking around and getting caught up in this.”

The woman's words made the younger female pause and think. A moment later, the raven-haired girl nodded her head, and made an about-face. As she began walking away, Lilian gawked at her back.

“H-hey! Where are you going?”

Pausing mid-step, the female with the ice blue eyes did not turn around, but she at least gave Lilian an answer. “That woman is right. I don't really know what's going on, but it clearly has nothing to do with me.”

“So you're just going to leave?” When the girl shrugged, Lilian huffed. “That's fine. It’s not like I want an annoying little girl here anyway, especially one as unhelpful and *tsundere* as you.”

The girl twitched. “I don’t know what that means, but I feel like I’ve just been horribly insulted.”

The young kitsune ignored the girl and turned her attention on Kiara. “And after I deal with you, I'll finally get to be alone with my Beloved.”

At the mention of the young man that she had fallen for, Kiara smirked. “I'm sorry to say that you won't be seeing your 'Beloved' any time soon. He's currently preoccupied with other, more pressing concerns.”

Lilian's eyes widened at Kiara's words and tone. The goth girl also went stiff. Seconds later, she was off, running down the hall. The other two ignored her in favor of each other, not even paying attention as the light tapping of her slipper-like shoes faded into the distance.

My Beloved is…” Lilian's eyes narrowed. “What did you do to my Beloved?”

“Me? Nothing.” Kiara’s sly grin boded nothing well. “He is simply being entertained by my boys at the moment. Don't worry, though,” she added upon seeing Lilian's horrified face. “They'll take *real* good care of him.”

Lilian didn’t hear that last part. She had stopped listening after hearing the part about her beloved being *entertained* by this woman’s *boys*.

Lilian made to leave, turning around to head off in search of her beloved, and rescue him from whatever this person’s *boys* were doing to him.

Kiara wouldn’t let her. She appeared in front of the girl once more, blocking Lilian’s path.

“I’m sorry.” Her smile said otherwise. “But I can’t let you go and help your mate. You and I still have unfinished business.”

“I see, so that's how it is.”

Lilian tilted her head toward the ground. Her red hair hid most of her face. The rest was cast into darkness, all except her chin and mouth, which was set into an ugly frown.

“Move,” she whispered harshly.

“Hm… how about, no.”

“I said move!”

“Not happening.”

“Fine,” Lilian growled, her voice harsh and grating. “I was simply going to use an enchantment to make you leave this place. But now… now I don't think that's going to be enough punishment for you.”

“Hoh?”

Kiara watched with a smirk as Lilian began to change. Her ears grew, becoming pointed and long as they moved closer to the top of her head. Red fur sprouted along her ears, covering them in crimson except for the tip, which became white. Her canines sharpened to finely honed points, and her pupils morphed into slits.

Finally, two bushy red, white-tipped fox tails sprang out from a hole hidden in the back of her jean shorts, writhing and twisting in obvious agitation, as if they were a reflection of the girl's stormy emotional state.

“Oh my, what an interesting transformation.” Kiara's smirk widened into a fanged grin. “It’s been a long time since I’ve seen a kitsune in their hybrid state—over one-hundred years, in fact.” She chuckled. “This is getting very, very interesting.”

Lilian hardly paid attention to the woman's words. Her outrage at the tomboyish femme overwhelmed of her. It consumed her every thought—this anger, this hatred. The need to destroy this woman who had let several men taint her Beloved surged through her, an unstoppable force.

"I'm going to break you," Lilian growled as two small, bright balls of compressed light appeared above the tips of her tails. "And then I'm going to find those friends of yours, and break them for daring to violate my Beloved in ways that he still refuses to do to me!"

An awkward pause ensued. Several crickets chirped. The annoying sound caused Lilian's ears to twitch.

"Wait. What?" Kiara gave her look a bewildered look. "I think you've got the wrong idea. My boys aren't going to—"

"You think you can sic your boys on my Beloved and have them play out your sick, twisted fantasy?!" Lilian interrupted. Her hair lashed out like fiery whips as she shook her head. "I'll never allow that to happen! No way! If you think I'm going to let those boys of yours commit acts of *yaoi* on my mate, then you've got another thing coming!"

"*Yaoi*?" Kiara blinked. "Isn't that also called Boys' Love in English?"

"Who cares what it's called in English, you disgusting, dirty old hag!"

Kiara twitched.

"Okay, now that was just rude."

"Your disgusting BL fantasies end here!"

"I'm trying to tell you, that's not—"

"Die!"

The tips of Lilian's tails moved like a trebuchet, shooting forward at speeds no human eye could track. The two spheres of light situated at the very tips of her tails were launched at incredible speeds, mere streaks of light that traveled toward Kiara.

They were dodged easily enough, effortlessly even. Turning her body to present Lilian with her profile, Kiara then contorted herself so that the light spheres sped past her on either side; one near her head and the other just inches from her lower back. The two spheres of compressed youki continued on, striking the wall at the far end of the corridor, leaving black scorch marks.

Looking back at the damage done, Kiara whistled.

"Phew, that was close." She turned back to Lilian and smirked. "You've got pretty good—whoa!"

She was forced to dodge another ball of light that came at her nearly twice as fast as the first two.

"Heh."

Kiara grinned. Two more compressed spheres of celestial energy burst into existence on the tips of Lilian's tails before they, too, were flung at her. Kiara shifted her body, easily avoiding the attacks and watching them strike the wall behind her again. She looked back at Lilian, who was already preparing to launch another set of spheres.

"I think I'm really going to enjoy this," she muttered.

The battle was on.

***

"Whoa, whoa, whoa, whoa! Hold up!"

Kevin held his hands out in a placating gesture. The men didn't stop their slow march toward him. Two of them even cracked their knuckles again. Kevin backed away.

"Why are you doing this? I don't even know you guys!"

While Kevin had recently experienced some pretty frightening stuff in the past two-and-a-half weeks, that didn't stop his spine from going rigid. It didn't stop him from experience terror at this new predicament. He would freely admit that he was petrified.

Not that he didn't have a reason to be. These people were not only much bigger than him, but looked like they meant business. And their business obviously wasn't going to be beneficial to his continued health.

"Like I said, it's nothing personal," said the tall one, seemingly the spokesperson. Kevin decided to call him Tall. "We were simply told by Kiara to rough you up some. And when Kiara wants something done, we get it done."

"Kiara? B-but wait!" Kevin continued trying to reason with them, or at least stall for time. Since he was still at school, Coach Deretaine must also be around as well. The man couldn't have left before him, right? Surely his coach would come to his rescue… he hoped. "Why would Kiara order you guys to beat me up? I never did anything to her!"

The three looked at each other for a moment, giving Kevin a small ray of hope that they'd stop advancing. That hope was mercilessly crushed when they began walking again, their footfalls sounding like a death knell to his ears. His back was soon pressed up against the nearest locker, which just so happened to be his.

"We don't know much about what you did. Not like it matters anyway," Tall answered. "Though, since I feel bad for you, I'll tell you why I think Kiara has ordered us to turn your face into mincemeat: her brother."

"Brother?" Kevin's expression changed from one of terror to one of stupefaction. He blinked several times before remembering something. "That's right. She told me that she has a brother who goes to school here, but what does that have to do with me? I don't know even her brother."

"You probably do and just don't realize it. Her brother is Chris Fleischer."

"Chris Fleischer?"

Kevin's mind only needed a few seconds to compute that sentence and realize what it meant. When that happened, his eyes widened.

"But that means—eek!"

A fist from Tall came flying at him, fast. Kevin reacted on nothing more than instinct, ducking under the attack and letting it pass by over his head.

BANG!

"YEOWCH!"

Tall yelled in pain as he pulled his fist back, the reddened, swollen flesh of his knuckles pulsing. He shook his hand frantically, as if doing so would somehow soothe the anguish. Kevin used the unintended distraction to scramble away from the big guy as quickly as possible.

The other two followed him, ignoring their injured comrade to close the distance between themselves and Kevin. Their menacing faces were a reflection of their ill-intent and made Kevin want to get away from them that much faster.

In his haste to escape, he didn't notice the article of clothing on the floor, a seemingly innocuous pair of running shorts. One of the other runners must have forgotten it in their desire to get home quickly. Regardless of who left it there and why, what really mattered was that Kevin didn't see it.

He stepped on the offending article of clothing.

And tripped.

"Waaa—oof!"

Falling flat on his belly, Kevin coincidentally moved just in time to avoid receiving a fist to the back of his head. Instead of being decked in the cranium with the force of a speeding semi-truck, the tightly-closed hand soared through the air where his head had been seconds prior.

It also caused the older man to stumble forward and trip over Kevin, who was sprawled out in front of him. His arms flailed as he began a very quick and painful looking fall.

As the loud *slam!* of someone's face hitting the tiled floor resounded throughout the room, Kevin scrambled to his feet, rushing toward the exit. If he could just make it out of the locker room, he could find someone—a teacher or his coach, maybe—and then he would be safe.

A figure stepped in front of the door, obstructing his path.

Murphy must have had it in for him. Or maybe he had just incurred some really bad karma.

Kevin skidded to a stop, immediately trying to backpedal. He didn't get far. His back crashed into what felt like a brick wall, hard and rigid and completely uncompromising.

He looked up, his face going pale as he saw it was the tall one again, staring him down with a hard expression. He looked kind of mad. Actually, he looked downright furious. His right hand had become a mass of swollen and red flesh.

Tall slid his arms under Kevin's armpits, gave a grunt, and then heaved. Kevin was lifted nearly half a foot off the ground, his feet dangling uselessly, no longer able to find purchase on a hard surface.

"Now we've got you," Tall said. "This is it, kid. The end of the line."

As if to emphasis his point, the guy who had been blocking his exit—the shortest of the trio, who Kevin had decided to call Short—charged forward. His fist reared back with the obvious intention of punching Kevin's lights out. Kevin knew that if he was hit with that fist, he wouldn't be walking away without extensive help.

He began to struggle in Tall's grasp, but nothing seemed to come of it. The man had him in a full nelson, he was dangling half a foot off the ground, and this dude was way stronger than him. It would take a miracle for him to break out of the hold.

Fortunately for him, a miracle came just in time. At least, that's how Kevin would refer to it later on, though it was really more of a case of blind luck.

Kevin's skin still retained some dampness from his shower, which had mixed in with the sweat he'd secreted due to his fear of these people. This combination of plain water and perspiration had created a slick coat that covered his skin and made him, for lack of a better term, slippery.

At the very last second, just when it looked like Kevin was about to sustain some serious brain damage, his arms slid out from Tall's grasp as if they'd been greased up with oil, and he fell to the floor in a heap.

Not quite understanding what had happened, but not wanting to waste this opportunity, he scrambled away on all fours. The tallest of the trio watched him go, gawking at his seemingly miraculous escape.

And since he was so busy gaping at Kevin, who took off like a pig that had just realized it was about to be gutted, he didn't even notice the fist coming at him.

"Oof!"

The power-punch hammered Tall in the gut with all the force of a freight train. He doubled over the extended fist like a folding chair as all the breath left his lungs.

Shocked by what he had done, Short pulled his fist out of his partner's gut and took several steps back. Tall fell onto his hands and knees, clasping his stomach with his right arm as he sucked in several lungfuls of oxygen.

"Oh, shit! You okay, man?" Short asked. Not that the other man could answer, busy as he was wheezing and gasping for breath that would not come.

Realizing that no one was paying attention to him anymore, Kevin tried to make for the door, but found his path barred… again. Naturally. It only made sense that he'd still have one more guy to deal with. It would also only make sense if that guy was standing directly in front of the only exit out of the room.

If Kevin wasn't so frightened, he would have cursed. This was like a bad plot device from a *Shōnen* manga!

"Now you're going to get it, bud," the man said, his abnormally large nose still bleeding from when he had fallen face-first onto the floor. For some reason, this made him look more menacing than before. "I'm going to beat your ass black and blue!"

"T-that doesn't sound very pleasant," Kevin muttered as he held a hand to his backside. "What did my butt ever do to you?" He blinked, then started in surprise. "And wait! You can talk!" It wasn't a question.

"Of course I can talk, ya moron! What, did ya think I was an illiterate baboon or something?!"

"Well…" Kevin wondered what this guy would do if he learned that Kevin had actually kind of thought that. It was probably best not to tell him.

"And it's a figure of speech, ya ignoramus! I didn't actually mean I would beat your ass, just that I would be kicking the crap out of ya so badly that you're going to need a bedpan, because ya won't be shittin' properly for weeks!"

"That sounds even less pleasant…"

"Raaagggg!" With a wordless battle cry, the man charged forward.

"Hiiiii!" Kevin squealed like a pig sent to the slaughter.

The muscular male's fist reared back in preparation to unleash a punch of such epic proportions that it would make the younger male's head spin. Kevin tried to back away, but his far stronger foe was quickly gaining on him.

Just when all hope seemed lost another miracle occurred—or another case of dumb luck.

Without even realizing it, Kevin had backed up into one of the locker room benches. The back of his legs smacked into the bench, and he began to tumble backwards.

His arms flailed as he tried to reestablish his balance to no avail. His feet kicked up into the air as he pitched over the bench.

At the same time, Kevin's attacker closed the distance between them. His right fist lashed out with a powerful jab, but missed by a hair as Kevin fell backwards. He also missed Kevin's feet as they were kicked into the air.

However, he did feel it when Kevin's feet slammed into his jaw with substantial force. With Kevin's head and torso acting as a fulcrum, the power put into the accidental attack was enough to force his jaw shut with a loud *clack!* followed by an equally loud *crack!* that rang out several decibels louder than normal.

"Ah! My toof!"

Holding his hands up to his mouth, the bulky male stumbled backwards. His voice rang out in a loud, keening wail of agony, as the sharp pain of his tooth cracking hit him full force.

Kevin continued moving backwards, his body rolling across the bench in a semblance of a back flip, his feet swinging through the air in a parabolic arc. As he completed his roll, his feet hit solid tile, and the rest of his body soon came with it. He stumbled a little, but remained upright and perfectly unharmed.

Kevin blinked.

Then took a look around.

The two that tried tag-teaming him were back on their feet and currently arguing.

"What do you mean it's my fault?! You're the one who hit me!"

"I wouldn't have hit you if you had kept a firm grip on the kid! Don't try and pin the blame on me! This is your fault!"

"You don't know what you're talking about, idiot!"

"Hey! Who're you calling idiot?! Idiot!"

Yeah, their argument went something like that. After a decently-sized drop of sweat coalesced into existence on his right temple, Kevin looked at the other guy. The drop of sweat increased in size. The guy was wailing on the ground, squirming around like some kind of inch worm. It was very disturbing.

"My poor toof! It's broken! Broken! Waaa!"

Kevin knew that he should still be frightened, but it proved incredibly difficult when faced with such stupidity. These were the people trying to beat him up? They were too busy arguing or, well, flopping around like a Magikarp out of water to even look at him. It's like they had forgotten that he even existed!

And that's when it hit him. They were no longer paying attention to him. This was his chance to escape. He would have to move quickly, though; the longer he waited, the more likely they were to realize he was still there.

Kevin bolted for the door posthaste.

"Hey! He's getting away!"

"Come back here, you little brat!"

He heard the shouting behind him as he ran out of the locker room, but paid them no heed. Seconds after he left, the door slammed open, but he refused to look back. Kevin was afraid that if he did anything other than continue running, they would catch him. And he knew that it would be all over if he let that happen. There would be no mercy then.

***

Warning: The previous scene should not be attempted in real life. What you saw was a mild case of someone who has been "Mistaken For a Badass." This is not to be confused with "Crouching Moron, Hidden Badass," which is where someone acts like a complete idiot, until their introduced to a certain kind of stimuli, like a loved one being in danger or something, and then unleash the biggest can of whoop ass known to man. A person who has been Mistaken For a Badass is someone who has absolutely no clue what he is doing. This person is just a normal guy who does normal things, and then suddenly finds himself thrust into an inexplicably abnormal and dangerous situation—like an alien invasion. In spite of the danger this man finds himself in, he always manages to escape. Of course, he does not just survive these dangerous situations. He survives them in such a way that everyone involved "thinks" he's the biggest, most hardcore badass this side of the multiverse.

You may now get back to your regularly broadcasted program.

***

Kiara dodged the twin balls of light that came flying at her. They moved so fast that a normal human would've seen nothing but a flash. Sidestepping to the left, then the right, she let the bright white spheres travel past her, the air around her crackling with repressed youki. They struck the wall several meters behind her and detonated in a brilliant explosion of light particles.

"Oh my."

Kiara looked back at where the light spheres had struck. The damage was minimal, merely two small burnt patches on the concrete where they'd hit, but that didn't mean much. Those attacks were meant to damage living matter, not inanimate objects.

The entire hallway was covered in burn marks; the walls, ceiling and floor had large black patches covering their surface. No part of the hall had been left untouched. It looked like someone had gone mad and started flinging miniature incendiary grenades all over the place.

She looked back at the still-enraged Lilian and smirked. “Those attacks of yours look like they might actually hurt if I let them hit me.”

“Shut up!” Lilian growled. The glare she gave Kiara was almost as potent as the vitriol in her tone. She was pissed! “For ordering your men to defile my Beloved, I'm going to make you wish you were never born!”

Kiara was amused. This girl had completely misconstrued the situation. The poor dear really had no clue that she had merely ordered her men to beat the crap out of Kevin (which honestly wasn't much better), not to defile his virginal self.

Ah, well. Who was she to correct Lilian on her erroneous assumptions? Besides, it was amusing to see the girl work herself into a fit over a misunderstanding. Seriously, who in their right mind would think she’d order her henchmen to commit BL on someone? Even she wasn't *that* cruel.

“Well, come on then,” Kiara grinned. “If you're so dead set on teaching me a lesson, then you'd better hop to it. I won't be waiting around all day.”

She gave Lilian a “come on” gesture with her left hand.

That was all the vivacious kitsune needed to begin firing off light spheres in rapid succession. Two spheres flared into existence, were flung forward, then two more appeared and were shot at Kiara with the force of a cannon. Faster and faster the spheres of light seemed to come, until Lilian was sending off two attacks every couple of seconds.

Kiara’s fanged grin showed off her sharp canines as she dodged the many light spheres. Left. Right. Duck. Tilt to the left. Tilt to the right. Jump. Spin. She was a constant flow of motion, letting each and every attack Lilian sent her way sail harmlessly past her by mere inches.

And while she exercised her abilities in evasion, she also began leading her attacker out of the hall, and into a venue of her own choosing. She had a plan for dealing with this little kitsune, but she needed a larger space to do it. The gymnasium would suffice for her purposes, so that's where she headed.

“Come back here, you coward!”

Of course, to the unknowing eye it looked like she was fleeing. That's exactly what Lilian thought as she chased after the woman. This enraged the redhead further, and she chased after Kiara, continuing to fling light spheres at her foe.

It was unfortunate that she only had two tails, and thus could only produce two spheres at any given time. It was also annoying because the other woman appeared to be quite agile, dodging each attack with ease.

This didn't mean she would stop. Quite the contrary. Seeing that woman's smirking face burned Lilian something fierce. This entire battle was about more than this vile woman sending several men to assault her beloved now—now, Lilian's pride was on the line! She would not allow a mere human to get the best of her!

Soon enough the two of them reached the gym. Without pause, Kiara spun around like a top, slamming a foot into the gym doors. The doors were blown right off their hinges, exploding with a sound reminiscent of a shotgun going off in an enclosed space.

She ducked into the room, barely managing to dodge another light sphere. The compressed ball of celestial youki was so close she could feel it grazing her hair.

“There's nowhere to run now!” Lilian shouted in triumph, thinking she had finally managed to corner the woman. All of this fighting was beginning to grate on her. She was a kitsune, and like most of her kind, she didn't like fighting.

Unfortunately for this woman, she had pissed Lilian off. Send those icky, disgusting men to hurt her beloved, would she? Lilian would show her!

“Who says I'm running?” Kiara asked, still keeping her back to Lilian. “Did it ever occur to you that I might be leading you here for a reason? That maybe I wanted to trap you here?”

The sphere of light that was just seconds from being launched at Kiara stopped. Lilian's brows furrowed.

“What are you talking about? In case you haven't realized it, that means you’re also trapped in here with me.”

“I'm saying that I couldn't do much in that hallway. Or more like, I didn't want to bring this building down around my ears when I went all-out on you.”

Kiara turned around, and Lilian noticed something about the woman that hadn’t been there before: her hands were clawed.

Sharp, deadly-looking nails glinted under the light from the large bulbs overhead. They looked like they could very easily rend flesh from bone if needed.

Realization struck Lilian like a bolt of lightning, sending a ripple of shock through her body.

"You're not human!"

"Finally figured it out, did you?" Kiara enjoyed the look of bafflement and shock that permeated Lilian's face. While not sadistic like her younger brother, she did so enjoy getting the drop on her quarry. "Didn't you wonder how I could dodge your attacks so easily? No regular human could've done that. You were so enraged by me sending men after your mate that you never even suspected that I might not be human."

"But... but how?" Lilian glared at the woman, shock and confusion warring for dominance over her features. "I would have known if you weren't human! I would have sensed it!"

"You may be able to sense yōkai that have no talent in suppressing their youki, but I've been around a long time. And in that time I've honed my skills to perfection—abilities that most yōkai have never heard of. My ability to suppress my own youki is so great that only the most talented sensors can even glimpse my power, and even then, it's only if I allow them to." Kiara smirked as Lilian's eyes widened. "Hiding from a young two-tails like yourself is well within my capabilities."

Now that the truth of her nature had come out, there was no more need to hide it anymore. With a large grin on her face, Kiara unleashed her incredible and potent power.

It came out of nowhere, appearing like a hurricane—the amazing power that Kiara possessed. Her body was suddenly engulfed in a bright, red light. Like a torrent of violent flames they licked and flickered across her body, covering her in a powerful aura that caused the ground around her to quake. Several loud sonic booms were unleashed as the air around her spontaneously combusted with her no longer suppressed youki.

Lilian was forced to raise an arm to shield her eyes. It was so bright that looking at it directly caused her retina to burn! But how could that be? How could someone possibly have youki that was *this* powerful? It was unlike anything she had ever felt before!

The light eventually died down, and Lilian risked lowering her arm. The moment she did, she really wished she hadn't.

Kiara had not changed much; nowhere near as much as Chris Fleischer had, but what changes had been made were drastic.

Her body emitted a potent-looking red aura. It covered her like a second skin, and didn't look like it would be pleasant to touch. Lilian was sure anyone who wasn't Kiara would be burned if they touched it.

Several additional appendages had become visible, allowing Lilian to figure out just what this woman was. Two floppy brown ears hung down her head, almost camouflaged by her hair. A single bushy-brown tail stuck out of a hole in her pants, wagging back and forth behind her back.

While discovering that the woman before her was an inu was certainly a terrible epiphany, it wasn't the worst part about this whole affair. With her dog appendages no longer hidden, Lilian finally realized why this woman looked so familiar.

"It's you!" She exclaimed, shock and fear coursing through her body, crashing into and overloading all other thoughts and feelings like a tidal wave as it swept everything away. "You're the one who nearly killed me when I first came to this city!"

"So you finally remember me, do you?" Unlike Chris, whose voice had been a horrible amalgamation of a dog's bark and human speech, Kiara sounded perfectly normal. "I had wondered why you looked so familiar as well. Were it not for your scent, I would have never realized that you were the kitsune I ran into nearly three weeks ago."

Lilian took a step back, but quickly stopped herself. She shook her head, trying to regain control over her fight or flight instinct. It was difficult, very much so, but she couldn't flee, not now.

"Not going to run?" Kiara sounded more curious than anything else.

"Even if I ran you would still catch me," Lilian sounded resigned. "You have my scent. I doubt I would be able to get very far, even if I used the enhancement technique to increase my speed. Besides—" the redhead's eyes narrowed into a glare, "—I can't leave when my Beloved is in danger. I'm going to beat you, and then I'm going to rescue him from those men."

"You must really care about this kid if you're willing to stand up to someone like me," Kiara observed.

"Of course. Kevin is my mate," Lilian declared proudly, using his name for the first time ever. "He means everything to me. There is nothing I wouldn't do for him. That includes fighting you."

After saying this, she settled herself into a light stance. She spread her feet slightly apart, though the action felt awkward, and raised her hands, even though she wasn't sure what to do with them. Like all kitsune, she was not a fighter, but that didn't mean that she didn't know at least a little self-defense.

The kitsune world was dangerous; the world of yōkai even more so. Many threats existed out there, especially to a young kitsune like herself. There were other kitsune who'd love to get their hands on someone of her status, yōkai that enjoyed violently killing others for no reason other than because they could. Her matriarch had made sure that she had at least been taught a little about martial arts, so that she would have something to fall back on in the event that her kitsune powers failed her.

Even then, she was not a fighter, and it showed in her awkward stance.

"But you're still afraid." It was not a question.

"Terrified," Lilian admitted freely. A glance at her legs, which were shaking, confirmed this fact. "But that won't stop me."

"Fighting for the one you love, eh?" Kiara gave a genuine smile. "I can respect that. Very few people are ever willing to fight for another. The fact that you would is impressive."

Her smile turned devilish, though, as she also took up a fighting stance. Unlike Lilian, whose stance was very basic and clearly untested by true combat, Kiara's showed experience. Her stance was narrow, right leg forward, an orthodox stance. Her footing was light as she bounced from one foot to the other.

Even the placement of her hands suggested that she was a very skilled fighter. Where Lilian simply held hers up as if she didn't know what to do with them, Kiara's were near her face in a guard position, a traditional boxing stance.

"However, I don't want you to think I'm going to go easy on you, just because I can respect your decision. I've never given anything but my best in a fight, and I'm not about to stop that just because you're young and inexperienced."

"I wouldn't expect you to," Lilian retorted, "nor would I want you to."

"Good." Kiara's smile became truly feral. "Then let us begin."

Chapter 8

Kiara Versus Lilian

Kevin ran down the hall as fast he could. He didn't know how long he'd been running; all he knew was that he couldn't afford to stop.

"Hey! Get back here, you little twerp!"

"Quit running and take your beating like a man!"

"Waaa, my toof!"

And those three were the reasons he could *not* stop running. The henchmen he'd inadvertently caused to injure each other were still in hot pursuit of him. They'd recovered pretty quickly—less than a few seconds after he'd escaped from the locker room, in fact. He'd scarcely ran more than a few meters before they were on him like an *Otaku* on a poster of Miku Hatsune in a bikini.

He raced down the hall in a mad dash, hoping to find a way out of the school, so that he could escape into the desert or something. He'd already tried the nearest exit and it had been locked. No surprise there, considering how late it must be, but he hoped there would be at least one door left unlocked.

Actually, he had been hoping to run into a teacher by now, but that hope had disappeared within the first few seconds of this chase. If a teacher hadn't come by to investigate after the ruckus they'd made in the locker room, chances were good that no teacher was present.

"Damn it… how can this kid run so fast?"

"He's a quick little bastard, I'll give him that! But don't think that will be enough to get away from me! YOU HEAR ME?! I'M GONNA CATCH YOU AND BEAT YOUR ASS!"

"My toof! It huwts so muff! Waaaa!"

If Kevin couldn't find an unlocked door and he really was trapped inside, then he would be in some serious trouble.

His breathing sounded harsh to his ears as he made a sharp turn around the corner. There were a number of hallways in this building. There had to be, it was a big building. Kevin knew from having walked them so many times that, not including the locker rooms, there were six rooms. Two gyms, a workout room, a theater, a dance room and a room that contained an indoor swimming pool. For this reason, there were several exits and a number of corridors to choose from.

Acting quickly, he ducked into the first room he passed, which turned out to be the weight room. Several dozen machines were scattered about, lined up in rows. The weight room also had six benches for people to exercise with dumbbells, and another six for free weights.

"He went in there!"

"Let's get that little shit!"

"My tooof!"

Eyes widening, fear pumping through his veins, Kevin rushed further into the room. The doors burst open soon after, and his pursuers ran inside.

"There he is!" Tall pointed him out as he ran to a bench with metal brackets protruding on either side. The brackets acted as a rack for the long metal pole used for bench-presses. "Let's get him!"

As they rushed towards him, Kevin, in desperation, jumped on one of the benches. He ran forward, hopped over the pole and landed on the ground. Short followed him. He ran along the bench and jumped—well, tried to jump, over the metal pole. Perhaps it was because of all that muscle, but he didn't make it over. His legs smacked into the long, offending pole, and he slammed face-first into the rubbery floor.

There was a loud crunching sound that reverberated through the room, sounding abnormally loud. Blood gushed from the now broken nose, pooling onto the floor and spreading rapidly to create a slick carmine puddle.

While Short rolled around on the ground, hands covering his now bleeding nose, the other two came in from either side, trapping him in a pincer maneuver.

Kevin darted through two of the benches before they could reach him. Both men had been running at a full-sprint, their hands outstretched to catch him. When they saw their prey slip away before they could beat him into submission, their eyes widened, and they quickly tried to halt their forward momentum.

They didn't succeed.

The sound of two bodies colliding rang harshly throughout the room, as the pair crashed into each other. The one with the chipped tooth ended up smacking face first into Tall's chest. Because of his height deficiency—especially in comparison to his stupidly tall friend—he was sent sprawling to the ground.

Tall stumbled backwards. His feet landing on the puddle of blood, causing him to slip. His arms frantically windmilling about, he fell backwards—

"AAEEIII!"

—and landed right on top of Short.

A loud shriek of pain rang out, echoing around the room. Kevin didn't wait around for them to recover. He bolted for the nearest door, slammed it open and rushed out. A quick right after exiting the room took him into a new hallway, one that contained an exit. Even at this distance, he could see it at the end of the corridor, two large double doors with a red exit sign over them.

He ran toward it in a full-sprint. Adrenaline pumped through his body, fast and powerful, increasing the amount of effort he could put into his muscles. His breathing went from ragged and harsh pants to loud rasps. His lungs burned, hot and painful; his esophagus was on fire. But he didn't stop. He couldn't stop. Not when he was so close.

The walls passed by in a blur. This particular exit had no other doors near it, which meant he would be more than a little screwed if it turned out to be locked.

Despite this, he continued to run. He no longer had a choice in the matter. Kevin had committed himself to this course the moment he turned down the corridor. He couldn't turn back now even if he wanted to.

"There you are, brat!"

"I'm gonna get you break your face in for what you did to my nose!"

"My toof! My toof!"

Those guys were following him again? Dang, they recovered quickly, didn't they?

Despite being tired from having run so hard and for so long, Kevin made it to the doors in record time. His body crashed against the hard and unyielding steel object, his shoulder pressing into the large handle that would open it.

The door didn't open.

"No," Kevin whispered. He rammed into the door again, harder this time. It still didn't open. "No, no, no, no!" This was not good. This was so not good! So, so, *so* not good! Oh god, he was so screwed! He was—

"Well, well, well, finally decided to stop running, did you?"

Kevin grit his teeth, his face draining of blood as his heart all but stopped. His mind began to panic. What should he do? He didn't want to turn around, didn't want to face these three; but really, what choice did he have?

None. That's what.

He turned around to see the three smirking goons who had tried beating him up—were *still* trying to beat him up. They were in pretty bad shape. Tall had a noticeable slouch and was rubbing at his chest, his face masked in a grimace of pain and agitation. Short was both bleeding from his newly broken nose, and the one with the cracked tooth was holding his mouth, from which copious amounts of carmine fluids oozed.

"You managed to get us pretty good," Tall said. He had a rather ugly, put-out look on his face. Kevin thought it suited him. "I admit, we greatly underestimated your skill at hand-to-hand combat."

"Uh," Kevin blinked. They thought he was skilled at hand-to-hand combat? Seriously? "No, I think you've got the wrong idea here…"

"But we've finally got you now," Tall interrupted him. Kevin would have normally been annoyed at being cutoff mid-sentence, but, well, he had other things on his mind—like the fact that he was about to get his face beaten in.

"There's no place for you to run, and nothing you can use against us here. You would have been better off sticking it out in the weight room."

Kevin pressed his back against the door. His breathing picked up. His heart began thumping like a battering ram in his chest. Fear and panic and a whole slew of other negative emotions raced through his nerves. Dang it! What should he should do? What could he do to get out of this?!

"Heh, you scared?" Short chuckled. A closer inspection of the man revealed that he was not only the shortest, but the one with the most pimples as well. The guy had a serious acne problem. "As you should be. After the amount of trouble you've given us, we're not letting you get off easy. Oh no. This is going to be very painful. It's going to hurt, a lot."

"My toof! Fow foing fu pay fow whaf you fid fu my toof!"

The man with the chipped tooth, whom Kevin decided to call Buck, was actually in tears. He had a hand to his cheek, covering the swollen flesh as he cried what appeared to be large rivers—or maybe waterfalls would be a more accurate word to use. Either way, a lot of water was coming out of his eyes. He must have gone through at least several dozen gallons already.

Three sets of ominous footsteps echoed down the empty corridor. They rang out loudly in Kevin's ears, who could swear he heard his death approach with each dull thud that sounded out. Each step the trio took increased his desperation to escape and the sheer terror he felt, because he knew there was no escape.

"I wanna say this is going to hurt me a lot more than it hurts you," Tall said, "But then I'd be lying." He chuckled, laughing at his own joke.

No one else laughed. It was a lame joke.

"That was lame, dude," Short sighed.

"Really lame," Buck added.

"Lame?!" Tall glared at the other two. "What are you talking about? My jokes are classics! Classics, I tell ya!"

"Yeah, yeah." Short waved a hand in the air, as if warding off a fly, or a really bad joke. "Why don't you just close that yap of yours and let's get to beating this kid?" He directed a venomous glare Kevin's way, causing him to let out a little squeak. "I have to pay him back for what he did to my nose."

"Argh! Why are you guys always dissing on my jokes?!"

As Tall began stomping around like an angry child that had his favorite toy taken away, a small bead of sweat ran down Kevin's forehead. This guy… how could someone be so terrifying one moment and look so silly the next? It was hard to take these people seriously when they did crap like this!

After several seconds of watching Tall act like a spoiled brat, Kevin realized something: their attention was diverted away from him. This was his chance! If he could just slip away while Tall was distracting the other two, then maybe he could…

"Don't even think of trying to get away, brat!"

Kevin froze as the three suddenly turned back to him, Tall's temper tantrum utterly forgotten.

"L-look," Kevin raised his hands in the universal sign of surrender. "Can't we work out our issues without violence? You guys don't really need to do this, do you?"

"Sorry," Tall cracked his knuckles as he closed the distance between himself and Kevin. He didn't sound very sorry. He didn't sound sorry at all. "But we really do need to do this. Kiara's orders and all that."

Tall grabbed the front of Kevin's shirt and yanked him up until he stood on his tiptoes. His feet kicked out uselessly, hitting the older man's thighs in the hopes that doing so would force the man to release him. Tall took his kicks without flinching, as if they were mere bug bites.

"You put up one hell of a fight, brat," Tall declared as he raised his clenched fist. "Much better than I would've expected from a runt like you, but it's all over now. Too bad that speed of yours won't be able to save you here!"

Kevin closed his eyes. He didn't want to see the fist as it descended towards his head with concussion-inducing force. His mind screamed at him, urging him to keep fighting, to not give up. He fought against those instincts, knowing that continuing to struggle wouldn't help him, and instead waited with baited breath for the attack that would likely knock him for a loop.

And he waited.

And waited.

And waited some more.

After several seconds of waiting, he wondered why Tall hadn't hit him yet? Not that he was complaining, mind, it was just that he'd been expecting to experience pain by now. And where was that pain? Why wasn't he on the receiving end of unadulterated violence already? And was it just him, or had the temperature taken a sudden nosedive?

"What the fuck?!"

"What's going on?!"

"Waa!!"

Kevin's eyes snapped open at the sound of surprised screaming.

In the years to come, Kevin would see a lot of strange and unusual things. More than half of those things would be the direct result of his actions. However, what he saw that day would forever remain in his memories as one of the most bizarre sights he had ever lay eyes on.

After all, it wasn't every day that you saw people with ice crawling up their legs.

Wait. Ice?

Tall's grip on his shirt loosened enough that Kevin pried himself out of the now shaking hands. He stumbled backwards, his balance skewed, knees reverberating from the sudden impact. Shaking himself out of his slight stupor, he looked back at the three shivering men.

He blinked, then rubbed his eyes and blinked again. Yep, he was not seeing things. That was definitely ice creeping up their legs. It had already made its way up their shins and calves and continued working its way up their thighs. Because of the bright sheen of the frozen liquid, it almost looked like some kind of mercury-type metal moving up their bodies as opposed to ice. Only the blue, semi-translucent appearance of the material, and the dropping temperature told him the substance really was ice.

At least he hoped it was ice.

Actually, he took that back—he hoped it was mercury. Wasn't mercury poisonous to humans?

"W-what the hell is this!? It's so cold!"

"My balls! My balls are freezing! They feel like they've turned into ice cubes!"

"Waa! Fuu muff informafion!" Buck said, which Kevin interpreted correctly as, "Waa! Too much information."

"What the…?" Kevin tried to process the sight before him. Okay, think Kevin, think. These goons were beginning to look like human popsicles. There was ice covering the floor underneath their feet, and the temperature had taken a sudden nosedive. It was almost as if…

"Are you okay?" a voice asked from behind Kevin.

"Gya!"

Kevin screamed like a little girl—a very manly little girl—and jumped nearly a foot into the air. When he landed back on his feet, he spun around toward the source of the voice.

Light azure met glacial-blue.

He blinked.

Then again, for good measure.

"Ah!" He pointed at the girl who gaped at him. "You're the girl I met back at the arcade!"

The girl looked at him for several more seconds, then scowled. "B-back at the... you IDIOT!"

Kevin stumbled back several steps.

"Are you telling me that you don't... that you don't..."

"Don't what?"

"N-n-n-nothing!" The girl squeaked. "Forget that! Are you telling me you only recognized me just now?"

"Just now?" Kevin tilted his head quizzically. "What do you mean? This is only the second time we've met."

A large vein pulsed on her forehead. The temperature began to drop some more. Kevin shivered, his breath blowing out and releasing a puff of steam.

"You idiot! Jerk! I stayed after school and came to that stupid track meet just to watch you, and this is the thanks I get?! You don't even recognize me!"

"Uh… sorry?" Kevin said, not quite sure what he was apologizing for. Then he registered the rest of her words. "Wait, you came to the track meet to see me?"

"Ah…" The girl's face turned bright red… and then went from red to ice blue. "Ah…" Her mouth opened to speak, but no words came out, just a strange monosyllable that sounded like a gerbil getting strangled. It was almost as if something got lodged in her throat.

"Hey," Kevin looked at the girl in concern. She really wasn't looking so good. "Are you okay? Your face is all red."

"S-S-S-SHUT UP! I-I-I-I'M F-FINE! JUST FINE!"

The girl exploded. Literally. Her voice was so loud it created a large gust of wind that blew Kevin's hair away from his face, and made his eyes water.

It was also extremely cold. Several strands of his hair froze over as her breath hit them, making him comparable to a young Jack Frost.

The girl continued ranting, her facial coloration growing more vibrant by the second. "I-it's not like I actually wanted to see you or anything! Idiot! I was simply staying after school for my own reasons, and decided to watch the track meet! That's all! Don't be so full of yourself! Hmph!"

"But you just said…"

"I-I-I didn't say ANYTHING!" The goth girl's face looked like a neon sign. And was it just him, or had the temperature finally reached sub-zero? He was freezing! "Y-you're just hearing things!"

"But I could have sworn I heard you say…"

"YOU'RE HEARING THINGS!"

Kevin opened his mouth, closed it, opened it again, and closed it one more time. Finally…

"You're right. I must just be hearing things." Just go with it, Kevin. Nod your head once or whatever and let it go.

Man, girls were so weird.

"So, you were at the track meet then?"

"Ah! Um! Y-yes," the raven-haired girl stuttered a bit. "B-but, don't think I came there just to see you! Like I said, I just happened to be in the area. Nothing more." She nodded her head, as if reaffirming something. "I certainly wouldn't stick around after school to watch your track meet. I had been doing other things when I finished early and decided to spend some time watching the track team compete."

Oh. Well that made sense. After all, how could she have known he was on the track team anyway? They'd only spoken to each other once, and most of that consisted of her yelling at him. It's not like he'd ever had a chance to tell her that he was on the track team. Yes, this was probably just one big coincidence.

"Right." Kevin scratched the back of his head, then realized something. "Wait." He studied the girl more closely, making her squirm under his gaze. "Were you the one arguing with Lilian?"

"O-oi! G-g-g-get us out of here!"

"F-f-fuck! This is g-g-g-gonna give me the w-w-worst case of b-blue-balls ever!"

“Shut up!” The girl shouted at the trio of complaining men. “Don’t say such crude things!” When the men opened their mouths to complain some more, ice gathered, taking the shape of three ball gags, which were then shoved into their open oral passages.

As their screams came out muffled and low, she turned back to Kevin and scowled.

“Yeah, I was the one arguing with that stupid fox! But she was the one who started it!” She crossed her arms and gave him a bit of glare, as if daring him to contradict her.

“Huh, so that was you,” Kevin mumbled, his head tilting down in thought. “I thought you looked familiar, but couldn’t get a good glimpse of your face. I was also in a bit of a hurry and didn’t—wait.” His mind ground to a halt as he finally registering everything she’d said, including something he’d initially missed. “How did you know Lilian is a kitsune?”

“Because I’m a yuki-onna,” the girl stated matter-of-factly “While yuki-onna don’t really specialize in sensing other yōkai, we can still tell when one is near us. I knew that Chris was a yōkai of some kind the moment I saw him, though I didn’t know what kind of yōkai.”

“He’s an inu,” Kevin answered absently. “So you’re a yuki-onna. Aren’t they also called Snow Maidens?”

yuki-onna were another race of yōkai found in Japanese mythology. Also known as Snow Maidens, they appeared as ethereally beautiful women who were found in the snow-covered regions of Japan. He remembered reading a manga where a yuki-onna had gone to a school for monsters and fell in love with a human… along with several other girls, all of whom competed for the hero's affection.

It was a harem manga.

Now that he was observing her more closely, she actually did resemble a yuki-onna. Her skin was so pale as to be nearly translucent, and her hair was darker than midnight. Lips of ice blue gave her a sort of frozen look, and those glacier-cold eyes seemed like they could freeze over hell. She was also very cute, like a porcelain doll that you wanted to take home and dress up.

“That’s right,” she nodded, “I’m surprised you know that. Japanese mythology isn’t covered in any of our classes.”

"I read a lot of manga," Kevin told her. "I also watch a lot of anime." He studied the girl, his mind brimming with wonder, curiosity and a hint of confusion. "But why are you telling me this? I thought yōkai weren't really supposed to reveal themselves to humans."

"There is a rule against yōkai letting humans know they're not human, but it's okay for me to tell you, because little miss fox-whore already spilled the beans about our existence." The girl paused. Then she gasped. This was followed by yet another blue-faced blush. "Ah! B-but, I don't want you to think I told this because I like you or anything! I was simply letting you know because you're already aware of the existence of yōkai! That's all! Got it?"

"Got it."

Kevin resisted the temptation to take several steps back. What the heck was up with this girl? Why was she getting so defensive?

"So if you were with Lilian, does that mean you know where she is?"

"The fox?"

The girl frowned at him, making Kevin wonder if he had said something wrong… again. He'd apparently been doing that a lot with this girl. Why else would she get so angry at him?

He knew that he should have been angry with her, or at least annoyed at her poor behavior, but was too confused to drudge up even minor irritation.

After several seconds of awkward silence, she spoke up. "I don't know where she is now. The last I saw of her, she was with that woman in the business suit."

"Woman in the business suit…" Kevin's eyes widened. "You mean Kiara?!"

He had known that she was responsible for sending those men after him, but he hadn't realized she was here at the school. And she was with Lilian?! This was not good, not good at all.

"What the—?" The girl in the lolita dress gawked at the boy as he bolted past her. "H-hey! Where do you think you're going?! Are you really just going to run off like that?!"

Kevin didn't even stop running as he turned his head slightly to wave at her. "I'm sorry, but I really have to go! I don't have time to stick around and chat!"

He had to make sure Lilian was alright. If Chris really was Kiara's brother, then it meant she was also a yōkai, and not just any yōkai, but an inu. And if she was an inu, then Lilian could be in serious trouble.

He did stop running, if only for a moment, as a realization crossed his mind. "Oh, before I go, I don't think I ever got your name."

The girl looked at him strangely, head tilted and face a mottled mass of confusion, before she seemed to realize that he was right. She had never given him her name.

"Uh, it's Christine, Christine Fraust," she answered him, then added, "But you can call me Christy. That's what my friend used to call me."

There was a pause, during which time Christine's face blanked as she went over everything she had just said.

Several seconds later she was a blushing wreck again.

"N-n-not that you're my friend or anything! Idiot! Jerk! Hmph!" She crossed her arms and turned her head away from him. What a strange girl.

"... Right. Anyway, I really do need to get going. Thanks again for the rescue." He grinned at the girl. "You know something, even though you're a little odd, you seem like a really nice person—I doubt you would've bothered rescuing me if you weren't. I hope we can be friends."

Kevin turned again and bolted down the hallway, his hurried footsteps echoing along the walls as he left a blushing wreck of a yuki-onna in his wake.

Several moments passed. Christine stared after the blond-haired sophomore as he disappeared from view. Then...

"He wants to be my friend," she whispered. She wasn't sure how to feel about that. It was kinda... well, there was just a lot wrong with it. She held a hand to her chest. Her heart was thumping rapidly. She wondered what this unpleasant feeling was.

And then she paused as the rest of his words caught up to her.

"Wait a minute, did he just call me weird?" Christine shook her fist, even though Kevin had long since left. "I am not weird you idiot! Jerk! Grrr..." She lowered her fist. "But he did say I was a nice person..." Her cheeks tinged ice-blue. She trailed off, her blush growing and her head attempting to hide in the collar of her black lace bodice, which didn't actually have a collar to hide in. It didn't stop her from trying, though.

Another moment passed.

"I wonder if I should have told him that Kiara is a yōkai as well…"

***

The moment the battle started, Kiara was already on the move. Bending her knees, she launched herself into a full-bodied sprint that put the speed Kevin displayed during his track meet to shame. She was so fast that her body became a literal blur, a streak of color that no human, and even few yōkai, would be capable of following. She covered the distance between her and Lilian in a split second, appearing right in front of the startled girl.

After reaching her red-haired opponent, Kiara's right hand lashed out. Lilian only got a brief glimpse of deadly nails flashing in the light, before they swiped across her face.

"Gah!"

A strangled cry tore itself from Lilian's lips as five sharp claws ripped through her face, shredding her flesh as if it were made of paper. Blood spurted out of the wounds immediately as her skin peeled apart. Dark red liquid splattered across the ground and Kiara's claws.

Lilian stumbled backwards, eyes dulling and her body becoming limp.

A second later, she slumped to the ground.

And then disappeared.

"Heh, not bad." Kiara smirked as she spun around. "But still not good enough!"

With her left hand making a wide, swiping motion, Kiara managed to smack away the two spheres of light aimed at her head. Each sphere flew off in a different directions. One headed toward the bleachers while the other hit the ceiling, exploding in a shower of light particles that rained down on the two supernatural creatures locked in combat.

"I'm impressed," Kiara complimented as she looked across the gym at Lilian, who stood several meters away. "You know that you can't compete with an inu up close, so you used an illusion to make me think you were right in front of me, while the real you snuck behind me. You even managed to fool my sense of smell."

As the name implied, an illusion was the act of distorting reality. Most people assumed this meant weaving a complicated set of false images to fool a person's sight, and while that was true, it was only a small part of what went into creating illusions.

Illusions didn't affect just sight, but also scent, touch, taste and sound. In other words, an illusion could affect any one of the five senses. Skilled illusionists could affect more than one sense at a time. Masters of the art could affect all five at once.

Lilian was not a master of illusions. It had only been fifty-nine years since she'd gained her second tail—not enough time to become a master at illusions, or even an adept at them. She was still just a novice.

However, she was also a kitsune—illusions were a specialty of her race; their greatest art. The power they excelled at beyond any other. She would even go so far as to say that casting illusions was in her blood.

So, despite being a novice, she was still capable of affecting more than one sense at a time, though it took a lot of concentration to keep the illusion up, and she could only do so for a short time. Thirty seconds was her limit.

Thirty seconds apparently wasn't long enough to fool Kiara. Lilian had used her ability to weave an illusion that fooled Kiara's sense of sight and smell, tricking the woman into *thinking* she was inflicting physical harm on her, when in reality, it had just been a well-crafted illusory image.

However, because neither her senses of touch or sound were affected, Kiara recognized the illusion for what it was, and reacted far more quickly than Lilian anticipated. The end result was an ineffective attack that Kiara swatted away like the light spheres were merely flies.

"But it will take more than a simple illusion to get the best of me," Kiara continued, grinning from ear to ear and showing off her fang-like canines. "Still, I have to admit it was a good attempt. My brother would have fallen for that illusion easily. Then again, he's an idiot, so I would expect nothing less."

"I don't want to hear any compliments coming from you," Lilian scowled. "And what do you mean your brother?" It took the girl a second to remember that Kiara had mentioned her brother going to this school. It took her one more to remember another yōkai she knew that went to this school, another inu that she and her Beloved had a run-in with not too long ago. Her eyes widened to the size of dishpans as she stared at Kiara, dumbstruck. "Don't tell me that…"

"Oh? Finally figured it out, have you?" Kiara said, her eyes glinting with a sort of amused joviality. She was obviously getting a kick out of the poor kitsune's reaction.

"Chris! Your brother is Chris!"

It was so obvious, thinking back on it. Lilian almost kicked herself for not figuring it out sooner. To be fair, Kiara didn't share Chris's last name. And they looked nothing alike. Not to mention the fact Lilian hadn't sensed any youki emissions from the older woman when they'd met before. She was still struggling with the concept that Kiara wasn't human, let alone that her brother was Chris Fleischer.

"That's right. You didn't think I was just attacking you for no reason, did you? While I may not like my brother, it doesn't change the fact that he *is* family. I've got to look out for him, and when someone hurts him, I need to make sure his recompense is paid in full."

Lilian couldn't have looked more stunned if she tried. Her eyes had gone quite wide, and round—too round to be human eyes. Likewise, her jaw opened so wide as to appear unhinged. She looked surprisingly fetching when surprised.

Had Kevin been there, he probably would have blushed at the sight.

Had Eric been there, he would have been knocked out via Nosebleed Express.

"But I think we've talked enough, don't you?" Kiara lowered her center of gravity, bending her knees at a 45-degree angle. She faced Lilian fully, her fists tucked into her torso. It looked like she was getting ready to unleash a giant beam of energy or something. "While I enjoy a little pre-battle banter, I think it's time we take things up a notch!"

Sucking in a deep breath, her chest expanding, Kiara held it in for but a second, then expelled it all in one large burst.

The effects were immediate and devastating; a large explosion of torrential winds shot from her mouth, expanding as they were unleashed from deep within her diaphragm. Before long the powerful, hurricane-like winds covered an extremely wide area as it sped forward. Floorboards were ripped apart by the brutal and deadly winds. Like a maelstrom, it destroyed everything in its path as it raced toward Lilian.

Realizing how dangerous this attack was, Lilian called upon her own youki. She channeled the supernatural energy through her tails, and then began spreading it throughout the rest of her body, enhancing her muscles far beyond the strength of a normal human, or even an Olympic athlete.

With her body now strengthened to inhuman levels, she threw herself to the left, speeding out of the range of the fierce-looking winds. Her hair whipped around her body as she just barely managed to avoid being hit. The ferocious winds sped past her, striking the wall of the gymnasium with such savage brutality that a large portion of the wall was destroyed.

Had anyone been walking along the adjacent hallway at that particular moment, they would have witnessed the entire wall exploding outwards, large chunks of brick and mortar soaring into the hallway at neck-breaking speeds. The debris moved so fast that each chunk acted like a deadly projectile, and was more than capable of tearing through bone and flesh with impunity. They struck the wall at the other end of the hallway, smashing *through* the wall and leaving large, gouging holes that made the entire area look like Swiss cheese.

The battle had just started and already the two were tearing school property apart at an alarming rate.

Even before Lilian had dodged Kiara’s attack, the inu was already on the move. She reached Lilian in record time, her right hand lashing out in a slash that would have torn the girl's chest open, but missed as Lilian jumped backwards with several deft leaps.

Kiara only managed to cut off several strands of hair, and in the time it took for them to fall to the ground, Lilian had fired off nearly a half a dozen spheres of light. She didn’t bother attempting to aim, merely flinging them in Kiara’s general direction. Only one actually made it to the woman, but it was knocked away with ease. Her business suit ruffling, Kiara charged forward, even as she swatted the attack out of the air.

“Come on! Show me what you’ve got!”

With startling speed Kiara was in front of Lilian, barely giving the girl any time to prepare as she attacked with a series of quick and vicious claw swipes and finger stabs.

Left without any other option, Lilian was forced to dodge each attack as it came, bending and twisting and weaving around the fast paced assault, as Kiara's clawed hands blurred with deadly intent.

As this deadly dance continued, Lilian soon realized that she would lose if the fight continued like this. Kiara was faster, stronger, had more experience and was an all-around better fighter than her. If she didn't do something soon, she might not walk away from this battle.

Gritting her teeth, she began to search for some kind of opening that would allow her to counterattack. When none were found, she tried to put some distance between them in order to attack at range.

Neither option was viable, she soon discovered. Kiara was too fast for Lilian. Even with her muscles being enhanced by youki, she could barely keep up. Every time she tried backing away, Kiara simply closed the distance before she could launch one of her light spheres.

Not that it would do much good, Lilian thought bitterly, *She'll just knock them out of the air again.*

Something had to change if she wanted to get out of this alive, much less pull off a victory over this damn dog.

Lilian ducked under a slash meant for her face. She backpedaled when Kiara's foot launched out in a kick. She blocked it by crossing her arms, but the attack still sent her skidding backwards across the wood tiles. It hurt. A lot. Lilian could see the red welts from where Kiara's shoe had struck her forearm. She was almost certain her ulna had cracked.

Lilian was given no respite as Kiara appeared before her, claws already coming in hot. She dodged and weaved and ducked around the older woman, doing her best to evade the inu's long claws. A plan soon formed in Lilian's mind—it was a long shot, but it worked once before so it should work again. Hopefully.

Kiara's grinning visage filled her vision.

"Too slow!"

Lilian's emerald eyes went wide as Kiara's clawed hand jabbed at her face. Seemingly distracted, Lilian was incapable of dodging the next attack. Kiara's claws struck her in the head… and ended up going right through her, like the redhead was nothing but a simple phantom, a figment of the mind.

"What?!"

"Got you!"

Kiara looked down to see Lilian crouched beneath her outstretched arm. Both of the redhead's tails were extended, the tips pointed at her chest. She had just enough time to realize that she had been fooled by another illusion, before a large explosion of compressed youki struck her.

Lilian jumped back as the fire from her kitsune-Bi expanded, engulfing Kiara and bathing the entire area in her youki-fueled flames. The smoldering, white hot conflagration didn't spread beyond the small, two feet circumference around Kiara, the fire being controlled by Lilian's will.

Lilian watched the fire burn, eyes narrowed. One moment passed, then two. After three seconds had gone by, she sighed in relief, and relaxed her tense shoulders. The fight was over. Surely there was no way the woman could have withstood a point-blank blast of Fox Fire? Right?

Her relief was short lived.

"That was a pretty sneaky move there."

Lilian gasped as a powerful burst of youki caused the hairs on her tails and ears to bristle. The amount of power unleashed generated a large gust of wind, snuffing out the flames in an instant.

"No…" Lilian whispered in horror. Standing in the exact same position before the engulfed her was Kiara, not a wrinkle on her suit nor a burn mark in sight.

She was smirking.

"I had forgotten how tricky you kitsune can be," she commented idly. Her lips quirked up, denoting her amusement at the situation. "If I'm not mistaken, that was actually two illusions, wasn't it? One layered over the top of the other. You created the first one to make me *think* you were standing before me, while the other made you invisible. An illusion within an illusion. Very clever. Had it not been for my protective cloak, that might have actually hurt me."

Lilian grit her teeth as she realized her attack had not only failed, but failed spectacularly. There was not a scratch on this damn dog. Not a scuff mark, a ruffle or even so much as a smudge. Kiara appeared just as pristine now as she had at the start of the battle, whereas Lilian had a number of thin cuts along her arms and shoulders, along with her shirt, which had torn up top and bottom, exposing a good portion of her cleavage and the underside of her breasts.

What made this even worse was that Kiara clearly wasn't taking her seriously. The fact that she spoke so much—verbally dissecting Lilian's techniques, showed that she didn't consider her a threat, not in the slightest. Lilian would've felt insulted were she not so terrified.

"You're beginning to tire out, aren't you?" It sounded like a question, but it really wasn't. Anyone with a pair of eyes would've been able to see how exhausted Lilian was. Her legs trembled, her body was covered in sweat, and her breathing came out in harsh, ragged gasps. "It's too bad you're just a two-tails. There's so much untapped potential in you. If you just had one more tail, you might actually be able to give me a decent fight."

"Shut… up…" Lilian tried to growl at the other yōkai, but it sounded more like a sigh due to her exhaustion. She did manage a pretty decent scowl, though. "I don't want to hear that… from someone… like you…"

"Someone like me?" Kiara looked nothing if not amused. "You mean an inu." Lilian grimaced, but didn't say anything. "Very well then. I suppose talking isn't something two enemies should be doing anyway, or so I've been told. Too bad, I kinda like bantering with my opponents." She shrugged. "Well, whatever. If you don't feel like a little friendly banter, I guess I'll just end this now."

Kiara took another stance, a much narrower one than before, and Lilian prepared herself, calculating how to handle the coming assault. She didn't have much youki left—only enough for two more illusions, three if she pushed herself. Enhancement was out of the question. Even if she only used it in short bursts, it would burn through her reserves faster than she could say "Beloved."

Knowing this, she prepared herself as best she could. If she could just weather this first assault, then maybe she could counterattack with everything she had. It was a slim hope. It was also her only hope.

All of her planning went out the window with what happened next. Kiara's left hand jabbed out, her entire arm blurring out of focus. At first, Lilian wondered what the woman was doing—she was too far away to hit her with a physical attack. They were several meters apart.

She received her unpleasant answer in the form of excruciating pain searing through her left shoulder.

"A-ah!"

Gripping her shoulder, Lilian very nearly fell to her knees as something pierced through skin, muscle and bone. She felt pain, but also confusion. What just happened? How did that woman hit her? And from that distance!

Lilian clenched her teeth as her hand pressed against the wound. Blood leaked from between her fingers, massive amounts of dark red that stained her shirt a deep crimson. It hurt so much that she could hardly think straight.

"You should never take your eyes off your opponent."

Lilian had just enough time for her eyes to widen before she doubled over like a fold-out chair. Spittle and blood flew from her mouth as a powerful fist plowed into her gut like the war-hammer of an angry god. Never in her life had Lilian felt anything more painful. She wanted to curl up into a fetal position until it stopped hurting.

Kiara pulled her fist back. Lilian would have fallen, but a powerful elbow immediately struck her in the chin. Her head was snapped forcefully back, blood spraying from her mouth.

As she lost her footing and stumbled backwards, Kiara's hands grasped Lilian's ears and pulled her into a knee. The loud *crunch!* of Lilian's nose breaking was accompanied by a small whimper of pain from the kitsune in question.

Kiara let go of Lilian's ears, allowing her to stumble around in a daze. Blood leaked from her nose and mouth, and her eyes had glazed over. Lilian was completely unaware of Kiara, until she had taken two steps forward and launched a powerful finisher: a double palm-strike to the solar plexus.

"Hya!"

"Gyaaa!"

There was a loud *bang!* like the clapping of thunder. Lilian was blasted off her feet and thrown backwards with explosive force, hurtling through the air like one of her light spheres. She plowed into a set of bleachers on the other side of the gym with a loud series of crashes and bangs. Plastic exploded and metal bent, screeching and squealing worse than someone who'd taken their nails to a chalkboard.

Kiara strode forward, surveying the damage done. The bleachers had caved in, a large amount of plastic lay scattered across the gym, and a good deal of the metal wire frame had twisted and warped around the young kitsune's still form.

It was an impressive amount of damage, if Kiara did say so herself.

Stopping several feet from the bleachers, Kiara looked down to see the girl in question lying there in a heap. Her body was bent at an awkward angle. Her left arm hung limply above her head, held aloft by a metal bar that had been distorted beyond recognition. Her left calf was folded underneath her thigh, while her right foot dangled limply off a warped beam of metal that hooked underneath her knee.

Her head was tilted toward the ground, bangs hovering over her face. Kiara couldn't see much of her features; just the partially-open mouth with a line of blood running down her chin and dripping onto her ruined clothes.

"Looks like you're finished." The girl twitched at the sound of Kiara's voice. "Too bad, I was hoping you'd be a bit better. Still," she mused to herself, eyeing the insensate redhead, "You may not have injured me, but you still did a pretty good job of fighting me, especially for someone who's obviously never been in real combat before." She smirked. "You should be proud of yourself."

Lilian didn't respond. While she was still conscious, it wouldn't be long before darkness engulfed her. Blackness already crept at the edge of her vision; everything was starting to blur out of focus. Her eyes, two lackluster orbs of dull green flickered, signaling her tenuous grasp on consciousness.

Kiara took a single step toward the girl she had so thoroughly thrashed—

"LILIAN!"

—And was promptly interrupted when a loud shout rang out from behind her. The sound of footsteps striking hard, varnished wood grew louder, and Kiara stepped aside just as Kevin rushed past her. He knelt down next to the girl lying in the ruined bleachers, eyes wide.

"Lilian! Hey, Lilian!" Kevin's voice was frantic as he called out to the girl. He carefully laid his hands on her shoulders, but he didn't shake her for fear of aggravating her serious injuries. "Come on, Lilian, look at me!"

Lilian lifted her face using what little power she had left. She blinked several times, her dull eyes becoming just a tad more vibrant as she saw the blurry but recognizable figure in front of her.

"Be… loved…" she said, voice little more than a breathy whisper.

"Hey," Kevin's voice was surprisingly soft as he spoke, as if afraid that speaking too loudly would injure her further. "Listen, you're going to be all right, but I need you to stay with me."

"Be… loved… run…"

Kevin shook his head. How could she expect him to run and leave her in this condition?

"You should listen to the fox." Kiara smirked when Kevin's body stiffened. He craned his head to glare at her out of the corner of his eye, which only caused her mouth to widen into a full-blown grin. "Oh my, what a scary expression. Are you sure you should be staring at me like that, boya?"

Her floppy ears twitched and her tail flicked out behind her. Kevin noticed the new additions to her body, as well as her very sharp and deadly-looking nails, but he didn't seem all that scared. Or, if he was, he hid it very well. Either way, she was impressed.

"You know that I could kill you faster than you can blink, right?"

"Be… Be… loved…"

Kevin ignored Lilian as she tried pleading with him to run. He couldn't do that. To run away while someone else was in trouble, especially someone who had helped him so much… It was just wrong!

He stood up and turned around.

Kiara raised a single eyebrow when he held his hands up in a protective manner. Was he actually trying to shield the girl from her? How cute.

"Please stop," Kevin pleaded with the brunette inu. "She's already been beaten, so there's no need for you to fight her anymore. You've done enough."

"Ho?" The look on Kiara's face betrayed how much entertainment she was deriving from this situation. "I'm surprised. I didn't think you liked her all that much. That's the impression I got whenever I saw you two together. She always clung to you, but you never returned any of her affection, always pushing her away, telling her not to get so close. I assumed you disliked the girl."

Kevin's grimace spoke volumes more than words ever could, yet still he spoke.

"It's true that when Lilian and I first met, I wasn't all that thrilled by her presence in my life," he admitted. At the sound of his voice, Lilian lifted her head, though her eyes remained dull. "She just sort of barged into my life without even thinking about how I felt about it, or how it would affect me. She has no sense of modesty, lacks common sense, tries to, uh, do, um, embarrassing things to me and… stuff…"

His face flushed a deep shade of red as his mind conjured images of all the embarrassing things that she had done to him. Embarrassing was a really, *really* mild euphemism that couldn't describe the things she had done to him—and it wasn't very accurate anyway. Seductive might be a better way of putting it.

"A-anyway," Kevin shook his head and tried to get back on track. "Despite all that, and all of the trouble she's caused me, Lilian is still important to me."

He looked back at the girl, who's glazed eyes blinked. The smile that he wore as he peered at Lilian instantly disappeared when he turned back to Kiara. In its place was an expression that looked far too serious and determined for someone so young, especially while facing such a dangerous entity.

"She's still my friend, and I won't let you lay another hand on her."

"Big words coming from a kid whose legs are shaking," Kiara said. Kevin looked down at his legs to notice that they were indeed trembling.

"I'm not going to tell you I'm not scared. I'm terrified." Despite his fear, Kevin still managed pierce Kiara with a surprisingly harsh glare. "Even so I… I won't let you hurt Lilian anymore. You've hurt her enough."

"Hmm…"

Kiara had to hide her smirk as she forced her face to take on a look of thoughtful contemplation. What an unusual human. He almost reminded her of another human she'd known long, long ago.

"Weeell…" She dragged out the word, and in turn, the tension. She could see how her lack of an answer caused the boy a great deal of stress, based on the trickle of sweat running down his face, as well as his Adams apple bobbing when he gulped. Finally, after drawing the moment out as long as possible, she shrugged, "Alright, I guess I can leave things like this."

Kevin blinked.

Twice.

"W-what?"

Kiara couldn't help but chuckle at the stupefied look on the boy's face.

"I said I'm done." She looked from Kevin to Lilian. Her lips twitched when Kevin moved to block the injured kitsune from her vision. "I only came here to get settle the score for what she did to my brother. I think this settles the score just fine."

"I see, so you did this because of what Lilian did to Chris?" Kevin crinkled his brow. He still didn't know what happened to Chris, because he'd been unconscious at the time, but it must have been bad if Kiara deemed this sort of revenge necessary. Come to think of it, Chris hadn't been at school since then.

"Yep. Anyway, I'm finished." As she turned around, Kiara raised her hand in farewell. "I'll see you around, boya."

Kevin watched Kiara embark, her heels echoing on the wooden floor until she left the gym. He then turned back to Lilian and knelt down.

"Lilian? Lilian? Hey, Lilian."

When Lilian didn't respond, Kevin gently placed his hands on either side of her face and lifted her head. He didn't quite manage to stifle his gasp as he stared at her face.

Though her eyes were still open, they had become dull and lifeless, blood leaked from her nose and mouth, and some trailed down the left side of her face from a head wound, which had split open like an overripe fruit. If it weren't for the rise and fall of her chest, he would have assumed she was dead.

"Dang it! Dang it, dang it, dang it, dang it!"

Kevin's gut clench. He should have been there when Lilian fought Kiara; he should have been there to protect her, to do something, *anything,* to help her out.

He knew these thoughts were dumb. His presence wouldn't have helped; it would have hindered Lilian, forcing her to protect him instead of fight. He would have been a liability to her, not an asset. That didn't stop him from feeling like he should have been around to help her. It didn't stop him from feeling like a failure.

Kevin shook his head. He might not have been around to help her with Kiara, but he *could* do something to help her now.

"Don't worry, Lilian, you helped me when I got hurt by Chris, so now it's my turn to help you."

After Kevin assessed the situation, he decided that the first thing to do was get her out of the big dent she had made in the bleachers.

First, he straightened out Lilian's limbs, grabbing the arm caught on the steel bar and setting it on her lap, along with her other hand. He then took her left leg out from underneath her thigh and set it straight, followed by lifting the foot of her right leg off the twisted steel bar. The girl's face twitched several times when his actions caused discomfort, but that was the only sign of activity she made.

With her limbs straightened, Kevin scooted closer. He pulled her out of the dent, her head lolling from side to side. Whimpers escaped her mouth, almost blocked out by the groaning of steel. After having to half drag her out of the bleachers, he laid them down on the ground. Now came the hard part.

One hand went to her upper back, lifting her off the ground. The other slide under her knees. With a grunt, he lifted Lilian off the ground, her legs swaying as he strained under her weight, tails dangling limply like soggy ramen.

"Ugh… geez…" Kevin grunted as he began walking toward the locker. There was a nurse's office in the locker room for minor injuries. While this could hardly be considered minor, he didn't have much choice. He needed some place where he could lay her down and bandage her up properly. "How do all those heroes in *Shōnen* manga make this look so easy?"

Making strange grunting noises with each step, Kevin slowly made his way out of the gym. Now that he wasn't facing a deadly yōkai who could potentially kill him, he finally had a chance to observe the damage done to the place.

"Dang… those two really went all out."

The ground looked like it had been ripped apart by a category five hurricane. There were burn marks all over the place, the bleachers were a complete wreck, and a gigantic hole in the ceiling made him think a Titan had torn it open in search of humans to eat. To his left, the wall appeared to have been blasted apart by TNT, and the wall beyond it was filled with holes. He didn't even want to know what had caused *that* kind of damage.

"I wonder how the school faculty is going to take this?" he mused. Probably not too well. He could only imagine how they would react when they came to school tomorrow.

The coaches and health teachers were going to flip.

It took Kevin nearly ten minutes to reach the small nurse's office, which was nearly nine minutes longer than normal. To be fair, he was tired from facing Kiara's three henchmen, and carrying an unconscious Lilian certainly didn't help, especially since he was being careful not to aggravate her wounds. At least he managed to arrive there eventually. That had to count for something.

He gently laid Lilian down on the examination bed, then went to grab the first aid kit located inside of the lass cabinet to his immediate left. It wasn't until he began pulling out medical supplies that another thought occurred to him, one that caused him to pause.

"Just how am I going to get her home like this?"

Chapter 9

Discoveries of a Heartfelt Conversation

Lilian woke up feeling absolutely awful, like a stampede of *Onikuma* (bear yōkai) had run her over at full-speed. Her entire body felt like it was one big, aching mess. It hurt so much that she wouldn't have been the least bit surprised if she looked in the mirror, and discovered that her body had turned into a giant bruise.

Some parts of her body hurt more than others. These parts of her anatomy were experiencing a very specific kind of pain—the kind that came from having what amounted to a metaphorical jackhammer bashed into them repeatedly. She also suspected that her nose, and maybe even a couple of ribs, were broken.

Wanting to know her whereabouts after running a proper damage assessment, Lilian slowly opened her eyes. There wasn't much light out. The room was dark, and she could see the velvety sky that marked the beginning of twilight through the open curtain. The dark hues of color painted across the atmosphere let her know that nighttime was swiftly approaching. She must have been unconscious for a good while, then. She also noticed, with no small amount of relief, that she was lying on a familiar bed underneath a familiar ceiling.

Rolling over onto her side, Lilian placed her hands on the bed and pushed herself off the mattress—or tried to. The moment she attempted to sit up, white hot pain like fire lanced along her sides. It felt like someone was stabbing her in several places at once with a dozen scorching blades.

She yelped. Her body experienced momentary shock, the feeling of unfathomable agony causing her arms give out. She fell back onto the bed in a heap.

Seconds later, hurried footsteps approached, getting louder, before the door burst open, and a figure entered.

"Lilian! You're awake!"

"Be… Beloved…"

Kevin rushed over to her side just as she made another futile attempt at sitting up.

“Hey, hey! You shouldn't be trying to get up right now! You're injured!”

Kevin placed his hands on her shoulders to gently guide her back onto the bed. A hiss of barely-repressed pain escaped Lilian's lips—even her shoulders were extremely sore and sensitive. Just that small touch sent jolts of what felt like raw lightning traveling through her body. Kiara had really messed her up, maybe even worse than she had initially thought.

“Beloved,” Lilian muttered as she fell back to the bed. She didn't struggle against Kevin's attempts to persuade her to lie back down. There really wasn't much she could do to fight him anyway, not with how hurt she was.

“How are you feeling?” Kevin asked, then paused. His face scrunched up a moment later, and he shook his head, embarrassed. “Sorry. That was a stupid question.”

Lilian smiled and shook her own head. His concern warmed her heart.

“I'm,” she paused, then grimaced, “Well, I'm alive. I suppose that's something.”

“Yeah, something.” Kevin frowned as he looked her over, checking to see if she had aggravated any of her injuries while trying to get up. “Where does it hurt?”

“Where doesn't it hurt?” Lilian answered his question with one of her own. Kevin opened his mouth to speak, but she beat him to the punch. “If you're asking me if there are any specific places that I'm hurting, then my face, chest and stomach hurt more than anywhere else.”

“I see,” Kevin looked at her pensively, as if he was unsure of what to say or do in this situation. She didn't blame him. “Is… is there anything I can do to help?”

“Just you being here is enough,” Lilian informed him, a soft smile curving her lips into a delightful shape. Seeing the love of her life acting so worried about her made her feel very good, content even, like so long as he continued looking at her with that expression of concern, nothing else mattered.

It almost made getting her ass kicked by an inu yōkai worth it.

"Ah… well…" He rubbed the back of his head with his right hand and looked away awkwardly. "T-thank you for that, I guess. But what I meant was… erm…"

Lilian almost giggled at the expression on her mate's face. He always looked so adorable when he got embarrassed. Maybe that's why she loved flustering him so much.

"If you really want to help, maybe you could make me something to eat? I'm a little hungry," she said, right before her stomach chose that moment to make its presence known by rumbling, loudly. It was so loud, in fact, that it sounded more like the dying roar of a prehistoric beast than the stomach of a hungry fox-girl. Hearing her stomach moan in such an unsightly manner caused two dark red spots to appear on her cheeks, as a good deal of blood gathered to her face. "Okay… so maybe I'm more than just a little hungry."

Now it was Kevin's turn to be amused. He chuckled, lips peeling back in a small grin.

"I kind of figured you would be hungry, so I took the liberty to making something for when you woke up. Hold on just a second, while I go get it."

As Kevin walked out of the door, leaving Lilian to her own devices, she realized something about her mate's room. It was a very lonely place without him. Despite the fact that nothing had changed about the room itself, without her beloved's presence to brighten it up, the interior space seemed dull, lifeless, and made her incredibly uncomfortable to be in. She felt like an intruder.

Thankfully, she wasn't left alone for long. Kevin returned less than five minutes later with a plate of food in his hands. He walked over to the bed and sat next to her, a small depression forming in the mattress as it accommodated for the new weight.

"Can you move at all?" he asked, remembering the last time they had been in this situation. Back then, their roles had been reversed. After Chris had nearly killed him, he hadn't been able to move at all, and the girl lying on his bed had been forced to feed *him.*

That had been embarrassing, at least for Kevin. Lilian had thoroughly enjoyed the opportunity to do something so intimate for her mate.

Lilian raised a hand, then hissed in pain. Her muscles went into a series of spasms, twitching erratically as her arm flopped onto the bed. She imagined this was what it would feel like to plug her finger into an electric socket.

"Don't strain yourself," Kevin told her, setting the plate on the nightstand. "Here, let me help you sit up, then I'll feed you."

Kevin scooted closer, sliding a hand behind Lilian's back to help her sit up, while steadying himself with the other hand. Lilian didn't resist, though she did wince several times as pain flared up in her stomach and chest. It was not a very good feeling, and Lilian hoped to never be in this kind of agony again. Once she sat up, Kevin fluffed her pillow, and placed another one behind her to make sure she was comfortable.

"Thank you, Beloved." Lilian's grateful smile caused Kevin to smile in return.

"You're welcome."

With Lilian sitting, the blond teen began to feed her.

Lilian wasn't really sure if there were any words in the human dictionary to describe how happy she felt in that moment. Her beloved, her mate, the person who had become more important than anyone else, was taking care of her; acting concerned, fluffing her pillows, and feeding her. He had even done a pretty decent job of bandaging her injuries. She was sure that she would look back on this moment as one of the happiest in of her life.

And it would be, but only until the next happiest moment of her life came along. There would be many of them, but they would come with a few hardships as well—let's call them bumps in the road.

This euphoria did not last long, as her mind forced her to remember the series of events that landed her in this position in the first place, along with the aftermath of those events.

"Beloved?"

At the sound of Lilian's strangely demure and soft spoken voice, Kevin stopped feeding her. Upon casting her a cursory glance, the young man easily noticed the pensive expression on her face; the way her head tilted slightly, causing her bangs to hover over her eyes, and the way she worried her lower lip between her teeth. He had known Lilian long enough by now to recognize when something was troubling her.

"What's wrong?"

"Am I…" Lilian hesitated for just a second before plowing on. "Am I a burden to you?"

Kevin looked startled for a moment. He stared at the girl, his eyes larger than normal and his mouth hanging open. He wondered why she would ask him something like that. It was only when he thought back to one particular moment, when he had arrived at the aftermath of her battle, that he realized there could only be one reason Lilian would ask such a question.

"You heard me talking to Kiara, huh?" He sighed. "Look, Lilian, I'm not going to lie to you. When we first met, you were the biggest pain in my backside that I've ever known. You barged into my life, not giving any thought as to how I might feel about you making me your mate. You didn't even ask me if I *wanted* to be your mate. You just decided this for yourself, without any regards for me or my feelings. Within a week you turned my entire world upside down, and not in a good way. You've caused me so many problems, and in such a short amount of time—I even thought about throwing you out several times."

It was surprisingly blunt for Kevin, but even someone of his saintly patience had their limits. He had likely exceeded those limits long ago, and was only just now beginning to crack under the pressure.

Lilian flinched at the honest words her mate spoke. It hurt to hear him say these things. And even though she tried to simply accept that he felt this way, her eyes soon began to water

"So… I guess… it would be better if I left, wouldn't it?"

Just uttering those words caused her throat to constrict, as if they brought about their own special brand of damnation. The mere thought of leaving her beloved was almost too painful to contemplate.

And yet, she knew that if he asked her to, she would leave, because she loved him. If leaving would make him happy, she would do so—even if it meant losing her own chance at happiness.

"Leave?" Kevin looked at the girl strangely. "I don't want you to leave."

"Huh?" Lilian blinked. Twice. "B-but you just said—"

"I said that when we first met, you caused me a lot of problems," Kevin interjected. "I didn't say anything about wanting you to leave. You can stay here as long as you want." His hand went to the nape of his neck, his face becoming bashful. "To be honest I…" He looked away, his cheeks staining red. "I kind of like having you here… now… it keeps things interesting, you know?"

Lilian stared at him with wide, searching eyes. Just what she was looking for was unknown, but if Kevin were to take a guess, he felt confident that any theory he came up with would be fairly accurate.

"Do you…" Lilian swallowed heavily. Her throat felt very dry some reason. Parched. Like she hadn't drunk any water in days. "Do you really mean that?"

"I do," he answered, "I never told anybody this, but I've never really liked living by myself. Everyone I know thinks it's awesome that I live on my own, because I don't have to follow any rules, and I can stay up as late as I want, but it's really not everything it's cracked up to be. It gets lonely, and there were times when I used to wish that someone lived with me just so I wouldn't be alone anymore. I, uh…" Kevin coughed into his hand, clearing his throat. "I haven't felt that way for a while now, though, ever since you came, so I… well, you know…"

As Kevin trailed off, there were several long seconds in which neither of them spoke. A startling silence permeated the room, broken only by the air conditioning kicking in.

Kevin shifted, flushing slightly as he waited for her to say something. At the same time, however, Lilian was kind of speechless.

Finally…

"So… you don't think I'm a burden? You don't find me annoying?" Lilian asked in a small voice, her fists tightly clenching the sheets that covered her legs.

Guilt welled up inside of Kevin when he saw the girl's shoulders begin shaking, and the barely constrained tears in her eyes. He wasn't exactly sure why he felt guilty, but he did.

"No," he said softly. His hand twitched, but he resisted the strange urge to raise it and brush Lilian's tears away. "I don't think you're a burden or an annoyance. I may have felt that way once, but I haven't thought of you like that for a while now."

The glance Lilian shot him was one of incredible hope.

"So… you like me, then?"

"Of course," Kevin stated with conviction, "You're my friend."

"Your friend, huh?" A sigh passed through Lilian's red lips. Emerald irises glanced at him from beneath a curtain of fiery red hair. "Just a friend?"

Kevin shifted uncomfortably.

"I… can't really offer you anything more than that."

"Because you like someone else, right?" Lilian's smile was resigned. When Kevin looked at her in surprise, she shrugged, and averted her eyes. "I know you like that Lindsay girl. I knew you liked her from the moment I first saw you talking to her. I guess that's why I always felt so threatened whenever she was around. I knew how you felt about her, and I knew that if I wanted to have any chance at making you fall in love with me, I couldn't let the two of you get any closer."

Contrary to what Kevin thought, Lilian wasn't ignorant to some of what happened around her—at least where he was concerned. Even her bad case of selective hearing was more of a defense mechanism than because she wasn't listening to Kevin's words. A part of her simply felt that if she were to give in and listen to him, it would all be over; her dreams of Kevin becoming her mate would end.

Although it was beginning to look like her dreams had ended before they'd even begun, but that was neither here nor there.

"I see," Kevin sighed, "I guess I should have figured that." He glanced at her, then looked away and sighed. "I'm sorry."

"Hmm?" Lilian blinked. Her head turned away from the wall to stare at him. "Why are you sorry?"

"Because I never really thought about how you must be feeling, I guess." He rubbed his left cheek with an open palm. "It must be hard, seeing the person that you have such strong feelings for every day—living with them even—yet knowing they like someone else. It's got to be tough."

"You really are an amazing person." Lilian smiled when Kevin's cheeks turned fifty shades of red. "Here I am, the person who barged into your life, and you're feeling compassionate toward me, regardless of the fact that I've caused you so much trouble."

"Uh… well… that's because… it's… uh…" Kevin scratched the bottom of his chin with his right index finger. Looking up at the ceiling, he tried to think of something to say, but couldn't, so he did what came naturally.

He changed the subject.

"You should finish eating before your food gets cold."

An excellent change of subject indeed.

Kevin started feeding Lilian again. He had made her spaghetti with marinara sauce, so he had to spear the noodles with a fork and twirl them around, before lifting the utensil into Lilian's waiting mouth. Her lips would then close around it in a way that was almost seductive—strange, since she was eating food, which could hardly be considered sexy.

Strangely enough, despite the fact that Kevin found himself gazing at those luscious, ruby red lips in a way that was *less* than innocent, he didn't feel embarrassed…

… Well, he didn't feel *too* embarrassed, and what little embarrassment he *did* feel was overcome by the strange sense of serenity that filled him. There was something incredibly therapeutic about feeding Lilian. He didn't know why, but the act had an unusually soothing effect on him. How strange.

After Lilian had finished the last bite of pasta, she watched as he stood up to leave the room.

"Be—I mean, Kevin." When he turned back to look at her in surprise, she asked a question that had popped into her head while he'd been feeding her. "What happened after I…" she trailed off.

"You want to know what happened after your battle with Kiara?" Kevin managed to phrase her question as diplomatically as possible.

Lilian didn't say anything, merely nodding with a deep flush of shame on her cheeks. She disliked recalling how thoroughly she had been whipped by that woman. Stupid dog.

Deciding that he could spare a few more minutes to explain things to her, he put the plate back on the night stand, and sat down again.

"Not much happened, to be honest," he informed her. "After your battle, Kiara just kind of left."

"Left?"

"Well, I may have asked her to leave," Kevin rubbed the back of his neck, recalling his small confrontation with Kiara. "Though, I don't think that made much of a difference. To be honest, I don't think she really intended to do anything more than defeat you in combat. She said it was for what you did to her brother."

"Chris," Lilian uttered distastefully. Just speaking that name aloud left a foul taste in her mouth. She still hadn't forgiven him for what he'd done to her mate. She likely never would.

"Yeah."

Even if Kiara's henchmen had not told him that Chris was her brother, Kevin would've easily figured it out once he saw the added dog appendages she'd been sporting. There was only one inu they knew of that went to Desert Cactus High School, after all.

"Anyways, after I asked her to stop, she just left."

"I see." A pause. "And how did we get back home? I can't imagine you were able to ride your bike while I was passed out on the back."

"Ah! Ahahahaha! W-well," Kevin gave a nervous laugh, his self-consciousness easily visible. Seeing her beloved so flustered made Lilian even more curious. "Let's just say that I'm going to need you to work that kitsune magic of yours to make a certain someone forget that her car is currently missing from the school parking lot."

***

"What happened to my car?!"

Ms. Vis stared in horror at the place where her car had been parked. The key word being *had,* because it clearly wasn't there anymore, no matter how many times she rubbed her eyes to see if it would randomly reappear.

She had no clue what happened. She had just gone to fetch herself a cup of coffee while she waited for Mr. Swift and that girl to leave the school. After getting her coffee, she had come back, only to find an empty parking space where her Toyota Corolla had been.

"My… my car? What happened to it? What happened to my car?!"

Ms. Vis felt like something was swallowing her up. Her mind was consumed with panic. Her car was missing! Gone! How could this be possible? She had only been gone for fifteen minutes! It wasn't like there had been anyone left on campus to steal it. Even most of the teachers had already left. The only people still around had been Professor Nabui, who'd only left a few seconds before her and…

"That girl…"

Yes. Yes, it had to be her. There was only one person who could have possibly stolen her car, who would *dare* to steal her car, and she would pay. Oh, but she would pay dearly for this. Ms. Vis was going to inflict a punishment of such epic proportions on that girl that the students of Desert Cactus High would speak about it in fear for decades to come!

Raising her fist to the sky, Ms. Vis' wrath was shouted out to the heavens.

"Damn you, Lilian Pnévma!"

***

"Uh huh." Lilian needed a few seconds to properly analyze Kevin's words. "So let me get this straight, you're telling me that you stole a car, and drove it home?"

"At first I was only going to wait for the owner to come back and ask for a ride," he admitted, blushing at the girl's blunt assessment of his actions. "But then, I realized that it might not be the best idea to ask someone for a ride while carrying you in my arms."

Yeah, because explaining why he was carrying an unconscious girl who looked like she had been put into a meat grinder would have been such an easy task. He could just picture what would happen if he did that.

"Excuse me, but could I ask for a lift?"

"What are you doing carrying that girl around? Why does she look so injured? Le gasp! I know what you're planning on doing to her, but I won't let you, you fiend!"

"M-ma'am, what are you doing?"

"Calling the cops. Excuse me, 911? I'd like to report a rapist…"

Kevin shook his head. Not a good idea.

"Beloved?"

Realizing that he had gotten distracted, Kevin coughed several times and continued speaking. "Anyway, after that, I noticed that the door was unlocked and the keys were in the ignition. One thing sort of led to another and, well…" he trailed off, but that was fine. Lilian managed to figure out the rest easily enough, and she had only one thing to say about it.

"That was surprisingly reckless of you."

"Ugh, don't remind me. I think you're beginning to rub off on me." Lilian managed to give a weak smile at his joke, while Kevin stood up again and picked up the plate. "Anyway, I'm going to go wash this."

"Kevin?"

Hearing his name called again, Kevin turned around to face her.

Lilian twiddled her fingers together. Her cheeks were a little flushed as she stared down at her lap. He'd never seen her act so bashful and shy before. It was absolutely adorable.

Kevin found his breath momentarily stolen from him.

Unaware of the effect she was having on him, Lilian began speaking. "Um, I was just wondering—what I mean to say is—I know this is a lot to ask after everything you just told me, but I… I really don't feel like sleeping alone, so I was hoping you would, kinda… you know…"

"I won't sleep with you, if that's what you're asking." When Lilian lowered her head, he grimaced and added, "But if you want, I'll grab my sleeping bag from the closet and stay in this room with you."

Lilian looked back up at him.

"Will you stay with me until I fall asleep?"

Once again, Kevin understood what she was *really* asking him. Maybe it was because of the amount of time they had spent together, or maybe it was because of how close they had grown, but it was becoming much easier to read between the lines behind Lilian's words lately.

"Yeah…" Kevin's countenance softened as he looked at her. "… I'll stay with you. Let me wash these dishes and grab my sleeping back. I'll be right back."

Lilian watched as the door closed behind Kevin. When his footsteps receded to the point that she could no longer hear them, Lilian allowed several tears to run down her cheeks.

What was she going to do now?

***

"I can't believe you three lost to a kid."

The three goons flinched at Kiara's words. While her tone was neither harsh nor reprimanding, the trio couldn't help but feel like they'd disappointed the woman that they looked up to so much.

"We didn't think he would be so formidable," Tall tried to explain. "He was a really cunning fighter, quick on his feet, and able to adjust to our styles like it was nothing. He was also really adept at using the environment to his advantage."

"Yeah, yeah," Short added. "You wouldn't think so from just looking at him, but the kid's got some serious fighting potential. I think he might be one of those battle geniuses or something."

Kiara didn't think their loss had anything to do with Kevin being some kind of battle genius, but was more on account of Kevin's incredible dumb luck and them underestimating the boy because of his young age.

She didn't say anything, though. It didn't really matter anyway. She had accomplished what she had set out to do. Anything else that happened was of no consequence.

"But don't you worry, Mistress Kiara!" Short smacked his fat right fist into the open palm of his left hand. "The next time we fight that brat, we won't show him any mercy! He's going down!"

The other two nodded in agreement. They had no intention of letting what happened to them go unpunished!

"No," Kiara cut the man off swiftly. "You will not be going after him anymore."

"WHAT?!"

"I've already accomplished what I wanted in regards to those two, so there is no more reason for me to go after them. You won't be going after them, either."

The three men looked like they wanted to argue. They all had a beef with that kid now! He had humiliated them! How could Kiara expect them to just let this travesty go unpunished?

Wisely, they chose not to dispute her decision. They knew better than to cross Kiara.

"Anyway, we're done here. You three can leave."

"Yes, Mistress Kiara!"

Kiara sighed as she watched them go, ambling along the dirt road as they walked to their beat up little Bimmer. It was kind of funny to know they'd been beaten by a kid with no combat experience to speak of, but at the same time, it was pretty embarrassing too—especially for her. She had been the one to teach them martial arts, and their loss reflected poorly on her. Ah well. Such was life, she supposed. At least it kept things interesting.

With her three henchmen gone, Kiara walked to her car. She had upheld Chris' honor, as was her job as an inu and a sister. Now it would be time for them to part ways again. She had to get back to work. Those fitness centers didn't run themselves.

Chapter 10

Tension

When Kevin woke up the next morning, he knew that something was different. He didn't know what. His mind, lost between the realms of Morpheus and the physical world, lacked the ability to pinpoint just what that difference might be. The only thing he knew was that there was something about this morning that differed from every other morning thus far, an intangible feeling that slipped from his grasp the longer he thought about it.

Light blue eyes opened slowly, blinking several times as they were greeted by the ceiling of his bedroom. A thin stream of light filtered in through the curtains, which were partially closed. Dim as the room was, Kevin could still make out his surroundings just fine.

A small frown crossed his face. That ceiling looked a lot higher than he remembered it. Why was that? And why was his bed less comfortable than he remembered it being? And just where the heck had his memory foam mattress gone?

As he stared at the ceiling, trying to ascertain the reason it looked so much farther away than he last recalled it being, he finally stumbled upon the reason why that morning felt different from every other one.

There was no Lilian. The warm and very gorgeous body of his sexy housemate was not resting comfortably against his side. He couldn't feel her body pressed into him, snuggling up to him like he was some kind of over-sized plushie. He couldn't feel her arms wrapped around his torso, or her leg hooked around his, or even her tails as they wrapped comfortably around his stomach. That comforting, lulling sense of contentment and fulfillment that his mind had subconsciously come to associate with Lilian's presence was gone.

It felt weird not having her sleep with him. Kevin couldn't help but feel like some aspect of his life was missing. The disappearance of Lilian from his bed left him with a strange sense of loss that he couldn't understand.

Ugh, get a grip, Kevin. There's no reason for you to feel this way.

That's right. This was what he wanted, wasn't it? He should be happy that she wasn't sleeping with him. Yes, it could only be a good thing that Lilian wasn't sharing his bed—um, sleeping bag. He'd probably just grown too used to her presence.

Rolling over onto his stomach, Kevin struggled to crawl out of his sleeping bag. Maybe it had been a bad idea to zip this thing closed? Well, too late now.

After clawing his way out of his sleeping bag and getting to his feet, the first thing Kevin did was look at his bed. More specifically, he looked at the figure sleeping in it.

Lilian lay there, looking as peaceful as could be, considering the circumstances. The covers had been thrown partway off her body so that he could see her bandaged chest and arms, and one of her legs had fallen off the side of the bed, exposing her perfect foot and cute little toes.

He shook his head. There must be something seriously wrong with him if he was thinking about someone's feet like that. God, he really hoped he wasn't becoming one of those feet people he'd heard some of his teammates talking about. How creepy would that be?

Dispelling the disturbing thoughts from his mind, Kevin turned his attention back to Lilian. She looked much better today than she had yesterday. He hadn't wanted to say anything about it when she'd regained consciousness, but she hadn't looked very good. In fact, she had looked quite awful. Her face, and in particular her nose and chin, had been swollen and black, and her chest and stomach had also been riddled with bruises.

Those bruises were gone now, leaving her perfect, cream-colored skin unblemished. Kevin suspected that this healing of hers was a side benefit of her Celestial powers. Or maybe all kitsune had the Deus Ex Machina ability to heal themselves. Yet, even though she looked much better physically, there was something about her that appeared… off.

It probably had to do with the way her nose scrunched up in displeasure, as she frowned sorrowfully in her sleep, but it was more than that. He couldn't figure it out, but something, some inextricable part of what made Lilian who she was, appeared to have vanished.

Kevin tried not to think about that, however, and instead focused on his relief that Lilian hadn't been more serious. He had been very worried about her.

Deciding that the best thing to do was start his day, Kevin headed toward the bathroom, where he took a quick shower, and dressed himself in a pair of black jeans and a white t-shirt.

He returned to his bedroom to see that Lilian was still asleep. Kevin decided to let her sleep a little longer and make some breakfast. She had done it for him every day since arriving, so really, it only seemed right that he reciprocated. Lilian had been spoiling him a bit too much in this area anyway, and while he felt all warm and fuzzy knowing that someone wanted to take care of him like this—God knows his mother didn't—he felt like he was taking advantage of her kindness.

Women weren't the only ones who could cook. Kevin might not have been a gourmet chef, certainly nowhere near Lilian's enviable talent, but he considered himself to be a decent cook.

On the way to the kitchen, he turned on the television and changed it to the news channel. He didn't usually watch the news, because it never failed to depress him, but he wanted to see if there would be any information about his school. Given the amount of property damage it had incurred the day before, he suspected there would be some mention about it.

And so, while the news anchor told him about some terrorist organization killing people in the Middle East, Kevin whipped up a breakfast of scrambled eggs with some milk, cheese, chopped spinach and minced red onions. It only took a few minutes to make. He also put some bread in the toaster, to go along with the eggs.

"And in other news, it appears that several vandals have destroyed the property of Desert Cactus High School." Kevin's ears perked up as he began paying closer attention to the newscaster. "The damage done was significant. The school's gymnasium was completely demolished, and we've been told that restoring the building to its previous condition is going to take well over a month. The police have begun a search for the perpetrators responsible, though so far, there have been no leads. Principal Corrompere has declared that the school will remain closed until the gymnasium has been restored."

Kevin walked into the living room, two plates of food in his hands to watch the rest of the announcement. He watched as the screen displayed the damage done to his school's gym.

"For some reason the damage looks much worse on television than it did in person. I wonder why that is?" The result of being more worried about Lilian than the school, per chance? Or maybe being given a view from the perspective of an outsider made the destruction look more catastrophic than he remembered? "Ha… whatever. Not my problem."

He paused as another thought occurred to him.

"Does this mean summer break's going to be shorter?"

"When asked how this would affect the student's schedule, Principal Corrompere had this to say."

The image changed to display the principal of his school. Eric's father looked nothing like his son. Where his perverted best friend was tall, lanky and resembled a monkey, his father was short, fat and resembled a beach ball with hair. They were a study in genetic contrast.

"We cannot risk the safety of the students, which is why we're closing down the school, until repairs can be made. However, we also don't want this to affect their education, which is why we'll be extending the school year into June."

"Dang it."

With a heavy sigh, Kevin turned off the television, and made his way back to his bedroom. Lilian was still asleep, so he set both plates on the nightstand, and sat down on the edge of the bed. Turning to face her, he reached out with a hand to wake the gorgeous kitsune up.

His hand paused. Then started again. It changed course halfway to its intended destination. Instead of moving to rest on her shoulder, where he would have lightly shaken her awake, it went to her face. Ever so softly, his fingertips brushed a few strands of her lustrous red hair away from her angelically-crafted face. Those same fingers gently touched against her delicate cheek, idly tracing a small circle along her soft skin.

A second later he jerked his hand back when Lilian mumbled something in her sleep. The girl stirred a bit more, then snuggled back into the pillows. Kevin watched her for several seconds, blinking, before shaking his head.

What the heck am I doing?

"Lilian," he called out. Putting a hand on her shoulder, he shook her awake. Or at least tried to shake her awake. "Come on, Lilian, wake up. I've got breakfast for you."

"Mmm… oh, Beloved," Lilian giggled in her sleep. "Come here, you naughty thing you."

Kevin's face turned red, but he kept from losing his composure. She must be having a dream. Yes. Just a dream.

He tried again.

"Lilian. You really do need to wake up. I've made breakfast."

"Ufufufu, I have no issues with swallowing if you want me to."

"S-s-swallowing?!"

Kevin wasn't sure if he felt like he had been metaphorically punched in the gut, or if his soul had been irreparably scarred for the rest of his life. Maybe a little of both.

"Oh, don't worry about a thing." It sounded like Lilian was trying to reassure him of something. Kevin was most definitely *not* reassured. "I've been practicing."

"Practicing?" Kevin wasn't really sure what to make of that statement. A part of him was curious to know what she was talking about. The rest was dreading it. "Practicing for what?"

"You want to know how I could practice something like that? Ufufufu, it was while you were sleeping."

"Geh!"

Even when she was asleep, Lilian refused to stop causing him trouble.

***

Several minutes and a good deal more embarrassment later, Kevin finally managed to wake Lilian up.

The twin-tailed kitsune slowly opened her eyes. She blinked several times as the image confronting her swam into focus. When the blurry outline above her head was revealed to be Kevin's face, she offered the boy a smile.

"Good morning, Bel—Kevin," she greeted.

"Morning, Lilian." He smiled. "I made you breakfast. I thought it would be a good idea for you to eat in bed. You're still injured, and probably shouldn't be moving around too much."

"Thank you," Lilian murmured, warmth spreading out from her chest to encompass the rest of her body. Her mate really was the kindest person she had ever met to treat someone like her, who'd messed up his life, with such kindness. Last night's events did put a bit of a damper on her spirit, but she tried not to let that show.

"You're welcome."

Lilian sat up and rested her back against the bed. Her movements were much smoother than last night, less strained. She didn't even twitch in pain. Lilian thanked Lord Inari that she was a Celestial kitsune. She'd spent all night in a healing trance, which seemed to have paid its dividends.

Kevin set a plate of eggs on her lap, then grabbed his own plate. Picking up their respective utensils, the two began to eat in silence. It was a very uncomfortable silence, broken only by the clinking of silverware on plates. There was a heavy tension in the air, and neither really knew how to break it.

"I forgot to ask last night," Kevin started, trying to break the disquieting silence by satisfying his curiosity. "But I wanted to know, what made you decide to start calling me by my name?"

Lilian paused mid-bite. Slowly, she set her fork down and looked at the plate in her lap. She hesitated for a second, worrying her lower lip, before saying, "I just thought you might prefer it if I called you by your name."

"Ah," Kevin nodded to himself. "That's probably a good idea." Lilian looked away, not saying anything, which he noticed. "Is something wrong?"

"No." Lilian shook her head. "Nothing's wrong. Why do you ask?"

"I don't know, you seem… different."

"Different?"

Kevin shrugged.

"I can't really explain it, but you seem a lot different now than before your battle with Kiara. You seem more… melancholy, I guess."

Her fox ears twitching, Lilian shook her head. “I'm fine.” She smiled at him. “Thank you for being so concerned.”

Kevin returned the smile.

“What are friends for?”

“Yeah.” Lilian's smile turned morose. “Friends.”

“The school has been shut down while they repair the gym that you and Kiara destroyed.” Kevin switched topics. He felt for Lilian, he really did, but there was only so much that he could do to alleviate her pain. And unfortunately, returning her affection was not one of them—he still liked Lindsay. He couldn’t just *not* like the girl that he had crushed on since middle school because some other girl had suddenly come into his life, right? “They say the repairs will likely last somewhere around a month, if not longer.”

“You say that like the damage done to the school was my fault.” Lilian frowned. “That damn dog is the one who did all the damage, you know. I don't have that kind of power.”

“I wasn't blaming you,” Kevin said gently. “I was simply stating that your battle with Kiara has forced the school to shut down. Not that it was your fault.”

“Oh, I see.” Lilian resumed eating, mostly so she could hide the flush of her cheeks. After a few seconds, she managed to get over her discomfort, and looked at Kevin. “What does this mean for us?”

“It means that we won't be going to school until the gym has been repaired.” Kevin finished his own breakfast and set the empty plate aside. “It also means that the time the school is closed will have to be made up during our summer break. Instead of having a three month break, we'll likely have a two month break.”

“Oh.”

“How are you feeling?” Kevin asked, once again changing topics. “You were really hurt yesterday. I was worried for a while there.”

“I'm fine now,” Lilian reassured the boy, smiling at his concern. “As a Celestial kitsune, I have very powerful healing abilities. Most of my injuries have completely healed—I'm not even sore anymore. I should be good to go in another hour or two.”

"That's good to hear." Kevin looked truly relieved to know that her injuries were all healed up. "That's a really impressive ability."

"You think so?" A tiny bit of warmth suffused Lilian's cheeks at the admiration in Kevin's voice. Regardless of what happened last night, of the painful truths that she had learned during their conversation, it was hard not to feel good when her mate praised her like that. "Celestial powers are pretty good at healing, but Water kitsune are better; all of the best healers are Water kitsune."

"Why water? I would have thought healing would be a Celestial specialty."

Lilian shook her head.

"Celestial kitsune do have the ability to heal due to our powers being divine in nature, but we are also capable of great destruction. Some of the most powerful and destructive techniques are Celestial attacks. Only the Void is more destructive, and that's just because of the nature of Void powers."

Kevin nodded at her words, even though he had no real clue what she was talking about. He didn't know what this *Void* was, but it sounded pretty bad. Didn't Void mean *nothing*? What kind of abilities would someone who had control over *nothingness* possess?

A shiver ran down his spine, as he imagined someone who could erase anything they touched from existence. That was a scary thought.

"Water, on the other hand, is not that destructive," Lilian continued. "Sure they have a few attacks, and there is certainly no denying that water can be very powerful. Anyone who's ever seen a tidal wave engulf a town knows this, but most water-based powers are healing in nature—at least until a Water kitsune gains more tails. I think four tails is when they have enough power to use the really big attacks. That's what Kotohime told me."

"Huh." Kevin rubbed the nape of his neck. "I would have never thought water powers would be mostly healing-based."

"That's because you read too much *Shinobi Natsumo*." Lilian gave the boy she loved an indulgent smile. "Not that there is anything wrong with that; it's an awesome manga, but the manga that you read aren't really conductive to kitsune powers."

"I guess." Kevin had the decency to look sheepish as he was called out on his attempt at comparing kitsune powers to something that he was more familiar with. "Anyway, I should probably clean the dishes."

"I'll help," Lilian scooted to the edge of the bed as Kevin stood up and grabbed the plates.

"You don't have to," Kevin told her, "I can do this. You should probably stay in bed and get some more rest."

"I've rested enough," Lilian declared as she swung her legs over the bed and stood up. "And my injuries have all healed. Plus, I don't really want to stay in bed. I would much rather get up and stretch my legs."

Examining the girl for several seconds with a silent gaze, Kevin eventually nodded.

"All right, we'll wash the dishes together like we usually do, then."

"Thank you!"

"But before that," Kevin's cheeks flushed with blood as he turned his head. Lilian looked at the boy curiously. Why had he turned away from her? Was something wrong? "Maybe you should put some clothes on."

That's when Lilian realized that she wasn't really wearing much of anything; just a few bandages around her chest, stomach and shoulders, and a pair of flannel pajama pants that belonged to Kevin. Nothing else.

"Oh, right," she muttered, looking down at her state of undress. When she looked back up at Kevin, a sly smile tugged at the corners of her mouth. "So, Be—Kevin, would you like to tell me just how it is that I've gone from wearing jean shorts and a shirt to pajamas and a couple of bandages?"

Cue massive blush.

"A-Ah! T-that is… w-well, you know, it's like…"

"Hmm?" Lilian's smile widened as she leaned forward, hands behind her back, and an expectant look in her half-lidded, sensual eyes. "It's like… what?"

"I-It's because you were so injured, and uh, well, i-it's not like I wanted to look or anything—I mean I did! No! Wait! I didn't! It's just, you know… I kinda had to… uh…"

Kevin was grasping at straws as he tried to find some excuse that *wouldn't* make it sound like he had enjoyed getting an eyeful of Lilian's gorgeous, generously proportioned body as he bandaged her wounds.

He didn't do a very good job.

"A-anyway, why don't you get changed while I wait outside! Okay? Good, I'llseeyououtthere!"

Lilian smiled as Kevin bolted out the door and slammed it shut behind him. It was good to see that she could still affect him like that.

Her mirth didn't last long, as she remembered last night's conversation. The smile on her face soon turned into a melancholy frown as her eyes dimmed.

With a sigh, she stripped out of the pajama bottoms, and unwound the bandages, before walking over to the dresser. Lilian outfitted herself in a pair of simple black stretch shorts that conformed to her bottom like a second skin, and a short-sleeved white shirt with black vinyl patterns running along the front, the hem and the ends of the sleeves. She couldn't find her sandals, so she decided to go barefoot.

Steeling herself, Lilian opened the door and gave Kevin a beaming a smile.

"I'm ready."

Kevin took one look at her outfit, then quickly turned around, and began walking down the hallway with an almost mechanical gait.

"Right. Well, let's go, then."

The pair made their way into the kitchen, Lilian discarding her dirty bandages in the restroom's trash on the way.

They took up what had become their standard positions: Kevin at the sink, blue rubber gloves traveling up to his elbows, and Lilian near the rack with a towel ready to dry the dishes once they were clean.

There weren't many dishes that morning, so they didn't focus too much on what they were doing, and instead made light conversation while they worked.

"What are we going to do today since we don't have school anymore?" Lilian asked. "I mean, it's Thursday, right? We'd normally have school, but since we don't, does that mean we should go and do something else?"

"I'm not really sure what we can do," Kevin admitted, "If it was summer, we could go to the pool and hang out there, or even go to a water park." He paused, thinking. "I suppose we could go to the arcade, but they won't open until ten, and it's only seven right now. That means we have a lot of time to kill before we can go there." His head tilted to the left as another short pause ensued. "We could also go to the mall, but none of the shops will be open until nine, so we wouldn't be doing much anyway."

"So basically, we have at least—" Lilian scrunched her nose up cutely. "—two hours to kill before we can really go anywhere." The inhumanly beautiful girl gave a soft hum, her two tails waving back and forth behind her. "We could play some of those video games you have here. Or we could watch one of those anime I saw on the bookshelf in your room."

Kevin glanced at Lilian out of the corner of his eye, then looked up at the ceiling and rubbed his jaw.

"I do have a few good anime, and it *has* been a while since I've seen any of them." Come to think of it, he hadn't watched any anime since Lilian came into his life. Maybe because his life almost felt like it had become an anime?

… He shook his head. No, that couldn't be it.

"Then that's what we'll do!"

Grinning at the enthusiasm that Lilian displayed, Kevin gave a light-hearted chuckle.

"All right, let's finish cleaning, then we'll decide what to watch."

***

After washing the dishes, the pair went back to Kevin's room, and looked at the large bookshelf filled with anime and manga—Kevin's biggest guilty pleasure. They searched through his collection, before deciding on one of the mecha anime, because nothing said romance better than watching giant fighting robots blow each other up.

The duo then adjourned to the living room, where they sat on the couch to watch *Full Metal Panic? FUMOFFU.*

For the second time that day, Kevin felt something inherently wrong with the situation. It took him a while to figure out what it was, and when he did, he found himself surprised.

Previously, whenever he and Lilian sat on the couch, even when they were playing video games, Lilian would sit as close to him as physically possible. And when they watched television, she would snuggle into his side, practically draping herself over him in a poorly-veiled attempt at smothering him with affection.

Now she sat at least six inches away from him. Far enough that there was no physical contact between them. He no longer felt the warmth that he had come to associate with her presence.

Have I really grown so used to Lilian's presence that it feels weird when she's not trying to get close to me?

He shook his head. No. Of course not. He just found it a little strange for Lilian to be this distant. He should be glad that she had finally realized that he didn't like her the way she liked him. Yes, this was exactly what he wanted.

So why do I suddenly feel like I'm missing something important?

"Is something wrong, Kevin?"

The sound of Lilian's voice had Kevin nearly jumping out of his seat in surprise. He looked at the redhead to see her staring at him in concern.

"I'm sorry, I wasn't paying attention. What did you say?"

"I asked if you were all right?" Lilian's frown deepened.

"I'm fine." Kevin's smile wasn't very convincing. "Why do you ask?"

"You're not watching the anime."

"Ah. I just got a bit distracted by something," he reassured the twin-tailed beauty, before turning back to the television just in time to see the main protagonist getting smacked in the back of head with a *harisen,* a Japanese paper fan, by the heroine for setting off an explosive that destroyed the school's shoe lockers. The main protagonist had done this under the apparent belief that someone had planted a bomb inside of his shoe locker.

It wasn't an explosive, however, just a love letter from a poor girl who didn't realize that the protagonist was a military nut with a distinct lack of common sense. Then again, she also didn't know that he belonged to a secret military organization, so Kevin couldn't blame the poor thing for her misconception.

Lilian looked at him for a second longer, her frown growing, but she eventually turned back to watch the show. If Kevin didn't want to tell her what was wrong, there was nothing she could do to force the issue.

Several more minutes into the anime, Kevin found himself sending occasional glances in Lilian's direction. Every time he did, she would notice and look his way, causing him to pretend he'd been watching the television. It was during one of these moments that he noticed Lilian was shivering slightly.

"Cold?"

"Hmm?" Lilian looked over at him. "Oh, yeah, a little. It's a bit cooler than I'm used to for some reason."

Probably because you're not trying to burrow your way into my side.

"Hmm. It might have something to do with the thermostat," Kevin said, "I like to keep it at a low temperature, though I'm surprised that you haven't felt cold before now. Especially since you wear such skimpy clothing."

Lilian pouted at him.

"I happen to like this clothing. It's not constricting like pants and long-sleeved shirts."

"Yes, yes, I know." Kevin waved his hand in the air, as if warding off a bug. "I wasn't making a dig at your choice in clothes." And how could he? She looked good in them. Even he would admit *that* much. "Though that does leave us a small problem." He studied the young woman for a second, before a small light flared briefly in his irises. "Hold on a second."

Kevin stood up, and Lilian watched curiously as he walked over to a small basket on the other side of the couch. Popping open the lid and reaching in, he pulled out a large, quilted blanket, which he took over to Lilian, and draped around her shoulders.

"Thank you." Lilian gave him a grateful smile as she wrapped the blanket around herself, folding the ends to engulf her like a cocoon.

"You're welcome."

As Kevin sat down, he eyed the girl with a semi-speculative look. She didn't fail to notice the expression, and gave an inquiring glance of her own.

"What is it?"

"Nothing."

Kevin looked away again, turning back to the television, and watching what had gone from the heroine beating the main protagonist with a *harisen*, to the hero undergoing a hilarious Extended Disarming while trying to rescue her from some thugs. Kevin eyed the pile of guns and ammunition that Special Agent Sousuke Sagara, pulled out of his clothes, absentmindedly wondering if he somehow had an Extra Dimensional Storage Space somewhere on his person.

Then he remembered that only women had Extra Dimensional Storage Spaces.

So how did that man carry all those guns around?

A good question, and one that Kevin was sure Otaku worldwide had asked themselves at some point.

"You're sure it's nothing?" Lilian asked. Kevin nodded, not taking his eyes away from the television.

"Positive."

Lilian frowned, unsure of whether or not she should call Kevin out on his strange behavior. He wasn't acting like himself. While she was no n*ekomata* (cat yōkai), as a kitsune, she held a natural curiosity toward things she didn't understand, and she didn't understand why Kevin was acting so differently.

In the end, she also turned back to the anime. As curious as she was, she didn't want to intrude.

The silence that soon engulfed the pair was truly unsettling, stifling even. After their heart-to-heart the night before, neither of them could really think of what to say to the other. All of their conversations thus far had been awkward and forced, or eventually became awkward after reaching a certain point.

For Kevin, the reason was simple. Ever since her appearance in his life, all he had wanted was for Lilian to leave. He may have been too nice to throw her out, but that didn't really change the fact that his life had become a mess ever since she had barged into it. Barring her leaving, he had wanted her to stop trying to seduce him. He hadn't thought that was too much to ask for.

She had finally done just that, yet Kevin didn't feel the satisfaction that he had been expecting, and he didn't know why. What's more, he no longer knew how they should define their relationship now that the key component defining it was gone.

It was a perplexing predicament to the young man, who had never really been in a relationship like this before. Too bad he didn't know anyone who could help him with this. As far as he knew, no one else had ever been in a situation like his—except for those anime characters that he loved watching so much.

Unfortunately, no amount of anime would help him here—unless he planned on trying to go the harem route, or something, which would probably end in a very painful and humiliating fashion for him.

Harem protagonists in popular anime never had an easy time, what with having to deal with tsunderes and yanderes and various other dere-type women either fighting over them, or trying to kill them—sometimes women who did both at the same time!

Yes, Kevin felt very fortunate that he was not one of those harem protagonists, because that would suck, regardless of what every ecchi-loving Otaku in the world thought. Just look at that poor bumbling fool from *To Love Ru.*

While Kevin struggled to cope with the new issues he faced, Lilian's thought process was a bit more complex, but still very simple.

For the whole of the time that she had been living with Kevin, she had dedicated herself to earning his love—or trying to seduce him, but that was merely semantics. To a kitsune, they were one and the same. However, having finally discovered what Kevin really thought about her, she understood that her attempts to make him love her were having the opposite effect, and she no longer knew what to do.

She wanted him to love her. She wanted him to hold her, to kiss her, and hopefully, eventually, make love to her one day. Her soul cried out for these things, yearning for them with a fervent zeal that she had only felt once several years ago.

But Kevin had no intention of committing any acts of passion and eroticism with her, and she had been unable to convince him otherwise. Because of that, she no longer knew how to make him fall in love with her. If showing off a little (or a lot) of skin and using her boobs didn't work, then what would? How could she make her mate love her the same way that she loved him?

Needless to say, they were in a problematic situation. Neither of them was really sure of their position with the other anymore; Kevin was confused about his feelings towards Lilian, and Lilian was just plain confused.

"So, I was thinking."

Lilian very nearly shrieked and jumped out of her blanket when Kevin suddenly spoke up, so lost was she in her own thoughts. A glance at the boy showed him looking anywhere but at her.

"Maybe when we go to the mall, we can get you some winter clothes. It's still a bit early, and it won't begin to get really cold until November, but if we do it now, we can beat the rush when all the snow birds come over."

Lilian blinked.

"Snow birds?"

"Old people who have retired and like to live in Arizona during the winter, because it's still the warmest state regardless of the season."

"Oh." That made sense. "That does sound like a good idea, but is it all right for you to buy me any more clothes?" She looked down at herself, or the blanket covering her body, picturing the outfit she had on underneath. "You've already bought me a lot, including all my toiletries and underwear." Kevin blushed at the mention of underwear, but Lilian either wasn't paying attention, or chose to ignore his reaction. "It wouldn't feel right if you bought me anymore."

"Why are you feeling this way now?" Kevin was curious. "You didn't seem all that bothered when I bought you clothes last time."

He sighed when Lilian flinched. She was obviously beginning to feel guilty, though he didn't know why.

"Listen," he said softly. "It really is all right. I don't mind buying you some more clothes."

"Really?" She turned her head toward him, her large emerald eyes looking entirely too vulnerable. There were so many emotions reflected in those bright green orbs that it would be impossible for most people to get a read on her mental state. Even an expert at interrogation and human psychology would be unable to read the windows to that soul.

"Really," Kevin told her. An interrogation specialist might have had trouble, but he could read her just fine—a side effect of living with Lilian for just under three weeks. He could pretty much read the girl like a book these days.

"Okay." Lilian looked down at her lap, where she was twiddling her fingers. It was impossible to see her eyes because they were hidden by a curtain of hair, but her cheeks were still visible, and they looked a touch pink. "Thank you, Kevin."

"Hmm." A small, unsure, half-smile appeared on his face. "Don't mention it."

Just then, there was a loud banging on the door. Kevin and Lilian shared a look. Who could be knocking at this hour? And why weren't they using the doorbell?

The knocking increased in intensity, until it sounded like the person on the other side was trying to break the door down. Kevin and Lilian stood up and walked to the door.

"I wonder who this could be," Kevin muttered as he opened the door.

And ended up staring at the person standing on the other side in shock.

What the heck was *she* doing here?

"You…!" Ms. Vis growled, staring daggers at the kitsune, who'd had the foresight to hide her tails and ears. The stern math teacher looked dreadful; large bags hung under her eyes, and her hair was in complete disarray. Her pale face was even paler than usual—deathly pale to the point of being almost translucent. The whites of her eyes were bloodshot, and her irises had shrunk to tiny pinpricks no larger than the tip of a pencil. She looked like a vampire who'd tried to cold turkey their blood addiction and had epically failed. "How dare you do this to me!"

Lilian looked at the woman in confusion.

"Um, what?"

"Don't act like you don't know!" Ms. Vis shouted, pointing an accusing finger at Lilian. "You know exactly what you did! And if you think you can get away with it, you've got another thing coming! Kukukuku…" Lilian and Kevin both took a step back as the woman let loose with the creepiest laugh they had ever heard.

It was remarkable, but Kevin actually thought her laughter was even creepier than Lilian's perverted giggling. "Oh yes, I'm not letting you get away with this! I'm going to punish you for thinking you can get away with stealing my car!"

"Car?"

While Lilian looked even more confused, Kevin gasped.

"Lilian!" He hissed in her ear. Lilian shuddered as his hot breath hit her earlobe, but she resisted the urge to jump him. Barely. "The car I took yesterday! It must be Ms. Vis's!"

"Oh."

Now Lilian understood what was going on. This woman thought that she had stolen her car—though, just why the math teacher had singled her out was beyond the girl's comprehension. What had she done to warrant such hostility?

"Don't worry, Be—Kevin." She frowned. Calling her mate by his name was going to take some serious getting used to. "I've got this."

She turned back to Ms. Vis, her eyes glowing a bright green. The math teacher's eyes glazed over, becoming dull and lifeless.

"I did not steal your car."

"… You did not steal my car."

"Neither did Kevin."

"… Neither did Kevin."

"You will take your car keys, drive back home, and forget this ever happened."

"… I will take my car keys, drive back home and forget this ever happened."

Lilian paused, then waved her hand in an exaggerated manner and said, "These are not the droids you're looking for."

"… These are not the droids I'm looking for."

As the dazed Ms. Vis left, stumbling down the stairs with an almost drunken gait, Kevin shut the door. He then turned to look at Lilian with a mile-wide grin. Lilian returned his look with a smile fit for a kitsune. A chuckle escaped Kevin's mouth. Lilian giggled. Soon, the two were in full-blown hysterics, their laughter ringing throughout the apartment.

"That was awesome!" Kevin compliment between chortles.

"You think so?" Lilian gave a grin that showed off her canines. "It was pretty cool, wasn't it?"

“Yeah, the way you went all Jedi on her was so cool,” Kevin praised the girl for her awesome abilities. “Makes me wish I had kitsune powers like that.”

“Given the number of contrived and clichéd plot devices this story has had so far, you might eventually gain strange powers. It probably won't happen any time soon, though.”

“Really? Well, I suppose I can wait for—wait. What did you just say?”

“Nothing.”

“It wasn't nothing,” Kevin insisted. “I could have sworn you just said something about plot devices and clichés.”

“I don't know what you're talking about. You're obviously imagining things.”

Kevin gaped at her.

“I—but you—but I know that—ah… man…” His shoulders slumped as he gave her a pout. “I really wish you would stop doing that. It always gives me a headache.”

“Sorry, B—Kevin.” She gave him an apologetic smile. “I can't help it. It's in my nature.”

“Whatever…”

The two looked at each other, the conversation trailing off. Silence filled the air again, uncomfortable, asphyxiating silence that felt smothering, like when someone shoves a pillow over your face. After several seconds of staring at one another, they finally looked away.

“We should probably head out soon,” Kevin said in an effort to fill the stifling silence.

“Yeah.” Lilian rubbed her left arm. “We should probably end this chapter anyway. It's getting a bit too long.”

“Would you stop that already?!”

Chapter 11

The Boy, the Kitsune, and the Yuki-Onna

It was strange, going to the mall during a school day. Whenever people thought of malls, they usually imagined this large, bustling building, or maybe a metropolitan plaza, filled with dozens of shops, stores and restaurants. They pictured busy sidewalks and walkways filled to the brim with pedestrians, all spending what little free time they had with friends and family.

What they did not think of was a large, empty building with only two or three dozen people walking around through mostly empty halls.

Because it was a school-slash-workday, the mall was more or less dead. The patterned walkways were free of traffic. There only seemed to be a few people here and there; a mother and father with their two kids, a few older teenagers who didn't have college classes that day, and some elderly people who had retired long ago and were able to enjoy life doing whatever they wanted. Kevin did notice one or two people that went to their school, but that was about it.

“Wow!” Lilian seemed surprised. “It's so empty!”

She also seemed intent on stating the obvious.

“Hush, you!”

…

“Lilian…”

“Ah! Right. My bad.”

Lilian poked her tongue out playfully, winking at Kevin as she bumped two knuckles against her head while saying, “Tee-hee.” Kevin decided to ignore the girl making a pose that she had likely seen in one of his manga. He quickly returned to their original conversation.

“It's usually like this on the weekdays,” he informed his red-haired friend as they walked down one of the many walkways, their footsteps echoing around them. The mall’s acoustics seemed different without hundreds of people in it. "I don't know how it is in kitsune society, but most people who work normal office jobs only work during the weekdays, which is why Saturdays and Sundays are so much busier."

"I see," Lilian muttered, poking an index finger against her lip. "So that's why people spend so much time at the mall on weekends, then?"

"Yes and no," Kevin said. "It's just the reason they don't spend time here on weekdays. People enjoy going out on their days off. They want to go somewhere they can spend time with friends and family outside of their home, if only to rid themselves of the monotony that's often associated with their daily lives. The mall is a great place to go on the weekends; there are shops and restaurants and the movie theater, all of which are perfect places to kill time."

"Oh," Lilian looked thoughtful. "kitsune don't have anything like that."

Kevin frowned at her.

"Then what do you do to kill time?"

"I used to spend time with my sister," Lilian answered. "Sometimes I'd spend time with my mom. Kotohime also followed me everywhere I went, and her sister was usually following Iris."

"So wait. You're telling me that you have *two* maids?"

"Did I not mention that before?"

Kevin twitched.

"No, I believe you forgot to mention that."

"Oh." A pause. "Well, now you know." Kevin twitched again. Lilian continued. "Let's see, I'd also go out into the village sometimes, but I never really liked it—too boring for my tastes, and all the people there are so old-fashioned. I also used to spend a bit of time with my cousins and nieces, but I don't think they like me very much."

Now *that* got Kevin's attention.

"Why wouldn't they like you?"

"Oh, no reason. We just had typical family arguments and stuff. Nothing to be concerned about."

Kevin didn't like the way Lilian waved off his question—he especially didn't like the bitter smile on her face. However, he didn't press her, either. She was entitled to keep her secrets, and he didn't want to make her uncomfortable.

He went back to their original conversation.

"It's better this way anyways. With so few people, we'll have an easier time shopping. No lines, you see."

"Mm, mm." Lilian nodded. "I get it."

Even though Kevin told her that it would be easier to shop, he didn't actually believe his own words. He didn't know why this was—no, actually, that was a lie. He did know why he felt this trip would be just as problematic as every other trip.

The people staring at Lilian. There may not have been as many this time, but what few people were present, eyed the gorgeous girl like she was a prime piece of meat hanging in front of a butcher's shop.

During their first shopping excursion, he had only noticed the stares people gave her objectively. They hadn't really been on his mind at the time. More like they had been the last thing on his mind.

That happens when you're too busy freaking out about the really pretty girl holding your arm within her bosom to pay attention to anything else.

Now he *could* see them, however. He could see the way people gazed at Lilian, their eyes brimming with lust as they stripped the redhead of her clothing—men, women, young and old, it didn't matter, everyone stopped to gawk as he and her walked past.

Kevin tried to put those stares out of his mind and focus on the task at hand. They had shopping to do.

While making their way to the nearest retail clothing store, the pair ran into a very familiar face.

"Is that Christy?" Kevin asked no one in particular, as he glanced at the girl walking down the opposite end of the walkway.

It was definitely Christine. There was no forgetting that gothic lolita dress, or that snow-white face, crystalline blue eyes, and pale blue lips.

Lilian took one look at the girl, then snorted. She forewent her earlier hesitation, and grabbed Kevin by the arm.

"Who cares? Let's just keep going."

"But wouldn't it be rude not to say hello?" asked Kevin, not quite understanding why Lilian didn't want to greet the other girl. Sure, they had been arguing during the match, but that didn't mean they couldn't learn to get along eventually. Right?

"Hey, Christy!" Before Lilian could pull him away from the other girl, without said girl noticing them, Kevin had begun shouting and waving the yuki-onna over. "Hey!"

Hearing her name being called, Christine turned toward the source of the voice. It wasn't long before she spotted the two very familiar figures. They weren't hard to recognize, nor were they difficult to spot in the sparse crowd. Kevin made it particularly easy to see him, what with the waving and yelling and everything.

With a slight smirk on her face, Christine walked up to the pair.

"Well, look who it is. I suppose I should have expected to see you two here, what with our school being closed and everything." The smirk on her face widened just a bit, as she turned her head ever so slightly to look at Lilian. "I'm guessing the damage done to our school was your handiwork? You're not very good at keeping on the down low, are you?"

A pulsing vein popped up on Lilian's forehead, throbbing angrily. The two-tailed kitsune glared at Christine, her left eye twitching intermittently.

"Don't try blaming me for what happened to the school. The one who did all that damage was that stupid dog, not me. Also, none of that would have happened if you hadn't run off like some kind of coward."

"You say that like I had a reason to stick around and get my ass kicked," Christine quipped, grinning when a low, menacing growl escaped Lilian's throat. "Unlike some people, I know the meaning of prudence."

The glare Lilian cast Christine looked like it could have cut through steel.

"And besides," the girl continued smugly as Lilian glowered at her, "Had I stuck around with you, Kevin here would have been on the receiving end of an epic beat down by those three thugs who attacked him."

Lilian stopped looking at Christine with DOOM in her eyes. She knew that Kiara had sent three people after Kevin, but had been so preoccupied with everything else that it had just slipped her mind.

"You protected Kevin from Kiara's goons?"

"That's right."

Lilian craned her neck to look at Kevin.

"She protected you from Kiara's goons?"

"Don't go asking someone else the same question you just asked me!"

"Yes," Kevin said, nodding. "She's actually the only reason I didn't get turned into a large bruise like you did."

"And you, don't go answering her, dammit!"

Lilian pouted.

"You didn't tell me that you almost got beaten up."

"There hasn't been a really good time to tell you." Kevin tried to shrug the girl's look off, but had some trouble. Her stare made him more than a little uneasy. "After our, um, conversation the other day, I didn't think it would be a very good idea to talk about it. And I had kinda forgotten about it anyway. Besides, I wasn't really injured or anything."

"Well… I guess so long as you're okay," Lilian mumbled. Despite her words, displeasure colored her voice. She was obviously bothered about not being informed of something so important. Actually, she just didn't like that Christine had been the one to save Kevin and not her. She was overreacting, she knew that, but that didn't stop her from feeling jealous.

While open-minded, kitsune are possessive creatures by nature. They don't like other non-kitsune coming onto *their territory.* And while Kevin could hardly be considered hers, Lilian still felt the desire to defend her right to be with him from the snow maiden.

"And speaking of yesterday," Kevin sent Christine a grateful smile. "I really am thankful for your help. I wouldn't have been able to get away from those three on my own."

"A-ah!" Christine gasped, her pale cheeks turning a mild red tinged with blue. "W-why are you saying this so suddenly?! Idiot!"

"Wha…?" Kevin was confused, naturally. "I was just thanking you for the other day." Seriously, what had he done to upset the girl now?

"You already thanked me yesterday, stupid! Or did you forget?!" When embarrassed, Christine resorted to insults. They were her fallback protocol for dealing with her own self-consciousness. "B-besides, I didn't do it for you! I just didn't want to be in your debt! That's it! Got it?!"

"All right, all right, I got it." Kevin held up his hands in a sign of surrender. "Sorry I brought it up."

"Whatever," Christine huffed, crossing her arms over her chest as she turned her head to hide the dark stain on her cheeks.

"Seems like someone here is a little *tsundere*," Lilian muttered. Christine whipped around to glare at her. She'd gone on the internet last night and searched for the term *tsundere*, so she knew what it meant now.

"What was that?! You wanna repeat that, ya damn vixen?!"

"I didn't say anything." Lilian's innocent smile didn't look very innocent at all. "And I certainly didn't say anything about you being a tsundere. Not at all. No tsunderes here. Did you hear me say anything about tsunderes?"

"Bitch!"

"Now, now." Lilian's smile contained massive amounts of victory and win. "No need to get so defensive. Otherwise people might think there's some truth to my words." Her smile grew when she saw the girl's face change from red to blue. "Then again, with the way you're acting, maybe I am onto something."

Christine grit her teeth.

"Bold words coming from a bitch in heat!"

"Don't compare me to a filthy dog, you loli wannabe!" Lilian's fierce expression began to match that of Christine's.

"Loli wannabe, am I?!" The girl in the gothic lolita outfit squawked in indignation. "I'll have you know that this outfit is authentic clothing from the late Victorian era! Besides, I don't need someone who dresses like a slut to tell me about fashion!"

"A slut?!" Lilian looked truly outraged. "I already told you that I'm still a virgin!"

"Doesn't change how gods-awful your sense of fashion is!"

"Says the girl who wears clothing made for flat-chested little girls!"

Glowering at the redhead, her face turning ice blue in outrage, Christine peeled her teeth back in feral snarl.

"People who wear this kind of clothing in real life don't have flat-chests, idiot!"

"Who are you calling an idiot?!"

"If you're too stupid to figure out who I'm calling an idiot, then that should obviously tell you who I'm talking about!"

"It was a figure of speech! And besides, the person who calls someone else an idiot is always the real idiot!"

"That doesn't even make sense!"

Kevin watched as the two began butting heads. Should he step in? He supposed coming between them before things could get ugly—uglier—would be the morally correct action to take. Then again, maybe he shouldn't. Christine and Lilian looked about ready to tear each other apart, and he really had no desire to inadvertently find himself on the receiving end of their hostility.

He looked at the two, whose argument had degraded to childish insults.

"Tiny-tot!"

"Whore!"

"Flat chest!"

"Pumpkin tits!"

"Pimple nipples!"

Yeah, those insults. Kevin sighed, raising his left hand to massage his neck as he muttered a small, fervent prayer under his breath. He then gave the two his attention again, having decided that, yes, he really should stop them before their verbal sparring came to blows.

I can't believe I'm actually gonna do this.

"Uh… hey you two…"

"What do you want?!"

"Yes, Beloved—I mean, Kevin?"

Under the combined glare of the two girls, Kevin shrank back, nearly crapping his pants at the vicious appearance his female companions held. The young man almost ran away screaming. Almost.

Taking a deep breath, Kevin gathered his courage and said, "Um, you two might want to, uh, you know, stop arguing."

"Why?" asked Lilian. Christine just frowned.

"Because you're making everyone else uncomfortable."

The two girls looked around to see that their little group had been given a wide berth. An *extremely* wide birth. There wasn't a single person within five meters of them. All of the people in the general vicinity had formed a large ring around them, gawking like they were a pair of wild beasts that might start attacking each other at any moment.

Several seconds of silence came and went in a tense form of peace. The two girls locked gazes, then just as quickly looked away with a mutual huff.

Kevin? Well, he just sighed in relief. Crisis averted, at least for the moment. He could only hope this peace would last.

Good luck, Monsieur Swift. You're going to need it.

“What's with the French accent?”

I thought it suited the moment.

“Oh. In that case, carry on then.”

Aye.

“Cut that out already!” A red-faced Kevin shouted at Lilian.

***

Despite how empty the mall was at the beginning of the day, as time went on, the crowd began to grow. By the time ten am rolled around, it seemed like the entire Desert Cactus student population was present.

Kevin felt very uncomfortable as he walked passed the many cliques that apparently had the same idea he did. He would like to say his discomfort was caused by the envious and jealous glares over ninety percent of the male population sent his way, as well as the occasional death threat muttered under someone’s breath.

That would not be quite accurate. While the angry looks he received usually caused discomfort, he had grown used to them. Sure, they had grown two-fold due to Christine’s presence, but that hardly meant much. No, these glowering looks were merely a symptom of the real problem, the one that made him feel like a small, insignificant ant standing between two giants—or a human standing between two incredibly angry yōkai who were leaking killing intent at each other like it was going out of style.

What did I do to deserve this?

“I thought you two were going to stop arguing with each other,” Kevin said meekly.

"We're not arguing," Lilian said, making it a point not to look at the other girl in their company.

"That's right. There's no arguing here," Christine added. "If we were, you'd know it. Little miss Fox-Whore here would be crying her eyes out."

"What was that?!"

"You heard me!"

With a sigh, Kevin pressed his left hand to his face. Maybe it hadn't been a good idea to say hello to Christine? Ah, well. It was too late to correct that oversight now.

"If you two aren't arguing, then what do you call this?"

While his words did not get rid of the tension, it did do a decent job of making sure the pair's argument didn't devolve any further. Both Lilian and Christine looked away with a huff, their arms crossed.

The trio soon arrived at their intended destination. It was one of the larger retailers that sold lower quality clothing for a cheaper price.

Kevin wouldn't normally shop at a place like this. Having a mom like his made him a bit more fashion conscious than most males his age. Actually, he was probably more fashion conscious than any straight man had a right to be, but that wasn't his fault.

Despite his natural dislike of shopping at department stores, Kevin didn't want to spend exorbitant amounts of money on clothing. He was already waiting for the hammer to fall with his use of the credit card that his mom had given him for emergencies. There was no need to get himself into more trouble when she found out that he had spent even more money on womens' clothing.

Mom's probably gonna think I'm cross-dressing or something.

Speaking of his mom, he wondered why he hadn't received a call from her yet. Knowing her as well as he did, he suspected that she wanted to discuss this matter with him in person, rather than on the phone, but had been unable to get away from her work. He was really not looking forward to that conversation.

Sometimes, I hate my life.

"So… what exactly should we be looking for?" Lilian asked as they entered the section that sold winter wear. It was located in the back of the building, because winter was still a couple of months away, though it would begin to get cooler once October hit. “I've never shopped for winter clothes before.”

Kevin looked at her, frowning.

“Doesn't it get cold in Greece?”

“Not really,” Lilian said, “I lived in a coastal village on a privately owned island, so while it did get somewhat cold during the winter, it wasn't enough that I ever needed clothing like this. And Florida almost never got cold, even during the winter.”

This wasn't necessarily true. As a kitsune, Lilian simply had a very different idea of what was and wasn't appropriate to wear regardless of the season.

It should be noted that kitsune didn’t really have any modesty… or shame, and their clothing reflected that. It was very rare to find a kitsune wearing something that wasn’t skimpy and designed to show off their unnatural beauty and incredible assets. It was also very rare to see a kitsune with small boobs, which explained their need to flaunt what they had.

“Besides,” she added, letting go of a jacket and standing next to Kevin. “If I ever did get cold, I could normally just use my tails to warm up. Or I could always change into my fox form if it got *really* cold.”

“Tch.” Christine tsked at the pair of them. From her expression, it would appear that she was annoyed by the topic of conversation. “Neither of you truly know what it means to live in the cold. I used to live in Alaska. It was always freezing there, twenty-four hours a day, seven days a week—the temperature always stayed well below zero.” She shivered involuntarily, as if remembering something unpleasant. “It was truly the most horrible place in the entire world.”

“You lived in Alaska?” Kevin asked. Christine nodded. “I remember visiting Alaska several years ago. When I was four, I think.”

“O-oh? Is that so?”

“Yeah, but like I said, it was a really long time ago,” Kevin said, then became curious, “So is that why you moved to Arizona? Because you don't like the cold?”

“Hnn.”

"Hmph!" Lilian snorted. "You hate the cold so you moved to a state that was hot for most of the year. Aren't you supposed to love the snow? What kind of yuki-onna are you?"

"Is that supposed to be some kind of insult?" Christine gave Lilian a frosty look. "Just because I don't like the cold doesn't mean crap!"

"But if you don't like the cold, wouldn't that mean you hate using your own powers?"

"Urk!"

"Before you two decide to start arguing over something pointless again, Lilian—" Kevin held out a dark red wool jacket with a double-breasted front that tightened around the waist and flared out at the hips, "—why don't you try this on and see how it fits."

"Uh, okay."

Taking the jacket from Kevin, Lilian quickly donned the article of clothing, putting her arms through the sleeves, and leaving it unbuttoned. She then looked up at Kevin and smiled.

"What do you think?"

"You look ridiculous," Christine declared with barely suppressed laughter. Lilian puffed out her cheeks as she gave the other girl a menacing look.

Naturally, the entire menacing appearance that she was going for was ruined by her childishly puffed-up cheeks. It was like looking at an angry chipmunk, if chipmunks could actually look angry.

"I don't want to hear anything from you! And I do not look like an angry chipmunk!"

Sorry, but you kinda do.

"!!!"

Eek! What a scary look! I-I mean, shutting up now!

"Lilian… you're doing it again."

"Oops! Sorry. Tee-hee!"

Kevin rolled his eyes as Lilian rapped her knuckles against her head.

"You really need to stop doing that. Anyway, Christine's right, you do look a little odd wearing a jacket with those shorts," he expressed his opinion much more diplomatically than the snow-girl. "You need some pants. Otherwise, you'll just look funny."

“So long as they're a pair of nice jeans that fit me really well, I guess it'll be okay,” Lilian grumbled a bit.

Christine just had to make an insulting comment.

“You mean jeans that look like they were painted on? How are you not a slut again?”

“Shut up, you!” Lilian growled. “I don't want to hear it from someone who dresses like a loli vampire!”

“W-w-what?! A loli vampire?!” Christine's right eye began twitching. “I'm nothing like Evangeline A.K. McDowel, you skank! Take that back right now!”

Evangeline A.K. McDowel—an all powerful, nine-hundred year old, immortal vampire from a popular ecchi manga.

She also looks like a nine year old little girl.

Lilian's smirk was one of victory.

“I never said anything about you looking like Evangeline. Something you want to tell us?”

Christine paled. The sly expression that Lilian wore didn't help her complexion any.

“Although…” The emerald-eyed vixen looked at the goth girl with barely concealed glee. She was on a roll. “Now that I've gotten a closer look at that outfit of yours, I have to say that the resemblance is uncanny. If you were a couple of inches shorter and had blond hair, you would look just like her. You're even as flat-chested as she is.”

Christine's face went from pale white to atomic red and then to deep blue in less than a second.

“Grrr! Shut up, you stupid, large-breasted bimbo!”

“Ha! You're just jealous that you don't have boobs like mine!”

“J-j-jealous?! Wh-why would I be jealous of those ridiculously-sized knockers of yours!? Whore! Skank! Slut!”

“Your insults are getting repetitive!”

“And yours are just as dull as always!”

“Whoa, whoa, whoa!” Kevin quickly placed himself between the two before the situation could escalate further. “Easy, you two. There's no need to start another fight now, is there?”

“I'm always up for showing this skanky little fox why she shouldn't mess with me!” Christine smirked, looking more than ready to put Lilian in her place. The air around her also began to drop in temperature, getting so cold that Kevin's and Lilian's breath came out as mist.

Strangely enough, while the two aforementioned people were cold (Lilian more so than Kevin), the one who looked the most uncomfortable was Christine. The poor yuki-onna was shivering horribly; her entire body shook like some kind of leaf caught in a stiff breeze. It seemed that when she mentioned how she didn't like the cold, she hadn't been kidding.

"I…" Lilian took another long, hard look at the other girl. She then looked at Kevin, and then back to Christine. Finally, she sighed and relaxed her posture. "If you don't want me to fight with her, Kevin, then I won't." She paused, then added, "At least not right now."

"Hmph!" Christine looked away with a huff, the temperature rising back to its normal 75 or so degrees as the yuki-onna relented her hold over her powers. "You're no fun."

"Thank you." The grateful smile that Kevin sent Lilian's way caused her heart to flutter. An odd warmth came to her face, like a good portion of the blood in her body had rushed up to her head. Light pink dusted her cheeks, traveling across her nose to form what almost looked like a bridge.

Feeling unusually bashful, Lilian looked down at the floor, the bangs of her hair hovering in front of her eyes, casting the rest of her face in shadow. Only the light blush on her cheeks and the small, almost shy smile on her face could be seen.

"You're welcome," she whispered softly.

Kevin gave her one last smile before turning it on Christine. "And thank you as well. I really don't feel like getting kicked out of this store because two of my friends were fighting."

"F-f-friends?!"

Looking like someone had just stuck her face in a deep fryer, only without all the oil, Christine did what she always did when she was embarrassed.

Tsundere protocols activated.

"W-who the hell said that we were friends?! Idiot! I-I never told you that we were friends!"

"Eh?" Kevin looked absolutely perplexed. "What did I do now?"

Placing her hand over her mouth, Lilian just barely managed to stifle her giggling with several coughs. "*Cough, tsundere Cough.*"

"What was that?! What did you just call me?!"

"Nothing, nothing."

"It wasn't nothing! You just called me *tsundere* again, didn't you?! I dare you to say that one more time?!"

"Hey, hey! No more fighting!"

"What makes you think I said anything? You must be hearing things."

"Bitch!"

"Flat-chested Loli!"

"My chest isn't flat!" Christine shrieked, shamelessly grabbing her breasts and mashing them together. "These might not be as large as those ginormous hooters of yours, but they get the job done just fine! Hell, it's even been proven that men don't always like big breasts!"

"Of course a girl with tiny lumps like yours would say that." Lilian thrust her chest out, causing her breasts to bounce enticingly. Several men that had decided to walk by at that exact moment passed out via nosebleeds.

"Oh, god! We've got more men passing out in aisle six! Someone, quick, call the paramedics!"

A group of paramedics appeared seemingly out of nowhere. Kevin watched absentmindedly as the unconscious men were placed on stretchers, and wheeled out of the department store.

"Huh." He scratched the back of his head. "Weird."

Kevin then turned back to the argument that was *still* going on.

"At least my boobs aren't so obnoxiously large that they'll cause me back pain in the future." Christine tried to look haughty and superior. She might have been able to pull it off, too, if she weren't still groping herself. "And besides, a couple decades from now when your tits are all saggy and gross, mine will remain just as perky as they are now."

"Are you two really going to talk about breasts here?" Kevin's question went ignored.

"You think my boobs will get saggy in a couple of decades?" Lilian looked smug. "Ufufufu, I've got a newsflash for you, frosty.

kitsune stop aging after they get their third tail." Lilian shamelessly hefted her "puppies" up and flaunted them to the blue-faced yuki-onna. "That means these babies won't be doing any sagging for a long, long time. Heck, my grandma is over a thousand years old, has bigger boobs than I do, and hers *still* don't sag."

Kevin covered his face with both hands. He couldn't believe they were talking about this.

"Must you two keep talking about saggy boobs? And do you really have to grab your breasts like that in public, Lilian?"

"Huh?" Lilian paused in her shameless groping to look at Kevin. "What are you talking about?"

In answer to her question, Kevin took one hand off his face to point at Lilian's chest. The fox-girl looked down to where her hands were currently cupping her superlative bosom. She blinked several times before responding.

"Oh." Lilian took her hands off her breasts. She looked back up at Kevin, her expression sheepish. "Sorry about that, Be—I mean, Kevin."

"It's fine." Kevin didn't even blush this time—which just went to show him how desensitized he had become to Lilian's antics. He felt like he had lost something important in all this. He didn't know if he should call it his innocence, or maybe an irreplaceable piece of his soul, but whatever it was, he could practically hear it giving one final cry of terror before going silent. "Let's… let's just finish shopping."

"Okay."

"And as for you."

"Huh?" Christine blinked as Kevin turned his attention to her. "What? Why are you looking at me like that?"

"You still have your hands on your chest. You might want to stop touching yourself."

"?"

Christine blinked. The time it took her to process his words. Eyes widening, she looked down at her chest to see that, yes, she was indeed still groping her breasts.

She then looked back up at Kevin, who was staring at her, waiting for her to take her hands off her chest. In a situation like this, Christine did the only thing that she could think of.

She screamed.

"KYAAA!"

***

After the moment of unintentional perversion had passed, the group of the human, the kitsune and the yuki-onna began their quest for several pairs of jeans anew. They walked to another section of the store, where various forms of female leg wear hung from racks, and lay folded up on shelves. There was a wide selection to choose from: jeans, capris and everything in between.

They headed straight for the rack with all of the jeans. Lilian had already made it perfectly clear that she would not wear anything else.

Lilian walked over to the first rack, which held several sets of blue jeans. As she perused the selection, Kevin rubbed at his sore cheek and glanced at the yuki-onna.

"Did you really have to hit me?" he asked Christine, taking his hand off his cheek to reveal the large red mark in the perfect shape of a hand print. "That really hurt, you know."

Christine just scoffed and turned her head.

"I-it's your own fault for saying something like that in the first place!"

"How is it my fault?" Kevin asked, only to sigh when she tossed him a glare. "You know what? Never mind. I don't want to know."

Turning back toward the red-haired member of their group, he saw that Lilian looked perplexed. In her hands were two different sets of basic jeans; one black and the other blue.

"Kevin?" she called as she held up the two articles of clothing for him to inspect. "I don't know which one I should choose. What do you think?"

"I think you should try them on before I can really give you my opinion," Kevin answered. "There should be a changing room somewhere nearby. Let's go find it, and you can try them both on."

"Okay," Lilian sighed. Together, they walked over to a small desk where a middle-aged woman sat.

"Something wrong?" asked Kevin.

"Not really." Lilian frowned as she looked at the jeans in her hands, as if they were the cause for her grievance. "I just never liked pants of any kind. They always feel so constricting, especially because I can't let my tails out. It's easy to let my tails out with shorts, but pants are too long for that. If I let my tails out while wearing them, I'd be forced to keep them stuck in one of the legs." She shuddered. "And that is not a pleasant experience."

"Really?" His brows furrowed a bit. "So that's the reason you always wear such skimpy clothing? Because it allows your tails more freedom?"

"Of course not." Lilian sent him a smile so wide that it forced her eyes closed. "I mean, yes, we don't like to wear clothing that keeps us from letting our tails out, but I only chose the clothes I have now because I wanted to look sexy for you."

Kevin twitched.

"So you were wearing them to try and seduce me."

"Yeah." A few seconds of giggling petered off as Lilian's beaming smile turned melancholy. She turned her head away from him, her lips curving downwards in a small frown. "Not that it really worked anyway."

"W-well, I wouldn't go so far as to say that." Kevin scratched his left cheek with an index finger. Lilian craned her neck to look at him, her eyes widening just a bit. His cheeks flushing slightly under her scrutiny, the young man nevertheless continued. "I mean, I always thought you were, um, like, really pretty, and everything. It's just…" he trailed off. He didn't want to mention Lindsay in this conversation. It would just hurt Lilian more. Besides, chances were good that she knew what he would say; they'd already had this conversation once.

"I understand." Lilian's countenance softened. Her eyes became warm and slightly misted, and a pretty pink coloration stained her fair cheeks. "And it means a lot to hear you say that to me. The compliment, I mean," she added after seeing him look at her strangely. "Thank you."

Feeling his own cheeks beginning to burn, Kevin looked away.

"You're welcome."

"Ugh, this is so disgusting." Christine grimaced at the two. "Would you two please stop making googly eyes at each other and get changed already. I don't want to be here any longer than I have to."

Lilian scowled. This girl just had to ruin the mood! Stupid, snow hating snow-maiden!

“Nobody asked you to come with us! If you don't want to be here, then maybe you should just leave!”

With one final huff, the redhead stormed up to the desk, and was assigned a changing room. Soon she was slamming the door to one of the changing rooms, leaving Kevin alone with the girl clad in gothic lolita garb.

“Do you really have to fight with Lilian so much?” he asked the girl with a small frown.

“I don't see why you care.” The yuki-onna had a bit of a frown herself. She crossed her arms over her chest, and looked at the changing rooms. “Besides, it's not like I was the one who started all of this. If that damn fox hadn't come up and started yelling at me during the track meet, I wouldn't have any problems with her.”

“Huh? So wait, you're telling me that Lilian was the one who started fighting with you?” Kevin was both surprised and not-so-surprised to hear this.

“Yeah.” Christine confirmed her words with a nod. “She just waltzed right up to me with that self-righteous attitude of hers and started yelling.”

“But why would she do that?” Kevin mused to himself. “Lilian's never been the type to just start randomly arguing with people. In fact, she generally tends to ignore anyone and everyone except for, well…” he coughed into his hand several times. “But, why would she argue with you if she didn't even know you? No offense, but that just doesn't sound like Lilian.”

“A-ah, w-well.” Christine looked away, causing Kevin to glance at her curiously. “She was asking me what my, eh, my, um…” pale, snow white cheeks became suffused with red as the girl began stuttering. “H-how we… I-I mean, how you and I…”

“Hey, are you okay? Your face is all red.”

A worried Kevin leaned in to get a closer look at Christine's face. Said girl leaned back, her scarlet cheeks quickly shifting from red to blue, as her embarrassment reached critical mass.

“I-I'm fine! Dummy! Idiot! Jerkwad!” The scowl was back in place. “Graaa!” Kevin stumbled several feet back when Christine shouted at him. “Why are you always doing this?!” He became concerned when she started pulling at her hair. “Getting all up in my face and acting all nice and stuff?! Huh?!”

"Did I… do something wrong?" Kevin asked uncertainly. He rubbed his cheek. He hoped she wouldn't slap him again. Once was enough for him. More than enough. That slap had really hurt. "I didn't mean to upset you or anything."

"Ugh… n-no, i-it's fine." Christine mumbled, turning her back to Kevin. She placed a hand against her chest, feeling the blood-pumping organ beating erratically against her ribcage. Why was her heart pounding so quickly? It felt like it was trying to beat its way out of her chest! "D-don't worry about it."

Not really sure what was going on, but realizing that he would probably be better off remaining ignorant, Kevin decided to do as Christine suggested.

"All right," Kevin said, shrugging.

While Kevin made what had to be one the most intelligent decisions in his life thus far, Lilian finally made an appearance. Stepping out of the changing room in a new pair of blue jeans that fit her beautifully shaped hips, heart-shaped bottom and killer legs perfectly, the stunning fox-girl looked at Kevin with a radiant smile.

"What do you think?" she asked, turning around and showing off her backside to the young man. Her hair long hair swished aside, allowing him to catch an unfettered glimpse of how well those jeans conformed to her small, shapely rear. "Do these look good on me?"

Kevin wondered why he found himself suddenly speechless by the sight of Lilian in a pair of jeans. Hadn't he seen her in far less? For the gods' sakes, he had seen her naked before! Multiple times! After being exposed to her beautiful, nude body, something as mundane as a pair of pants should be nothing to him! So why did he feel so strange? How come his stomach felt like it was being tied into knots? And why were there butterflies fluttering around in his chest?

Kevin took a deep breath.

I'm overreacting again. I need to calm down. This is just Lilian. Yes, just Lilian.

Feeling his heart rate slow done, he said, "You look really nice."

"You don't sound very enthusiastic." Lilian frowned. "Do they not look good on me? I can try on another pair if you want."

Kevin's eyes widened.

"No!" He flushed when several women who were shopping looked at him after he shouted. Trying not to let his shame bother him too much, he continued in a much softer voice. "I mean, of course not. You look really good. I was just…" *Come on, Kevin, think. Think!* "Thinking!"

Lilian stared at him.

"Thinking?"

Kevin nodded effusively, his head bobbing up and down like a bobble head found on the dashboard of cars.

"Yes, thinking. I was thinking and it distracted me."

Lilian did not look like she believed him, but was willing to go along with it.

"What were you thinking about?"

"That I really want to see you in the black pair next." It was only a second after saying this that Kevin realized what he said. His eyes went wide and his face began to burn. "I-I mean, I just meant… so I could decide which pair looked better on you… you know?"

Lilian had to hide her smile at Kevin's reaction. He looked so cute when he got all embarrassed like that. That he had essentially just admitted that he wanted to see her in more cute clothes was simply the icing on the cake.

Christine stood off to the side, silently tapping an agitated foot against the floor. She didn't have much of a part to play in this scene. She wasn't one for googly eyes and lovey-dovey crap like this. But she didn't say anything because, well, she just didn't.

Lilian decided not to embarrass him anymore. While it was fun, she didn't want to jeopardize their already fragile relationship and drive him even further away.

She did, however, toss a vicious glare at Christine when the other girl began to make gagging noises. She really didn't like the yuki-onna.

Several seconds later, Lilian stood before Kevin again, this time in the black jeans. Kevin was more prepared now, and didn't overreact this time.

"How do these look on me?"

"Really good," Kevin said after taking a moment to remember that breathing was necessary if he wanted to get any oxygen to his brain. Lilian gave him a beaming smile, which made his insides feel strange, like someone had stuck a furnace in his chest or something. Weird. "They really suit you. They outline you figure well, and allow you to show off your hips and legs while still remaining modest. And I like the black pair much better than the blue."

"Why black?"

"Because black goes better with your hair." Kevin nodded to himself. "Maybe it's my mom's influence, but I always felt like black goes better with red than blue."

"Huh. I see." Lilian appeared thoughtful for a second before smiling again. "In that case, I'll grab several black pairs."

"Does that mean we're done here?" Christine asked impatiently, a scowl marring her cute face. "Good. Then let's get something to eat. I'm hungry."

"If you're that hungry, you could always just leave and get something to eat on your own," Lilian taunted. "Really, ever since we ran into you, all of you've done is complain." She paused, then looked at the girl with a combination of curiosity and a hint of condescension. "And just why are you following us around anyways?"

As the question was asked, Christine looked at Kevin out of the corner of her eye. Kevin noticed her gaze and gave her a smile, which caused her to quickly look away.

"T-that's none of your damn business! Just hurry up and buy those clothes so we can get something to eat!"

"Maybe we don't want to eat. Did you ever think of that? Some of us might not be hungry." Just as Lilian said this a loud, rumbling gurgle, like the roar of a hungry lion, sounded out from her stomach. Two sets of eyes stared at the emerald-eyed fox-girl, who suddenly found herself blushing under the attention. "Okay. So maybe I'm a bit hungry too. It's been a while since breakfast, so…"

"Right." In a completely out of character display, Kevin decided to take charge. "Let's get those pants and that jacket, then we'll head to the food court. I'm getting a little hungry myself."

The group left the department store after buying Lilian's clothes. The redhead eyed the bag with a bit of distaste, which Kevin noticed.

"Do you really not want those pants?"

Lilian deadpanned at him, causing some sweat to run down Kevin's face.

"Right, stupid question. Forget I asked."

"I'm sorry," Lilian apologized. "It's not that I'm not grateful. I was just thinking about what a pain it's going to be to create a flap for these. I'm not really good at sewing."

"Flap?" Christine asked.

"I can't very well just cut out a hole in these, can I?" Lilian said, as if the answer was obvious. It wasn't, because neither of them were kitsune. Lilian pouted at the two. "I may not be able to let my tails out in public, but I'm not going to hide them at home. Therefore, I need to create a flap so no one sees my butt when I am in public."

"I didn't know you foxes cared so much about being modest," Christine uttered.

"We don't," Lilian admitted, her eyes narrowing. "But that doesn't mean I'm going to give everyone a free show either."

Kevin groaned when the two started butting heads again, sparks flying back and forth. Several people who had been walking near them backed away when a few errant bolts struck the ground, leaving black scorch marks in their wake.

"Please don't fight anymore. I don't know if I can take it."

As Christine scoffed and Lilian puffed her cheeks up like a balloon, Kevin sighed. These two were such a handful. He could only pray that they would stop fighting once they started eating.

Chapter 12

Possible Lunch Time Romance

Maybe it was just Kevin's imagination, but the mall seemed to be much more crowded once noon rolled around. The walkways were filled to capacity with pedestrians; the stores had hordes of men and gaggles of gals. There were also a lot more people staring at them.

This included a significant amount of stares from numerous boys Kevin's age—and even a few who were quite a bit older, too. Most stared at Christine or Lilian, but a few were glaring at him.

Kevin knew why they were glaring, of course, but he honestly didn't see what the big deal was. How could they possibly think this was fun? Did they truly believe that he was enjoying himself?

Probably. None of these guys knew what it was like to have two girls constantly fighting around you, always arguing, always glaring at each other, making constant snipes about each others' physical appearance, or just throwing about random insults like they were something everyone said in normal conversation. They didn't know how frustrating it was to deal with these two.

All they saw was a single male with two hot females sticking close to him. That was all they *wanted* to see.

Idiots. The whole lot of them.

It should not have come as a surprise that the mall became more active in the afternoon. People were getting off work and schools were letting out. It was only natural that a number of them preferred spending time at the mall instead of home. Kevin also suspected that most of the Desert Cactus High students had decided to visit the mall since school was closed. They had probably just woken up a little while ago.

Teenagers were lazy like that. It didn't help that most of them probably stayed up all night playing *Halo, Call of Duty, Dragon Age: Inquisition, Destiny* or any other number of games.

Now that it was nearing lunch, there were plenty of teenagers with voracious appetites wandering the walkways.

"Why the hell are all these people staring at us?" Christine snapped.

It seemed that Kevin wasn't the only one who had noticed the stares, and the yuki-onna made it readily apparent that she did not enjoy being gawked at like a maid at a cosplay café.

Kevin didn't particularly enjoy it either, but couldn't really blame everyone for doing so. They were a noteworthy group; the blond-haired, blue-eyed young man walking alongside two girls whose beauty differed vastly from one another: the gothic cutie with raven hair and snow white skin, and the gorgeous redhead with enchanting emerald irises, fiery red hair, and a body that supermodels would gladly commit genocide for. That was a lot of sexy in one place—too much for the average male to handle.

"I'm surprised you're just now noticing them," Kevin said.

Christine gave him a dirty look.

"It's not that I'm just now noticing them. It's just that all these stares are starting to get on my nerves."

Kevin shrugged. "You get used to them after a while." He sure had.

"Grr! Whatever!" Christine huffed. "That doesn't make being gawked at any less annoying!"

He didn't say anything, but Kevin did agree with her. It was bothersome. You'd think people would have something better to do than stare at a trio of high school students, but apparently not.

"Are people really staring at us?" Lilian looked around at all the other people they walked past. It was in that moment that she *finally* noticed the looks every single male in their vicinity was giving her—looks that she had been getting for the past three weeks.

She walked just a little closer to Kevin, as if subconsciously trying to use him as a shield. Now that she was actually aware of the men's leering gazes, Lilian felt very uncomfortable.

"You mean to tell me that you've been living in human society for Kami-only-knows how long now, and you haven't even noticed how many people stare at you?" Christine looked like she didn't know whether to be impressed or disgusted by Lilian's lack of awareness.

"Not really." Lilian shrugged, doing her best to ignore the lustful looks she only just now realized people were giving her. "I've been… preoccupied with other matters."

Yeah. Other matters, such as trying to get into Kevin's pants. It's hard to focus on the people around you when you're so caught up in your own fantasies of someone bending you over the table, taking you like a vixen in heat, and—

"Do you really have to say it like that?"

Are you denying it?

"Well, no, but the way you say it makes it sound so dirty."

It is dirty.

"Yeah, but still, you don't have to say it like that."

"Who the hell are you talking to?" Christine asked.

"No one."

Christine's right eye twitched.

"That didn't sound like no one to me."

"It was no one," Lilian insisted.

"Don't mind her," Kevin said, gesturing to get Christine's attention. He didn't want them fighting again. "She does this all the time. I find that it's best to just ignore her when she gets like this."

"Really? All the time?" At Kevin's nod, Christine gave him a pitying look. "I feel really sorry for you, then."

Lilian puffed up her cheeks and glared at the two.

"Thank you." Kevin nodded solemnly. "Your sympathy is appreciated."

"You're welcome." A pause. "But really? All the time?"

"All the time! She's always saying weird things that make no sense, and constantly holding conversations with herself, and then she'll say that she's talking to no one every time I ask her. It's really weird."

"You're right, that is weird. Who the hell holds conversations with themselves?"

"Trust me, you haven't seen anything yet."

While Kevin and Christine talked about her, Lilian's face had been growing steadily redder.

"Do you two really have to talk about me like I'm not here?"

"Do you have to talk to break the fourth wall every other paragraph?"

"… Touché." Lilian gave Kevin an appraising look before returning to their original subject. "Anyway, I don't really care about these other people. Why should I care if they stare at me?" she asked, though it sounded more like she was trying to comfort herself than because she actually believed her own words. "They don't matter to me."

Kevin looked at her, his eyes compassionate.

"They make you uncomfortable, don't they?"

"… A little." Lilian admitted reluctantly. She didn't want to admit that she disliked the looks people gave her—she was a kitsune for Inari's sake! They reveled in attention! Or they were supposed to. But she couldn't lie to her mate. "There's only one person in this entire world who I want looking at me like that. I don't care about anyone else. The only person whose eyes I want on me is the one that I love," she finished softly.

Kevin felt odd; a combination of guilt and elation. He truly wished that he could give Lilian what she wanted. But how could he when he still had feelings for Lindsay? Lilian wouldn't want him like that anyway. She wanted his love, not his pity.

He would admit that Lilian was one of the most beautiful girls he knew; prettier than Lindsay, cuter than Christine, and hotter than any supermodel. Lilian was like those females you see in popular *Shōnen* anime; too beautiful to be human. Her beauty made his chest flutter, and his stomach twist, but he just couldn't love her.

He loved Lindsay.

He had to.

If he didn't love Lindsay, then why did he spend the last three years of his life pining after her from a distance?

"I doubt any of these guys would actually bother trying to hit you up," Christine informed the other girl. She eyed the many lecherous gazes lingering on them scornfully. "Most of them will simply be content to lust after you from a distance, acting like you're some kind of untouchable goddess or something equally stupid. Tch." She scowled. "They're just a bunch of cowardly, perverted idiots."

"You said it." Lilian nodded in agreement. Christine's words made her feel a bit better.

The two shared a look of camaraderie, for once completely in sync with each another. Kevin resisted the urge not to facepalm.

"Of all the things that you two could agree on, of course it would be *that.*"

"KEVIN SWIFT!"

Kevin groaned. Christine blinked. Lilian actually sighed.

"YOU'VE GOT SOME EXPLAINING TO DO!"

Three sets of eyes turned to look at Eric Corrompere, who marched toward them, an enraged look on his face. Kevin wondered what he'd done to upset the idiot this time—and then remembered that he was standing between two beautiful women.

Before he could even begin talking to his unreasonably angry friend, Eric grabbed him by the front of his shirt, and began to violently shake him back and forth.

"What the hell are you doing here?! Never mind that—what the hell are you doing with two boob-dacious babes?! Why is it that you're always the one attracting the hotties, huh?! HUH?!" Eric began crying as he continued shaking his best friend, though right then, it seemed more like they were hated enemies—or at least the results of unreasonable jealousy. "First you steal my Tit Maiden, and now you've managed to sink your claws into another sexalicious cutie!" The shaking increased and blackness was soon creeping into the edges of Kevin's vision. "Grr! You have no idea how much I hate you right now!"

Once the shock of watching someone manhandle her love wore off, Lilian stomped over to the boy.

"What in Inari's name do you think you're doing to my Beloved?!" In her outrage, Lilian used her normal term of endearment for Kevin. Her voice was also loud enough that most of the people in the area stopped walking to stare at the scene. "Let go of him NOW!"

"I'll be with you in just a second my lovely Tit Maiden," Eric declared as he continued to shake Kevin like a ragdoll. "But first, I need to show this pompous ass what happens when you don't spread the boob-love!"

The shaking increased with renewed zeal. Kevin's eyes rolled into the back of his head.

While Lilian tried to get the stupid pervert to stop manhandling her mate without resorting to using any kitsune techniques—which never seemed very effective on Eric once he went into his pervert-mode—Christine wrinkled her nose in disgust.

"Ugh, don't tell me you two know this stupid pervert."

Eric stopped shaking Kevin as this new voice reached his ears. It was so beautiful, so heavenly; like the tinkling of a wind chime, soft and enchanting. It passed through his ear like a soothing melody. He *had* to know who that beautiful voice belonged to.

Lilian was still trying to get Eric—who, surprisingly, was ignoring her—to let go of her love.

"Hey, you stupid pervert! Let go of my Beloved!"

She wasn't having much success.

"…"

Kevin was unconscious by now. His head lolled back and forth, and his body had gone limp.

Slowly, very slowly, Eric craned his neck, the movement almost mechanical, like a machine that hadn't been oiled in several years. As his head turned, his eyes sought the girl whose voice had enchanted him so.

She stood there, looking like some kind of gothic sex doll straight out of one of his erotic fantasies. He had been so caught up in teaching Kevin a lesson that he had not taken the time to truly see just how frickin' delicious this goth loli was. If she was dessert, then he would definitely skip the main course to get a piece of her.

Her long black hair shone and sparkled like a thousand stars at midnight. Her gothic lolita outfit accentuated her delicate body; those soft, feminine curves, not at all like Lilian's bodacious figure, but definitely drool-worthy in its own right. While her boobs were kinda tiny—make that really tiny—there was something appealing about her smaller-than-average chest.

Never let it be said that Eric only liked girls with big tits. He wasn't the kind of pervert who discriminated against small breasts. He loved boobs of all sizes!

Seconds later, Kevin was lying on the ground in a crumpled heap.

"Inari blessed! Beloved!" Lilian stepped around to kneel beside her abused mate. She wrapped her arms around his torso and lifted him up. His head flopped around uselessly as she tried to shake him awake. “Kevin! Are you okay?! Talk to me, Kevin! Beloved!”

Kevin didn't respond, naturally.

While Lilian tried to bring her beloved back to the land of the living via more shaking—which did more harm than good—Eric appeared directly in front of Christine. It happened so quickly that the yuki-onna could only gape. One second the boy had been standing several feet away, and the next he was right in front of her. How could a human move that fast?!

The young man ignored the way the new object of his lustful gaze leaned back in disgust and surprise. His nostrils flared like a bull and steam shot from his nose, a rather prominent flush of red staining his cheeks. This blush, which could only be salacious in nature, spread from his cheeks to the rest of his face, going all the way down his neck to disappear beneath his shirt.

“You are one of the hottest pieces of meat I have ever seen!” He declared fervently. It was a declaration that did not mean much, since he made it to almost every woman he met, but Christine didn't know that. “Please let me rub my face between your wonderfully-tiny tatas!”

Christine stared at the boy for several seconds, gawking at him with an open mouth and wide eyes. Her mind went blank as she tried to comprehend his words. It took a while, because really, how many people were prepared to hear something like *that*? Not many. Despite this, she eventually managed to catch up with the lecher's comments, and react in an appropriate manner.

“FUCKING PERVERT!”

“GYA!”

Exactly one second later Eric was lying on the ground, his arms and legs twitching intermittently. There was a very large lump on his head where Christine had smashed her fist against him. Perhaps not so surprisingly, this bump—which looked like a miniature mountain rising out of his hair—was covered in a thin layer of ice, giving it a light, silvery sheen.

Standing over the now insensate boy was a blushing, shaking and very enraged Christine. She glared down at Eric with righteous anger—and humiliation, but mostly righteous anger. Her left was hand clenched into a fist near her face, and it shook with the after effects of her fury. It also had a layer of ice covering it, due in no small part to the pervert's audacity.

Strong emotions always affected the powers of yōkai.

"You… you… you perverted IDIOT!"

STOMP!

"Gya!"

"Die!" STOMP! "Die, die, die!" STOMP! "I'll kill you dead!" CRUNCH!

"GRAA!"

Lilian and a now-recovered Kevin stood on the sidelines, watching uncertainly as Christine proceeded to stomp a mudhole into the back of Eric's head, further increasing the size of the lump, and causing the tile underneath the licentious boy's face to crack.

"Maybe we should stop her before she kills him?" Kevin suggested, though it was clear that he did not want to get between Christine and the target of her vengeful wrath.

Lilian stared at the scene for a second longer, then slowly shook her head.

"No. Let's just let this run its course. Better him than you."

Kevin took one look at Christine and Eric again. Slowly, he nodded his head in agreement.

"You know what, I think you're right. And besides, Eric did bring this on himself." He adopted a sagely pose, arms crossed over his chest as he nodded his head and "mm-hmmed" several times. "I keep telling him that he shouldn't be so crass and to treat women with respect, but he never listens. I suppose this is his divine punishment."

"Yeah, divine punishment. I suppose we could call it that."

After all, a woman's wrath is very similar to divine punishment.

By now, Christine had kicked Eric onto his back, and was smashing her heel into his face.

"Ack! Not the face! Not the face! OH GOD!" His squealing cries went up several dozen octaves. "YES, THE FACE! YES, THE FACE!"

Kevin winced as Christine switched targets and proceeded to stomp on Eric's manly bits. All around them men covered their own groins, grimacing and wincing as if they could feel the phantom pain the teenage boy was suffering through. A few of them even keeled over, as if the agony that Eric felt had been transmitted to them.

Teenagers could be such drama queens sometimes.

"DIE, PEON!"

"GYAAAA!"

Though it might be warranted in this case. Maybe.

"DAMN PERVERT! HURRY UP AND DIE ALREADY!"

"NOOOOO!"

Okay, it was definitely warranted. Poor, poor Eric. You only have yourself to blame. That's what you get for being perverted when there's a *tsundere* in your vicinity.

"DIE! DIE, DIE, DIE!"

"MERCY!!!"

***

After Christine's anger had run its course, the trio left for the food court.

Eric, who'd made a miraculous recovery after having faced Christine's Righteous Female Fury, followed them. Of course, seeing how Christine was still pissed, he followed from a distance of several meters. Meanwhile, the other three did their utmost to ignore his existence.

Despite having his gonads pretty much ground into a fine mulch, and his face smashed into the walkway, Eric looked right as rain, except for the lump on his head… and the very pronounced limp. Other than that, it was almost as if the whole "Christine beating him into near catatonia" had never happened.

Kevin wondered if it was some kind of perverted Deus Ex Machina that allowed his friend to recover so quickly. Or, maybe he should call it a Deus Sex Machina? That sounded more appropriate.

Eric grumbled as he walked through crowds of mall goers, staring at the trio in front of him, tears of despair pouring out of his eyes and streaming down his cheeks like two giant waterfalls.

"I can't believe this! They're ignoring me! How could they ignore me like this?!" he shouted to no one in particular. A few people stopped walking to stare at the strange boy as he yelled out his displeasure, but the group he was following continued ignoring him. Eric's shoulders slumped as he trailed after them in silence, a literal cloud of despair hanging over his head.

The life of a perverted high school student sure was tough.

"Here we are." Kevin gestured grandly as they finally reached their destination. "The food court."

"Oh wow." Lilian's eyes widened as she looked at the area before her. "It's so big."

"That's what she said."

"Die pervert!"

"Gya!"

Kevin sighed and rubbed a hand over his face. He saw Lilian looking at him out of the corner of his eye, her head tilted quizzically. Shaking his own head, he gave her a "shall we?" gesture and said, "Let's get something to eat."

Beaming at him, Lilian nodded.

"Okay!"

They walked into the food court, Christine hurrying to catch up, leaving behind a battered and broken Eric, who was forced to pick himself off the ground and trudge after them at his own pace. He did so, grumbling and crying in despondent discouragement all the while.

"I don't get it. Why am I always the one getting beaten up by girls? How come this crap only happens to me and not Kevin?"

He didn't expect anyone to answer, but Lilian apparently decided to throw the boy a bone.

"It's because you're a pervert," her declaration, complete with shameless pointing, made Eric cry. "And also because you're the Butt Monkey."

"The Butt Monkey?" Christine looked both confused and curious. "The hell is that?"

In response to Christine's question, Lilian reached into her Extra Dimensional Storage Space, and pulled out a book called *TvTropes for Dummies.* Then she began flipping through the pages.

"Let's see, I know it's in here somewhere... no... uh uh... nope! Nu uh. Ah-ha! Here it is!" Clearing her throat, Lilian proceeded to speak with a sort of lecturing tone of voice. "The Butt Monkey is a character who, to put it bluntly, is merely added into a story for comedy purposes. They are the butt end of every demeaning joke, are always the ones to suffer under physical abuse, and generally tend to end up in humiliating yet strangely hilarious situations. In some ways, it is almost like the Butt Monkey goes through life with a giant 'kick me' sign on their back, one they cannot see, but one that everyone else is more than aware of. For that reason, nothing ever goes right for the Butt Monkey. If something bad is going to happen, it is almost always guaranteed to happen to him. To make a long story short, it sucks to be the Butt Monkey."

While Eric began crying even more, Christine just facepalmed.

"I already regret asking."

The food court was a large, open space within the mall that contained numerous fast-food restaurants arranged in a line of booths. In the center of this space were several dozen long tables all lined in neat rows, surrounded by flat-screen TVs that cycled through a variety of music videos to provide ambient background noise for the crowd.

There were a number of places for people to satiate their hunger; eateries like Sub Hub, Burger Queen and McDuffin's were a dime a dozen in malls like this. The sheer variety found there was such that everyone, regardless of their palate and eclectic tastes, could find something to enjoy—provided you were into eating fast food.

"I don't know about you two, but I'm going to get myself a burger." With these parting words, Christine walked—or rather, stormed—over to Burger Queen. She had every intention of getting herself a Raging Whooper or two, *or three*, and gorging herself until she couldn't eat another bite.

For some reason, the act of shoving inordinate amounts of food down her gullet was very therapeutic. And she was angry.

Kevin and his red-haired housemate watched the girl stomp off with matching beads of sweat rolling down the sides of their heads. After a second or two, Kevin looked away from the sight of the angry goth and focused on the girl by his side."What do you want to get, Lilian?"

"I don't really know." Lilian looked unsure, her green eyes gazing at the fast-food restaurants. They hadn't gone to this area of the mall last time, having been more concerned with buying Lilian's clothes—not to mention how Kevin had fainted before they could get lunch. That kind of put a damper on things. "I've never eaten fast-food before. We only have a few cafés in the village, like, one or two, but most of our meals came from Kotohime or Ivy."

"Is Ivy a relative of yours?"

"Yes. She's technically my cousin, the daughter of my grandmother's second eldest daughter, Daphne. In case you were wondering, Ivy has three tails."

"Gotcha." Kevin confirmed with a nod. He was tempted to ask about her family, but there were more pressing concerns, like filling his empty stomach. "Since you've never tried fast-food before, let's try something a little more, ah, refined than hamburgers."

He pointed toward one of the many booths located in the food court. It was a small place like the others—built into the wall, and lined with a black marble countertop with a cash register on one end. Large, thick, transparent plastic panels blocked off a section of the counter, where several large pizzas sat. Behind the counter was a giant oven constructed from dark red bricks. The bright, glowing sign above the booth read *Fat Fizoli's Pizza Parlor.*

Turning to look at Kevin, Lilian tilted her head.

"Pizza?"

"Do you not like pizza?"

"No, I do." Lilian shook her head, then smiled. It was a smile of nostalgia. "I only had it once, but I remember when Kotohime baked us pizza. She normally sticks to either Greek or Japanese cuisine." Lilian chuckled at Kevin's "wtf?" look. "Don't ask. Anyway, my sister complained about how we never had any variety with our meals, so Kotohime decided to make something different."

"And that something was pizza?"

"Yes."

"Right, then I think that's what we'll get. I'm partial to pizza myself."

A quick tug on Lilian's hand had the girl getting pulled along behind him.

An electric jolt surged through Lilian's body, starting from their conjoined hands and moving up her arm, across her shoulder to flow down her back and traveled all the way to her feet, making her entire body tingle pleasantly. It felt nice. *Really* nice. She wished this feeling would never end.

However, end it did. They eventually reached the counter, and Kevin let go of her hand, much to her disappointment. She looked at him out of the corner of her eye, which he eventually noticed. Turning his head, Kevin met her stare.

He tilted his head in quizzical curiosity, causing Lilian to shake hers and smile at him. Kevin returned her smile easily enough, and then it was their turn to order.

"I want one slice of Sicilian pizza with all the toppings and a medium Coke, please." Kevin was quick to place his order, knowing what he wanted before reaching the counter. While not one to indulge in unhealthy food often, when he did allow himself to eat something that wasn't necessarily good for him, he liked to go all out. He was a go big or go home kind of guy.

"All right, one Sicilian pizza with all the toppings," the young man behind the booth said; a decently handsome male that stood head and shoulders over Kevin, and who was obviously not in high school anymore. After taking Kevin's order the man looked at Lilian, his eyes trailing up and down her body. Then he smirked. "And what would you like, gorgeous?"

Kevin's hands clenched into fists. This guy was just like all of the others. He stared at Lilian with lust filled eyes, stripping her bare without regard to her feelings, as if she was some kind of doll without any emotions to call her own. All he saw was a pair of tits and a nice ass. He probably didn't even notice Lilian's emerald eyes sparkling with unusual innocence, or her bedazzling smile that could brighten whole continents. Guys like this looked at a girl and only saw a quick screw; one and done and all that crap. People like this pissed him off so much.

Taking a deep, shuddering breath, Kevin tried to release the strange, pent up rage brewing within him like the roiling of a terrible tempest, and turned to the girl next to him.

"Lilian?"

"Um," Lilian looked at the menu for several seconds, her nose scrunching cutely. She shook her head, then looked at him. "I don't know. What's good?"

"All of it's good, it just depends on your preferences." Knowing that Lilian likely didn't have any preferences due to her lack of knowledge about anything outside of Greek (and Japanese, apparently) cuisine, Kevin began a very lengthy explanation about the wonders of pizza.

"So pizza comes in several different types, and you can get a number of different toppings?" A nod. "And you got a Sicilian pizza with all the toppings?" Another nod. Lilian made her decision. She turned back to the man behind the counter. "I would also like a Sicilian pizza with all the toppings." She looked over at Kevin and gave him a beaming smile. "Since I don't know much about pizza, I'll follow your example."

As Lilian's smiling face gazed upon him, Kevin found himself unable to look away from her gorgeous, emerald orbs. Those eyes, which could enchant men with just a glance, and yet were so innocent, so pure. For some reason that was beyond him at the moment but would come to him in time, he found himself incapable of thinking about anything other than how beautiful those eyes were.

Lilian seemed to be of like mind. She stared up at him, twin pools of bewitching green gazing into his with something akin to longing. She could see something in her mate's eyes, an intangible emotion that she could not place. The only thing she knew was that it had not been there before now, and it was sucking her into the depths of those clear blue irises.

If asked, neither would be able to explain what came over them. It could have been a spell or just simple hormones. Whatever the case was, neither could look away from the other.

Their faces began drawing closer together. Lilian's eyes fluttered shut while Kevin's mouth became strangely dry. His mind, which should have been screaming at him to stop, had fallen silent.

Their heads slowly inched closer and closer. Kevin leaned down at the same time that Lilian's head tilted up. Just a few more inches and their lips would meet.

"Kevin! Lilian!"

Naturally, someone would arrive to interrupt the two before they could actually kiss.

They jerked away from each other like they had been shocked, their cheeks flushing red and their hearts beating frantically, as the spell that had been cast over them shattered into a million, irreparable pieces.

As the strange feeling that had come over him dispelled, Kevin shook his head. What… what had happened just now? What was that? Why would he… he had been mere seconds away from kissing Lilian! What had possessed him to do that?

Kevin tried to calm his raging heart. He needed to calm down. He needed to be serene. Tranquil. He couldn't let this get the best of him.

Once he had calmed down, he found it much easier to think rationally. He decided not to let himself be bothered by what had nearly happened, his almost-kiss with Lilian. Whatever strange spell had come over him was gone. Thankfully, they had been interrupted before he and Lilian could actually kiss—that would have been a mistake that he didn't want to make. After all, he didn't love Lilian… right?

Kevin would learn in due time that no spell had been cast over him, but that wouldn't come until later… after a certain kimono-clad, katana-carrying kitsune came into the picture.

"Hey, Kevin! Lilian! Over here!"

Two sets of eyes blinked as they saw the person who had broken them from their trance standing just a few feet away, a tray of food in her hands. Kevin was the first to respond.

"Lindsay?"

***

"It looks like everyone had the same idea to come to the mall," Lindsay said as she sat down at the large table that a few of her soccer teammates were already sitting at. Kevin didn't know any of those girls personally, but he recognized them from when he went to watch Lindsay's soccer games. "I guess it's not that surprising that I would see you guys here." She looked at the bags Kevin set down by their table. "And I see you've done some shopping."

"While winter's still a ways off, I thought it would be a good idea to buy Lilian some clothes for when it gets colder," was the answer that Kevin gave as he and the fox-girl sat down at the table with their plates of identical-looking pizza. All around them conversation flowed, some of it was about him and Lilian, but most of it seemed to be centered on the school shutting down. Which was actually kind of about them in an abstract *they were responsible for the school shutting down* sort of way.

“I see, getting clothes for your girlfriend.” Lindsay grinned at the duo. “That's really sweet of you.” Kevin and Lilian shared a look. One of them looked away uncomfortably, while the other gave a sad frown. The soccer-playing tomboy noticed their strange reaction and frowned as well. “Is something wrong?”

“No,” Kevin answered quickly, shaking his head, “Nothing's wrong.”

The frown on Lindsay's face grew. She wondered if something had happened to cause a rift between the two—an argument, perhaps?—but decided that it would be prudent to just let things lie, rather than trying to wheedle out whatever was wrong with them. Instead, she decided to let her curiosity turn to something else.

Or rather, *someone* else.

She looked at the raven-haired goth girl, who had joined up with Lilian and Kevin a few seconds ago. Sitting at the table in front of the goth were three Raging Whoopers, one of which she was already biting huge chunks out of. She was scowling as she chewed.

“I don't think we've met before, I'm Lindsay,” the tomboyish blond greeted the angry-looking girl. When Christine didn't respond, but instead continued angrily chomping on her food, the soccer player continued. “So what's your name?” she asked politely, but with an inquisitiveness that could not be masked. How could she not be curious when she had never met this girl before? First Lilian and now this cutie… just where did these girls keep coming from? “And how exactly do you know Kevin and Lilian?”

“That's none of your business,” Christine declared impudently, right before taking another monstrous bite out of her giant burger filled with bacon, pepper jack cheese and jalapenos, all of which was smothered with a spicy sauce. The heat of the food matched her anger perfectly.

“Don't mind her,” Kevin told Lindsay as she stared at the goth, dumbfounded. The tomboy looked from Christine to him, her head tilting to convey her perplexity. “That's Christine.” He hiked a thumb at the girl angrily chowing down on her Raging Whooper. She had already finished one and was starting on her second. “We met at the arcade a while ago, but I hadn't seen her again until she showed up at the school track meet yesterday.”

"So she's a friend of yours, then?"

"Yeah, I guess you could say that."

While Lindsay looked at the girl curiously, and Lilian huffed at the very idea that she and that stupid loli goth were friends, the snow-maiden in question began making a very accurate imitation of a tomato at the North Pole. It was a good thing she had already swallowed her food, or she might have started choking on it.

"F-f-f-f-friends?! W-w-who the hell ever said we were friends?! I-I-I already told you we're not friends! Hmph!"

She tried glaring at the boy. Unfortunately, the sheer amount of blue on her face made her glare less than intimidating. The steam pouring from her ears like a steam engine didn't help matters. Everyone there watched the steam in mute silence, wondering how such a thing was possible.

Lindsay looked from the girl, whose face had taken on the general coloration of a Blue Whale to Kevin. She raised a single, delicate eyebrow, as if asking, *"what's up with her?"*

"She's been saying that ever since we met," Kevin told her, rubbing the back of his head. "But she's still been hanging out with us ever since we met her today."

"Th-th-th-that's… that's just because I have nothing better to do! Stupid! A-a-and it's boring walking around on my own! That's all!" Huffing, Christine crossed her arms over her chest and turned her nose up at them. "Don't go thinking you're special or anything just because I decided to stick around! I'm only with you because I was bored, not because I want to spend time with you or anything!"

"Uh huh."

Lindsay stared between Kevin and Christine uncertainly. After several seconds of awkward silence, she shrugged, and decided that she wouldn't bother trying to figure out what the strange relationship between her friend and this new girl was. She had a feeling that trying to understand the dynamics between them would simply give her a massive headache.

"Oh!" While Lindsay decided to ignore the last few seconds of conversation in order to retain her sanity, Lilian had just tried her first bite of Sicilian pizza. "This is really good!" Taking another bite, she gave an almost sensual moan of satisfaction. "It's so light and fluffy!" Another bite. Another moan. "And the sauce is so thick and robust!" Another bite. A third moan. "Mmm! It's soo good!"

"Uh… Lilian?"

"Hmm?" Lilian blinked, snapping out of the small trance that she had been in since she began eating. She craned her neck to see Kevin staring at her with wide eyes and a very mild flush coloring his cheeks. "What's wrong, Kevin?"

"You may want to stop eating like that."

Lilian tilted her head, her confusion more than evident.

"Eating like what?"

"Like… you know, making all those noises and stuff while you eat."

Lilian just looked more confused.

"Eh? Why? What's wrong?"

"You're making the others uncomfortable."

Lilian looked around the table to see almost everyone staring at her with a look that could only be described as, *"Oh my god, I can't believe she just did that!"* Their eyes were wider than dishpans, and their faces redder than anything a tomato could ever hope to achieve. They all looked like someone had shoved their heads into a convection oven set on high for several hours.

The only one among them who was not a blushing wreck was Eric, and that's mostly because he had passed out some time after Lilian started eating, and was currently lying in a puddle of his own blood, which ran freely down his nose in massive quantities that should have killed him.

"Huh?" Lilian gazed around at everyone, bewildered, and then looked back at Kevin. "I don't get it. Did I do something wrong?"

As he sat there next to Lilian, and saw the varying expressions on everyone's faces, Kevin felt like banging his head against the table.

Christine was the first to recover.

"You really don't get it, do you?"

Lilian glared at the other girl.

"What's that supposed to mean? What am I supposed to get?"

"You're sitting there, eating pizza and moaning like some kind of slut. It's disgusting everyone else." The pale-skinned snow-maiden scoffed derisively. "I guess I really shouldn't expect anything less from a fox. Your kind has always been the most whorish creatures among us."

"Says the girl with the loli fetish!"

"It's not a loli fetish! And this outfit is a classic! A CLASSIC!"

"A classic for loli vampires maybe. Have you looked at yourself in the mirror lately?"

"What's that supposed to mean?!"

"It means you look ridiculous! You have a horrible sense of fashion!"

"Like you're any better! You dress like a cheap hooker! Why don't you go back to whoring yourself out on the Vegas Strip?"

A low, deep growl escaped Lilian's throat. She shot to her feet. Christine followed suit, glaring at the twin-tailed kitsune, her lips peeled back to show pearly white teeth grit in anger.

"You take that back!"

"Fuck that! I won't do anything of the sort! Not unless you take back your insults to my outfit!"

"I was only telling the truth!"

Lindsay looked at the two girls as they began to literally butt heads, both trying to overpower the other, glaring into each other's eyes, teeth bared in barely suppressed choler. She could almost see the sparks flying between the two as the battle of wills heated up.

"Are they always like this?" Lindsay asked Kevin, who buried his face in his hands, as if ashamed of being seen with the two arguing yōkai.

"Usually," he sighed. Peeking out from between his fingers, the young man saw the two supernatural creatures from Japanese myth still glaring at each other. He then looked over at the girl that he had been crushing on for the better part of three years.

He stood up rather suddenly, startling the tomboy and several others. Kevin looked down at Lindsay, who tilted her head up to look at him.

"Lindsay, would you mind if I talked with you?" He looked at all of the people around them, then back to her. "In private, I mean."

"Huh? Oh, yeah, sure." She stood up as well and began to follow Kevin, wondering what he could possibly want to talk to her about.

As Kevin left with Lindsay in tow, Christine saw the pair leave and stopped arguing with her two-tailed adversary.

"Hey, Kevin and that girl are leaving." Christine's statement caused Lilian to stop arguing as well and turn around. A small ache spread through her chest as she saw the pair walk off together. "Do you think we should follow them?"

Lilian stared after the two as they disappeared around the corner. She wanted to follow them, to spy on them and see what they were doing, to hear what they were talking about. Another part of her was even thinking up ways to sabotage whatever conversation was about to go down. It wouldn't be that hard to implant a suggestion into Lindsay's mind. She was positive that she could make the girl say something that would irreparably damage her relationship with Kevin.

That would certainly pave the way for her to truly work her way into Kevin's heart and confidence. She could lend him an ear, listen to his woes, and offer him a shoulder to cry on after Lindsay tore his heart in two. He would feel so grateful to her, and before long, his gratitude would turn into affection and affection into love. He would freely give his heart and soul to her, and she would be able to remain by his side, ensuring that he was never alone for the rest of his life.

It was the perfect plan.

A plan worthy of a kitsune.

Her matriarch would have been so proud of her for conceiving it.

"No," she decided, sitting back down with a sorrowful sigh. With her head tilted down, silky red bangs overshadowing the upper half of her face, Lilian stared at her plate of half-finished pizza. "Let them be. Whatever they have to talk about isn't for us to hear."

"Never thought I'd hear you say something like that." Christine looked back to where Kevin and Lindsay had gone. "Whatever. You do what you want, I'm going to follow them."

With that she took off, leaving Lilian surrounded by a group of girls that she didn't know and didn't care about. In this crowd of unknown people, all of them now gossiping about Lindsay and Kevin, making wild assumptions and speculations that she didn't care to hear, no one saw her shed a single tear.

***

Lindsay leaned against the wall, arms crossed under her chest, as she looked at the young man that she had befriended back when they were in elementary school. He stood across from her, messy blond hair hovering over light blue eyes that looked a tad nervous. His arms crossed, only to uncross a second later. He did this several more times, as if he was undecided on just what to do with them. In the end, he simply let them hang at his side.

"So what did you want to talk about?" Lindsay asked. "It's gotta be pretty important if you want to talk to me alone, right?"

"It is," Kevin admitted, closing his eyes and sighing. "It's something that I've wanted to tell you for a while now, but couldn't for… well, reasons," he finished lamely.

"But you can tell me now," she smiled at him. "You've changed quite a bit this past month."

"You really think so?" Kevin scratched the back of his neck and looked away. "I don't think I've changed that much."

"Well, maybe not so much." Lindsay grinned at him. "But you have to admit, you have changed some. You're a lot more confident than you used to be. I haven't seen you blush, or heard you stutter for a while, either."

"Eh? I guess." At this unexpected praise, Kevin felt his cheeks become warm. Lindsay chuckled.

"Though it looks like you still have trouble accepting praise."

"I don't have trouble accepting praise." Kevin frowned. "I just don't think I've changed all that much, and I've never been lacking in confidence."

"You just couldn't talk to girls."

"Yeah." Kevin ran a hand through his hair and let out a long breath. "Something like that." He looked thoughtful. "Maybe I have changed a bit. But if I have, it's thanks to Lilian."

"That girl really is something else." Lindsay's smile became wistful. "She's helped you get over whatever issues you had with girls, *and* has managed to charm her way into your life. That's no easy feat."

Kevin couldn't help but snort.

"Right. Charm her way into my life. I suppose that's one way of putting it."

More like barged into his life with all the subtlety of the Hulk at an anime convention. Regardless, he supposed there was some truth to Lindsay's words. Even if they had started off on rocky terms, Kevin had come to accept the pretty fox-girl as a part of his life. These days, he would even go so far as to say that he enjoyed having her around.

He wouldn't tell her that, though. Who knew what kind of chaos that would unleash?

"So what did you want to talk about?"

Kevin looked at Lindsay, gathering his courage.

Several feet away from where the two youngsters were standing, a certain yuki-onna was peeking out from around a corner, watching the two as they spoke. Unlike Lilian, who seemed to have lost whatever inclination she may have had to follow the pair, Christine wanted to know what they were talking about.

I-it's not like I like Kevin or anything! I'm simply doing this to satisfy my own curiosity! Hmph!

"I like you, and I don't mean as a friend." Two sets of eyes widened. "I've liked you for a long time now. Part of the reason I had so much trouble talking to you was because I wanted to tell you, but couldn't. I was afraid that if I told you how I felt, you wouldn't return my feelings and it would ruin our friendship."

Christine reared back as if struck. Pressing her back against the wall, a hand went to her chest, clutching at the fabric of her black lace bodice tightly. She closed her eyes and took a deep breath, ignoring the way her heart felt like a giant fist had decided to crush it in an ironclad grip.

Moving forward again, Christine peeked back around the corner. While a part of her felt like running off and crying, another part needed to hear more. Actually, a good deal of her wanted to go over there and shove a dagger of ice up Kevin's ass, but she resisted the urge and looked back at the couple.

Lindsay had gotten over her shock, and looked at the boy with a melancholy smile.

"I had been wondering if you were ever going to tell me how you felt about me."

"What?" It took Kevin exactly one second to process her words. It took him another second to come up with an appropriate response. "Wait! Are you telling me you knew how I felt about you?"

"I've known for a while now." Lindsay confirmed with a nod. "You're not very good at hiding your feelings, Kevin. Actually, you're downright awful at it."

Kevin felt an unusual combination of embarrassment and frustration, which bled into his voice as he said, "Then why didn't you say anything?"

The smile Lindsay gave him was odd, a combination of emotions that Kevin didn't recognize but were plainly visible for him to see.

"Because I wanted to hear you say it yourself. It wouldn't have as much meaning if I told you that I knew how you felt about me, would it?"

"I guess not," Kevin admitted with a small frown. "So… what now? What does this mean for us?"

Christine wanted to know that as well. She was so set on figuring out what Lindsay's answer was that she didn't even notice that she was losing control of her powers. Starting from her fingertips and moving across the wall, hoarfrost began to spread, slowly creeping along the white painted bricks like the tendrils of some eldritch horror. It wasn't long before a good section of the wall around her became covered in a light sheen that reflected her features against the surface.

And it wasn't just the wall that her powers affected. The air around her became colder than a winters breeze in the middle of the Arctic Circle. All around her people nearby had stopped walking, and gaped in wide-eyed surprise at their exhaled breath as it came out in puffs of misty white.

Christine ignored all of this, only noticing the change in temperature enough to release a shiver.

She really did hate her powers.

"I'm definitely glad you finally worked up the courage to tell me." Lindsay still had that smile on her face. Kevin wondered what that smile meant. "I've been waiting for you to tell me that for so long now that I wasn't sure you would actually do it."

Kevin didn't know how to feel as he looked at the girl. Happy that she had been waiting for him to confess his feelings? Or upset that she hadn't believed he would ever confess?

In the end, he decided not to be upset. Considering his problem talking to women, it wasn't like her feelings were unjustified. He wasn't sure if he felt happy either, though, for some weird reason.

"So then… what does this mean for us?" Kevin asked.

With her hands behind her back, Lindsay gave him a kind, yet slightly sad, smile.

Chapter 13

Clearing the Air

“I'm home!” Lindsay called out as she entered her house. Frowning when no reply came, the blond absentmindedly took off her shoes and set them in a small alcove near the door. Her parents didn't like her tracking dirt on the floor, especially the carpet. They were clean freaks like that.

She walked further into the house, white marble tiles transitioning to beige carpet as she entered the living room.

“Mom! Dad!” She called out again. After another second in which she received no response, Lindsay shrugged. “Dad must be at work or something.”

She didn't know where her mom was, though—that woman didn't even have a job. Maybe she was at that “Aesthetic Appreciation Club” of hers, which was just a really fancy name for a group of middle-aged women who got together and drooled at pictures of males half their age, sometimes younger. Lindsay's mom was the “president” of the club and arranged all of their meetings.

It was one of her mom's more disturbing hobbies.

On a side note, she really should apologize to Kevin on behalf of all the women of that club.

Since her parents weren't home, and she wasn't hungry, Lindsay walked to her bedroom. She closed the door behind her, then strode further in, stepping over a number of soccer balls and volleyballs that lay scattered along the floor. Lining the walls were a variety of posters featuring her favorite soccer teams and players. Her unmade bed looked kind of like a pig had been rolling around in it, making her grimace at the sight. Those sheets would have to be washed.

“Maybe I should clean up?” she wondered out loud as she studied the sty-that-was-her-room. “Ah, whatever. I'll do it later.”

With a shrug of her shoulders Lindsay wandered up to her desk, which was just as messy as the rest of her room. The top was littered with papers, pens, pencils and several other knick-knacks that would have most people scratching their head in confusion, wondering what sort of function they served.

As she stopped in front of her desk, Lindsay's eyes landed on a very specific object—one that she found herself looking at often these days. It was a picture of her and Kevin when they were younger, back when her friend wasn’t girl-shy, and she had just been one of the guys.

She player picked the picture up and looked at it. She and Kevin were standing side by side, their arms around each other's shoulders. Kevin had the biggest grin plastered on his face, a smile so wide that it threatened to split his face in half and forced his eyes to close. She was grinning, too, and her free hand was held up in front of the camera, giving it the peace sign.

A sad smile crossed her face. She missed those days. She missed how Kevin had been able to talk to her like a normal person. She missed being able to spend time with him. In some ways, Lindsay found herself longing for those days again.

In other ways… not so much. The more she grew up, the less she found herself wanting to be seen as one of the guys, and the more she wanted Kevin to see her as a woman.

He did see her that way now, but he hadn't been able to talk to her once it dawned on him that girls weren't just boys without boy parts. It was cute at first, but after a while, she had really been hoping that he would get over his shyness. This desire had gotten especially bad after she had realized that he had a crush on her.

Her eyes dimmed, and her smile turned into a frown. He had gotten better now. For nearly one and a half or so weeks—ever since Lilian appeared, now that she thought about it—Kevin had been talking to her like a normal person, but it wasn't because of her. It was all due to Lilian.

A single tear fell from her eyes. It traveled down her cheek, all the way to her chin, where it dripped off and splashed against the glass frame in her hands. Another soon followed the first, which was followed by another and another, until she was crying in earnest.

Her face turned into a combination of a smile and a grimace as she brushed her fingers against the photo.

"Lilian was able to do what I couldn't…"

That was a bitter pill to swallow.

"… She's a much better match for Kevin than I am…"

That knowledge didn't stop her from hurting.

"… I hope she can bring you the happiness that I couldn't…"

Alone in her house, Lindsay cried as she realized that her desire to hear Kevin confess his love for her of his own gumption had allowed another girl to worm their way into his heart.

***

Kevin took in a deep breath as he entered the apartment that he shared with Lilian and his mom—when she was home. A second later, he released it in a large gust, before a smile broke out across his face.

"Man, it feels good to be back home."

Closing the door behind him, the young man raised his hands above his head, stretching them as high as they could go. He could feel his joints crack in a most satisfying manner.

"Today was definitely a nice break from school and all that monotonous homework they give us. Though I think we should do something a bit more fun than clothes shopping tomorrow." He turned to look at his housemate. "Hey, Lilian, how would you like to go to the arcade to… mor… row…?" Kevin trailed off when he saw the disquieted expression on the two-tailed kitsune's face. "Lilian?"

"Hmm?" Lilian blinked. Her head turned toward him. "I'm sorry, were you saying something?"

"Nothing. Forget about it." The frown deepened. "Are you okay?"

The smile she gave him did nothing to convince Kevin of her sincerity.

"I'm fine. I was just thinking about something."

Her words didn't do much to reassure him, either.

"So!" Her smile widened as she clapped her hands together. "Why don't I get started on dinner? I'm thinking of making ground beef gyros. I've never made them before, so it should be interesting."

"I've never had gyros before," Kevin admitted, "But don't you think it's a little early for dinner?" He looked at the clock. "It's only two-thirty."

Lilian frowned, looked at the clock, then back at Kevin.

"Then what should we do until then?"

"We can start by talking," Kevin suggested. Lilian seemed to interpret something in his words, because she turned away, presenting her back to him.

"I'm not sure if there's anything that we can talk about," her voice was even, but off. Kevin could sense that something was amiss. The tone of her voice, the pitch and timber, it all sounded wrong. "I mean, we did just spend the entire day together."

"We spend every day together and still find things to talk about, so don't give me that," Kevin quipped, looking at the back of Lilian's head. Long crimson hair cascaded down her back like a shimmering waterfall. Kevin would have normally admired how it glimmered in the light, but his concern overrode his appreciation of her glamorous locks. "You've been quiet ever since we had lunch. You've hardly said a single word. I want to know what's wrong."

"Nothing's wrong."

"Something is obviously wrong," Kevin countered. He would have rolled his eyes, but that seemed a tad redundant. "You can't fool me." He took a single step toward the girl, and placed a hand on her shoulder, but Lilian shrugged it off. "Lilian, please, tell me what's wrong."

"As if you don't know!" Lilian whirled around suddenly to face Kevin. His heart lurched as he got a good look at the twin-tailed beauty's face, at the tears running down her fair cheeks, and the slight redness in her eyes. "I know what you and Lindsay were talking about! I know that you confessed to her!"

Kevin's eyes went wide.

"Lilian…"

"That's why you're so happy, isn't it?" Lilian continued as more and more silvery droplets of salty liquid fell from her eyes. "Because you were finally able to confess your love to the girl you've had a crush on for so long, right? Well, I'm glad for you. I'm glad that you were finally able to confess to the girl of your dreams." Lilian sniffled as she tried to futilely wipe the tears from her eyes. “But don't expect me to be happy just because you and Lindsay are now dating. Because I can't be happy when I… when you…”

“Dating?” Had Lilian's vision not been blurred by her tears, she would have seen the confused look on Kevin's face. “Lilian… that's not…”

“Don't try to reassure me,” Lilian hiccuped as she continued wiping at her eyes. Her cheeks were now heavily stained with her tears, streaks of wetness that glistened on her fair skin, catching the light. She turned again, not wanting to look at him. “I know what happened, so don't try to make me feel better. I hope you have a very happy life with Lindsay.”

“Lilian.” Kevin placed his hands on her shoulders. Lilian shook them off, but this didn’t deter him. He placed them back on her shoulders gain, his grip firmer this time. “Lilian, would you just listen to me? I have something important to tell you.”

“No!” Lilian tried to struggle out of his grip, but kitsune were not very strong physically. They could boost their physical capabilities through enhancements, but Lilian’s mental state was such that the idea never occurred to her. “I don't want to hear whatever you have to say. Why don't you just call Lindsay and tell her!”

“Lindsay and I aren't dating!”

The words penetrated her brain seconds before her body stopped shaking. This time when Kevin tried to turn her around to face him, she allowed it. She looked at the boy who meant the world to her; her tear-stained eyes red and puffy.

“What did you say?” she asked, her voice a mere whisper.

Kevin sighed, closing his eyes for a moment of respite now that she was no longer fighting him. He opened them a second later, and looked at Lilian once more, hands relaxing their grip on her shoulders, though he didn’t remove them.

“I said, Lindsay and I aren't dating.”

Long red locks of hair swayed as Lilian tilted her head to look at their bare feet.

“I don't understand.”

She looked up again, her hair parting like the Red Sea. Every flash of emotion that crossed her face was visible for him to see.

Lilian's eyes were like an open book. She was completely vulnerable.

Kevin saw the confusion on her face. Despite the tense situation, he allowed himself to feel amused by her baffled expression. “Yeah, I kind of got that. But it's like I said, I'm not dating Lindsay.”

“But, didn't you confess to her?” Lilian questioned. “I thought that's why you went off with her; to confess your feelings.”

Kevin removed his right hand from her shoulder to scratch at his cheek. “Well, yeah, that is why I asked to talk with her alone. But we aren't dating. She turned me down.”

“Turned you down?” It only took Lilian a second to realize what that meant. Her eyes softened. “Oh, Kevin, I'm sorry. I know how much you liked her.”

“Why are you sorry?” Kevin chuckled a bit. “You've got nothing to be sorry for. It's not your fault Lindsay didn't feel the same way about me.”

“Yeah, but…”

“If anyone should be saying sorry, it's me,” Kevin interrupted the girl before she could even think of apologizing again. “I know it hurt you when I confessed to Lindsay. I can't imagine how I would have felt if our positions were reversed, but I know that I wouldn't be very happy.”

“I guess.” Looking at Kevin's smiling face a small, tentative smile appeared on her own. The smile soon left, however, replaced by furrowed brows and irises flickering in confusion. “But, if Lindsay turned you down, then why are you so, well, what I mean is that you don't seem very sad that Lindsay doesn't like you like, well, like *that*. So then why…?”

“Why am I not depressed and feeling sorry for myself?” Kevin finished for her. When Lilian nodded, the smile on his face became different. Lilian couldn’t place the emotions hidden behind that smile, but it seemed… relieved? No. Maybe disencumbered was a better word. He looked like a large weight had been lifted off his shoulders.

Little did she know that the reason for his smile was because Kevin was remembering his conversation with Lindsay.

***

"Even though I'm glad you finally told me, I can't return your feelings. I just don't like you like that."

"I see. So that's how it is. Strange," he muttered softly to himself, "I thought hearing you say that would hurt a bit more."

"Did you say something?"

"Not a thing."

"So now that you've told me how you feel, and I've told you how I feel, where does that leave us?" asked an uncertain and nervous-looking Lindsay.

Kevin tilted his head.

"What do you mean?"

"I mean that you just made a very heartfelt confession to me, and I shot you down like someone out of a bad romance novel."

"Ouch." Kevin flinched. "That was kind of harsh, don't you think?"

"Maybe, but it's also true. It takes a lot of courage to tell someone you like them, and it absolutely sucks when someone turns you down. And I guess what I'm trying to say is that I'm worried." Lindsay looked off to the side, grabbing her right elbow with her left hand. "I mean, can we even be friends after something like this? Do you even *want* to be my friend now?"

"I don't see why not." When Lindsay looked at him, her face perplexed, he gave her a bit of a smile and shrugged his shoulders. "I mean, yeah, it does kind of suck to be shot down. But you know what? Even though you turned me down, I actually feel pretty good about all this."

"Why is that?" An honestly curious Lindsay asked. "I thought you would get depressed and start moping around your apartment the moment you got home."

"Okay, first of all, men do not mope," Kevin declared, frowning, and puffing his cheeks out like a child who'd been denied the chance to have a 24-hour *Pokemon* marathon, but mostly frowning. "We just don't. And secondly, you said it yourself, didn't you? I've matured. I'm not going to act like a spoiled brat, or get all teary-eyed and mopey. Moaning over how unfair life is, and how the girl you like doesn't feel the same way never helped anyone, and it's not going to help me. Yeah, it sucks that you don't like me, but we're in high school. For all we know, our relationship might not have lasted more than a few months before sputtering out anyway, or we could have ended up hating each other when our relationship went down the drain. High school romances seem to have this tendency to sputter and die before the year is out. I mean, how many people do you know who ended up marrying their high school sweetheart?"

"None." Lindsay shrugged. "But I think that's just because we're still in high school."

"Semantics." Kevin waved a dismissive hand. "My point is, most high school relationships don't last that long—I know for a fact that Chase's current girlfriend is the fifth girl he's dated this year, and he dated ten last year. I asked you because I really like you, but I'm also aware that teenage relationships aren't known for their longevity. People's feelings can change, or they move away from each other, or something happens and the relationship stagnates. I know this, which is just another reason I was so hesitant to confess to you."

"You mean aside from the fact that you couldn't talk to me without the risk of fainting?"

"Ugh." Kevin felt like he'd just been physically slapped. "Do you really have to bring that up?"

"Sorry, couldn't help myself," Lindsay grinned guiltily.

Kevin mumbled under his breath. Lindsay chuckled softly.

"But I guess you do have a point," Lindsay said, continuing where they left off. "So does that mean we're still friends?"

"Of course." Grinning like he used to back when they were in elementary school, Kevin thumped his chest. He used to do it a lot back in elementary school, too—probably something he picked up from his anime, Lindsay guessed. He'd watched a lot of that stuff back then as well. "Something like this isn't enough to end our friendship. Sure, things might be a little awkward for a while, but soon enough, we'll be hanging out just like we used to."

"Like we used to?" Lindsay whispered, sighing.

"Something wrong?"

"No." She shook her head. "Nothing's wrong. I was just thinking about how much you've grown. That's an awfully mature way of looking at things," Lindsay complimented. She rocked back and forth on her heels as she spoke, looking at him with a smile. "Then again, you've always been a bit more mature than most of the kids our age."

"Comes with living alone since I was in middle school, I guess. So anyway." Kevin stuck out his hand toward the girl. "Friends?"

Clearly understanding what the gesture meant, a large smile spread across Lindsay's face as she stuck out her hand, grasping it. As the two shook hands, Kevin completely missed the way Lindsay's eyes dimmed.

"Yeah… friends."

***

Kevin returned back to the present. Lilian still stood in front of him, and his hands still rested on her shoulders.

"I guess that's because I didn't like Lindsay as much as I thought I did," Kevin admitted, then paused. "Or at least, I didn't like her as much as I used to. It's really strange. A few months ago, Lindsay was all I could think about, but recently, she just hasn't been on my mind that much lately."

Kevin wondered why he'd undergone such a swift change of heart. Maybe he'd only liked Lindsay because she was the only girl who kept talking to him after he became so shy around girls, or maybe it was because they'd been friends since elementary school. He didn't know what the reason was, and he supposed it didn't really matter in the end. It didn't change the fact that he no longer had strong romantic feelings for the girl that he had originally believed was his dream girl.

"So then, you and Lindsay aren't dating?" Lilian confirmed. Kevin nodded. "And you just found out that you don't really like Lindsay as much as you thought you did?" Another nod. "I see."

Lilian allowed a smile to appear on her face. While it hurt to know that her beloved had confessed to another girl, hearing this made it all worth it. With Lindsay now a non-factor, she had a chance to truly earn Kevin's love. It was an opportunity that she would not be wasting.

"Right, so now that we've gotten all that cleared up, why don't we see if there's anything good to watch on TV," Kevin suggested. "I know there's an anime playing on Cartoon Network right now that you might be interested in. Or, we could watch one of the anime I have on DVD; I know you haven't watched all of them. Barring that, we could also play video games."

"I want to play video games!" Lilian, thrusting her hand in the air as a show of enthusiasm. Kevin stared at the girl for a second, then grinned.

"All right, then, video games it is. Why don't you choose what we play while I set up the console?"

As Lilian scurried toward the large display case filled with movies and games, Kevin went to grab the video game console. The rest of the day would be spent peacefully—or at least as peacefully as a day could be when you were involved with an enthusiastic and eager kitsune yōkai.

As they began playing the game that Lilian chose, Kevin decided that he wouldn't have his day any other way.

***

Ms. Vis had been in a foul mood ever since she and the other faculty members arrived at school to discover the extensive amounts of property damage. Actually, she had been rather detestable several hours before then, but hearing about the utter destruction of the gym certainly hadn't helped. How could she properly facilitate her student's education if they weren't even at school?

To top it all off, she had been stuck at school last night because someone had stolen her car. Her car! Stolen! It was absolutely unbelievable! The nerve of some people!

Of course, it had been inexplicably returned to her that morning—even though she couldn't remember how or when. She'd just woken up to find herself lying on her bed, unable to remember when she'd gone to sleep, and her car sitting out front. There seemed to be a large gap in her memory that she couldn't explain.

She blamed Lilian.

If all of that wasn't enough, then she and the other teachers now had even more work to do. Most people wouldn't understand how that worked. They were teachers, right? How could they work if there was no one around to teach and no papers to grade?

The truth was that, with school being closed down for the unforeseeable future, all of the teachers had to scrap and redo their previous lesson plans in order to fit this new, unprecedented situation.

Some had more work than others. Ms. Vis was actually lucky in that regard. She only needed to move a good portion of the school work over to make room for an extra week's worth of reviews. Some of the other teachers—especially those who were in charge of clubs or sports—had a lot more work to do.

She knew that Coach Deretaine was currently in meetings to see what could be done about keeping their track team going through the potentially long hiatus. Apparently, not even the utter annihilation of the gym would keep him from running his students ragged.

Just because Ms. Vis didn't have much work to do did not mean that she couldn't, or wouldn't, complain—she did, with great fervor in fact. She complained to anyone who was willing to listen.

At the moment, only one person had the misfortune of being the recipient of her current tirade. Professor Nabui, the Social Sciences teacher.

His short, combed back black hair was flecked with gray to give him a very distinguished look. Despite his prematurely-graying hair, the man held a youthful appearance. It was quite clear that he kept himself in good physical shape from the way his suit fit him, showing off his broad shoulders, and straining against his pectorals. He honestly didn't look anything like a teacher, even if he did wear a pair of studious-looking glasses over his sharp, hawkish eyes.

"That little cretin stole my car! It couldn't have been anyone else! Only she and Mr. Swift were here so long after school hours!" Ms. Vis continued ranting about Lilian. "I'm certain that girl was responsible for the damage done to the school as well! Oooh! Just thinking about that horrid child gets me so riled up!" The crazed math teacher raised a clenched fist up to her face, her irises burning with an inner fire, one that took on the physical manifestation of flames behind her eyes. "Just you wait, Lilian Pnévma! Once I get some dirt on you, you'll be gone for good! For good!"

Before Ms. Vis could continue ranting, Professor Nabui stood up from the small chair that he had been occupying, the leaflets that he had been reading in hand. The pale-skinned, vampire-esque woman looked up at her older compatriot with a startled glance, having not expected him to stand so suddenly.

"Are you leaving, Professor Nabui?"

"Yes, I have to put the grades for these reports in my computer," the Japanese professor informed the crazy teacher slowly. His accent was so thick that people often had trouble understanding him, which explained why he spoke at a snail's pace.

"I understand. I should probably do that as well. Take care."

"You, too."

With hardly a backwards glance, Professor Nabui walked out of the teachers' lounge, gently closing the door behind him and beginning the leisurely walk back to his classroom. It was a nice day outside. The air was crisp and cool. The cloudless September sky was a light azure blue, and the sun's rays didn't seem to affect the cool temperature. There was no sense in rushing on such a beautiful day.

Still, all good things must come to an end, and Professor Nabui eventually arrived at his classroom. Unlocking the door and entering, he closed it behind him and quickly re-locked it. After taking a second to ensure that the room was secure, he made his way behind his desk and sat down.

He then picked up the phone, placed it against his ear, and began carefully dialing a number that he hadn't used since coming to work at this school.

The phone began to ring. After several seconds of this ringing, someone answered.

"Taka-kuuuunnn!" A voice squealed from the other end. Professor Nabui winced as he jerked the phone away from his ear.

"Do you really have to scream into the phone?" asked the now-disgruntled Nabui. "And don't call me Taka-kun. We are not familiar enough for you to even think of adding that suffix… and you are not Japanese."

"Muu," the female voice on the other end moaned in complaint. *"You're so cruel, Taka-kun."*

"That isn't my name!" Professor Nabui took a deep breath. "I am Agent Inagumi Takashi, ID number 22AD10001. Not Taka-kun."

"I like Taka-kun better," the perky female voice said. Nabui, or Takashi, twitched. *"Ne, ne, Taka-kun—"*

"It's Takashi!"

"What are you calling for anyway? You know better than to call me at this time. I'm playing Air right now, and you know I don't like it when people interrupt me while I'm playing a visual novel."

"I wish you'd stop playing those eroge," Takashi sighed. "And this is important."

"Hmm, important enough to interrupt my ero-ero time?"

Takashi twitched at his superior's words. By all eight-million Shinto gods, he hated it when she talked like this. "As a matter of fact, yes. I have discovered another yōkai that I believe our superiors will be interested in; a student who just transferred here one week and four days ago."

"Really? Ha, well, I suppose that is important enough to interrupt me. Just make it fast, okay? I've got important stuff to do."

"Right."

Takashi rolled his eyes. His free hand grabbed hold of his desk's top left drawer handle, which he pulled back to reveal several dozen files inside. He reached in and felt around. There was a deft *click* as he hit the catch that opened a hidden compartment. He then pulled out a file titled, *Subject LP,* and placed it on the desk. Opening the file revealed the student transcript for a beautiful girl with red hair and green eyes.

"I have reason to suspect that she is a kitsune. Her name is Lilian Pnéy̱ma."

ABOUT THE AUTHOR

Brandon Varnell first got into writing when he was in college. Before that, he wanted to be a video game designer—until he realized that he couldn't make a video game to save his life. And before that, he wanted to be a rock star—until he realized that whole sex, drugs and rock-n-roll stopped being a thing in the 80s. His life has been filled with ups and downs and various moments of ADHD driven high-jinks. It wasn't until he discovered his love for writing that his mind gained the focus necessary to commit himself to something as a possible career choice. When not sitting in front of his computer typing, he can usually be found watching anime or reading a variety of books, manga and Japanese light novels. He also enjoys taking long walks on the beach, watching the sun set and... you're not even reading to this anymore, are you?

Made in the USA
Columbia, SC
02 December 2020

26095853R00167